T0156450

The Blonde Effect

Daine Myles

iUniverse, Inc.
Bloomington

The Blonde Effect

Copyright © 2012 by Daine Myles

All rights reserved. No part of this book may be used or reproduced by any means, graphic, electronic, or mechanical, including photocopying, recording, taping or by any information storage retrieval system without the written permission of the publisher except in the case of brief quotations embodied in critical articles and reviews.

This is a work of fiction. All of the characters, names, incidents, organizations, and dialogue in this novel are either the products of the author's imagination or are used fictitiously.

iUniverse books may be ordered through booksellers or by contacting:

iUniverse
1663 Liberty Drive
Bloomington, IN 47403
www.iuniverse.com
1-800-Authors (1-800-288-4677)

Because of the dynamic nature of the Internet, any web addresses or links contained in this book may have changed since publication and may no longer be valid. The views expressed in this work are solely those of the author and do not necessarily reflect the views of the publisher, and the publisher hereby disclaims any responsibility for them.

Any people depicted in stock imagery provided by Thinkstock are models, and such images are being used for illustrative purposes only.

Certain stock imagery © Thinkstock.

ISBN: 978-1-4697-8783-1 (sc)
ISBN: 978-1-4697-8784-8 (hc)
ISBN: 978-1-4697-8785-5 (e)

Library of Congress Control Number: 2012922419

Printed in the United States of America

iUniverse rev. date: 11/27/2012

Acknowledgment

First and foremost, I want to thank God, for without him, nothing is possible. I would also like to thank my sister, Leona. She is the inspiration behind this novel. She is a very intelligent woman who holds a master's degree in education, but when she has her "blonde moments" after getting her hair dyed, you wonder if the dye didn't have something to do with those "moments." She is the one who helped me through this whole writing process. She was my rock. She had input on this novel and helped me review everything that went into this book.

I would like to thank Peter Kirsch for the excellent job at line editing. You are a great friend and your assistance is greatly appreciated.

I want to thank my parents for their continuing support. My father is the one who came up with the idea of Cindy dying her hair brunette and getting smarter. He has helped me so much in this process, more than he will ever know. I want people to know that most of the characters in this book are based on my family and people around my small town of Muldrow, Oklahoma. The family dynamics in this book are based on the way I was raised. I have a very close family, and that will never change. I am proud of my upbringing. I want to thank my parents for all the support, love, encouragement, and discipline they have given me during my life.

I want to thank the Larssen family from Newberry Springs, California, for allowing me to use their names and family dynamics for this book. They are a wonderful, close-knit family that portrays the families in this book. They not only encouraged me to keep writing but also helped with suggestions along the way.

I want to thank my best friend, Susan, for her encouragement through this process. She has been very supportive. I saw in her the strength that a single mother needs to get through every day. She has shown great courage and resilience from the hard life that she has had. She has survived against all odds for her children. She not only has encouraged her children but also found the time to help a friend achieve a goal that seemed impossible. I also want to thank Susan for allowing me, not only into her life, but also into her children's life. I want to thank my goddaughter, Mary, for assistance with this book. She is one of the reasons I decided to write this book.

I wanted to write a book that was clean and family oriented, something I could give my twelve-year-old godchild or to my grandmother or mother that they could read without me being embarrassed by the content. I wanted something that described my childhood and the pride that I have for my community. I wanted something that had no cussing, sex or drugs but still sent a clear message.

I want to thank David Foltz for his input on the characters and for being the inspiration for certain characters in this book. I also want to thank him for the patience and understanding of the late hours in writing this book. Thank you from the bottom of my heart.

I also want to thank my brother-in-law, David, for understanding the many phone calls to his wife regarding this book. I thank you for the input and for being the inspiration for certain characters in this book. You really don't know how much I appreciate you and love you.

I also want to thank my late uncle, Kenny. He showed me what being an optimist really is all about. He also showed me courage. He was a paraplegic and was the most amazing man I have ever known. The strength and courage he showed everyone was amazing. He always had a smile on his face and never said anything bad about anyone. He was and still is with me wherever I go, and I will never forget him. I love him very much and wish he was here to see my accomplishment.

I want to thank my mother. You will find in this book that the female characters are very loving and encouraging characters. That is my mother and grandmother wrapped up in those characters. The grandmother figure in this book is a combination of my mother and my grandmother. She has always stood beside me and encouraged me through some of the most difficult times in my life.

I would like to take this time to tell my family how wonderful they are and how much I love them. Without them, I would be lost. They have been there for me through adversity and helped me come out on the other side. I want my parents to know that they are my rock. I respect them and thank them for the support. I am proud to call them Mom and Dad. I want them to know that they raised two daughters who are so proud of them. I want to say, "Job well done. You achieved what you set out to do. You raised two daughters who are professionals, college educated, and doing what they always wanted to do in life. *Thank you*, and I love you very much."

To my late Uncle Kenny.
I miss you more every day
and love you very much.

Chapter 1

Deni sat in her bedroom in front of her computer, typing away. She was always researching something; if it wasn't something for school, it was something she was just curious about. Today's topic was alternative energy resources. She wanted to come up with something on a small scale that was affordable for everyone, but it had to be environmentally friendly. She had already scaled down wind energy so that it was affordable for everyone. Last year's science fair winner was her small windmills for rooftop installation. Her parents had spent the money to help her build the project and installed it on their rooftop. As she sat in front of her computer, she just could not believe how much energy that project produced. Her parents no longer had to pay for electricity; in fact, the electric company was paying them for the energy produced by those small windmills and solar panels.

She knew it was just a matter of time before someone came up with that one invention that would change the world and help reverse the effects of global warming. She wanted that someone to be her.

That's when she heard her door open and her mom, Cathy, ask, "Are you still on that computer?"

Deni replied, "Yes, you know I have only three months until school starts then only three months until the science fair. I have to start on this now if I want to change the world."

Her mother laughed. "Yes, but you just finished school yesterday. Can't you just enjoy the summer?"

Deni had not "enjoyed" a summer in a very long time. She always had some project to work on for school. She also liked to get a jump-start on the next school year. The principal was so proud of her that he allowed her to take books home for the next year to help encourage her to excel even more. She had already skipped a grade and was in all the honors classes. If she continued on this path, she should be able to graduate high school two years early. She had already applied to all the top universities in the country and already received confirmation from five of them, offering her scholarships. All she had to do now was choose which one.

Her mother was sitting on her bed, watching as she continued her search on her computer, trying to figure out how her daughter had gotten so smart. She started swelling up with pride.

"What are your friends doing this summer? Are they gonna be working, participating in internship programs, or just kickin' back and enjoyin' it?" She was hoping Deni would say, "Kickin' back."

Deni just shrugged her shoulders. Her mom stood up to leave, not having much success at distracting her daughter. Deni turned around just in time to catch her mother's sleeve. "I'm sorry, Mom, I know you think that this is just a waste of time, but it's important to me."

Her mom turned and brushed a piece of hair out of her daughter's eyes. "I know, sweetheart, but just once I'd like for you to enjoy your childhood while you're still a child. Is that too much to ask?"

Deni replied, "No. I understand what you're saying. How's this? We have a slumber party to kick off the summer. Is that all right with you and Dad?"

Her mom smiled. "I think that's a wonderful idea. I'll start calling now to get approval from your friends' parents. Come downstairs when you finish but make it soon."

Deni smiled back at her mom. "I'll be there in a minute."

As Deni approached the kitchen, she heard her mother on the phone with Cindy's mom. Cindy was Deni's best friend. They were born on the same day, at the same time, at the same hospital, and their bassinets were side by side. You could say they were born to be best friends. They were, and are, inseparable. Deni was very intelligent, but Cindy was lacking in the smart department. Both had skipped a grade in school.

Now they were in the same classes. The only reason Cindy had these opportunities is because of Deni. Deni was always pushing Cindy to greater heights, but truth is Cindy just could not reach those anymore. The higher the grade in school, the more Cindy sunk. Both had been accepted to the same colleges and universities, but Cindy wasn't sure she deserved them.

Deni heard her mother. "I'm just trying to get Deni out of her room, away from that computer," Cathy said. "She needs to have fun during the summer, not spend it on the next science project or any project. With your help and help from Cindy, maybe we can all just have fun and actually go on a vacation without computers this time." She heard her mother saying "yes" and "okay" or "that sounds nice" before she hung up the phone.

Deni walked into the kitchen just as her mother hung up. Cathy turned around and smiled at Deni. "I made us an appointment at Hair Station Salon for in the morning. I thought you might want a makeover and a girls' day out. We can go to the salon, go shopping for some summer clothes, and then eat lunch before we come home to get ready for your party."

Deni laughed at her mother's excitement but agreed without hesitation. Then Deni thought of something that she had not thought of in years. When she was younger, she had always wanted to dye her hair and make it lighter. She had beautiful hair—long, light brown, and with gold and auburn natural highlights. However, she wanted something different. Now that she was getting older, she felt it was time for a change. She would go research, as she always did, and try to find the best color choice for herself, but she wanted to lighten her hair slowly. Deni was thinking of going lighter, maybe blonde but not platinum blonde—that would be too drastic. Maybe a dark blonde to start with and then dye it lighter gradually. She would wait and see what her research said about hair color and the effects it had on the hair and the person.

As Deni researched about hair color, she happened upon an article written by someone much like herself, always researching, but this time the person had written an article on hair color and the effects color has on a person's personality. She observed that someone going from natural blonde to brunette seemed to get more respect from people in public. Brunettes who colored their hair red were assumed to have bad tempers when in fact they have very sweet, docile dispositions until provoked. The biggest change and most interesting information she found was when brunettes or redheads changed their hair color to blonde. Those women that did change their color to blonde found they had less respect. People treated them as if they really were dumb blondes and did not even consider them as having a brain or feelings. They also found that people did not listen to them as much and disregarded their thoughts.

Deni turned to leave when her mom appeared. "You remember when you were younger?" Cathy asked. "You always wanted to dye your hair. Why don't we try that tomorrow?"

Deni laughed and said, "I was just coming downstairs to talk to you about that. What do think of this color?"

Deni showed her mom the color she had found on the Internet. The color was very subtle but very pretty at the same time. Her mother loved it and thought Deni would look great with her hair changed. Deni agreed also and decided to go all out and have her hair cut also. Deni had never done this before. She didn't want it cut short but wanted her hair trimmed to a modern long cut. She decided she would consult the stylist tomorrow to see what kind of cut she suggested. That was her decision and nothing could change her mind now.

Deni was so excited about the change she was going to be making that she could hardly contain herself. She wanted to keep everything a secret until her friends arrived tomorrow afternoon for the slumber party. She told her dad all about the new color and haircut she was going to get the next day and asked him to not tell anyone until her friends saw it the following night. Her dad agreed, of course, but wasn't aware of what was going to take place the next night.

Deni had forgotten to ask her father's permission for the slumber party. Therefore, she said, "Dad, is it okay if I have a slumber party tomorrow night? It's just gonna be the usual crowd. Cindy, Mary, Leah, and myself. Mom and I are gonna go down to the salon in the morning for a girls' day too. I am so excited. I cannot wait till everyone sees my new hairdo. Is it okay? Please, Dad, please."

Her dad looked at her very seriously and said, "Yes, it's okay. But are you sure you're not going to explode before morning?"

Deni started laughing harder and said, "Yes, Dad, I'm sure. But what are you and Mom gonna do tomorrow night?"

He just laughed and said, "We are staying here to make sure nothing gets out of hand. Is there a problem with that? I want to make sure you don't spontaneously combust from all the excitement."

Deni just agreed and said it was okay for them to stay but to leave the extinguisher in the garage. They all had a big laugh and finished dinner.

That night before Deni went to bed, she looked again at the pictures of her new hairstyle and color. She was still so excited she didn't think she would sleep that night. However, when she lay down and started listening to her ocean sounds, she fell fast asleep. Her dreams were weird that night. She kept having dreams that she was driving a convertible down an oceanfront road with the wind whipping through her long thick beautiful blonde hair. She had contacts in and a pair of Electric Sunglasses on, driving a classic Thunderbird. She had on a beautiful outfit with red lipstick, and her nails were done in a French tip, with a thumb ring on her left thumb beaming in the sunlight. She saw herself stopping at a stoplight, taking off the sunglasses, and seeing the most brilliant teal eyes she had ever seen. She thought it was someone else driving the car because she had hazel eyes. Was this some kind of a subconscious longing or was this some kind of a premonition?

The next morning she got up very tired but excited still about what the day was going to hold. She couldn't shake the restlessness of her dream but she wasn't going to dye her hair platinum blonde, get contacts to change her eye color, or wear makeup. That was just not for her, and she would never give in to the peer pressure of wearing makeup when she was quite happy the way she looked. She felt that people who had to wear makeup were trying to cover up their true self or hiding something. Therefore, she got out her journal to write down what the day would hold and to write down what she could remember about her dream.

After she finished with her journal, she decided to take a shower to get ready for the big day. She heard her mom yelling for her to come down for breakfast. Deni walked into the kitchen in her robe, her hair up in a towel, asking her mother what's for breakfast. She sat down at the table just as her mom put a plate of blueberry waffles in front of her. She looked at her mother a little strange and asked, *"Mom, you made my favorite waffles?"*

Her mother turned around and smiled. "I just thought since we were going to spend the day together, we should start with a good breakfast. I thought after we get our hair styled, we could go the nail salon and get a mani-pedi. Does that sound good?"

Deni replied, "I guess. What did you have in mind, exactly, about the manicure?" Deni described her dream from the night before and how it made her anxious. "I just don't get it," she said.

Deni finished her breakfast and went upstairs to finish getting ready. She was trying to decide on an outfit when she ran across something she had bought for the beginning of school. She fished out the halter top and a pair of cute jean shorts. She then pulled out her favorite sandals and looked in the mirror. She remembered she wasn't sure about the halter when she bought it, but now was the time for change. She normally didn't wear fuchsia, mauve, or prints of any kind but her mom had talked her into trying it since she was starting a new year. Well, that year was over and now it was summer. She was beginning a new chapter in her life; she decided it was about time to wear the beautiful electric-blue halter. She looked at herself in the mirror, and what she saw blew her away. She saw a young woman instead of a girl standing there. Then she thought of actually putting on makeup, but she just couldn't bring herself to do that after the dream she had last night.

Cathy was finishing putting on her clothes when her daughter walked into her room looking beautiful as usual. She also was stunned that Deni had chosen the blue halter to wear today. It was completely out of character for her, but it was a great shirt, and the color made her daughter look more like a woman. It was very sophisticated for her age. She was only fourteen but looked like she was eighteen in this, even if she refused to wear makeup. She told her daughter how stunning she looked and then asked, "Are you ready to go?"

Deni said she was, and she insisted on taking her laptop. In case the hairstylist didn't understand what she wanted. She could just show her the picture of the hairstyle and the color. Deni wanted to make sure the stylist got it all correct. Cathy just chuckled at how her daughter was acting. It reminded her of her first date. How that date had to perfect. She could not help but laugh aloud and just shake her head.

They both walked downstairs together and stood in the doorway. It was sunny when they were getting ready, but now it was starting to cloud up and sprinkle. Cathy grabbed an umbrella, and they headed for the car. Just as Cathy pulled into the parking space in front of the salon, it started to pour. There was a bright flash of lightning and a loud clap of thunder when they opened the car doors. Then the rain hit them hard and fast. They made a mad dash for the door but still got soaked. Luckily, the hairstylist, Sabrina, saw them pull up and held the door for them.

The salon was small. A few clients sitting under the driers with rollers in their hair joked with Cathy about how wet she got. The salon's walls were a beautiful warm teal color, and a gorgeous mural of a beach with the waves easing their way up the sand adorned one side. The salon had recently been renovated, and it looked gorgeous. Rain pounded the windows of the small salon, making it sound as if the waves were just on the other side of the glass.

Sabrina brought them towels, and after they dried themselves off, Cathy and Deni looked through books for the hairstyle Deni had picked out on the computer.

Sabrina brought hot cocoa to warm them from the cold rain and said, "What kind of magic can I work on y'all today?"

Deni asked if she had been on the website *hairforyou.com* to keep up on all the latest styles. Sabrina said she had. "Which one was you lookin' at? The blunt with bangs? The blunt without bangs? Do you want to block your hair? What kind of color can I put on this beautiful long hair?"

Deni looked at Sabrina as if she was speaking a foreign language. Then she said, "I brought my laptop to show you what kind of hairstyle I wanted and what color I picked out. If you think they will look okay on me."

Sabrina looked at the pictures and said, "That's gonna be the purtiest thing I ever done for a young lady. Yer gonna leave here lookin' like a movie star, girl. Now get over in this chair and let me go mix your color."

Deni sat in the chair and put her laptop on top of Sabrina's work space, just waiting for the miracle worker to start her magic on her long dull hair. Then what Sabrina had said about being a movie star hit Deni, and she was a little unsettled by the statement. She kept telling herself to get over it because it was just a stupid dream.

Cathy sat and watched her daughter settle into the chair and wondered how much more beautiful could they make her. She was so proud of Deni for the decisions she had made about her life so far that she knew Deni was making the right decision about changing her hair. She also knew Deni was getting older and wanted to help encourage her daughter to pursue her dreams.

Deni prepared for the slight changes she was about to undergo. She made Sabrina turn the chair around so she could not see the transformation take place. She wanted to be completely surprised.

Sabrina turned the chair around and just chuckled. She did tell Deni and Cathy that she was going to be using an all-natural dye on both of them from a new company. Sabrina also said they had been having very good results with this product. It would make their hair more manageable and would help reverse the damage to the hair. It would also help the hair follicles and nourish the scalp.

They both agreed that the new company was at least being environmentally friendly, which made Deni very happy. All she could think of was, *Bring on the all-natural botanical dye.* How funny that a company could develop such a wonderful product that would dye your hair without any kind of side effect. Deni made a mental note to research this company later.

As Sabrina worked on putting the color on Deni's hair and finished with the last foil, Deni found she just could not wait to see the magic Sabrina had worked. She sat watching Sabrina work on her mother's hair. Sabrina was very meticulous about her work. Deni noticed how careful Sabrina was with each stroke of her brush on her mother's hair. She also noticed how pretty her mother was.

Deni had never really noticed the beauty that her mother possessed. When her mother laughed, her eyes just lit up. The way her mother's mouth was perfectly shaped for her face. She also noticed the very small wrinkles starting to form at the corners of her mother's mouth and the very small crow's feet around her eyes when her mother laughed.

Deni realized her mother was aging right along with her. Right before her eyes. How unappreciated she must have felt because Deni thought of her as just a mom. Moms don't age, get sick, have sex. Deni didn't want to think about that last one, but she vowed to spend more time with her mom and to make sure both her parents knew how much they meant to her.

This day had certainly been a great day so far, and Deni was so enlightened. She wanted more and more to make sure that her mother was going to be happy today. While Deni sat there watching Sabrina finish her mother, she heard the sound of a bell. Sabrina's assistant came over to take Deni to the washbowl to wash out her hair. Deni's heart was pounding so hard when she walked back to the chair. She glanced at the mirror and was amazed at what she saw.

Deni refused to look at herself any longer. She sat down for Sabrina to cut her hair in what Deni described as a one-length blunt cut in the back with a textured cut around the face. She felt this would help frame her better. Sabrina made cuts with precision, and when she finished, she put more product in Deni's hair so she could style it. Deni waited until Sabrina blow-dried her hair, and then she took out the flat iron for further styling. When Sabrina turned Deni around to face the mirror, Deni didn't believe it was her sitting in the chair looking back. She saw a beautiful haircut flattering the face of this very pretty young woman. The color was perfect—light brown on the bottom with pale blonde highlights in the front. She loved it. She really felt like a movie star. That's when Deni turned to her mother and said she wanted to buy makeup.

Cathy was so shocked at the sudden change in her daughter that she would agree to anything. She was so happy and so proud of Deni. Sabrina turned to Cathy to finish styling her hair. Cathy decided to go a little lighter with her blonde hair, which made her look ten years younger. Deni looked at her mother now and saw someone who was not her mother but someone who looked like her sister. They both were ecstatic with the results. They made return appointments to keep the color fresh and headed to the nail salon across the street.

Deni decided to take her mother's advice and get French tip nails. She had always made fun of girls at school for keeping their nails so manicured. She felt that only those who were not eco-conscious got their nails done regularly. After all, it was acrylic, and the smell in the shop could not be good for the environment. It had already made Deni dizzy. Deni knew that acrylic nails had harsh chemicals in them, such as formaldehyde, which is used for embalming people, toluene, and dibutyl phthalate—all harmful chemicals. Deni had made sure to research the effects the acrylic nails had on the environment, and what she found made her question whether she wanted to get her nails done. She didn't want nails at all until she found an alternative for acrylic nails. It's called ethyl methacrylate, or EMA to nail specialists, and that made Deni happy to know she could still be fashionable without filling the landfills with more waste.

Cathy had decided to do the same but wanted a flower on her toes. Deni thought it was cute, so she did the same. They sat side by side in the chairs, getting their nails done. Then they moved to the massage chairs to get the pedicures. They were so relaxed and so happy. This was the perfect day. They made a vow that since they have to have their nails done every two weeks and their hair done every six weeks, those days were just going to be for them. Those were the days they planned to have lunch and go shopping just to spend more time together.

When they left the nail salon, they started looking for a place to eat lunch. Deni suggested a Chinese restaurant a couple doors down from the nail salon.

Cathy laughed and said, "Usually it's pizza or some other fast food. What's gotten into you? Don't tell me you're starting to grow up on me."

Deni smiled, blushing a little.

They walked into the Chinese restaurant. When they finally sat down and ordered their food, Cathy got out a pen and paper from her purse. Deni started right in on the slumber party plans. "Do you think Dad would mind grilling burgers and hot dogs? Everyone loves those. Then all we have to get are paper plates and plastic cups," Deni said.

Cathy agreed and called Stanley to okay the grilling with him.

After they ate, they headed to the Party Planner to pick up supplies when Deni noticed a Help Wanted sign on the door. She asked her mom, "Is it okay if I pick up an application?"

Cathy replied, "I don't know if your father would approve of you having a job so young. I'm afraid your schoolwork would suffer."

Deni shook her head. "You know I'm not going to do anything to jeopardize my chances of going to college, but this might be a fun place to work. Besides, I need this experience. Come on, Mom, it's just an application. They might not hire me anyway. But at least let me try."

Cathy could not resist her daughter's plea. Deni picked up the application and talked to the manager that day. The manager told her they had only one opening, and she would be considered for the job, although she was very young.

Deni and her mother picked up the lanterns and some paper plates, napkins, cups, and other miscellaneous items for her Japanese-themed party. Now she felt that everything was complete, except she had forgotten about the food. Cathy didn't forget and went straight to the grocery store to pick up the necessary items for the barbecue. Deni picked out the chips and snack foods while her mother went to the butcher to have fresh sirloin ground into hamburger meat. Then Deni and her mother proceeded to the checkout. Before leaving the store, Deni had the feeling she should ask for an application. She proceeded to the manager's desk to ask when she noticed a boy from school working there.

Josh was a wannabe jock in school and hung out on the outskirts of the in- crowd. Deni had known him all her life and considered him a friend. She approached Josh to ask if he liked working at the store. Josh said, "It's okay. I mean it's a job, right?"

Deni replied, "I guess, but I was just looking for something to fill the time."

Josh asked, "Don't you usually work all summer on the next year's schoolwork? I mean, isn't your time filled with all kinds of scholarly junk? Have you already started on next year's science project?"

Deni shook her head and said, "No. My mom wants me to take the summer off this year, and I thought a job might be the thing to keep my mind off the school year. Besides, I could always make a science fair project out of the life experience I get from this job. Now who do I talk to around here to get an application?"

Josh took Deni over to the shift manager. The manager told Deni there was an opening for an after-school checker but couldn't guarantee anything without talking to her parents first. Deni agreed and took the application.

As Cathy loaded the car, she noticed Deni coming across the parking lot with a light spring in her step, holding a piece of paper. Cathy asked, "What took you so long?" Deni showed her the application and smiled.

Cathy turned to finish loading the car. "I thought we agreed to only the Party Planner, not every place we stop. We haven't even talked to your father yet to see if it's okay for you to have a job. What do you think he's gonna say to all this?"

Deni replied, "Mom, I don't think he will mind, especially if I say this is for a science fair project. I really think I could come up with a good project from the experience I get from this job."

Cathy just shook her head. Her own words used against her. What could she do but accept what Deni had said. She did want her daughter off the computer, but she thought maybe Deni could just enjoy being a kid for once. She finally realized that this probably would never happen, and she should just face the fact that her daughter was a typical overachiever who didn't know how to have fun in the summer. To Deni, fun was working on the next school year's subjects or the next science fair project or whatever else she could think of to keep her mind growing and expanding. Cathy swelled with pride again at how mature her daughter was becoming and how smart Deni was. She was always thinking of her next move.

They arrived home just as Stan arrived from the office. They all helped unload the car, and Deni was about to ask her father about the applications when Stan turned around and asked Deni, "Hey, I got an interesting phone call today. Homer down at the Pig-n-Tote called and said you asked for a job. You want to tell me something?"

Deni looked embarrassedly at her father and explained the conversation with her mother and the application.

Stan looked his daughter in the eye and chuckled. "Yes, it's okay. I think Homer is looking for a cashier just for a few hours every evening. It might not be very many hours a week, but it's a start." Deni was so excited that she could hardly contain herself.

Shortly after hanging the lanterns, the doorbell rang. It was Cindy. She had come early to see if Deni needed help with anything. Deni was glad to see her and told her about her mom and dad agreeing to the summer job. She had already filled out the application and was ready to take it to Homer the next day. She asked Cindy, "Do you want to come with me tomorrow?"

Cindy nodded her head excitedly and could hardly contain her excitement for Deni. Cindy couldn't help but wonder if maybe she could get a job at the Pig-n-Tote also. She would check tomorrow. Meantime, Cindy kept answering the door as each of their friends arrived. Cindy greeted them as if she was the host. Deni didn't mind though; she and Cindy had been friends forever, and it was as if they had agreed to cohost the event.

Deni was just starting to set the table when her father announced that in five minutes the hamburgers and hot dogs would be ready. Deni hurried to set each place with accuracy and speed. She had made funny little place cards and now thought they were silly, so she just let everyone sit where they wanted. Deni's father placed two large platters on the table, one containing the hamburgers and the other containing hot dogs. Cathy had also placed similar platters holding the buns on the table. Deni had already put the potato chips and pork and beans on the table and was hollering for all to come eat. Just as everyone was sitting down to eat, the phone rang. It was Homer asking for Deni. Deni came to the phone. "Hello."

Homer replied, "Deni, this is Homer. I was just wondering if you would be interested in the after-school job as a cashier. It won't be very many hours a week, but it should be enough to buy school clothes. I've already approved it with your dad."

Deni didn't know what to say. She had filled out the application but hadn't even turned it in yet. She was so excited. "Yes. Yes, I want the job. You wouldn't happen to have another opening, would you? My best friend, Cindy, is also looking for a summer job."

"As a matter of fact, I do have another opening. That's the reason I'm calling. You see, today when I closed the store, one of the checkers came up and just quit. Said she was moving to Kentucky," replied Homer. "Both of you show up in the morning, and we'll start on the paperwork. Can I have Cindy's home number to approve this with her parents?" Deni gave Homer the number and hung up the phone.

She ran to the backyard and blurted out the information so fast no one could understand her. She proceeded to tell them all again very slowly. Cindy was so excited she jumped up to go call her parents to tell them Homer was going to call them, but the phone was busy. Cindy kept dialing until finally she got an answer.

"Mom, Homer from the Pig-n-Tote is going to call you to see if it's okay if I work there for the summer. Please, please, tell him I can. Deni is going to work there tomorrow. Her parents don't care. Please say it's okay for me to get this job."

Cindy's mom was just laughing. "Wow, you need to slow down. Homer did call us and ask if you could go to work for him. He also told us about Deni, and of course, we had to say yes. Your father and I both feel this will be a good opportunity for both you girls. Congratulations, honey," replied Cindy's mom.

Cindy hung up the phone and sprinted outside to tell the others. Everyone congratulated the girls but decided they should go to bed early since they had to be at work at nine.

They all started passing food around the table so the girls could get a good meal before bed. They all sat and talked about the upcoming day. Then they went upstairs, and Cindy asked to see the application Deni had picked up earlier that day. Deni pulled it out of her desk drawer and showed it to Cindy.

Cindy looked at it, asking, "How did you know what to write on here?"

Deni answered, "My mom helped me fill it out. She also said I have to have my social security card to take with me. You do have yours, right?"

Cindy nodded her head and continued to look at the application, as if memorizing it so she would know what to put on hers.

Deni noticed this and said, "If you want I can help you in the morning when we get there. It should be easy. Probably be just all paperwork and Homer said he would help us fill everything out since it was going to be our first job."

Cindy looked at Deni. "Well, thank goodness for that. I've never seen an application before. Actually, I never dreamed I would have a job this easy. I know you have something up your sleeve. So what gives?"

Deni told her about the Help Wanted sign and the rest of the story about the Pig-n-Tote. Deni also proceeded to tell Cindy about Josh working at the store.

As the others came into the room to get ready to go to bed, they all gathered around Deni's computer to look at the newest edition of Hollywood gossip slathered on all the top websites. Deni wasn't too concerned about the Hollywood scene. Cindy was totally into all the latest trends and gossip. For that matter, Cindy was into gossip about anything or anyone as long as it was gossip. Deni couldn't understand why anyone would go to such lengths to find out about stars and who was dating whom or who had broken up over the weekend. She thought it was just appalling how everyone could snoop into other people's personal lives so willingly. Especially Cindy. Deni had always thought that Cindy was too smart and intelligent to be interested in gossip. What Deni didn't know was that Cindy was so into all the Hollywood scene and gossip that it just wasn't funny. Cindy dreamed about going to Hollywood after graduation wanting to become an actress. Cindy was also the blonde of the bunch. She was not always the brightest crayon in the box, but given enough time, she could catch on. Deni has always been the intelligent one. But Cindy knew she could not hold a candle to Deni.

Chapter 2

Deni and the other girls got in bed early so she and Cindy could get a good night's rest. The next morning they all woke up bright and early. Leah and Mary said their good-byes as they left and wished Deni and Cindy good luck with their new jobs. Deni and Cindy finished getting dressed and getting ready for work and then had a big breakfast Cathy had made for them. Because of all the excitement over the barbecue, sleepover, and jobs, no one had noticed Deni's hair.

Cindy finally said something in the car while they were waiting for Cathy. "Hey, Deni, did you do something different to your hair? I was going to mention it last night when I saw you, but with all the commotion going on, I simply forgot. I'm sorry."

Deni said, "It's okay, I completely understand. I almost forgot I had it done till I looked in the mirror this morning. Do you like it? I didn't want something drastic, just very subtle."

Cindy studied it for a moment and then said, "I love it. I was just thinking I've wanted to do something different with my hair. Where did you get yours done? I want something subtle too, but I want to go darker. You think that would be good for me?"

"I think it would be great. You really like it? I'm thinking of going lighter next time I go. Hey, why don't we make your appointment with Mom's and mine? Then we can all get our hair done together. That would be cool," Deni said.

Cindy agreed. She and Deni vowed to research the colors when they got home so they could pick out their colors for the next visit. When Cathy got in the car to go, Cindy and Deni laid out the plan for their next visit to Hair Station Salon.

Cathy agreed, "That would be a wonderful idea. Cindy, what do you want to do with your hair? It's gorgeous the way it is, why change it?"

Cindy replied, "I was thinking about dying my hair a little darker and maybe a trim. I want something subtle but noticeable."

"You two girls sound so much alike it's not even funny," Cathy said. Then they all laughed.

Cathy dropped the girls off in front of the store and wished them good luck. She said she would be there at 7:00 p.m. to pick them up. Homer had promised the girls' parents they would work no later than 7:00 p.m. every night due to their ages.

Deni and Cindy walked into the store to find Homer standing there waiting for them. He had a big smile on his face and extended his hand to welcome the girls. He asked them to follow him to his office so they could start filling out paperwork. Then he said, "Cindy, I'm gonna need you to also fill out an application."

Cindy nodded her head nervously. The girls were so nervous because they didn't know what to expect from the paperwork. As they sat in that tiny office filling out the stack of papers Homer had given them, they started laughing nervously.

"What do you think they do with all this paperwork? Think how many trees were killed just to go to work," laughed Deni.

Cindy replied, "I don't know what they do with all this, but I know what I'd do with it. I can't believe you have to fill out this much stuff just to go to work. This is nuts." Just as writer's cramp was starting to set in, Homer walked in to check on the girls and pick up what paperwork they had finished. He asked the girls for their social security cards and made copies. He then took them on a tour of the store and showed them their personal lockers. He gave them store T-shirts, showed them the break room, and gave them aprons to wear. Homer was talking so fast they almost couldn't keep up. They had to run to catch up with Homer at this point. Homer was on his way to the front of the store to one of the registers. He introduced the girls to Martha, who would be training

Cindy. Then he introduced both girls to Peggy—she would be training Deni. Both girls were eager to get started, so Peggy and Martha showed them first how to bring the registers up for the day.

At around noon, business started picking up, and the girls could do nothing but watch Martha and Peggy as they scanned all the items the customers brought to them. It was kind of fun watching how fast these two women were but then came some smaller orders. It was Deni and Cindy's turn at the register with Peggy and Martha watching. Deni and Cindy started scanning the items just as they had seen their trainers doing. All went well till it became time for coupons. As always, coupons were a hassle but well worth the time. They noticed that people using the coupons were saving a lot of money. Deni knew that already but couldn't convince people to use them. Maybe that could be what their project could be about—coupons. She would make a note to talk to Cindy later about that. Right now, she had her hands full with the long line of people.

Deni glanced at Cindy to see how she was faring on her first day and noticed Cindy was still watching Martha. Cindy's line got too long, so Martha took over. By the time they had checked out the last customer at around two, Martha and Peggy sent the girls on break. The girls walked into the break room and hung up their aprons as everyone else had done earlier. They picked out a little table in the corner and opened up the bag Cathy had given them when she dropped them off. Cindy and Deni were so surprised when they looked in and saw a note lying on top of the lunch Cathy had packed. They began to read it and tears began to roll down their cheeks. The note told them how proud Deni's parents were of both of them and how grown up they'd become. At the end of the note was signed, "Love always, Stanley and Cathy." Cathy hadn't written the note; it was Stan. Deni was as shocked as Cindy. They saved the note and dug deeper into the sack. Cathy had packed a nice lunch for the girls.

After lunch, they put everything up and grabbed their aprons off the hook to go back to the register and see if they could finally get things together. Sure enough, both girls were pretty much on their own by the end of the day. They also learned that during down time, they had to restock the candy counter and the magazine racks. Unfortunately, there was not much down time, and the girls were so looking forward to the end of the day. To their surprise, Homer let them go at 5:00 p.m., before the evening rush. They were happy to be off work but so tired. Homer told them to be there at noon the next day, and their new schedule would be noon to five most of the days they work. The girls headed to the break room, to their lockers, to pick up their belongings and headed to the front of the store.

Outside, Cathy was waiting for them. She explained how Homer called and asked how their first day went. Both girls told Cathy about the whole day, almost cutting each other's sentences off, each trying to talk over the other. Deni left out the part about seeing Cindy fall behind a bit, but most of the day was wonderful. Both were excited about the next day but were growing more and more tired the closer they got to Deni's house. Cathy turned to Cindy to ask her if she wanted to spend the night again when she noticed that Cindy was nodding off, just like Deni. Cathy pulled into her driveway with two very sleepy girls in the car. She woke them up to go into the house so she could start supper.

Cathy was preparing supper when Deni walked in asking about the note her dad had written and slipped into their lunch sack. Cathy turned to look at her daughter to ask further about the note. Deni noticed the look on her mom's face and then pulled out the note from her back pocket. Cathy unfolded the note, and while reading it, she began to become misty eyed. When she looked at Deni, tears started streaking down both their faces.

Deni asked, "Did you know anything about this?"

Cathy just shook her head. She told Deni that when she had come downstairs to cook breakfast, Stan was sitting at the bar looking at something. She started packing their lunch first so she wouldn't forget it. After she packed it, she turned back to the refrigerator to get the breakfast stuff out when Stan left in a hurry.

"That's when he must have put it in the lunch sack. I had no idea," Cathy replied.

Deni said, "It's okay. Just tell him thanks from Cindy and me. We really liked it. It surprised us but we liked it." Cathy agreed and gave the note back to Deni.

When Cathy called everyone for dinner, the girls had fallen asleep again. She sent Stan to wake them up; when he opened the door, there was no one there. Stan looked around the room but noticed no one. He went back downstairs to see if the girls were there, but he still couldn't find them.

When Stan reached the kitchen, he saw Deni and Cindy coming in from the living room and said, "There you are. You two had me worried. I went looking for you in your room and no one was there."

Deni replied, "We heard Mom call us for dinner and took the front stairs. Sorry, Dad, we didn't mean to worry you."

"That's okay. Just don't let it happen again, you little Houdini." They all just chuckled, not finding her Dad's joke funny, if you can call it a joke.

Cathy had set the food on the table and called everyone. When they all settled in, she started asking about their day. Everyone tried to speak at once, and then they started going around the table. She had already heard about the girls' day but wanted Stan to hear about it. As the girls recapped their day to Stanley, he got just as excited as they were. He also said that Homer had called to let him know how the girls had done. Homer said he was proud at how fast they picked everything up today.

Stan passed this on to the girls and told them to keep up the good work. Then it was Stan's turn. He told them about his day at the office, but no one really understood what he was saying because he was an architect, and they really didn't understand all the terms he used.

After supper, everyone headed into the living room to watch TV, but they couldn't find anything to watch but reruns. The girls finally said they were going upstairs to do some research before bed. They couldn't wait to look at the newest hairdos and colors for Cindy's hair. They downloaded her picture so they could see just how she would look. They laughed at some of the styles and, just for fun, looked at the punk styles with all the different colors. They really got a laugh out of the purple with the green stripe. It looked like a funky skunk. They finally settled on a style, so now the color was next. They tried several but it was too drastic for Cindy. She just wanted a subtle change. She finally settled on a blocking of the color, and then she said she would just wait and see what Sabrina thought.

They finally decided to go to bed when the phone rang. Cathy yelled for Deni to pick up the upstairs phone. When she answered, it was Leah and

Mary. "What are the working girls doing?" both girls asked simultaneously.

Cindy and Deni both answered, "Going to bed. What are you two doing? Wishing you had a job so you could shop more?"

Deni couldn't help but be a little sarcastic since her friends always wanted to hang out at the mall. Deni hated shopping unless it was for a project or something for school. Deni couldn't understand what was so exciting at the mall, but her friends thought the boys were interesting. Still Cindy only went for the fashion. She didn't really care for the boys; she wanted to achieve her goals first before she would allow herself to think about boys? Leah and Mary laughed but still asked about the girls' days. They all talked for about thirty minutes. Cindy and Deni had to hang up to get ready for bed.

They each took their showers and put on pajamas. They both lay in bed that night recapping their day and wondering about tomorrow. Deni was talking to Cindy but Cindy didn't answer. Deni continued to wait for an answer. Cindy still didn't answer her. Deni rolled over to look at her friend and realized she was fast asleep. Poor girl. Deni was just as tired but couldn't go to sleep yet.

Deni got up to go to the computer to research what she could about people using coupons and how much money it took to even make the coupons. That was the one thing Deni was concerned about—what the bottom dollar was and if it was eco-friendly. She couldn't care less how many people use them. It's what the companies did with the coupons after they entered an establishment. That was what Deni wanted to focus on for the project. That's when Deni noticed that most of the coupons people used were all printed on recycled paper and wasn't worth the paper they were printed on. Deni had to laugh to herself. Now she had to come up with a completely new plan. She decided to sleep on it for tonight and discuss it with Cindy in the morning.

The next few days went by without incident, and Deni just couldn't figure out what she wanted to do for her next project. Usually by now, she would have already been gathering information, but right now, she was finding it hard to focus on projects. Deni talked to Cindy about the next school year and what they wanted to do for the next science fair. Cindy talked Deni into just having fun this summer. Cindy didn't want to worry about the next school year; the only thing she wanted to worry about was what to do with her hair.

Deni and Cindy went to work every day and one night they would stay at Deni's, and the next they would stay at Cindy's. It went on like this for about a month. One night when both girls were staying at Deni's house, her mom reminded them of the hair appointments they all had the next day. Both girls were so excited they could hardly sleep. Both girls went upstairs and turned on Deni's computer to see the new styles and color they had both picked out. Deni wanted to go a little lighter on the blonde, and Cindy wanted to go brunette or just a little darker on the blonde. They just kept looking at the pictures when Deni came up with a brilliant idea.

"Let's print out the pictures to show Sabrina tomorrow, and that way, there will be no confusion on her part," suggested Deni.

Cindy agreed, so they printed the pictures and set them aside.

They both headed downstairs to see what was for supper and if they could help. Cathy had everything prepared and was transferring the food from the pans to the plates. She asked the girls to get Stan for supper. Deni rounded the corner to the living room and heard her dad on the phone with Homer. It didn't sound like a pleasant conversation, but she couldn't figure out what was going on. Stan hung up the phone and turned to go into the dining room but instead was facing two curious teenagers.

He looked at them and shook his head. "You two need to wear bells around your necks to let people know your coming. I just got off the phone with Homer. He said both of you are doing fine. He says you're really go-getters."

Deni and Cindy had a hard time sleeping that night. They just knew if they got makeovers before the school year people would respect them more at school. Truth is the only people respected at schools are teachers and other staff members. Students, on the other hand, respect each other's property and personal space but don't always respect each other the way they should. Well, Deni wanted to change that and teach people that respect is something earned. But it was something everyone deserved. Finally, the girls got ready for bed. They were just lying down when the door opened. "Are you two ready to go to sleep?" Cathy said.

"What's up?" replied Cindy.

"Well, I was just wondering if you two would mind if I go to the library while you're in the salon. There are some new books I want to check out," said Cathy.

Deni sat up and then said, "Mom, you can't do that. We were looking forward to the day with you as much as getting our hair done. We can make time to go to the library later if you think you can wait a while."

Cathy nodded her head and looked so proud that these two young ladies wanted to be with her.

Cathy hugged them both before leaving the room, and then Cindy turned to Deni, asking, "What do you think that was all about?"

Deni said, "I don't know, but sometime she goes through this depression thing where she thinks I don't want to spend time with her. She is so wrong though. I think my mom and I have a great relationship. I just wish she wouldn't worry so much."

Cindy said, "Yeah, it's that way with my mom too. I think they just need reassurance like we do. They all just need to chill. How long do you think it will take for our transformation tomorrow?"

"You make it sound like Frankenstein or something. I don't know but it's gonna be fun. Afterwards we can go eat at the Chinese place. They have such good food," said Deni.

"Okay, sounds good to me," said Cindy.

The next morning, both girls got up slowly and just dragged. Cathy caught them going down the hall to the shower and looked to see if they were actually awake.

She stood there watching them approach and then decided to speak very softly. "Are you two tired or what? Just what exactly did you two do last night before you went to bed?"

Both girls mumbled something inaudible to Cathy, and Cathy just shook her head and finished getting ready. After she was ready, Cathy opened the door to see if the zombies were still moving about but instead found them getting ready and very cheerful now. The showers woke up the dead, so to speak, and both girls were picking out *the* right outfit to wear for the outing today. Cathy thought this was a little odd for Deni since she never cared before about what she wore or who saw her. She didn't think too much about it since Cindy was here, and Cindy was the one who was really into the fashion scene. Maybe being around Cindy so much was finally having an impact on Deni. Thank goodness for that. Maybe Cindy was just the ticket for Deni to stop worrying about next school year, not that this was a bad thing, but she needs to spend time as a child. Cathy hollered for the girls to load up, and both girls came running down the stairs just as Cathy opened the door. They ran to the car, laughing and giggling.

Cathy backed out of the driveway with the girls still laughing. When she got to Hair Station Salon, there was not a parking place that she could see but as she turned onto main street in front of the salon, there was a car pulling out. Cathy waited so she could pull in. The girls were still laughing and giggling. They all walked into the salon laughing.

Sabrina heard them come in and walked over to them. "What can I do for you today, Miss Deni?" Deni looked at her in astonishment

"I can't believe you remembered my name. Here's a pic of what I want, and my friend Cindy has a pic too."

"Well, you brought a friend this time. I'm flattered. Okay let me take care of Miss Deni then I'll take care of Miss Cindy. That okay with you?" asked Sabrina.

Both girls agreed, and Deni walked over to the chair. Sabrina draped her and said she would be right back. She had to go mix the color and she had a surprise for her. Deni couldn't wait to see what Sabrina had in store for her. Sabrina reappeared from behind the curtain and turned Deni away from the mirror. She immediately went to work parting Deni's hair and applying color. When she finished with the last foil, she called Cindy over and looked at the pic she brought with her. She draped Cindy and disappeared behind the curtain.

When she returned, she asked, "Do you want to watch? Or you want me to turn you around like Miss Deni?"

Cindy said, "Go ahead and turn me around. That way I can be surprised like Deni."

Sabrina turned the chair around and started her magic on Cindy. When she was finished with the last foil, her assistant took Deni over to the shampoo bowl. Sabrina called Cathy over and disappeared again behind the magic curtain. When Sabrina reappeared, Cathy was sitting there patiently, looking bored. Sabrina started on Cathy's hair. When she finished with the last foil on Cathy's hair, Sabrina's assistant took Cindy over to the shampoo bowl. Deni sat in the chair again for Sabrina to start her trim and style. When she turned Deni around to look at herself, Deni couldn't believe her eyes. Sabrina had not gone a shade lighter—she had gone two shades lighter. Deni was stunned. She saw this beautiful young lady sitting before her, looking more like a movie star. Cindy and Cathy were just shocked at the change it immediately made in Deni's personality. She sat up straighter and seemed much more proud of herself than she had been before she walked in.

Now it was Cindy's turn to have her makeover. Sabrina turned the chair around and started on Cindy. When she was done, she spun the chair around facing the mirror. Cindy was stunned at the result of Sabrina's magic. Cindy wanted to go a shade darker, but Sabrina had mixed the color too dark, and Cindy ended up a brunette with blonde streaks. It looked beautiful, but she wanted something a little more subtle. Everyone in the salon loved Cindy's hair and told her how flattering it was on her. She absolutely loved her hair now. She thought she looked older and more sophisticated.

Cathy looked at the girls in astonishment and the changes their hair made in them. Cathy was next in line. Sabrina's assistant had already washed Cathy's hair, and Cathy was waiting patiently, hoping her hair would transform her as it did the girls. Sabrina worked her magic on Cathy, and indeed, it had transformed her. She was so proud of her hair, and it showed on her face and the way she carried herself. She exuded pride and confidence. Sabrina made them all return appointments in about a month.

Deni and Cindy led Cathy to the Chinese place for lunch. All three were just beaming. It's so amazing how good you can feel after getting your hair done, and these ladies showed how good they felt. The waitress remembered them from the last time they were in there and commented on how beautiful they all looked. Deni couldn't believe how everyone could remember them from just one meeting. The fact is her memory was starting to fade a little. She couldn't understand how she could forget seeing these people when it was just six weeks ago. Reality was, it was only five weeks, but Deni didn't bother keeping up with the days anymore.

Cathy told them it was time to go shopping for school clothes, and Deni was shocked it was already time to go back to school. She got out her wallet to see if she had her school-clothes money with her. She had forgotten some of it at home but had the majority of it on her. She had saved every dime she made this summer so she could get some really cool clothes for school. That's weird—Deni had never cared about what she wore or what anyone ever thought about the clothes she wore. Her thinking was, "If you don't like what I wear, then don't look at me. I mean, as long as you are comfortable with yourself, why should it matter what anyone else thinks? You're the one who has to live with yourself, so you might as well be happy and learn to love yourself."

Deni looked at her mom and said, "Let's go to the mall. I think I want something trendy to go with my new do. Is that okay with everyone?"

Cindy and Cathy looked at Deni confused. Deni had never wanted to go to the mall for anything. Usually if she needed something from the mall, she always sent her mom or one of her friends to pick it up for her. Deni never went to the mall.

Finally, Cathy spoke first. "What did you say? Because it sounded like you said you wanted to go to the mall."

Deni nodded her head, saying, "Yeah, that's what I said. Well, don't sit there looking at me as if I have a zit on my nose. I want to check out the mall and see what's poppin' for the school year. Do I have a zit on my nose?"

Cathy and Cindy both shook their heads and continued to eat.

"Besides, Cindy is up on all the latest trends, and both of you could help me update my wardrobe," said Deni.

After they paid the bill and walked to the car, Cindy turned to Deni, asking, "Are you sure you're okay? I mean, you have never used those words before. Why now? Did this happen after she changed her hair color? Is that blonde going straight to your brain?"

Deni laughed, just shaking off all the questions but was ready to start shopping. Deni thought all this was a little too weird but didn't pay much attention to it. The problem Deni was starting to experience was memory lapses. She couldn't figure out why she kept forgetting everything. And to top it all off, now she was talking about the mall. What was going on with her? Was this color going straight to her brain or what? She made a mental note to look it up tonight and see if there have ever been any reports of anyone having this side effect from hair color.

Chapter 3

Deni could see the Swaying Pines Mall sign a mile away. She was both excited and nervous. She hadn't been to the mall since she was a little girl. Now she was almost out of high school and almost into college. She still couldn't believe she wanted to come here to shop for school clothes. She usually hated everything trendy and prided herself on being different. Now all she was starting to care about was what's hot for this year and where to get it. She wasn't going to worry about it today. She was here with the two most important people in her life, women in her life anyway. She wanted to buy her mom something nice to say thank you for all the time they had spent together and being there for her. They pulled into the parking lot into a sea of cars. It looked like there were not enough parking spaces for all the cars that were in line. They finally found a parking spot after what seemed like an eternity.

As they entered the mall, Deni was at a loss for words. There were so many people. Every store in this place was having a back-to-school sale, and people were running around grabbing things even if it didn't fit. Deni saw a small woman with her child beside her shopping quietly. She had an armful of clothes, and the little girl was hanging onto her momma's skirt for dear life. Out of the blue, this girl runs by and grabs a sweater out of the woman's arms. Deni couldn't believe it. The sale had people going mad. Deni looked at the teenage girl in shock when all of a sudden she recognized her. It was a girl from Deni and Cindy's school. She was a popular girl, but Deni had no idea how obsessed the girl got over a sale or a sweater.

The quiet woman turned around just in time to catch the girl by the arm and grab her sweater back. Deni couldn't hear what the woman told her but was sure it wasn't pleasant. Deni laughed to herself, thinking, *Good, she deserves whatever the woman had said to her.* Deni didn't realize how bold and pushy people got at the mall. She vowed she would never be that way over anything, least of all clothes. She didn't care that much about fashion to snatch an article of clothing from another person's pile.

Cathy looked at her daughter, amazed at how smart she was and how she had changed over the summer. She couldn't believe all the changes that had occurred so quickly. Deni was becoming a woman in her own right. Cathy started swelling with pride over the two girls. A tear came to her eye and she quickly wiped it away. She didn't want the women to see her crying for fear it might embarrass them. And that was the last thing she wanted to do to them. They were growing up so quickly. Soon they would be going off to college, and Cathy would only see them on holidays, but she couldn't think about all that right now. She had to focus on school clothes and finding something hip but still tasteful.

Deni was so excited to be here for the first time in her semi-adult life that she just couldn't contain herself. She grabbed Cindy and her mom's arm and headed for the first sale rack. Everything she picked out she looked around to see if anyone else had that garment. Then she looked for Cindy to get her opinion on how cool it really was. Cindy was up on all the latest fashions in Hollywood and on what all the stars kids were wearing. Cindy would tell Deni either "Yes" or "That doesn't match with the other stuff. Try this instead" or "No no no. You have to wear things like this that flatter your boobs or your figure. That's what the magazines say. I don't really have boobs yet but let's try this one." Cindy didn't realize what a big help she was being to Deni and Cathy.

Cindy even tried to help Cathy become a diva by bringing her clothes that complimented her figure and face. Cindy was good at picking out clothes and very color coordinated. Deni realized Cindy's dream by bringing her here. Deni finally knew what it was like for Cindy—the excitement of finding the right outfits for each person. Deni could see the excitement and satisfaction on Cindy's face each time she found the perfect matching outfit. Deni thought all this was a little weird, but she loved seeing her friend this happy, and really, Deni was having fun.

The shopping trip was such a blast, but it was time to start gathering their bags to go home. Cathy realized it was after six and didn't even realize how hungry she was until she looked at the clock.

They loaded the packages into the car and were ready to leave when Deni asked if they should stop and pick up something for supper. Cathy thought this was a wonderful idea and called Stan to let him know.

As they pulled into the drive, they saw Stan standing on the front steps, waiting for them so he could help unload the packages. Then all three started talking at once, bombarding him with the day's events and how, after supper, they were going to hold a fashion show for him to show off their new outfits. Stan got caught up in the excitement and was rushing to eat so he could put a makeshift runway in the living room. He had not seen his wife this excited about something in a long time. Come to think of it, he hadn't seen Deni this excited about clothes since she was a baby. He was happy they spent a fun day together.

In a way, he wished he could have been there to spend time with Deni too. He missed his little girl but had to face the fact that she was growing up. He knew she would start pulling away but was happy she wasn't pulling away from her mother, as most teenagers tend to do. Still, she was growing up, and it wouldn't be long till she left for college. He shook his head; he didn't want to think about that. He just wanted to revel in this moment, seeing all of them excited and happy.

After the fashion show was over, they all decided to watch TV for a while. They popped popcorn and decided to watch the movie that Cindy's mother had dropped off a few days ago. It was supposed to be a romantic comedy but turned out to be a total chick flick. Stan was bored with all the crying in the room and decided to go to bed. The girls didn't even know he had left. They were all so into the movie they were watching that nothing could have interrupted their cry fest. After the movie, they realized Stan had left them, and all decided it was time to go to bed.

Cindy and Deni walked into Deni's room and immediately turned on the computer. Cindy had to check the latest gossip and make sure that the clothes they bought that day were actually the latest and hottest things in fashion. Her suspicions were confirmed by all the gossip magazines, so she was thrilled and couldn't wait to show Deni the pics of the stars wearing the clothes that they just bought. Deni was excited about the outcome of the shopping spree. But there was something she wanted to investigate on the computer. She couldn't remember exactly what it was.

They got up the next morning still feeling giddy from the day before. Deni hardly recognized herself when she looked in the mirror. Her hair was so much lighter than she wanted, but it was growing on her. Deni finally remembered what she wanted to research—the hair color company but she couldn't remember the name of the company now. She made a mental note to call on Tuesday and ask Sabrina the name of the company again. What was with her memory lately? This was really weird, but she blew it off, thinking it was just the excitement of the previous day.

Tuesday came and went without Deni remembering to call Sabrina, but work was going good. Cindy was doing so well that Homer promoted her before Deni, but only by a few hours. They each got raises and decided to take their parents out to celebrate. They went to Deni's house that night and told Deni's parents about their promotions and the plan to take them and Cindy's parents out to dinner on Friday night. Cindy called her parents to report all the happenings of the day and asked if her parents would be free on Friday for dinner at the Chinese restaurant. Her parents agreed with great enthusiasm. They congratulated both the girls on their promotions and were thrilled about the raises. Deni and Cindy couldn't wait till Friday to get dressed up, go out, and eat with their families.

Finally, Friday came, and the girls were so excited that they went shopping that day for a new outfit for dinner that night. They each picked out what they thought were the perfect outfits for the Pig-n-Tote's newest junior checkers. Deni felt so excited that she actually bought makeup to wear that night. Cindy was right there to help with the color choices and decided to get herself some new eye shadow. They both looked so pretty that night that their parents couldn't stop looking at them. Deni noticed her mother choking up occasionally but quickly turning her head so no one would notice, or so she thought. Later, Cindy asked if she was okay, but Cathy burst out in tears and just grabbed her. Cindy didn't know what to do or what to think. What was happening? Why was Cathy breaking down like this? Cathy never did explain what happened, but both girls could figure it out. It was because they were growing up and there was nothing Cathy could do about it.

They arrived home still excited from the evening, but Cathy and Stan were a little somber. The girls couldn't figure it out. They said good night and headed for Deni's room. They dressed for bed and lay down just to stare at the ceiling.

Deni started, "Did you see what happened at supper? What is going on around here?"

"I don't know, but you have a great relationship with your parents. Why don't we just ask them?" said Cindy.

"I will in the morning. I have a hunch it will all be okay," Deni replied. As they drifted off to sleep, both girls started to dream about Leah.

The next morning they awoke to a very strange noise. Cathy was still acting weird and didn't wake them like she usually did when they had to work. They got up and headed downstairs to see what was going on.

"What is that noise?" asked Deni.

Cathy turned to see both beautiful faces and said, "There is a tree trimmer outside, and he's butchering the neighborhood. I tell you this city needs to hire people that can actually do the job right."

The girls noticed that Cathy had been crying again. Cathy sat breakfast in front of them and said she needed to talk to them after they ate.

The girls finished and cleaned their plates when Cathy told them to sit down in the living room. Cathy sat across from them on the coffee table and grabbed their hands.

"I have some bad news about Leah," she began.

That was weird because the girls had a dream about her last night. They remembered Leah waving good-bye to them. Two days after the slumber party, Leah left for Nashville with her family. They were going to visit her grandmother. The girls haven't heard from her all summer but knew she was to return any day to spend the remaining summer days with them. They remember saying good-bye to her and her family though.

Cathy started saying, "I spoke with Homer, and you both have the next five days off."

She held up a hand to hold off the questions until she could finish what she wanted to say. Cathy just kept thinking about what to say without breaking down.

"Leah and her family were on their way back home when a semi crossed the divider and hit the car head-on. I'm so sorry, girls, but none of the family made it. The police say that it happened quickly, and there was no suffering or pain."

Cathy began to break down now. She continued, "I'm so sorry, but we are going to help her family plan the funerals and help clean out the house for them. Since you two were her closest friends, along with Mary, we are all going over there later today to meet with Leah's grandmother. Mary and her family will be there along with Cindy's family."

The girls just sat there stunned. Neither had ever experienced a death this close before. How could this happen? They were just in a daze. They didn't know what to say. All they could do was grab each other and cry. They all sat there for what seemed an eternity, crying and talking about the good times they shared with Leah. All Cathy could do was look at the girls and cry.

The girls went upstairs to change from their work clothes to something a little more appropriate for this somber moment. As they waited for the time to come for them to leave for Leah's, they were on the computer putting up a memorial on Leah's Facebook page. They included how much they would miss her and how they loved her.

Cathy came in the room and said it was time to go. The ride to Leah's was very silent. When they got there and saw all the people gathered they couldn't help but cry. They met Leah's grandmother, Bea; they noticed how much Leah looked like her.

They asked, "What needs to be done?"

Bea quickly opened the front door of the house and sent the girls to Leah's room to pick out the outfit for Leah to wear. The girls weren't quite sure what to pick out, but Mary and her mother came in to help. They picked out a nice dress that Leah loved to wear in the summer.

She always looked so beautiful in this purple shirt with the flowered skirt. Purple always looked good on Leah. They wondered what would happen to Leah's belongings but didn't dare ask about all that right now. Things were just too busy to ask questions now. They all headed downstairs to show Bea what they had chosen. Then they asked if there was anything else they could do for her. She said she would handle the rest. Bea thanked them and asked if they could all write down a story about Leah for the preacher and asked if they could come by tomorrow to help clean the house for the guests that would be arriving for the service. They all agreed to be there at 10:00 a.m. the next day.

They all went home for lunch and decided to pick out what they would wear for the funeral in two days. They made some phone calls to see who would be willing to help them with the cleanup and decided to start cleaning up their own house just in case people showed up there. Cathy came up to see what all the commotion was about and asked the girls what they wanted for supper. They both looked at each other and decided to have one of Leah's favorite dishes. They wanted hamburgers and hot dogs on the grill. Cathy called Stan to ask him to stop for groceries on the way home and told him that the girls were holding up fine.

Stan arrived home with the supplies and started the grill. He ran upstairs to see the girls while the grill was heating up. He opened Deni's bedroom door to find both the girls on the computer, looking at pictures of the last sleepover. He started to tear up. He cleared his throat to get their attention, and both girls turned, wiping tears. He sat down on the bed to talk to them.

Somberly he asked, "Do either of you have any questions about what happened or what happens next?"

Both girls just sat there when finally Cindy asked, "*Why?*"

Stan sat there not knowing what to say. He looked at her and said, "I don't know. Sometimes things like this just happen. I don't know why. I wish I did." He got up to hug the girls and found that both girls clung to him for dear life.

As Stan walked into the kitchen to retrieve the hamburgers and hot dogs, he looked at Cathy and started to cry. Cathy came to him, and they just stood there, hugging each other.

After supper, they all sat in the living room. Deni's parents thought the girls might want to talk, but to their surprise, the girls asked if they could have some friends over. Stan and Cathy thought this was a rather odd request considering what just happened. Deni's parents couldn't understand why the girls wanted to celebrate at this time. The girls elaborated on this request, saying they wanted to organize a cleaning crew for tomorrow to help Bea. Deni's parents quickly agreed and felt a little relieved.

As kids started pouring through the door, the girls started writing down the names and tasks that everyone would be taking on tomorrow. Even Josh showed up to lend a hand. He offered to mow the lawn and weed the flower beds. He asked if there was anything else he needed to do for them. He told them how sorry he was for what happened.

The next morning Deni and Cindy got up early to get ready to go to see Bea. Most of the kids that had come over last night were starting to show up at Deni's to go with Deni and Cindy to Leah's. Cathy had prepared a truckload of pancakes for everyone to eat. After breakfast, everyone loaded up in Stan's truck to go to Leah's. Stan had taken the car today and was planning on meeting everyone at Leah's to help with the heavy stuff and the lawn. Everyone arrived to see Bea watering the plants and complaining that the yard looked like a barnyard.

Everyone laughed at what Bea had said and started working. The girls went inside to start on the house while Josh and a couple of other boys from school started on the yard. Bea went into the kitchen to start cooking lunch for everyone and make some sweet tea when the phone rang. Bea answered and then dropped the phone and fell to her knees. The girls ran to her in a hurry to help her to a chair, screaming for Cathy to come in and help. Cathy ran to the kitchen, where Bea was sitting in a chair with Deni, Cindy, and Mary standing by her side, holding her up.

"What's wrong? What happened?" Cathy asked.

"We don't know. We just heard the phone ring and a bunch of commotion. When we came in to check on her, she was on the floor mumbling about it being a mistake," said Mary.

Cathy went to get a glass of water and handed it to Bea. She grabbed another chair and pulled it over next to Bea. Cathy gently took Bea's shaking hand, asking, "What happened?"

Bea took a sip of the water and looked at Cathy, crying. "That was the Tennessee State Troopers. They said they were sorry but the information they gave me was wrong. It was a mistake. The car had broken down and my family is fine. They said that all of them were trying to reach me, but I wasn't home. The troopers came to my house, but one of the neighbors told them where I was at and reported that back to my family. They had the police call to tell me what had really happened and that they were coming home. The police said that the car broke down. The family called AAA to have it towed then they went and checked into a hotel until the repairs were complete. The car involved in the accident was my family's, but it was not my family in it. It was the mechanic and his workers taking it out for a test drive to make sure they had fixed the problem. Can you believe this?"

Cathy just looked at the girls and Bea and started crying. Then they all started hugging and jumping around and yelling for joy. About that time, the boys that were working in the yard heard all this and ran into the kitchen to see what was going on. Stan drove up, saw everyone running in the house, and ran in the kitchen as well. All stood there gasping when Cathy started to explain what had happened.

Everyone was crying, hugging, and shouting for joy when the phone rang again. This time it was Leah. She wanted to know if Bea was there and why her grandmother had come there. Cathy told her what happened and how happy everyone was to hear from her. Everyone was yelling into the phone how happy they were that she was alive. Everyone continued to clean up around the house. With everything that had happened, they wanted to make sure that Leah and her family returned to a clean house and yard. Bea decided to go to the market and get something special for dinner. Stan decided to go with her and offer to have a big welcome home barbecue for the whole neighborhood.

When Stan and Bea returned from the store, they saw a beautiful house and yard awaiting them. They also noticed more people had shown up and the decorations. Everyone was singing, laughing, and having a good time. Stan pulled out the grill and started to barbeque.

Leah had said when they would be home, but everyone was so busy they didn't realize the time. That's when they heard the noise.

The local police had heard about what had happened to the family and was waiting for them to escort them home. Everyone was waiting on the porch and lawn when Leah and her family pulled in front of the house. They were welcomed with a huge banner. They stepped out of the car to the wonderful smell of meat cooking on the grill. A crowd of people rushed to them to give them hugs and kisses. Deni, Cindy, and Mary practically tackled Leah. They were all so happy to see each other.

Everyone came into the house, including the police, to a feast sitting on the dining room table. Bea told everyone what exactly happened and how sorry she was for worrying everyone but thanked everyone there for the outpouring of affection shown to her the past two days. Bea was so excited to see her family that she decided to move to town to be with them. Leah was so happy to see everyone and to hear the news about Bea that she told her grandmother that she could move into her room with her. Bea told her granddaughter no, that she had picked up a flyer of homes for sale in the area and was planning on buying a home close to her so they could visit as much as Leah wanted. Bea also asked everyone there to please come see her once she was settled and specifically told Leah's friends to look forward to slumber parties at her house.

Finally, everyone started to calm down from the excitement of the events and decided to give the family the peace and quiet they so deserved. Stan cleaned the grill, and Cathy put all the leftovers up in the fridge. Leah and her friends were upstairs looking at pics that Leah had taken of her grandmother's house, Bea's neighbors, the Grand Ole Opry, Music Row, and other places around the town. Cathy came in to give Leah a big hug and to tell her how happy she was that everyone was okay. Cathy also wanted to invite Leah over for another slumber party if it was okay with Leah's parents. Cathy told Deni and Cindy to get ready to go home and walked downstairs.

Deni and Cindy gave everyone a hug and told Leah they would call tomorrow and walked downstairs. At home, Deni decided to call Leah and tell her about her Facebook page, which she and Cindy had changed. Leah told them how sorry she was for the mix-up and that she would change the page. Deni and Cindy decided that today had been a very stressful day and decided to call it a day. They lay there staring at the ceiling and unable to believe what had happened. They both fell asleep and had another dream about Leah. This time she was waving good-bye but not with the same meaning. Deni felt the emptiness she had felt yesterday fade, instead filled with joy.

Chapter 4

Deni and Cindy slept in the next morning thinking they didn't have to work. But now that Leah was back, they didn't know. They decided to go downstairs and call Homer. Cathy was standing in the kitchen making breakfast when the girls came in and saw that Cathy was hanging up the phone.

"Homer said you can still have the time off. He knows how important Leah is to you both and wants you two to go and spend time with her. He also said bring her by the store if she wants a job," said Cathy.

The girls were so excited about the job for Leah that they couldn't contain themselves. They called Leah and told her immediately, but Leah was already aware of this because Homer had called earlier to ask for her parents' permission. She said Homer also told her to come by there sometime today for some donations he had to give her.

They hung up the phone with Leah and told Cathy what had happened and then started to plan their day. First, they wanted to go see Leah. They ate in a hurry and then barreled up the stairs to get ready for what would become a very busy day. They left for Leah's house around ten on their bicycles. Leah was waiting on the porch for them, and they all rode off together to the Pig-n-Tote to see Homer.

Homer decided to put Leah on the same schedule as Deni and Cindy so the girls could spend as much time together as possible. Homer knew the importance of childhood friendships. When Homer was a kid, his best friend was taken from him when they both joined the army.

Homer's friend Leon lost his life during routine maneuvers at the base. Homer was so devastated that the army finally kicked him out. It took Homer a long time to get over Leon's death. They had been friends since they were three years old. They were neighbors, and their mothers were friends and would get the boys together for play dates. Therefore, Homer knew what Leah meant to her friends, and he did not want to mess that up. Homer also told them to have Mary come see him when school started if she needed a job too. Homer was the best boss anyone could ever hope to work for in town.

Leah filled out all the paperwork, and Homer gave her the T-shirt and schedule. Deni and Cindy were so happy Homer gave Leah the same schedule, so that they all could work together. Leah was introduced to Peggy and Martha and then she said hi to Josh. Leah also thanked everyone for showing up at her house for the welcome home party. Homer also went in the back and carried a huge box out to the girls.

"What's this?" asked Leah.

Homer said, "That's the donation I told you about."

"Why was all this donated and by whom?" Leah asked.

Homer just laughed. "By the people who care and love you and your family. That's all you need to know. Now do you want me to load this into your mom's car?"

The girls just looked at him and shook their heads. Deni stepped up, saying they had ridden their bikes and didn't have a car waiting. Cindy offered to call her mom to pick it up and take it to Leah's house. Cindy returned from talking to her mom and told Homer what time her mother would be there to pick up the box.

The girls left the store on cloud nine but had to keep their feet on the ground because they had ridden their bikes. Now they headed for Deni's house. They all had so much to say. Leah couldn't believe what Deni and Cindy had done to their hair but loved it anyway. She asked if she could go next time. Deni said she would ask her mom and see if all four of the friends could go and get their hair done. Deni knew what her mom would say but felt a little guilty about all of them going. This day that was supposed to be for Deni and her mom now turned out to be about Deni and her friends and her mom. Deni would talk to her in private about all this soon.

Cathy was watching TV when the girls came through the door. "What are y'all up too now?" she asked.

Deni and her friends all replied at the same time. "Nothin'." Everyone laughed. Cathy patted the couch where she was sitting, and the girls walked over and flopped down beside her.

"What's on?" asked Leah.

"Oh just some stupid show. What do you want to do?" asked Cathy.

"Let's go to the mall. We can shop and then have a late lunch and maybe a matinee. What do you think?" said Deni.

Leah was shocked that Deni had actually said the word *mall*. Cathy and Cindy agreed, but Leah was still sitting there with her mouth open, wondering what had happened to her friend while she was gone.

Leah finally was able to form words when she said, "What did you just say? Did I really hear you say *mall*? What exactly happened while I was in Nashville?"

Everyone else laughed, and Deni replied, "I don't know. I just thought that we could all enjoy the mall. There's a nice place to have lunch at if everyone wants to go there. Don't you want to go, Leah?"

Leah started to laugh and got up to follow them outside to Cathy's car. Leah called her mom to see if she needed anything and to ask for some money. Cathy dropped by Leah's house to get the money and to check on everyone.

They hit the mall around 1:00 p.m. and saw that every store was still having a sale. It was not as crowded today but still bustling. Deni felt the adrenaline rush hit her as she stepped into the first shop. What was going on with her? She had never gotten that worked up over a sale and especially a sale at the mall. Of course, Cindy stepped into her role as the fashionista that she is and started grabbing what would look good on each of her friends. She started handing out clothes for everyone to try on, and she didn't forget Cathy. Cathy was becoming more than just another mother to her. Cathy was becoming a friend. Cindy wasn't the only one feeling this connection with Cathy. Deni was also starting to feel that her mother was becoming a true friend.

After they made their purchases, the next thing was to decide where to eat. They looked at the mall directory for suggestions. They finally decided to eat at the Burger Stop, located on the second floor. It had a terrace with umbrellas. They made their way to the second floor only to see the line for the Burger Stop a mile long. Now what? They all decided it was better just to go home. On the way, they passed by Leah's house to drop her packages off and talk to her grandma, Bea. Bea was helping Louise, Leah's mom, reheat leftovers from the cookout the night before. Leah asked her mom if she could spend the night with Deni and Cindy. Her mom agreed but told her to be home early the next day to take Bea to the airport.

"Why do you have to go now?" asked Leah.

Bea replied, "Because I have to put my house on the market and arrange to have everything brought here. I would like to live in this neighborhood, but it doesn't look like there's anything available."

Deni spoke up, "Bea, I think there's a house on our street. Mom, is the Nelsons' place still for sale?"

Cathy said, "You know I think you're right, Deni. I remember seeing that sign still out there a few days ago. We can drive by there on the way home, and I'll call when I get home and give you the number. How's that?" Bea got excited about the prospect.

They drove by the Nelsons' house and saw the sign. Deni wrote down the name and phone number of the realtor so Cathy could call. Leah got even more excited about her grandma maybe moving into this house. It was not a big house like the others on the street, but it was very nice. Bea should be very comfortable here. Then Leah and the gang can meet at Bea's for a slumber party.

Leah gave the information to her mother so she could call the realtor. Louise said she knew the realtor and maybe could get the price down on the house. An hour later Louise and Bea knocked on Cathy's door to let them know they were going to look at the house and wanted to know if they wanted to come with them. Everyone agreed, and since the house was only two doors down from Deni's, they all decided to walk to the Nelsons' old home.

The realtor was waiting there for them and opened the door. Bea was shocked at how well they had taken care of the house. There was furniture left in the living room that was to stay with the home. Bea was happy to see that the furniture looked new. She was also shocked to see that this family had decorated their house in the same fashion as her: early American with lots of antiques. She could tell by the rugs left and the furniture that the family had bought. Her furniture would fit in here nicely. She was delighted with the neighborhood and that Deni was only two doors down. She was growing attached to Leah's friends and wanted to spend more time with the girls.

This was a plus for Deni because her grandparents had passed away. Stan's parents passed when he was eighteen, and Cathy's father died five years ago while her mother just passed two years ago. Now Deni would have a grandmother to help teach her those special things in life. Like how to can the peaches from the peach tree in the backyard. How to make homemade bread from scratch or how to sew. But the most important thing was how to make a boy fall in love with you.

Louise was a little concerned about how big the house was but was elated to find it was only one story. Most of the houses in this neighborhood were two stories. Still it was big for one person, and Louise was concerned about how her mother would be able to clean the house and mow the lawn. The girls seemed to read her mind.

Deni said, "I think this house is very nice but kinda big for one person. Do you care if I come over once a week to help out?"

Cindy said, "I could come with her, and that way it all gets done twice as fast."

Mary told them, "I think my brother is looking for a lawn-mowing job for the summer. I'll call him and find out."

Leah agreed to come with everyone. "Maybe we could have our slumber parties on that night. If it's okay with you, Grandma." Bea was shocked at how helpful these girls were and how willing they were to step in and start in with the work. Louise was relieved to hear all this and was willing to take that deal.

Louise turned to the realtor and asked about the price and if they could work out something. Bob told her that they could work on a price, and he would have a figure for her tomorrow morning. Louise told Bob about Bea leaving in the morning, but he could talk to her about negotiating a price, and she would call her mother. Louise also asked if Bob knew anyone in Nashville to help sell Bea's house.

Bea spoke up. "That's not necessary. I've had someone trying to buy my house for over ten years. All I have to do is make a phone call as soon as I get home. I bet he comes right over and buys it."

"That's great, Mom. How long do you want to take to get everything moved out and back here?" asked Louise.

Bea looked at Bob and asked how long it would take for the paperwork on this house. Bob replied that it would take about thirty days. Bea said that was perfect; it would take that long to get her things in order and rent the truck to get her moved.

Bea signed what papers Bob needed to get the figures together and to negotiate with the previous owners. Bob shook everyone's hands and locked up the house. Cathy invited everyone to her house for coffee, cake, and to talk about the house. On the walk back to Cathy's, Bea was talking about the flowers in the front yard and how she wanted to plant even more flowers.

Mary spoke up then. "My brother and I are really good at planting and maintaining flower beds. My dad has a landscaping business and we go with him sometimes. He's taught us a lot about plants and maintaining a yard. You'll like the way my brother mows it and keeps it up. He's really good. He likes to mow patterns in the yard." Bea was happy to hear that and was hoping everything would work out.

They reached the house and went straight to the kitchen. Cathy cut them all a piece of cake and started the coffee. The girls got milk from the fridge. The adults waited for the coffee. Everyone started eating and talking at the same time. They were all excited about the prospect of Bea moving in the neighborhood. Everyone had ideas about what to do to the yard and what to do to the house. Bea was excited about the house but couldn't get too excited until she sold her house and finished up there. It was going to be hard to leave the home that she has lived in for over thirty-five years. All her friends were there, and it was going to be sad to leave all them.

Deni did notice that the backyard was fenced in and asked Bea, "Do you have plans to get a dog? I noticed the backyard is fenced already, so all we have to do is put in a doggie door."

Bea looked at her and said, "That's a great idea. I think I would like to have a little dog. I could use the company and something to take care of besides that big house. I hope it's not too much though. Let's wait on the dog till I get moved in and see how hard this is going to be. Deal?"

"Deal," said Deni. They couldn't wait to see how all this was going to unfold.

Louise and Bea left so that Cathy could start fixing supper. Cathy asked the girls what they wanted and got the typical teenager reply—pizza. So Cathy called Stan to see what kind of pizza he wanted and called Roscoe's Pizzeria. She ordered the regular three large pizzas—one with pepperoni, one with sausage, and one with the works. Roscoe told her that it would be there in forty-five minutes. As the girls waited for the pizza to be delivered, they went to Deni's room and looked up the latest Hollywood gossip on the computer.

Deni was at the helm, soaking up the latest gossip and talking more about it than anyone else in the room. The others just looked at each other with a "what's up" look on their faces. They couldn't believe that Deni was actually participating in this activity, let alone reading the news aloud to everyone. Deni turned in her chair to see her friends sitting in her room with their mouths wide open.

"What's wrong? Why aren't y'all sayin' anything? Usually when we do this there's so much talkin' you can't hear anything," said Deni.

"Yeah. What's up? Usually when we do this, you don't participate. What's up with you?" said Leah.

Cindy was the next to chime in. "You will find that Deni has been changing. I think it's the hair color going to her brain." Everyone laughed and Deni shrugged it off.

The pizza arrived, and the girls took the sausage pizza to Deni's room and went back for another box. Stan came in to see the pizzas disappearing at a phenomenal rate. He couldn't see how four young paper-thin girls could eat so much pizza. He decided to jump in the middle of this feeding frenzy and get some food before it all was gone. He was afraid of being bitten and cautiously reached in to retrieve some for himself. Cathy was standing there watching and laughing sarcastically. "What's wrong, big man? Scared to get pizza from a few girls?"

"Have you seen how these kids eat? It's like a shark hunt. I think I have a bite mark on my hand," said Stan. Both of them were trying not to choke because they were laughing so hard while eating their pizza.

When the feast was over, there were only empty boxes left. Stan and Cathy cleaned up and went in the living room to watch TV. Stan asked how Cathy's day was, and Cathy told him about Bea wanting to buy the Nelsons' house. Stan was excited about the prospect of Deni having a grandmother figure around. Cathy voiced her concerns to Stan about Bea being able to take care of such a big place. Stan told her not to worry, that Bea was a strong woman and could take care of herself. He saw that when all the mix-up about Leah and her family took place. Bea was very strong during that time and was surprisingly able to orchestrate all the people who came to her aid. He was impressed with her strength and ability during that time.

Bea returned home and immediately called George. He said he would be right over with the cash for Bea's house. Bea waited for George but started calling moving companies to inquire about pricing from Nashville to Catfish Holler in Oklahoma. The prices were good, but she was afraid to hire someone till she had the money in her hand. She heard George's vehicle pull in the drive and screech to a halt. He knocked on the door with such enthusiasm that Bea thought he might knock it down. Bea answered the door, and George immediately started counting out hundred-dollar bills. Bea was shocked. George took all the money from his mattress and gave it to Bea to buy her home. She asked if George wanted to keep the couch and chairs in the living room and George agreed. Bea got a fair price for her home and was a little sad that night when she laid down to go to sleep. She had walked from room to room remembering everything that had taken place in this house. When her husband died ten years ago, George had come over to help her with her grieving and take care of the yard work for her. George had been trying to buy this house since Harold died. Now it was his, free and clear. All Bea had to do now was hire a mover.

Bea got up the next morning and called Power Movers. They showed up an hour later and asked what room to start packing first. Bea showed them to the living room and told them what to pack. Then she told them what rooms to pack next. By the end of the day, they had everything packed but the kitchen and her bedroom. She needed something to sleep on for the last night in her house. Bea had signed all the paperwork over to George, and both parties were satisfied with all that had happened. Bea's neighbors saw the moving van show up and started coming to Bea's house in to ask what was going on. Bea explained the mix-up and how she felt after hearing the great news that everyone was okay and that she decided to move there to be closer to her family. Everyone understood and wished her well. They promised to write, and Bea promised to stay in touch with everyone.

The movers showed up the next morning to finish the packing and loading the van. Bea called Louise to ask about the Nelsons' home and to inquire about where to take her things. She told Louise about the selling of her house and how quickly the movers had packed everything, but she didn't know where to have her things stored. Louise told her she would call her back once she found a storage area. It didn't take long for Louise to find a place. She told her mother to give the movers her address and she would direct them. Bea loaded her car with the rest of her personal things and pulled out of the drive for the last time. She waved good-bye to all her friends and called her daughter to say she was on her way. Bea arrived at Louise's house around 5:00 p.m. and was shocked when Louise gave the movers the Nelsons' address. She asked what was going on, but Louise just looked at her and smiled.

"Mom, everyone in town knew what happened to us and the situation you were in and decided to help out. The Nelsons reduced the price so much that no one could resist. All our friends pitched in and paid cash for the house so that you could be close to your family. It's been a miracle here the last forty-eight hours. Bob reduced his fee and signed the papers this morning. The house is yours free and clear."

Bea couldn't say anything. She couldn't believe that this beautiful little town would pull together like that for a stranger. How wonderful the world was becoming. Now she would be able to do all the things she wanted to do with that yard and still have plenty of money to live.

When Bea and Louise pulled up in front of Bea's new home, the whole neighborhood was there waiting to help her. Bea and Louise started to cry and Bea got out of the car to a sea of cheering. Bea thanked everyone for helping her and didn't know how she was going to repay these people for all the love and kindness they had showed her. Bob was waiting on the doorstep to hand Bea the keys to her new home and to welcome her to town. Bea opened the door, and everyone started grabbing boxes to take inside Bea's new home.

Homer showed up with a carload of groceries to fill Bea's fridge and her pantry. Bea was overwhelmed; she could not thank everyone enough for all they had done for her. Howard, Leah's father, showed up with the crew from Dave's Real Pit Bar-b-que with ribs, pork, beef, and all the fixings. They had enough food to feed the whole town while the whole town was helping Bea move.

After the last box was unloaded and put away, Bea sat on her new sofa and examined her belongings in her new home. She was so happy she couldn't stop smiling and her face was sore from all the smiling she did today. She was dreading moving in for fear she would be lonely, but coming here was the best thing she could have done. Everyone left and went home to leave Bea alone for the evening, but Bea was so tired from the day that all she could do was take a bath and fall into bed.

She awoke the next morning with the birds singing and the sun shining so bright. She heard a light noise coming in through the window and thought she heard someone in her house. She grabbed her robe and went into the kitchen to find Leah and her friends cooking breakfast.

Leah turned around, frightened from the noise Bea made coming in, and said, "Grandma, we were just fixin' you breakfast and was goin' to serve it to you in bed. Did we wake you?"

Bea shook her head and was delighted to see everyone there. She sat at the kitchen table while the girls finished cooking and waited for her breakfast. Everyone sat at the table, eating, talking and having a good time. Cathy came over to help the girls and to see how Bea was this morning.

Cathy didn't dare tell Bea that the trucks were showing up to help Bea with her gardening. Bea was in such a good mood that she couldn't stop talking. It didn't take long for Bea to figure out that everyone was trying to keep her in the house. Bea got suspicious and went to the window. She saw people milling around her yard and planting all the flowers that she had talked so much about.

Owen, Mary's father, was overseeing the operation. Bea walked outside before everything was completed and started weeping. Owen walked over to her and introduced himself, and Bea just hugged him. Owen hugged her back. Bea told Owen how special this was to her. Owen told her they would be by once a week to maintain her yard and asked about the peach tree out back. Owen wanted to know what to do with all the peaches. Bea asked if he like peach cobbler, and Owen said he did. Bea told him how many peaches to leave for her and to give the rest away to anyone who wanted them. Bea promised Owen peach cobblers all summer to thank him for the work he and his crew had completed. She offered to pay him for his services, but Owen said it was taken care of but didn't say who had paid.

The girls cleaned up the kitchen and went outside to see Bea, who was sitting under the tree, looking at the flowers Owen had just planted. She was crying. Cathy asked, "Are you all right?"

Bea said, "Yes. I was just thinking how Harold would have loved to see all this and how I miss him. Harold was my husband for forty years. He always kept the yard lookin' so nice, and he always planted flowers in the spring. I hope these will last through the winter."

"They should last for a long time as long as my dad takes care of them," Mary said.

Bea asked if she knew who had paid for the services, but Mary said she didn't know anything about it.

It didn't take long for Bea's house to be known as Mamaw's House. Every kid in town could be found there helping Bea do some kind of chore around the house or yard or baking cookies. All the parents couldn't be happier. They wanted Bea to feel welcome.

Chapter 5

I t was time for Deni and her friends to get their hair done again before school started next week, and everyone was at Deni's looking on the computer to see how they wanted their hair. Cathy came in to look at pics with the girls and decided to look at some new styles for herself. They were all sitting around the computer laughing at the purple Mohawk Deni had put on her mother when Stan knocked on the door. He couldn't believe that all of them were looking at hilarious pics of his wife. Deni decided to take a pic of her dad and see different styles on him. Stan was laughing along with the girls at the "funky skunk" hairdo Deni had put on him. He asked what else was going on and decided to go fire up the grill for burgers and hot dogs.

Deni continued her quest for the perfect hair color and style for each and every one of her friends. Cathy had picked a beautiful strawberry-blonde color with a bob haircut. Deni decided to keep hers the same but just get her hair trimmed. Cindy decided to do the same while Mary and Leah decided to go blonde with auburn highlights. They wanted something cool for the new school year. This was definitely going to be different, but who cares—you only live once. All the girls printed out pics to take to Sabrina the next day and decided to go downstairs to help Stan with the food.

Stan was just finishing up when everyone filed downstairs and out in the backyard. Cathy was setting the table and putting the chips and condiments out when Deni stole a chip. Cathy hugged her daughter and kissed her on the cheek.

Deni asked, "What was that for?"

"For being you," was all that Cathy said.

They all sat down to eat when the doorbell rang. It was Josh asking about Mamaw. He thought that she was there since there was no answer at her house. Stan went with Josh to Bea's to check on her, and Leah stayed by the phone. She tried to call Bea but got no answer. When Josh and Stan got to Bea's house, they heard an awful sound coming from inside.

"It sounds like a scream," said Josh.

"Yeah, and did you hear that? It sounds like glass breaking," said Stan.

They knocked on the door and got no answer but could still hear all the commotion going on inside. Stan turned the doorknob and the door opened. All they saw was something scurry across the floor in front of them and some wild, crazy woman coming at them with a broom. Stan grabbed Bea and asked what was going on.

Bea said, "I opened the back door to go sit at the picnic table and look at the stars while I ate my supper when this thing came running in, and I can't catch it."

Stan searched the house for the "thing" but couldn't find anything when Josh starting yelling from the living room. Stan and Bea ran to the living room to see Josh crouched behind the sofa, telling them to get down and be quiet. They both crawled over to where Josh was hiding and asked what was going on.

Josh told them, "While you two were searching, I saw it run in here and up the chimney. I think it's a squirrel."

"Oh no, how am I gonna get it out of there?" asked Bea with a sigh.

Stan crawled to the kitchen and called Cathy. He told her what was going on and told her to call Leon and get him over there. Leon was the town sheriff and also the animal control officer. Leon would know what to do.

Leon arrived like the cavalry charging in to the rescue. Leon brought with him a shotgun and a noose, just in case. Stan looked at him like he was crazy and told him to get down and be quiet. Leon put his things on the floor and crawled over to where Stan, Josh, and Bea were hiding behind the sofa, watching the fireplace.

Leon asked about the situation and Stan brought him up to speed. Leon didn't know what to do about this. He crawled to his gear, grabbed the noose, and took out his flashlight.

Stan asked, "What are you gonna do with that?"

"I'm gonna see where that critter is hidin' in there and see if I can lasso him outta there," said Leon.

Stan just chuckled and told Josh to take Bea to the kitchen and shut all the doors to the other rooms. That way if Leon can lure him out he won't go anywhere else. Stan crawled to the front door and opened it so if that thing comes flying out he could coax him out the front door.

Leon crawled over to the fireplace, carefully looked up the chimney, waving his brightly lit flashlight, trying to illuminate every dark nook and cranny . The only thing Leon saw was a set of eyes and teeth. Leon screamed, hit his head, and the thing flew out like a bullet. Stan was trying to coax it out the front door when it decided to get even with Leon for shining a light in its eyes. The squirrel jumped on Leon's back and proceeded to crawl to Leon's head. Leon looked like a woman trying to get a spider off of her and was screaming at the top of the his lungs. Stan pushed Leon out the front door and slammed it shut. Leon was doing his dance on the front lawn for all the neighbors to see when Bea and Josh opened the kitchen door to see if the coast was clear.

Stan reassured them that everything was okay now and to wait till Leon had composed himself enough to get in his truck before he and Josh could leave. They assessed the damage that Bea had caused with the broom and found nothing of any value broken and no one hurt. Bea was still shaking when she heard Leon drive off. She assured Stan and Josh that she would be okay and sent them on their way.

Stan and Josh walked home quietly but shaken. When they arrived at Stan's house, Stan invited Josh in for supper. Josh agreed, saying he couldn't drive home even if he wanted to right now; he was still too shaken up to do much of anything. Stan and Josh recapped the evening for everyone there and got a big laugh out of all that happened. Cathy was really laughing when she told Stan that she heard a scream and thought something had happened to Bea.

She said, "It sounded so much like a woman screaming that I was sure it was Bea."

They all got a bigger laugh out of that one. All Stan could say, "You should have been there to see all that commotion."

The girls helped clean up the mess from the cookout, and Josh went home. Homer called to check on everyone and to see if the girls wanted to take a permanent hiatus for a while. He had over hired and had to let some go because school was starting up again.

"It slows down when school starts. If I need you, can I call you to come in for a while though?" Homer asked.

The girls agreed, saying yes to everything. Deni and Cindy saw this as an opportunity to help Mamaw more and to spend more time with Mary and Leah. This was a good day. They all headed upstairs to try to get some sleep.

They all woke up the next morning still laughing about what happened at Mamaw's house the night before and wondered if she would like to go with them to the salon today. Leah called Bea to see if she wanted to go but she said no. Bea said she needed to clean up the mess that the squirrel had caused. They all said they would go another day. Bea promised the next time they go that she would go with them.

They all piled into Cathy's car and headed to the salon for their makeovers. This was going to be a great day for Sabrina. They arrived just as Sabrina just finished with a customer. Sabrina welcomed them and took Leah first. She asked Mary if it was okay for her assistant to do her hair and asked the others to have a seat.

She also told them, "If you keep adding people to this outing, I'm gonna have to hire another girl to help me out here. Thanks for the business, and I'll be lookin' for that other girl," said Sabrina.

Leah spoke up and told Sabrina that next time they would be bringing her grandmother with them, so she should be prepared. Sabrina smiled and said thank you again and said she couldn't wait to meet her.

Sabrina and her assistant, Tasha, were working hard on the girls' hair so that they could finish their day. Around 2:00 p.m. they were finished and said good-bye to the girls. They all scheduled return appointments and added Mamaw to the mix. Cathy and the girls headed to their usual Chinese place, to eat lunch. Everyone there remembered them and asked if they wanted their usual. Deni thought this was funny because they had only been in there a few times, and they already had a "usual." It was nice that they remembered them, they thought, and remembered what everyone ate. This time they had extra girls with them, and they ordered the usual for them too.

When the food arrived, everyone was starving. Not a word was said till all the food was gone and they were sitting back waiting for the check to arrive. Deni rubbed her tummy, saying she wanted to take a nap. Everyone agreed with Deni but Cathy. Cathy was so jazzed by the day that she wanted to go shopping.

"Does anyone need to buy more school clothes?" asked Cathy.

All the girls thought and nodded. So Cathy suggested going to the mall to burn off some calories. Everyone piled in the car and headed to the mall. Of course, this was going to be the busiest time because it was the last weekend before school starts. There were sales and people everywhere.

Deni was really overwhelmed when they walked in the door and saw all those people. Women were walking around grabbing things off racks, tables, and out of other people's hands and running to the checkout to grab the last bargains of the summer. Cathy saw the look on Deni's face and reassured her that it was going to be okay. Deni's friends dragged her across the floor to the first sale table. Her friends started grabbing and shoving things in Deni's hands till she was loaded down. Then they started grabbing till they were loaded down. Then they steered Deni to the checkout without even looking at what they were getting. Cathy was right there with an armload of her own when finally they were at the checkout.

Cathy stepped forward, grabbed the stuff from Deni, and put hers on the table to pay for all that was there. The others followed suit until they were all through checking out. They walked out of the mall with a stunned Deni being led to the car. They put Deni in the backseat and loaded the bags in the trunk. Cathy started the car and turned to look at Deni. Deni looked as if she were catatonic, but she was looking around at all of them as if they were all crazy and needed to be locked up.

Cathy asked, "Are you all right, sweetheart?" Deni just looked at her. Cathy backed out of the parking space and headed for home.

When they pulled into the driveway, Deni was starting to come around. All the others had talked all the way home, but Deni just sat and stared at them. Deni was able to get out of the car without assistance and even carried some of the bags into the house.

Cathy told them, "Take all the bags to the living room, and we can clear a space to sort through what we bought. Then we can dump them all out and pick what we want. Does that sound good to everyone?" Everyone agreed with Cathy's plan and took the bags to the living room.

When Stan arrived home, he found all five girls in the living room and clothes flying everywhere and girls saying, "I want that one" or "That's so me." He just stood there watching in amazement and couldn't figure out what they were doing. When he approached to ask what was going on, he was hit in the face with a flowered skirt that someone had meant to throw on her pile of clothes.

Mary stood and walked over to where Stan stood frozen and grabbed the skirt off his head, saying, "Sorry, Mr. Rosen. I didn't mean to do that. I meant to throw that on my pile of clothes."

Stan started laughing, saying, "I didn't know if you wanted me to model that or what." They all busted out laughing.

Stan could always get a laugh out of the girls and usually kept them laughing throughout their stay at his home. All the girls love Stan because he was so at ease around them and made them truly feel at home. All the girls felt that Stan was a dad to them too. The girls loved Cathy just as much but were starting to accept her as a friend and not look at her as a mother anymore. They were constantly asking her to join them in whatever adventure they wanted to try and always asked her opinion on what they should wear or advice about school. Cathy couldn't wait for the day when the girls started asking her about boys and what to do about the boy they liked.

After all the clothes were divided up and all were content with their choices, they all went up to Deni's room. Deni started hanging up her new clothes and was very pleased with her choices. Of course, all her friends helped pick out her clothes. Deni was also noticing the changes in herself and her friends. She couldn't quite put her finger on what was happening to her, but she could certainly tell that her friends were growing up. She was so proud to call these girls her friends and have them over all the time. Cindy was her best friend, but something was changing in her too. Cindy's parents called to check on Cindy and wondered when she was coming home.

Deni and Cindy decided to spend the night at Cindy's and to take their new clothes over for Hal and Samantha to approve. Cathy drove them to Hal and Sam's and talked to Sam for a while. Cathy couldn't help but ask about what Sam thought of all the things that happened over the summer. She also told Sam about Bea moving in down the street. Sam had met Bea and was very happy for Bea being there for her family.

They all went to bed exhausted from the day and slept in the next day. Deni and Cindy got up looking for Cathy but remembered they had slept at Cindy's house. They went to the kitchen to find Sam cooking breakfast and looking a little tired. Cindy offered to finish cooking so Sam could go lay down, but Sam insisted on cooking breakfast. Cindy and Deni cleaned up the kitchen and asked Sam what she wanted to do today. Sam had no plans so they called Cathy to see if she had any. Cathy said she had no plans. They all decided to go to Mamaw's house and spend their day with her.

They arrived at Mamaw's in time to help bake cookies and to feed the birds. Owen was there with a crew cleaning the yard. He had asked about the squirrels. When Bea told him what happened the other night, Owen said he would have someone come over and fix the chimney so this won't happen again. Bea was so pleased with Owen and his crew that she made them all peach cobblers.

Chapter 6

School started two days later, and the neighborhood was busy with school buses and children walking to school. Deni was up bright and early to get ready for school and to pick the right outfit. She called Cindy to see what she was wearing and to try to pick something out for herself. Cindy told her what to wear. As usual, the fashionista that she was, she knew what Deni had in her closet and picked it out for her over the phone. Deni knew exactly what she was talking about, put that on, and fixed her hair the way Cindy told her to.

They rode their bikes to school and walked in together. Cindy was so excited about this school year. Then it hit Deni that she hadn't brought back the books she had borrowed and hadn't accomplished anything this summer. She didn't get a jump start on the science project, didn't study for the first day of school, and didn't even pick up a book all summer long. Then it hit her—this was the best summer ever. She was finally able to be the kid her mother wanted. Deni was proud of herself despite all the stuff she skipped out on. She was able to hold a job for a while and even dealt with the grieving process over the summer. And to top all that off, she had a Mamaw now who she could depend on at any time.

Deni and Cindy went to their first class with great anticipation because of their makeovers and decided that they were going to start the new trend this year and become the most popular smart girls in the school. They went to the back of the class, which was so out of character for them, and picked two seats across from each other. Mary and Leah walked in and found that Deni and Cindy had saved them seats in the back of the class. Deni proceeded to tell the other two about their plan to become the most popular smart girls in the school, and they all made a pact to set the trend this year.

The school year started with an announcement of the upcoming events for the week and for each student to remember to pick up their locker assignments at the office. Also, they were reminded to pick up the social events calendar when they get their locker assignments. All four girls went to the office to stand in line after first period and finally received locker assignments. Deni and Cindy decided to locker together, and Mary and Leah decided to locker together right beside the other two. All was well in school until they saw the Twit Clique. This consisted of all the so-called rich kids and their boyfriends following along behind with their tongues hanging out like dogs looking for water.

Natalie decided to stop and inspect Deni and her friends but thought at first they were new students. She didn't recognize the foursome after their makeovers. She was impressed and decided not to say a word. She led her friends elsewhere to wreak havoc. The new kids didn't know what hit them when the Twit Clique showed up. They were all knocked down to size and put in their by Natalie and her crew. Deni thought this was appalling and vowed to not get into a fight this year with the witless wonder.

The four of them decided to go to class and were late, of course, to second period. They all had excuses. They blamed it on the long locker assignment line. Ms. Bell excused them all and told the girls to take a seat. Of course, the only seats available were the ones in the front now. They had all vowed to take the seats in the back of the class and to continue to be the smartest girls in the school.

They arrived to the third period early enough to get the seats they wanted in the back of the class. Mr. Larson started passing out the books and the plan for the year. His class was going to be fun this year. He taught biology, and they were going to be able to dissect animals this year. He worked really hard to get the required animals needed for each class. Deni was excited about the prospect of getting to dissect a shark or a squirrel this year. She was also hoping that during deer season, someone would hit a deer and Mr. Larson could bring it in for dissection. That would be the coolest to Deni. What was going on with her now? All she could think about until now was where to sit and how she was going to change the school by being the most popular. Deni had never been concerned with being popular. All she cared about was schoolwork.

Deni's favorite subject, Mr. Keen's science class, was their fourth period. This was not just any science class. This was honors' science. Deni knew this year was going to be a challenge but knew that she could handle it. She was mostly concerned with Cindy doing the work. Mr. Keen did the normal routine of handing out books and the syllabus for the year. He also asked Deni for a rundown on her science project for the year. He knew Deni very well and had assisted her in the past with her projects. He was shocked that Deni said she had no idea what her project was going to be. She said she would discuss possibilities later with him if he were available.

Next period was the least favorite of all, honors' English literature with Mrs. Cane. She was a cool teacher, but Deni didn't like English lit that well. She had excelled in it in the past but wasn't so sure about this year. Something had changed in Deni over the summer, and she was really concerned about the schoolwork for this year.

Cindy sensed what was going on in Deni's mind and said, "I don't know about all these honors classes this year. I think I'll discuss with my parents about dropping some of them and going into regular classes. What do you think?"

Deni said, "I think that might be a good idea. I don't know about this either." Cindy thought that was a little odd for Deni. She had never questioned a class in her life, and now she looked utterly terrified about these honors classes. Cindy wanted to talk to Mr. Keen about a secret project of her own.

Next was going to be the best class of the year for Deni. It was an elective she decided to take that was only offered to those in honors classes. Bowling with Mr. Hill. Every day they would load up in the school bus and drive to the lanes to take the bowling class. This was going to be great. There were a lot of boys in this class, and Deni was going to make it a point to meet at least three of them. When class started, Mr. Hill handed out the syllabus and permission slips for the year. Deni didn't know how they were going to bowl all year but found out that half the year was for bowling and the other half was for ice-skating.

Now how was she going to meet boys while ice-skating? All she could think of was meeting the perfect boy to take her to the winter dance. Now she was really losing her mind. She had never cared about boys or dances. She made a mental note to talk to her mother about what was going on and to see if Cathy had noticed the changes that were going on with her. For now, she had to get to know the boys in class and ask her dad to take her bowling one night so she wouldn't make a fool of herself.

First day of school out of the way, Deni and Cindy rode their bikes to Deni's house to recap the day with Cathy. Cathy got excited as the girls talked but was concerned about what Deni was telling her about the workload. Deni said good-bye to Cindy and asked her mom if she could talk to her. Cathy sat down, concerned for her daughter. Deni started with a syllabus from each class and asked her mother to tell her the truth about whether she could handle this schedule or not.

Deni continued to tell her, "Mom, I don't know about this year. I'm really concerned that this is too much for me to handle. I don't think I can do all this work this year. I'm thinking of dropping out of honors classes and going into the regular required college classes."

Cathy didn't know what to say. She had seen Deni upset before and overwhelmed with homework, but Deni never showed stress like this.

Cathy asked, "Why do you feel this way? I've never seen you this upset over school. What has happened to make you feel this way?"

Deni said, "I don't know what's going on. Have you noticed any changes in me this summer? Like memory problems or anything unusual?"

Cathy looked at her daughter and said to her, "Yes. I have noticed that you have changed. I didn't know that you were this bad though. I have noticed that you forget a lot of things, and do you know that you didn't even open a book this summer? I thought that was fantastic, but I also know how you are about schoolwork. Why don't you tell me how you are really feeling? Do you feel any different than you did last year?"

Deni thought about what Cathy had said and started to cry. Cathy hugged her daughter and asked her to talk about it.

Deni started, "I don't know, Mom. I don't feel any different, but I know there's something going on with me. I can't explain it or put my finger on what's happening. I felt like such a fool when Mr. Keen asked about my science project this year and looked at me like I had lost my mind when I told him I haven't even thought about it. Oh my gosh! I completely forgot to go by there and talk to him after school about some ideas I have on some projects. See what I mean? I can't remember anything. I don't know what's going on with me. This is so frustrating."

Cathy didn't know what to say to Deni. All she could do was sit there and hold Deni as she cried. Cathy felt so sorry for Deni and sent Deni to her room to rest before supper. Deni went up to her room, and Cathy waited till she heard Deni's bedroom door close before picking up the phone to call Cindy. Sam answered the phone, and Cathy explained what happened after Cindy went home. Sam said that Cindy had been telling her about changes she had noticed in Deni but couldn't pinpoint when it all began. Cathy asked if she could talk to Cindy for a little while tomorrow afternoon. Sam agreed with that but asked Cathy how she was going to get Deni out of the house so she and Cindy could talk. Cathy said she would think of something.

Cathy hung up with Sam and called Mamaw. She asked if Bea could call Deni to help her tomorrow afternoon with cleaning to get her out of the house so she could talk to Cindy in private. Bea agreed and asked if Deni was okay. Cathy explained the situation, and Bea said that she hoped everything was okay. She also offered to talk to Deni tomorrow to see if there was anything she could do to help the situation. Cathy thanked her and asked for Bea to call back tonight to talk to Deni.

Cathy called for Deni to come down for supper after Stan got home, and Cathy explained what was happening to him. Deni came to the table in a depressed state, but Stan was there to help cheer her up.

"What's up, kiddo?" said Stan.

"Nothin' really, Dad. How was your day?" replied Deni.

Stan said it was okay and wondered how her first day at school was. Deni explained the events of the first day and asked her dad if it was okay for her to drop the honors classes and go to required college courses at school. Stan agreed with this decision but asked if she was really okay with this herself. Deni said yes and had her parents write a note to the principal explaining why she needed to drop honors classes. Both Cathy and Stan signed the note and gave it to Deni to give to the principal the next day.

Deni went upstairs and called Cindy to tell her the good news about dropping honors classes. Cindy reported that she had a note signed too and that they could take them together so they could get the same schedule again. Deni agreed to wait for Cindy in the morning at the bike rack. Cindy told her what outfit to wear the next morning so Deni could lay it out tonight and not stress in the morning. Deni did what Cindy told her and decided to go to bed.

The next morning Deni got up feeling good about the day. She dressed and rode her bike to school and waited for Cindy. Cindy got there just in time to go to the office and change schedules. They both got the same classes. At lunch, Mr. Keen asked Deni why she had dropped her honors classes and said he was sorry to hear that she was not going to be in his class anymore. Deni explained that she just had a lot on her mind and felt that the schoolwork would suffer. Mr. Keen accepted that excuse but thought it was really odd for Deni Rosen to worry about schoolwork suffering. She always had a lot on her mind and was still able to perform at above optimal level.

This day finished with a bang, and Deni was on cloud nine. Not once did she run into the Twit Clique or have an exchange with Natalie. It was always a good day when she didn't run into them. It was a little unusual for Natalie to steer clear of them, but Deni thought, *Whatever.* Oh no, now she was starting to pick up the clique lingo. Oh well, whatever.

Deni arrived home in time to change and go to Mamaw's house to help with the cleaning of the fireplace. Cindy arrived five minutes later. Cathy quickly told her to take her bike around the side and to come into the living room. Cindy did as she was told and met Cathy in the living room.

Cathy began, "What's really going on with Deni?"

"I don't really know. I have noticed some changes, and it seems to get worse every time she gets her hair done. I don't know what that has to do with anything, but maybe it's just a coincidence and maybe I can check on that with Mr. Keen," said Cindy. Cindy asked if Cathy had noticed anything different about Deni and if she could remember when it first started happening.

Cathy said, "You know, now that you mentioned it, it first started right after we got our hair done the first time. I have noticed that she is very forgetful and she's not as interested in school anymore. She asked us last night about dropping those classes, and the look in her eyes was pure terror about that schoolwork. I don't know what to think of all this. As long as you stay aware and can keep an eye on her for me, I would appreciate it."

Cindy said she would keep an eye on Deni and report any other changes she saw in her. Cathy thanked her and told her to leave before Deni came home.

Deni came home with a homemade peach cobbler looking like she had been working in a coal mine. Cathy laughed at her and told her to go immediately to the laundry room and throw her clothes in the washer. She didn't want them mixed in with the other clothes. Deni did what she was told, took her clothes off in the laundry room, and put them immediately in the washer. Deni couldn't wait to dig into that cobbler that she and Mamaw made before they started working on the fireplace.

Cathy fixed ribs for dinner that night, and Deni couldn't get enough to eat. All the ribs were gone before anyone even noticed how much Deni ate, and the cobbler was brought out with a fantastic scoop of vanilla ice cream. Deni scarfed that down in a hurry and cleared her dishes. She helped her mom clean the kitchen and switched the load in the laundry room before going to bed. Cathy thanked her for all her help and kissed her good night.

Deni got up the next morning ready for school with renewed energy. Deni was so happy she had gotten out of those honors classes, and she looked forward to starting the school year with a good attitude. She knew now that she could conquer anything that was thrown at her. She met Cindy at the bike rack again so both could walk in together and pick seats at the back of the class. She and Cindy arrived to first period early to get the seats they wanted in the back of the class. Ms. Linn was calling roll when this gorgeous creature walked in and sat in the seat in front of Deni. He was the picture of a gorgeous male model. He had blond hair, blue eyes, and a body that was so hot. She thought she had seen him in a magazine before. Wow, what was she thinking? She had never been this attracted to the opposite sex as she was with him.

She looked at Cindy and gave her that love-struck look when he turned around and caught her. Her whole body turned an indescribable shade of red. Jack stuck out his hand and introduced himself. He said his name was Jack. Deni just sat there, red as a beet and blushing even more.

Jack looked at her again. "Are you okay? Most people usually shake a hand that is offered to them."

Deni reluctantly took his hand and introduced herself. She also introduced Cindy to him. Jack shook Cindy's hand and asked what there is to do in this "one-horse town." Deni and Cindy looked at each other and started to say something about Mamaw's house but stopped themselves. They told Jack about the mall and how everyone goes there and hangs out on the weekends. Jack just looked stunned that this was the only activity in town. He proceeded to ask if there were any beaches or lakes around for him to be able to scuba dive or kayak. Cindy spoke up on this one and told him about Lake Blackbird and all the things they offer there. Jack was impressed and asked if anyone wanted to go with him. Deni and Cindy said they wanted to but would have to check with their parents first.

Lunch was interesting. Everyone was talking about the new guy and how gorgeous he was when Cindy and Deni walked up and sat down. Mary asked if they had seen the new guy, and Cindy told her about Jack asking them to the lake this weekend. Mary and Leah were shocked, their mouths wide open, with the strangest look one can imagine. Just then, they heard him clear his throat. Jack was standing behind Deni and asked if he could sit down beside her. Of course, she said yes. Jack introduced himself to Mary and Leah and asked about the lake again. Mary and Leah said they would ask if they could go and proceeded to ask for his phone number so they could call him and let him know.

He gave his number to all four of them and asked for their numbers in return. Deni was shocked he asked for hers too. I mean why did he want her number? He had all those others. Then it hit her—he's being polite and asking for everyone's so that they don't feel left out.

About that time, Natalie and her goons showed up asking Deni who her new friend was. Jack stood up, introduced himself, and sat back down. Natalie tried to sit down next to him, but he moved his books there and turned his back on her. Natalie was so stunned and bewildered by his actions, especially because he was a guy, that she didn't know what to say. She walked off in a huff, and one of the dogs told Jack that he had just messed up by turning his back on Natalie. Jack just looked at him and laughed and then proceeded to tell this goon that he was messed up for following around a wannabe for most of his life. Then Jack turned his back on this boy and continued his conversation with the girls.

Deni was impressed by the boldness Jack showed and for standing up to Natalie and her clique. Jack explained that at his last school he had seen people like that kick people when they were down and never consider anyone else's feelings but their own. He also explained how he never wanted to be a part of that crowd again and hoped he could change the way people perceived these so-called cliques, which were the stupidest thing he had ever seen.

Mary looked at him and asked the question that was on everyone's mind, "Did you say 'again'?"

Jack looked at her and started to explain. "You see, when I was younger, I was involved with a group like that because I was the star football player. Naturally, I thought I had to be with the prettiest girl in school. I still feel that way, but I realized that the prettiest girl in school wasn't in the cliques I realized that the prettiest girls are the ones with inner beauty and brains, not what people could see on the outside. That's not what makes a person. That's what makes a shallow person. I'm deeper than that. You know."

They all sat there and listened intently, and Deni started to blush at the part about being with the prettiest girl in school.

Jack took all the trays to the washers and turned to wait for the girls. They all left the cafeteria together and asked Jack where his next class was. Jack showed them his schedule and noticed that Deni was in every one of his classes. Deni was thrilled at this and started to show him where his next class was at and showed him to his locker. At the end of the day, Deni noticed Jack was standing beside her at her locker, watching some kid clean it out and then proceeded to put his books in there.

Deni had to ask. "What are you doin' here? Your locker is down there."

Jack just smiled a sly smile and said, "No, it was down there. I paid this kid to trade with me so I could be close to the newest in-crowd and to be next to the prettiest girl in school." Deni blushed at this and smiled.

Chapter 7

Deni got home from school so excited she couldn't contain herself. She ran to find her mother and found her in the laundry room. Deni burst in, talking ninety miles an hour and couldn't stop herself. Cathy grabbed her and made her sit down at the kitchen table, and then she told Deni to take a breath and slow down. Deni did what she was told and told her mother about school. She also told her mother about Jack—how cute he was, how nice he was—and asked if he could come over for supper one night so they could meet him. She also told her mom about Jack asking if the girls could go to the lake this weekend and begged her to say yes. Cathy told Deni they would have to discuss that part with Stan and that it would be nice if Jack came over for supper one night so they could meet him.

Deni asked what night was good to invite him and showed Cathy the note that Jack gave her. It had his phone number on it along with a short note saying, "I hope to hear from you soon."

Wow, Cathy couldn't believe that her little girl was developing a crush. This was a first, and Cathy wasn't sure she knew how to handle this. She gave the note back to Deni and said they would talk about it over supper tonight. Maybe they could talk Stan into having Jack over tomorrow night. Deni was so excited that she ran to her room and called Cindy.

Cindy was excited for Deni but also a little jealous. She was the one who usually got the guy, and now Deni was stealing the cutest guy in school. What was she thinking? This was Deni, her best friend, and Jack wasn't hers, so this was going to work out. Deni asked if she had talked to her parents about the lake this weekend, but Cindy said they would wait to see if Deni's parents approved. If Deni could go then the other girls' parents would let them go. That's the way it always worked.

Deni sat at the table patiently waiting for her dad to ask about her day but couldn't wait any longer. She started to talk about her day and told her dad all about Jack and how cute he was. She also asked if Jack could come over for supper tomorrow night to let her dad check him out and make sure he was okay. She also told her dad about Jack asking about going to the lake this weekend and had invited all the girls to go.

Stan raised his eyebrows at this request and suggested this in return: "Why don't we just start with supper tomorrow? Tell him to be here at 6:00 p.m., and then we can discuss the weekend plans."

Deni agreed and finished her supper in a hurry. She ran upstairs to call Cindy and told her what her father had said. She then called Jack to see if he was available for supper at her house tomorrow night. She heard Jack ask his mother if that was okay, and she approved. She told Jack she would give him the address tomorrow at school. Jack agreed and hung up. Deni called Cindy back and told her about the conversation with Jack and talked a bit more about this weekend, hoping that her father would approve of Jack and let her go. Deni hung up with Cindy in time to get ready for bed before Cathy came up to kiss her good night. Cathy could tell that Deni was still excited and offered her something warm to help calm her nerves. Deni refused and said that she was starting to come down from this wild ride and starting to get sleepy.

Cathy left Deni's room and climbed in her own bed. She started telling Stan about Deni coming in today from school and told him about the conversation she had with Cindy yesterday. Stan said he was glad that Cathy finally noticed what was going on and said that he noticed this a long time ago. He couldn't understand what took so long. Cathy rolled over to look at him and was stunned to see how serious he was about Cathy taking so long to notice. She also told Stan how she had noticed but was afraid to talk about it to anyone. Stan laughed and said he was afraid to mention it to her for fear she might freak out and start to worry about Deni even more. They both laughed and vowed to never keep anything from each other when it concerned Deni.

The next morning Deni got up excited about the day and started talking from the time her feet hit the floor. Cathy couldn't even ask her what she wanted for supper tonight. Oh well, she thought, she would figure it out before supper tonight. Deni left for school, and Cathy was finally able to breathe again. Cathy cleaned the kitchen and made a grocery list. She headed to the Pig-n-Tote around noon and stopped to see Stan on the way. Stan suggested they go eat lunch and discuss this special supper.

They headed to Dave's and thought better since Stan knew that he would probably be cooking out tonight. Instead, they went to the local drive-in burger joint, ate a light lunch, and made a list for groceries. Cathy decided she would stop and get groceries and spruce up the house before Stan got home and recruit Deni to help when she came in from school. They finished their lunch and went their separate ways. At the market, Homer caught up with Cathy and asked how the girls were doing. Cathy filled him in on all the excitement from the first week of school and was wondering if Homer knew anything about the lake activities that these kids participate in these days.

Homer told her, "I don't think you have anything to worry about. I've heard people in here talking about this Jack and his family. They say that this kid is really a good kid. He is a bit rebellious at school, but what kid isn't?"

Cathy looked concerned about that last statement and asked, "What do mean by 'rebellious'? What exactly does he do to rebel?"

Homer laughed and said, "I don't think it's anything wild. I've heard that he mostly rebels against the popular kids who seem to rule the school. He just hates those cliques that so many schools allow. I think he tries to make everyone equal, which is a good thing. He's not a bad kid or doing bad things. I think he just wants to fit in, in his own weird way. Going to the lake might be a good thing for the girls. Might get their mind off everything that's happened over the summer." Cathy agreed and thanked Homer for his input on Jack.

Cathy arrived home and was just finishing putting the groceries away when Deni came in like a whirlwind. Deni was running through the house looking for her mother. She found Cathy in the kitchen, cleaning up, and was so excited that she couldn't sit down or stop talking. Cathy sent her upstairs to take a long bath to calm her nerves and to get ready for supper. Cathy went into the living room and started cleaning and vacuuming. Before long, she heard Stan come through the front door. He stepped into the living room to help Cathy with last-minute cleaning when Deni came running down the stairs, talking a mile a minute and running around like a chicken with its head cut off. Stan finally caught up with her and sat her down on the sofa, saying, "Stay." Deni looked up at her father in astonishment and finally shut her mouth.

The doorbell rang at precisely at 6:00 p.m., and Deni got nervous again. Stan answered the door and led Jack to the living room. Deni was sitting there waiting for Jack and her father. Looking for any sign from her father about his first impression of Jack. Stan introduced himself and Cathy and told Jack to come out to the patio. Stan led everyone out to the patio and offered some sweet tea to Jack. Deni got the dishes to set the table, and Stan checked on the grill. Jack was making small talk and didn't seem a bit nervous, like he was an old friend of the family.

Cathy followed Deni into the kitchen to get the condiments out of the fridge, and Deni turned, saying, "Well, what do you think?"

Cathy laughed, saying, "I think he's nice. Don't be so nervous. You act like this is a date or something."

Deni took a deep breath and let out a sigh. It's true Deni did think of this as a date instead of just having a friend over for supper.

Deni and Cathy walked out to the patio and sat down. Jack was talking about school and how everyone there was very welcoming except for Natalie.

Stan choked back a laugh and said, "Yeah, I've heard a few things about her over the years."

Jack asked about the lake and if it was okay for Deni to go with him and his family over the weekend. Stan told Jack that he would think about it and wanted to speak to Jack's parents before letting Deni go anywhere. Jack agreed with that and said he would have his mother call tomorrow to speak with Cathy and then call Stan if that's what he wanted. Stan said that it was fine, that she could talk to Cathy and then they would make their decision.

Jack left to go home, and Deni suddenly got a headache. Stan and Cathy cleared the rest of the table and walked into the kitchen, where they found Deni sitting there in a daze. Stan asked if she was okay, but Deni just nodded.

Stan and Cathy returned to cleaning the dishes when finally Deni spoke. "So what did you both think of Jack?"

Stan said he liked him and that Jack seemed very nice. Stan also made a suggestion about all of them going to the lake this weekend, and Deni's friends could come too. He wanted to see Jack and his family this weekend and watch Jack to see how well he got along with his parents. Deni was so excited that she ran upstairs to call Cindy. Cindy got all excited because she knew she would get to see Jack this weekend and get to meet his parents.

The next day at school was very interesting. Deni and her friends couldn't stop talking about the lake trip, and even Jack was getting excited about this trip. His family had a boat and said he would take them out skiing if they could ski. All of them laughed. He told them he would show them some new tricks on the water. Now the girls couldn't wait to go this weekend and be in a boat, alone with Jack.

Deni rode her bike home from school and ran into the house to tell her mom about Jack saying his family was taking their boat this weekend and how she couldn't wait to go skiing. Cathy looked at Deni exasperated from all the excitement that had been going on this first week of school and told her to slow down and start at the beginning. So Deni sat down and started telling her mom the whole story that Jack had told them about the boat and that he knew how to ski and how he would show them some new tricks. Cathy told them how great that would be and told Deni that Stan was going to take a boat also.

"Wait, we don't have a boat," said Deni.

Cathy replied, "I know, but one of the your father's coworkers overheard Stan talking about Lake Blackbird this weekend and told Stan we could take his boat there if we wanted. I called and told Sam, so she said they would take their boat this weekend, and she told Owen and so forth. So everyone is going this weekend and taking boats. So we all decided to take camping equipment and really make a weekend out of it. How does that sound?"

Deni was overjoyed and grabbed the phone to call Cindy.

Cathy stopped her and said, "Wait, I'm not through telling you all my news yet. Ruth called today, and when I told her what everyone was planning they decided to go along with the camping."

"Who is Ruth?" asked Deni.

"That's Jack's mom," replied Cathy.

Deni was really over the top now and immediately started dialing the phone. Cathy started to laugh.

Cindy answered on the first ring, and she and Deni were both talking at the same time.

Deni told her, "Wait, hold on, what did you say?"

Cindy started talking so fast Deni could barely keep up with her. "I said my mom told me that your mom called today to say that your father is taking a boat and camping equipment and that Leah's and Mary's family are goin' to do the same and that Jack and his family were goin' to go and everyone gets campsites right next to each other so that we could all hang out together. Isn't that cool?"

"This is the best weekend ever. I can't believe Jack's family is going to camp with all of us. This way they can get to know the best families in town," said Deni.

Deni couldn't wait for her dad to get home so she could inspect the boat they were taking. She wanted to know if it was a ski boat or not. About an hour later, Stan pulled up in front of the house, pulling the boat. Deni ran out the front door to give her dad a hug and inspect the boat. Deni couldn't wait to get to the lake and see Jack. Stan was laughing as Deni went to the boat and climbed in and asked how she looked in it. Stan laughed harder when Deni realized how silly she looked sitting there in the boat, on dry land, in the middle of her neighborhood, acting like she was talking to someone. Stan told her she would look good wearing anything, even a boat.

Deni climbed out laughing and hugged her dad. "Thanks, Dad. You're the greatest," said Deni.

"Remember this moment in another year or two when you're mad at me," replied Stan.

He and Deni walked arm and arm to the front door. Stan opened the door for Deni and followed her in the house.

Deni helped make supper that night and, immediately after eating, went upstairs to call Cindy to ask what she should pack for the camping trip. Cindy was having problems deciding on what to pack for herself and was asking Deni for her advice. This was a major change for the two girls. No one ever asks Deni for fashion advice. They were afraid Deni would tell them to wear jeans and a T-shirt. Deni started telling her what to pack, and Cindy did the same for Deni.

Deni went to bed that night and couldn't get to sleep. She was so excited that she thought her heart might jump out of her chest. Deni got up the next morning and couldn't wait to get on the road. She ran downstairs, after showering and some last-minute packing, with her bag in hand and was headed to the front door when Stan yelled for her to stop and drop the bag. Deni did as she was told and went into the kitchen.

Stan said, "Sit and eat. You need a good breakfast before we get on the road. Besides, we have to wait for your friends to get here. We are all leaving from here. They should be arriving any minute."

Cindy came running up the front steps and banged on the front door. Deni ran to let her in, and both were talking too fast for anyone to understand. They ran upstairs to see if there was anything that was left behind, and Deni grabbed her pillow and favorite blanket. Stan yelled for everyone to load up when the others arrived, and everyone went outside to help Deni load her stuff into the truck, then the caravan began. They passed by Jack's house and stopped to help them load.

The trip wasn't that long, but when you're this excited, it seemed an eternity. They arrived at the campgrounds raring to go but were soon stopped by how crowded the grounds were. They had to get campsites across from each other, but that was still okay although it wasn't the same as side by side. The fathers all went to unload the boats and brought them around closer to the campsites. While they were gone, the mothers set up camp while all the kids went down to the water. The moms waited for the dads to get back to set up tents and to blow up mattresses. The kids were all ready to get out to the water but couldn't stop talking long enough to even ask Jack how he liked the lake.

Deni finally stopped talking to her friends long enough to turn to Jack and ask how he liked his first week of school.

Jack said he liked it and loved the lake. He also said, "I'm a water baby and love to hang out at lakes. Is this the only lake in this area?"

They all nodded and thought he looked so cute standing there, staring at the water. Jack said he also brought his fishin' pole so that he could catch fish later that day. Deni hadn't thought of her pole till after Jack had mentioned his. Now she wished she had brought hers so that maybe she and Jack could go fishing together. One more thing they would have in common.

They all decided to head back to camp before skipping one more rock across the water. Jack was the best at it, but Leah was giving him a run for his money on that one. They got back to camp and noticed no one around. They looked for the boats but didn't see them either. That's okay; they decided to walk back down to the docks and see what kind of trouble they could get into. They heard a lot of yelling, on the walk to the docks, and looked out across the water to see their parents coming in to the dock for gas and supplies. Deni ran to her father and asked about her fishing pole. Stan went to the back of the boat and picked up several poles. Deni was surprised to see that he remembered the special pole that she liked, so she gave him a quick hug. She asked if he could pick up some bait so they could go fishing before everyone started cooking supper. Stan asked the others if they needed anything and went in Chuck's bait shop to purchase snacks, bait, gas, and sodas to take out on the boat.

Chuck was behind the counter. "What can I do you for today?"

Stan chuckled and said, "I need some bait so I can take these kids fishin', some snacks, and some gas for the boat. Where is the best place to fish out here now? It used to be in the coves but I don't know now. I haven't been here in a while."

Chuck first asked, "Well, that depends on what you're fishin' for. The coves are good for crappie and catfish, but experience tells me to go to the furthest cove, just at the mouth, and there you can catch some bass. Now what kind of bait do you want? I got worms, minnows, fake bait, jigs, all sorts of bait."

Stan told him, "I think I'll take a box of worms and a dozen minnows. Thanks for the information, and I'll let you know how the fishin' is."

Chuck thanked him for his business and Stan paid for everything and left. Chuck followed him out to the dock, helped with the gas, and waved goodbye to them.

Deni and her friends climbed into each of their family's boats, and all headed out together. Stan led them to a little cove that was known as a good fishing spot and had little traffic. He was sure that if they got loud they would not be disturbing anyone.

Once anchors were dropped and fishing poles baited, Deni and her friends threw out their lines at the same time. Deni loved to go fishing and knew Cindy did too. She could sit there all day and wait for the fish, but it was still fun to be out there on the water. Mary got the first bite but broke her line. Finally, Cathy was the first to catch a fish. They always had a contest to see who could catch the most fish and who could catch the biggest. Stan was the winner of all this, but sometimes Deni would come close.

They fished till the bait ran out and decided to explore the lake. Stan wanted to show Jack's parents, Harvey and Ruth around the lake. He took them slowly around all the banks and showed Harvey the best places to fish and the best places to camp. He also asked if Harvey liked to hunt and showed him some really good hunting spots for deer, squirrel, rabbit, quail, or whatever they could hunt. Harvey made mental notes, and Jack was especially paying attention to the deer and fishing grounds.

They headed back to the campsite to park their boats and to just sit and relax before the women starting cooking supper. The ladies had all gotten together and made meal plans, and each brought specific food for each meal. Every meal was a feast, and all of the work was shared equally. Deni and her friends always pitched in to help clean up and help with any other chores that needed to be done. Even Jack helped everyone. He cooked breakfast for everyone the next morning and cleaned everything up.

Deni's parents really approved of Jack and his parents. They felt that Jack was a good person for Deni to hang out with and to help her and her friends. Jack was good to have around. Stan could tell that he had a special place in Deni's heart already but didn't want Deni to get hurt. He would make a mental note to talk to Deni about this later. Jack asked all the parents if it was okay for him to take the girls out in his boat to go skiing. All the parents agreed, and Harvey told Jack to be very careful. Jack also reminded the girls to get their life jackets. "Make sure you wear them. I don't let anyone ride with me without a life jacket." The girls all went to their boats and grabbed the life jackets and was putting them on as they were climbing into Jack's boat. Jack untied the boat and pushed it off and then jumped in and started the boat. He took off slowly, cautiously, and made sure the girls were all sitting down first before he sped up.

The parents all gathered at Harvey and Ruth's camp to congratulate them on how they had raised Jack. Stan told Harvey that he had a fine son and said that he would consider it a privilege for Jack to be friends with Deni. Harvey looked at Stan and said the same to Stan. Cathy made immediate friends with Ruth, and both had been talking all day. Cathy admitted to Ruth that she thought Deni had a crush on Jack. Ruth laughed and admitted that Jack hasn't stopped talking about Deni since the first day he met her. They both agreed that it was cute that the kids liked each other. Cathy remembered her first crush and wondered if she was really that giddy all the time.

The kids were having a ball out on the water. Jack showed Deni how to run the boat, and Deni was driving now while Jack was skiing. All her friends were watching as Jack told Deni to speed up and make a turn so it would whiplash him around. As Deni did this, Jack was whiplashed over the wake, jumped and twisted in the air. Deni was excited and all her friends cheered him on. All the girls had turns skiing and tried to make the same jump without success. All of them, including Deni, crashed. They were starting to tire when they heard the air horn that Stan carried with him, indicating it was time for them to come in. They headed for the campsite and parked the boat.

They got there as lunch was set out, and everyone sat down to eat. They discussed what to do this afternoon, and all decided to go fishing again. They went back to the spot they were at yesterday to try their luck again. Today was really slow, but in the late afternoon, the fish started coming in the cove in schools. The fishing picked up so much that Deni was starting to get tired. All the kids looked tired and started curling up on the boat seats to take a nap. Everyone headed in and parked the boats, and the women immediately started preparing supper. They wanted something light since it was getting late. The men went down by the dock to clean the fish that had been caught. They planned a big fish fry for the next afternoon before heading home.

They all ate their supper and quickly got ready to go to bed. Deni had no trouble sleeping that night. She and her friends all slept late the next day. When they got up, they had cereal for breakfast since all the cooked breakfast food had already been put away. As they ate their bowls of corn puffs, they started talking about what to do that day. They decided to go to the docks to go fishing. Jack noticed that the girls were holding their own on the fishing end of this trip but never said anything about it to anyone. Jack was hoping that Deni would need assistance with something this weekend. He wanted to look like a hero to her and wanted to show her what a big strong man he was becoming, how he wasn't scared of anything, but instead he learned that Oklahoma girls can take care of themselves. He also learned that Deni knew how to fillet a fish and tie her own hooks. Deni even had her own tackle box. He was impressed by all that but wanted her to be more like … like … what was he thinking? That was how all those other girls acted, like they were too dainty to do any of the stuff that Deni and her friends did. He was proud of his new friends and was proud to call them friends now.

Chapter 8

They arrived home to find everything okay. Stan always worried when they left for the weekend. Deni took her stuff to her bedroom and started unpacking her clothes. She was so tired that all she could do was take a shower and go to bed. Cathy came upstairs to check on her and found her passed out at 8:00 p.m. Stan and Cathy unpacked everything and put it away before taking their showers and hitting the hay. It's amazing how a weekend getaway to relax can wear you out so much.

Deni woke up at her usual time and got ready for school. She rode her bike, put it in her usual spot, and waited for Cindy to show up. Jack came, put his bike up, and stood talking to Deni when Cindy rode up. They all walked in together and went to first period. This day was dragging for all of them because they were still tired from the weekend. Cindy had made an appointment to talk to Mr. Keen about Deni and a possible science project.

School went on as usual but not fast enough for Deni and her friends. Halloween and Deni's birthday were fast approaching. All the buzz around school was the Halloween party at the gymnasium and all the fun activities. Deni was more concerned with her birthday party which was the next week. Deni was also excited about the Halloween party and was deciding what costume to wear. Deni asked if everyone wanted to visit the Halloween store to pick out something that all five would like.

Deni wanted them all to dress as characters from one of their favorite movies, *Shrek*, but didn't know if Jack would be willing to be Shrek. Later she talked to Cindy about it, and Cindy suggested they could dress as the four musketeers and Jack could be the king. Mary came into the conversation and suggested that they all go as classic characters, with Jack being the vampire. Leah came in and said that her grandmother would be making her costume, and they could check and see if Bea could make all of them. Deni thought that was nice. Cindy wanted to know what costume Leah was wearing.

Leah said, "Grandma found this pattern on the Internet for a beautiful queen's dress and cape. She was so excited about making it that she started it a month ago and is already finished. I just have to go over there for the final fitting. Hey, y'all want to come with me this afternoon? Then we can check with her about your costumes." Everyone agreed with that and decided to ask Jack what he wanted to be in this royal court.

Jack came with them to Mamaw's house and asked Bea what she suggested for him. She told him to let her think about it for a bit and she would let him know. She had already figured that if one girl wanted to go as queen that the others would probably want something to go with that same theme. So when Bea purchased the pattern and materials for Leah's dress, she went ahead and picked up patterns and materials for all the girls. She kept this from Leah so Leah wouldn't tell her friends about the surprise Bea had for them. Amazingly, Bea had already finished all the costumes and gave them to the girls to try on.

Meanwhile, she looked at Jack and said, "I'm thinking you're not the king-type person. You seem more like Lancelot or Merlin perhaps. Which do you prefer?" Jack thought Merlin was a fantastic costume for him and asked how Bea had figured that out without really knowing him.

Bea told him she had heard quite a bit about him from Leah and her friends, and by looking at Jack, she could just figure out that he wasn't mainstream.

Jack laughed and said, "You're good, Mamaw."

Bea hugged him and laughed and then said, "Well, then, let's give you something to try on."

Jack was amazed that she had already made him a Merlin costume and went in another room to try it on and model it for the girls. The girls came out looking fantastic and all the dresses fit perfectly. Mamaw was really good at guessing sizes. Jack came out of the other room looking very magical. Mamaw was pleased to see him in his costume, which also fit perfectly. Jack was so pleased with this that he couldn't thank her enough. He offered to pay for his costume, and all the girls also offered to pay. Mamaw would not take money for these costumes. She was delighted to make them and so glad the kids liked them. She loved to sew and it gave her something to do.

They all left Mamaw's and went to Deni's to model for Cathy and Stan. Deni's parents were so pleased with the work that Mamaw had completed they offered to have her over for supper one night and to give her a special present to thank her for all she had done for them and for the kids. Leah was very happy that so many people in town cared so much for her grandmother. It made her tear up a bit, thinking about it. Leah turned to them and told them how Mamaw loved all her friends and loved living so close to her family now. She said she had never seen her mamaw so happy before. Cathy gave Leah a hug and told her that it was such a pleasure to have Bea right down the street and how much she enjoyed having her there. Cathy had always told Bea and Leah that if they ever needed anything, all they had to do was ask and she and Stan would be there for them.

Deni's friends left for the night, and Deni asked her parents about going to the Halloween party at school. Her parents both said that she could go but was surprised she asked since she goes every year.

But there was one thing Deni had not mentioned to them, and now it was time to jump in and say it. "Yeah, I know I go every year, but this year I was wondering if you cared if me and my friends went by ourselves? Do you think that would be okay?"

Deni stood there looking shy and afraid. Her parents looked at each other and smiled and then turned to Deni and said that it would be okay only if they could take Deni and her friends there and pick them up at 9:00 p.m. Deni agreed to this and softly asked if they would take Jack also. Cathy and Stan knew that was coming but didn't expect it so soon.

Of course, they said, "Isn't he one of your friends now too?"

Deni said, "Yeah, but I think he's a little more than a friend. You know what I mean." Her parents just nodded and told her to go to bed.

Deni went upstairs and crawled in bed. Today had been a very trying day for Deni. There was a pop quiz in math class, which she didn't do very well on, and she was really starting to worry about her grades this year. Cindy was doing well but couldn't figure out why her grades were dropping. Usually she was the one with the straight As, and Cindy was the one with Bs and Cs. Now it seemed that the roles had been reversed. What was going on with her and with Cindy? This was starting to get really weird. Last time they went to the Hair Station, Sabrina let her former assistant, Tasha, mix all the color. Did she mix it wrong or put something extra in it that was affecting Deni? Deni couldn't think about this anymore. She was too tired to think.

Cindy was keeping a log of everything that was going on with Deni and herself. She had taken early entries from her diary regarding Deni and how smart she was and entered them into this new log so there would be a baseline behavior pattern to compare Deni's recent developments to, and she also wrote things about herself in the new log. She wrote in the log every day about both their behavior and what happened on pop quizzes or tests. There was a pattern starting to form, but Cindy wasn't sure she was doing this correctly and decided to keep on with what she was entering and then check with Mr. Keen later to see if he could make any sense out of it.

Cindy went to sleep thinking that something was happening to Deni and herself but just could not put her finger on it. She didn't feel any different, and Deni didn't report having any problems that she was aware of, so this must all be in her head. She tried to shrug it off, but things just kept leading her back to the same question. What was happening to her and her best friend?

Cindy woke up at nine on this beautiful Saturday morning, and a wonderful aroma hit her nose. Mom was cooking bacon. *Yum*, thought Cindy. She loved bacon, and her mother just didn't make it enough for her. She would eat it every day if Sam would let her, but Sam liked Cindy to eat semi-healthy. She limited Cindy's junk food and limited her daughter's intake of grease and fat. Sam knew Cindy loved bacon and also knew it would get her out of bed. Cindy came downstairs into the kitchen and hugged her mother.

Sam hugged her back, saying, "I knew this would get you out of that bed. How'd you sleep, sweetheart? I know you've been working hard at school and at home and wanted to give you a special breakfast for being so special yourself." Cindy liked when her mother was like this and hugged her even tighter. Cindy loved her parents very much and wanted so much to spend more time with her mother, but sometimes that was hard.

Sam suffered from depression and sometimes didn't want to get out of bed, but Cindy could always cheer up her mother. Cindy had to admit though that sometimes it was hard to go in there and ask her mother to spend time with her. The doctors had been changing Sam's meds, and it was really messing her up. If they had just left everything alone, it would have been all right. Sam was in a good mood this morning though and was feeling great. Maybe the meds were starting to work, at last. Cindy asked her mother if they could go hang out at the mall today or go to a movie. Sam thought it would be a great idea and asked Cindy if she wanted to invite Deni and Cathy along. Cindy went to the phone and called Deni. Deni and Cathy agreed and said they would meet up in about an hour to go to the mall.

Cindy went upstairs to get ready while Sam cleaned the kitchen. Deni and Cathy came over within an hour, and they all left in Cathy's car. Sam left a note for Hal to let him know where they had gone and about what time they would be home. Deni and Cindy were happy to see something in their lives that seemed back to normal. Deni never mentioned to Cindy about the weird feelings she had or how she felt that she was changing. It just scared her too much to admit that to anyone but her own mother. Cindy knew this was going on because she and Cathy talked almost every day about what was happening, and Cindy would even send Cathy copies of her new journal so Cathy could add anything just in case Cindy missed something. Cindy would never let Deni know this but knew what was going on inside Deni's head. Cindy felt bad for keeping such a secret from her best friend but felt that in some way she was helping Deni through this tough time in her life.

They arrived at the mall in great spirits, and Sam seemed so happy that they were all together. Cindy and Deni decided to cater to their mothers today and to make this day about the ones they loved the most. Cathy had convinced Sam to help her watch Deni today to see if there was something special Deni might want for her birthday, which was coming up on November 7. Sam told Cathy she would ask Cindy to help with that task and had told Cindy about all this before Deni and Cathy came over. Cindy told Sam she would watch to see if there was something in particular Deni really wanted, and then she would secretly pass it on to her and Cathy.

Cindy led Deni to their favorite store and started looking at clothes. Deni wanted something new to wear for her birthday but didn't know what she wanted. She still had money left over from her summer job and wanted to spend it on a new outfit today for her and her mother. Cindy helped pick out the perfect outfit for Deni and then started picking out Cathy's outfit. Sam came over to see what she was doing. Cindy explained to her mother that she was Cathy and Deni's stylist, and she immediately jumped in to assist her daughter.

Cathy came out first to model her outfit and then Deni came out. Much to everyone's surprise, the outfits matched. Sam and Cindy decided to get outfits like that and chose the same style but in a different color from the other two. They all didn't want to be twins. After the purchases , they decided to go see what was playing at the theater. Today was supposed to be a special at the *Reel-2-Reel Theater*. They were supposed to have a matinee of old movies but didn't see it on the marquee. Cindy decided to ask someone at the ticket booth and found out that they were having a special showing of *An Affair to Remember* with Cary Grant and Deborah Kerr.

They all bought tickets and then headed to the concession stand to pick out snacks. They bought popcorn, sodas, Junior Mints, and Whoppers to share and headed into the theater. It was already dark when they headed in, and it took a minute for their eyes to adjust to the darkness. They realized they were the only ones in the theater. They picked the best seats in the house and propped up their feet on the seats in front of them when the door opened and in came the flood of people. They had forgotten to post what movie was being played today, and when Cindy asked, they posted it on the marquee. A mall-wide announcement came that the movie was starting, and it seemed like everyone decided to see this movie. What Cindy thought was going to be a quiet movie now became a loud movie.

They had grabbed extra napkins at the concession stand and it's a good thing they did. There was not a dry eye in the theater by the time the movie was over. They decided to go to the Burger Stop for a late lunch and headed up the stairs. It was a nice day when they went into the mall, but now it was starting to cloud up and thunder. They wanted to sit out on the balcony, but that plan was spoiled by the few raindrops that started to fall while they waited in line for a table. They sat by the indoor waterfall and found it just as relaxing as the balcony. After they ate and everyone was on the escalator to leave, they heard someone screaming at Deni. They all turned around to see Jack coming down the stairs, trying to get their attention.

Jack ran up to Deni so fast he couldn't stop and he ran smack into her, almost knocking her down, then kissed her right on the lips. Cathy, Sam, and Cindy started to giggle but turned away. Deni was so embarrassed that she immediately turned a bright shade of red, and Jack was so overwhelmed that he forgot what he was going to say. After an awkward silence, Cathy cleared her throat, and that seemed to snap Jack out of his daze. Jack said he was sorry and walked off.

Sam just watched as he walked away and said, "Huh, wonder what he wanted?" They all shrugged and turned to leave.

They got to Cindy's house just as the clouds let go of the hardest rain they had ever seen. Cathy and Deni decided to stay there till the rain eased a bit, and Cathy called Stan to let him know where they were. Sam suggested that if Stan could make it over, they could all eat supper together. Cathy told Stan and he said he would try to come over as soon as the rain let up a little bit. About an hour later, Stan showed up soaked to the bone, and Hal came in from work. Hal had to work most of the time and rarely got a weekend off for anything. Hal gave Stan a towel to dry off and went upstairs to fetch a pair of sweats for Stan to put on while Sam dried his clothes for him.

Sam and Cathy were preparing supper for everyone, and Cindy and Deni were setting the table. Everything was done by the time Stan came out of the bathroom with his wet clothes, and he handed them to Sam. She immediately took them to the laundry. They all sat down for supper and the phone rang. It was Jack; he had finally remembered what he was going to say to Deni. Hal answered the phone, and Jack identified himself and asked to speak to Deni. Deni got on the phone and Jack started talking really fast. Deni could tell he was nervous, but why? Jack had never been nervous around Deni, so why start now? Jack said that he wanted to be the one to escort Deni to the Halloween party at school and asked if that was okay with her. She said he would have to ask her father. Deni hollered for her father to come to the phone. Stan said yes and told him to be at the house at 6:00 p.m. Jack thanked him and said he would be there.

Stan returned to the table smiling and proceeded to tell everyone what Jack wanted. Deni was shocked by this tell-all story her father was saying that she got up and ran to Cindy's room. Cindy ran after her and consoled Deni while the adults just sat down there having a good time. Stan made his way to Cindy's room and wanted to talk to Deni alone. Stan sat down on the bed next to Deni and stroked his daughter's hair while she cried.

He started by saying, "I'm sorry. I didn't mean to embarrass you like that. Deni, honey, please look at me. I am sorry and it will never happen again. It's just that I thought that was one of the sweetest things that could happen and was so proud of you both for asking my permission. Well, I've never dealt with anything like this before and just thought it was sweet, that's all. I just wanted to share that with everyone. I'm so proud of you and love you very much." He got up, Deni rolled over, and jumped up to hug him.

"Thank you, Daddy. I love you too. I've never been through anything like this before either, and I'm not sure how to do things. I felt like you were making fun of me but you weren't. I'm sorry too." Stan took Deni back downstairs and apologized to everyone there for making Deni feel uncomfortable.

Deni and Cindy cleared the table and cleaned up the kitchen. Cindy told Deni that it was nice of her father to do that for her, and then she hugged Deni. Deni had always told Cindy that Stan was like that, and

Cindy got to witness it tonight. She believed Deni now about Stan being a special father.

The adults retreated into the living room and asked the girls to start coffee for them. Cindy went to make coffee and decided to cut everyone a slice of the cake that her mother had made that morning. Cindy put it all on a tray, and she and Deni took the desserts and coffee to the living room. They served their parents and made sure everyone was happy before going upstairs to Cindy's room. Cindy had her computer up and on the gossip page. Deni sat down to review the latest gossip while Cindy lay across the bed. She was still shocked to see Deni looking at the latest celeb gossip and started laughing. Deni turned to see what was so funny.

Cindy said, "You are, silly. Remember six months ago you thought that was all just a load of poop, and now you can't get enough gossip. Who's dating whom and who's sleeping with who? Wow, I'm proud of you for evolving into this person. Now we really are alike." Deni laughed at her friend's analogy and turned to read more about Brangelina.

Cathy came upstairs to get Deni to go home, but Cindy insisted that Deni spend the night if it was okay. Cathy agreed and told Deni to be home before noon to help her clean for Mamaw's supper surprise tomorrow night. Cathy also asked Cindy to come over if it was okay with her parents. The girls tired of looking at the gossip and started to get ready for bed. Cindy told Deni she would be back in a bit and disappeared downstairs.

Cindy had left her Deni journal downstairs that morning and went to retrieve it from the laundry room. She needed to write down tonight's events and to make a note to tell Cathy about the computer thing. Cindy decided to fix a snack to take up to Deni as an excuse for leaving and took a piece a chocolate cake with a glass of milk back upstairs for them to share. Deni was starting to worry about where Cindy had run off to when the door opened and Cindy walked in with a wonderful treat. Shortly after that, Sam came in to kiss the girls good night and to thank them both for the wonderful day. Both girls thanked Sam and kissed her good night.

They finished the milk and cake and still weren't ready to go to sleep. They lay there staring at the ceiling when Cindy spoke up. "Well, how do you like our classes so far? I like these classes better than I did those honors classes. I'm sure we can cruise through this year without any problem."

Deni sighed. "I don't know. I like the classes better, but I'm not sure if it's gonna be easy for me. You seem to be doin' good though. I'm really scared about my grades this year."

"Yeah, that's unusual for you. You always get good grades. I'm usually the one struggling," said Cindy.

Deni looked at her and said, "I know, but this year is different. I don't know why but something has changed. Haven't you noticed anything different?"

Cindy replied, "I have noticed some subtle changes but nothing too drastic. You need to quit worrying and concentrate on the task at hand." Deni agreed and said good night to her best friend.

Cindy rolled over and finally fell asleep. She had a weird dream about seeing some blonde girl driving an old car down an oceanfront road. The girl had blonde hair, teal eyes, red lips, manicured nails with a French tip, and an absolute fabulous outfit on. Who was this mysterious woman?

Cindy and Deni woke up feeling refreshed. Cindy didn't dare tell Deni about her dream. She just couldn't bring herself to do it, but she did make a note to write it down in her journal. Deni got to the shower first and dressed in a hurry. Cindy got in and out so they could go to Deni's to see Mamaw and surprise her. Sam offered to take the girls, but they both decided to walk. It was always nice outside this time of year. Besides, it was only two blocks away.

The girls got to Deni's and told Cathy they were going to Mamaw's to tell her about the surprise. Cathy told them to make sure to tell Bea to be there at four so they could visit while Stan cooks. The girls left and walked the two houses to Mamaw's and heard Bea singing. They knocked on the door but were sure Mamaw couldn't hear them because of the music playing. They opened the screen door and walked in, following the sound of the singing voice. Bea was standing in her kitchen, kneading bread and singing to the birds outside her window. It was a funny sight, but the birds didn't seem to mind. They were singing right along with Mamaw and putting on a show in the birdbath under the peach tree.

Mamaw turned around to get more flour and saw the girls standing in the kitchen door. Startled and a little embarrassed, she asked what they were doing there.

Deni spoke up and said, "We are here to formally invite you to my house for a special supper in your honor."

Mamaw looked shocked and said, "What do you mean my honor? Whatever for? I haven't done anything to deserve that."

Cindy said, "Oh yes, you have. You made our costumes for Halloween, and we want to say thanks for all the hard work. Please say you'll come. It's real important to us." How could Bea resist those faces? She agreed to come but only if she could bring this loaf of bread she was making. Deni and Cindy didn't mind that at all and offered to help.

Mamaw put the bread in the oven and went upstairs to get ready. Deni and Cindy waited in the kitchen, watching the birds and squirrels outside playing. Cindy wondered if Mamaw would ever get that dog that they had discussed when she looked at the house. But Deni thought it best not to bring it up. Mamaw seemed happy as a lark with the way things were. Why mess that up? Cindy agreed and said she wouldn't mention it anymore.

Mamaw came down to visit with the girls while the bread finished baking, filling the house with a wonderful smell. This was going to be a grand feast with Mamaw's bread at the table. Finally, the bread was baked, and they wrapped it in a tea towel and headed to Deni's. They came through the front door with Mamaw carrying the bread and saw Cathy sitting on the sofa. Cathy got up to help with the bundle Mamaw carried, and the smell of the bread hit her nose. Cathy drew in a deep breath and closed her eyes. She was transported to a time in her childhood when her grandmother made homemade bread. She opened her eyes and thanked Mamaw for bringing this wonderful treat. She asked if anyone wanted something to drink and began filling glasses with ice for the sweet tea she had just made. Mamaw asked for a glass of tea and thanked Cathy.

Everyone loved Cathy's sweet tea. They don't know what it is about her tea that made it so special, but it is just better than anyone else's.

Cathy also made a pitcher of raspberry tea to accompany the steaks that Stan was grilling. They retreated to the patio while Stan prepared the steaks. Cathy had already put the taters on the grill and fresh veggies. Mamaw wanted to keep the bread covered till it was time to eat. Stan was having a good time watching the ladies laugh and smile.

Finally, everything was cooked and the table was set. Mamaw brought out the bread on the cutting board and started cutting off slices. Stan's mouth was watering just from smelling the bread.

After finishing this magnificent meal, Cathy got up to clear some plates and brought out Mamaw's special dessert. She brought out a big box that said Mike's Bakery on it. Then she left to get the plates and forks for dessert. Mamaw sat there in anticipation.

Cathy returned with a present in her hands. Mamaw just looked at her in astonishment and started to tear up.

Cathy cleared her throat and started to speak "I just want to say thank you for moving to our little town. We love you very much and want to spend more time with you. It's a good thing you live so close or else I would never get to see my daughter and her friends."

Everyone laughed, including Mamaw who was still dabbing her eyes. "I want to say you are truly a part of this family, and we want to say thank you for being, not only Leah's grandmother, but for being Mamaw to all of us. We love you and hope you enjoy this small token of our appreciation," said Cathy as she handed the present to Bea.

Bea tore off the wrapping and opened the box to find a brass door knocker and a gift certificate. She picked up the knocker and just started to cry. The girls looked around bewildered as Bea told them that it was the knocker from her house in Nashville.

"How ever did you get this?" she asked, looking at Cathy. Cathy hugged her and told her that Louise called George and asked if he could send it for her house here and he overnighted the knocker to Cathy's house. Bea was so overwhelmed that she almost forgot about the envelope that was still sitting in the box.

Bea put the knocker back in the box and set it aside. Then she went around the table hugging and thanking everyone for the tasty meal and the wonderful present. Stan told her that he would come over tomorrow and put it on for her. Then Stan told them to cut the cake. Cathy took the cake out of the box and saw that Mike had put a little something extra on it. He added a little sewing machine to the top of the cake and wrote on the cake as well. Bea looked at the cake and laughed. Mike had written, *"Thank you SEW much for being you."* Everyone got a laugh.

After the cake was served, Bea got up to go home, and the girls decided to walk with her since it was dark out. They made sure Mamaw was safe and secure before leaving to go back to Deni's house. Mamaw gave them another hug and kissed them good night.

Bea set the box on the table and took out the knocker again. All she could do was clutch it close to her heart and cry. Then she looked up, as if seeing someone, and said, "Harold, can you believe this has happened? I miss you so much. I remember when we got this knocker. It was on our honeymoon. You got me this knocker and promised to get the house to hang it on. I will never forget that moment. Now I will always have it with me. Thank you, Harold, for watching over me. I love you."

Then she noticed the envelope in the bottom of the box. She took it out and opened it. Inside was a note saying, "We love you, Mamaw. Hope you enjoy this day." Then she pulled out a gift certificate for Sew and Sew, the material store in town. She couldn't believe it was for $200. That was just the sweetest thing Mamaw had ever received.

Chapter 9

It was just three days before Halloween and Deni was getting excited. Jack was taking her, and they were gonna have a wonderful time; Deni was going to make sure of that. She was standing by the bike rack when Cindy came up, and they both stood there talking till Jack got there. They all went in the school together and went to the computer lab. During class, Jack kept sending Deni e-mails and instant messaging Cindy. They were all enjoying themselves when Ms. Linn walked by and caught them. She asked how far they had gotten on the assignment, and all of them hem hawed around the subject.

School flew by and now they were in the last period. Deni wished she could have stayed in her bowling elective but was forced to drop it when she dropped honors classes. Now she has a math class that's really kicking her in the pants. They had another pop quiz today, and Deni just knew she failed it. What was she going to do? Report cards would be coming out in two months, and she was really worried about her grade. After class, she approached Mr. Taylor to inquire about her grade. Mr. Taylor did not give her a good report, and Deni asked if there was anything she could do to bring up her grade. Mr. Taylor said he was quite surprised by Deni's grade. He had heard she was an excellent student and asked her what was going on.

He told her, "I know you're getting older, but maybe you are just too young to be a junior right now."

Deni told him, "No, that's not it. I've just had a lot on my mind and want to do better. What can I do to bring this up? Is there any extra work I can do before Christmas break?" Mr. Taylor finally gave in and gave Deni makeup work and told her to have it in by December 15. Deni said she would.

Cindy and Jack were waiting at the bike rack for Deni. Deni told them what had happened and showed them the makeup work she was going to have to do. Jack told her he could help, and Cindy said she would help as well. Deni told them that she had to do the work and would only let them help if they promised to stick with her till she caught on, no matter how many times they had to go over it. Jack and Cindy agreed and knew they were in for a challenge. Cindy made a mental note to write this down in her journal as soon as she got home, but first she wanted to call Cathy and tell her the latest news on Deni.

Deni got home and went straight to her room. Cathy was on the phone anyway. Deni went to her room, unloaded her book bag, and started on her homework. This was going to be a trying year, but Deni knew if she wanted to graduate early, she would have to get cracking and really apply herself. That night Cindy called to set up a work schedule with Deni and see if it was okay with Cathy and Stan. Jack would also be informed of the work schedule and get that approved with all parents involved. Cindy talked to her mom about all that was happening and asked if it was okay for her to help Deni out with her homework.

Sam told her daughter, "After all Deni has done for you, I think it's the least we can do for Deni. Is Cathy aware of what is going on with Deni's math class?"

Cindy said she did and told her mom everything that she and Cathy had been discussing. Cindy also showed her mom the journal she had been keeping on Deni's behavior.

Sam was shocked at what her daughter was telling her and asked if there was anything she could do to help. Cindy told her to just be aware around Deni and to let her know of any odd behavior.

Sam agreed and said, "Anything for you two girls." Cindy felt relieved finally that her mother knew about the weird behavior Deni was exhibiting. Now to call Jack and let him know about the plan.

Jack was onboard with the plan and approved it with his parents. They decided to start the next day at Deni's house. Jack said he was going to ask if he could do extra work in that class too so that he would be sure to get an A. Cindy said she would ask also just to make sure, and that way Mr. Taylor wouldn't get too suspicious about all of them working so hard on Deni's extra work. Jack thought it might help Deni if Deni thought she was helping someone else. Kinda reverse psychology goin' on for Deni's sake. He only hoped that Deni didn't catch on with his plan.

The next day they all met at the bike rack and walked into school. Jack was excited to ask about the extra work, which was really weird for Jack because he hated homework, and to ask for extra work was not Jack. He couldn't believe he was doing something this crazy for a girl. But he liked Deni not only as a friend, and he felt something deeper for her. He thought of Cindy as a close friend but thought of Deni as more. He didn't want to admit that to anyone, but he had talked to his father about Deni and the plan they had and how stupid it was to do this for a girl.

His dad just laughed and said, "Son, when it comes to girls, nothing is stupid. Just remember that it's for a friend as well. She seems like a nice girl and I want to help her too. Is there anything I can do to help?"

Jack told him, "Maybe, but I would have to see how the first few lessons go first. Then I'll let you know if I need your help."

They all decided to go to Art's Drive-In after school before starting on the extra work. Jack could tell this was going to be a long lesson. He had been trying to assist Deni earlier in math class, and she just could not grasp the concept of this lesson. Jack wondered what to do, and then it hit him while he was eating his burger. *I need to start at the beginning and see what she knows then go from there.* Jack and the girls sat eating and visiting with Deni's friends Mary and Leah before heading to Deni's to start on the extra math homework. Mary and Leah offered to help but had so much homework of their own they could barely breathe. Mary and Leah were still in the honors classes and doing okay but were overwhelmed with all the assignments. They had barely seen anyone since school started. They were always together and were missing Deni and Cindy. They wanted to drop the honors classes, but their parents wouldn't let them. So they were stuck for the rest of the school year.

Deni said she was sorry for all the confusion earlier in the year about the honors classes, but she just felt that she couldn't put her 110 percent into those classes this year. The other girls understood and wished that their parents would let them drop those classes as well.

Deni asked Mary and Leah to be at her house Saturday at 4:00 p.m. to get ready for the Halloween party at school. She asked Jack if he wanted to come over that early but really preferred to have him over at 5:30 or 6:00 p.m. Jack said no and that he had some things to take care of before he came over. He told her he would be there at 6:00 p.m. with a big surprise. Deni could hardly wait now to see what this surprise was going to be. Jack had asked her to go but was still being very secretive about the whole thing. Deni wondered what he had in mind.

They arrived at Deni's and brought a bag of onion rings for her mom. Deni knew that her mother loved the onion rings at Art's. Cathy was so surprised to get these. She had no idea that her daughter was going to Art's after school but was glad Deni went just so she could have those onion rings. The three kids headed to the kitchen to have a little quiet time for study. Deni started unloading books and setting her supplies out on the table. Jack started asking questions to probe Deni's mind and see how much she understood about trigonometry. Deni answered his questions correctly since he was asking her some very basic questions.

Jack was impressed and realized he didn't have as much work to do with her as he thought. Jack got out his books and supplies and opened to the first chapter, which was on the extra assignment list. They all were doing quite well. Jack and Cindy were baffled at why Deni felt she needed their help. Once she was alone with them and sitting there working on the problems, she was teaching them things about trig that they didn't know. She was not giving herself credit for all she knew.

Cindy stopped her and asked what was going on. She could do all this and more at home. Why couldn't she do this at school? Deni told her, "I don't know. I just get so nervous in class. It seems so advanced to me when Mr. Taylor is writing this on the board." Cindy was confused. Deni had never been this intimidated by any type of schoolwork. Why now? Why this class? She knew she had to get to the bottom of what was going on with Deni.

They all sat and worked till Cathy came in to inform them that supper was ready. Deni didn't even hear her father come in and was surprised to see him there. They all put their books away and cleared the table.

Cathy came in to set supper down and asked Deni, "How did it go? Did you get a lot accomplished?"

She said this to Deni but was also looking at Cindy for any hint that might tell her how Deni was doing. Cindy didn't give anything away. Deni told her mother that everything was going well and that she had already gotten half the extra work completed. Cathy was proud of her daughter, gave her a hug, and told her how proud she was to have her as her daughter. Cindy told Cathy that Deni was teaching her something about trig. Jack told Cathy that Deni was smarter than she gave herself credit. He said he knew a lot about math and was really good at this sort of thing but Deni was smarter at it.

Cindy made a mental note to make sure she wrote down everything that happened tonight. She also made a mental note to talk to Jack sometime and let him know what was going on with Deni and all the changes that had been going on. They all sat down to eat, when Stan came in stretching his arms wide and making an awful noise that was supposed to be a yawn. Deni looked at him and started laughing. Cindy and Jack covered their mouths but looked embarrassed for Deni. Stan had no inhibitions. Especially when it came to making Deni's friends laugh. Stan felt this was part of his job when Deni had friends over. He'd do anything for that girl and felt the same about Cindy. Jack was just an extra bonus to him.

Stan took his seat and started passing the serving bowls. Jack still couldn't look at Stan for fear he would burst out laughing and squirt tea through his nose. But eventually he was able to look up long enough to see Stan sitting there staring at Deni with a quizzical look on his face. Deni wasn't even aware of her father looking at her till Jack kicked her under the table. Deni looked at Jack, and he motioned for her to look at her father. Deni looked at Stan and just sat there.

Finally, she said, "What? Do I have food in my teeth or what?"

Stan just sat there staring and finally said to his lovely daughter, "I was just wondering what was going on with you that you need tutoring? I thought that if I stared enough I might be able to figure that out."

Deni didn't know what to say, so Jack took over for her. "You know she told us she needed our help, but I think she lied. She taught us a thing or two," said Jack. Deni looked at Jack with relief on her face.

Stan said, "Oh, well that makes sense. I mean you did meet a very nice young man this year. Although that sounds like something a guy would pull instead of a girl."

Deni's face turned red. She was so embarrassed that she couldn't speak. Jack just looked down at his plate and couldn't even look at Stan or Deni.

After everyone finished eating and plates were starting to be cleared, Jack got up to get his book bag and took his plate to the kitchen before turning to leave. Deni thanked him for the assistance with the homework and apologized for her father and the way he acted tonight. Jack laughed and left for the night. Cindy started to get her things together also and leave before it got too late. Deni thanked her as well and asked if she could spend the night the next night so that way they could sleep in Saturday. Cindy said she probably could and left for the night.

When Cindy got home, her mother met her at the door. "Well, how did it go? Did she really need that much help?" said Sam.

"No. I think she just got overwhelmed with dropping honors classes, and then Jack came along, and it just messed up her grade early on, and she couldn't get over it," said Cindy.

Cindy also got her journal to start writing down everything that had happened and finish telling her mother the events of the evening.

Cindy also told her mother, "I think she has test anxiety. Is that what you call it?"

Sam nodded and said that Deni just has to be sure and be calm before going into that class from now on. She told Cindy what to do to help Deni calm down. Cindy told her she would do what she could but would also pass it on to Jack.

The next day they all met at the regular place, and when sixth period rolled around, Deni couldn't wait to hand in the extra assignments that she had already completed. Mr. Taylor took them and was shocked at what Deni had accomplished. He asked why she couldn't have done that well in class and on her tests. Deni didn't know what to tell him. All she could say was that she would try harder. He took the work from her and told her what a good job she did.

Cindy went home with Deni. She had her mother drop everything off to Cathy earlier in the day. She was excited to see what accessories Deni was going to wear with her dress and couldn't wait to show Deni the shoes Sam had picked up for her to wear. Deni was so impressed by the shoes and wished she had a pair when Cindy started digging in her bag for something. What Cindy pulled out of that bag made Deni scream with delight and made Cathy come running into the room. Cathy was breathing hard and clutching her chest, scared to death. When she saw what Deni was screaming about, she calmed down and grabbed the shoes and started screaming herself. They were gorgeous and she couldn't help feeling the excitement too. It was a girl thing when it came to shoes, handbags, and clothes.

Then Cathy looked at her daughter and said, "Don't you ever do that to me again. Next time just holler at me or say it's shoes. Okay?"

"Okay. Sorry, Mom, I didn't mean to scare you," said Deni. Cathy hugged her daughter and kissed her forehead. Then she tried to put on Deni's new shoes.

Deni couldn't wait for her dad to get home to show him the shoes that Sam had gotten for her. Stan came in late and went to the kitchen to heat his supper. Deni came downstairs and asked how his day was. Stan looked so tired, and Deni wondered if he would stay awake long enough to even eat his supper.

Stan just looked at Deni and said, "It was okay. I'm just really tired. It's hard when all you do all day is sit behind a desk and stare at a computer."

Deni laughed and said, "Dad, I know that's not what you do all day. It would be nice if that's what you could do, but I know you don't."

Stan just patted his daughter's knee and kissed her forehead. He tried to finish eating but was just too tired. Stan could hardly make it up the stairs to his bedroom.

Deni went back to her bedroom and told Cindy what had happened downstairs with her father. Cindy and Deni felt really bad for Stan and decided to get up early to make a special breakfast for him in bed. They set their alarm and went to bed.

When the alarm went off the next morning, the girls got up very quietly and snuck down the stairs. They were trying their best to be as quiet as possible while trying to cook breakfast. Deni found the bed tray in the cabinet. She set it on the counter and went outside to cut a fresh rose from the bush in the front yard. She thought her dad would appreciate it even though he was a man.

She got out a bud vase and put the flower in it on the tray. She got out her mother's best linen napkins and place mats then placed them on the tray. Cindy was putting the eggs on the plate and getting toast out of the toaster. They sat the plates on the tray along with a cup of coffee and walked up the stairs. They got to Stan and Cathy's bedroom and didn't hear a sound. They opened the door very slowly and quietly and approached her dad's side of the bed. They wanted so bad to surprise him, but it was so dark in the room they couldn't tell what side of the bed they were on. Just then, they heard a door open and saw Stan coming out of the bathroom with just a towel around his waist. Deni was so embarrassed that she dropped the tray on the floor, grabbed Cindy's arm, and ran for the door. Stan was shocked as well and ran back into the bathroom. He had forgotten how hot his shower was and how steamy the bathroom was and went sliding across the floor. He hit the shower door and fell flat on his back. Stan lay there moaning in pain, unable to move. Deni heard the crash but was too embarrassed to walk back in there. She knocked really hard on her parents' bedroom door to see if her mom was awake but didn't remember seeing her mom in the bedroom.

Deni started yelling for her mom and heard somebody coming up the stairs. Cathy had gotten up and went down the front stairs to the kitchen while Deni and Cindy went up the kitchen stairs to her mom and dad's bedroom. Cathy went into the kitchen and saw the dishes sitting on the counter and thought Stan had cooked something last night because he couldn't find his supper. When she thought she heard something hit the floor upstairs and someone running, she took off up the kitchen stairs and scared Deni and Cindy so bad that all of them screamed and jumped.

Cathy opened the bedroom door and started hollering for Stan. She couldn't find him but heard him moaning from the bathroom. She ran to the bathroom door and could barely open the door because Stan lay sprawled in the middle of the floor. She attempted to help him up but couldn't. She went into the bedroom and grabbed the phone. She dialed 911 and gave the lady the information. When the ambulance arrived, Deni directed them to the bathroom where her father lay moaning in pain. Deni felt so bad for causing her father to fall and injure himself that she could barely look at him when they carried him out on a stretcher.

Cathy had gotten dressed while waiting for the ambulance and ran to her car to follow the ambulance to the hospital. Once at the hospital, they took Stan immediately to a room where a doctor was waiting to examine him. Stan had a bump on his forehead from hitting the shower door and one on the back of his head from hitting the floor. The doctor didn't think he had a neck injury but wanted an x-ray just to be sure. Since Stan was complaining about his back hurting the most, the doctor decided to do a full-body scan. Stan was whisked away to a huge machine that would take the necessary x-ray and was brought back to the room where Cathy was waiting.

Stan lay on the backboard with his head strapped down for another thirty minutes before the doctor came in and started removing the straps. Dr. Joe Kinsky was explaining that his x-ray showed no broken bones. He did say that Stan had a concussion. Dr. Kinsky also said that Stan had a severe problem with his back. Stan tried to rise to help the doctor but was unable to due to the pain. Dr. Kinsky pushed him back down and told Stan not to move. He explained that when Stan fell, one of the discs in his back had blown out. He further explained that he needed to have surgery to help relieve the pain and to replace the disc. Stan begged to go home. Dr. Kinsky told him that usually with this problem, most patients stay in the hospital till surgery can be performed or, if nothing else, stay for pain management; but Stan insisted on going home with oral pain meds and promised the doc that he would stay in bed. Dr. Kinsky agreed to this but told him that if the pain got worse or if he started losing feeling in his feet or legs he needs to come back to the hospital.

Stan and Cathy agreed to those terms, and Stan was taken back to the house by ambulance. He was taken back to his bed and the paramedics left. Deni stood in shock at what she had done. She went in to talk to her dad, but he was sleeping soundly from the pain meds. Deni left in tears and went to find her mother. Cathy was sitting at the bar in the kitchen, wiping tears from her eyes.

Deni sat by her mother and hugged her. All Deni could say was, "I'm so sorry, Mom. I didn't mean to hurt him. I just wanted to do something nice for him. I didn't mean to hurt him. I'm so, so sorry."

Cathy grabbed her daughter and starting wiping tears from Deni's face. "Honey, what are you talking about? You didn't do anything. He slipped and fell in the bathroom. It was an accident."

Deni was shaking her head and saying, "No, Mom, I made him fall. I saw him last night when he got in from work. He was so tired. I felt so bad for him working so hard. I just wanted to do something nice for him. Cindy and I got up this morning to fix him breakfast in bed. When we went in, he came out of the bathroom in a towel. I was so embarrassed that I just ran. That's when he ran in the bathroom and fell. Oh, Mom, it's all my fault. I'm so sorry. Please tell Dad I'm sorry for hurting him." Deni grabbed her mom and sobbed.

Cathy could do nothing to console her daughter but was trying her best to help her. Cathy took her upstairs to her room. Cathy went to check on Stan and saw that he was awake. He asked where Deni was and started to tell Cathy what had happened. Cathy told him that Deni had told her the same story and felt horrible because she thought she hurt her dad. Stan told her to get Deni. Cathy knocked on Deni's door and took her to her father.

Deni sat down beside her father, still crying, unable to look at him. Stan reached for her hand and told her it was not her fault. She fell to the floor beside him and tried hugging him without hurting him. Stan held his daughter tight and reassured her that he was going to be okay. He told her that his back has been bad for a long time, and this was just what he needed to make sure it was fixed. He told her that it was an accident and that she had nothing to worry about. He also told her to make sure that when her friends come over they should all come in there to model their costumes before they leave for the party tonight. Deni tried to tell him that she didn't want to go now, but he insisted that she go and have a good time.

Deni went back to her room and lay on the bed, trying not to cry. Cindy was there waiting this whole time and not saying a word. Deni told her everything Stan had said. She said that he wanted them to still go to the party and show him their costumes.

Cindy laughed and said, "Your father is the best guy I've ever known. I hope one day to meet someone as special as him."

Deni said, "Yeah, he is pretty special. I still feel bad about everything." Cindy agreed, and they both sat there praying Stan would be okay.

Deni's friends arrived at four, and Deni told them everything that had happened that morning. They all agreed to model for him and asked if there was anything they could do for Deni or her family. Deni thanked them but told them they were okay. They all started getting ready for the costume party and tried to be quiet at the same time. When they were ready, they all paraded in to see Stan.

Stan was just waking up and thought he was still having a dream. He rubbed his eyes and looked again at the girls standing in the doorway. He told them to come in so he could take pictures of them. He told them he wanted each one to remember this night for a long time. He took pictures and told the girls how wonderful they all look. He asked where Jack was at though. Deni remembered Jack saying that he had a surprise for her and also started to wonder where he was.

They heard a horn honk from outside and ran to the window. They saw Jack standing through the open sunroof of a stretch limousine. Stan was wondering what was going on, and all the girls started talking at once. He couldn't take all the excitement and they all left his room. He gave the camera to Deni and told her to take lots of pics for him to look at tomorrow. She promised she would and kissed him good-bye.

They all ran downstairs to the front door. Jack was getting out of the limo and asking the girls to hurry up or they would be late. He whistled at the girls as they came out the door and told them all they looked terrific. They all told Jack the same and stood while Cathy took pics of them. They all turned to get in the limo and stopped. Cathy yelled to see if they were okay. They all stood back, and out came three other guys who Jack had made friends with at school. Josh was among the guys in the limo and was looking a little sheepish as he got out. He had never done anything like this before in his life.

There in Deni's front lawn stood Josh, who approached Leah and asked if he could escort her to the party. Leah turned red and accepted. Christian approached Cindy and asked for her hand. Cindy reluctantly held it out. She had always liked Christian but thought that because Natalie was his sister he was out of her league. Christian never really hung out with his sister because he didn't like the way his sister treated people. They were always fighting about something and Cindy thought she never had a chance with him. She was glad to see him there and that he wanted to go with her. Last was Kurby. He approached Mary and asked if she would mind if he accompanied her to the party. Mary was so happy she threw her arm through his and took off for the limo.

Deni stopped Jack and asked, "How did you do all this?"

Jack laughed and said, "I don't spend all my time with you, just most of it. Besides, I got a good deal on the limo, and the guys approached me and asked about the girls. So we all got together and decided to surprise you all with this fantastic night. Now are we going or what?"

Deni walked to the door of the limo and turned to wave at her mom. Then she got in and they all took off to the party.

Chapter 10

A t the high school gym, the limo driver pulled right up front so everyone could see them as they got out of the long car. Everyone who was walking to the door stopped to turn around. They had never known anyone who could afford a limo before. As Jack got out to assist Deni, everyone took a deep breath and watched. They were all in awe of the costumes and who was in the car. Josh and Leah got out next, and then Kurby and Mary got out, followed by Christian and Cindy. There was an extra gasp as everyone saw who Christian was with, and all started looking around to find Natalie.

Deni and the gang walked to the gym door, walking past the other students who were still in awe with their mouths wide open. This was really weird. Deni felt self-conscious as she approached the door. Jack held her hand and walked with his head held high and with pride. Jack opened the door for them all. They could hear the music playing and couldn't wait to get inside to see all the decorations and all the fun games.

The foyer was decorated in the usual Halloween garb, with witches flying around the room and goblins standing guard at the main doors leading into the gym. The gang made their way through the crowd and walked into a dark gym with colorful lights flashing all along the walls and floor. The decorating committee had done a fantastic job. There were booths set up for apple bobbing, a spook house, a drink station that had smoking cups sitting on the table with a punchbowl that had eyes floating in it, and on the stage they had the witch hunt contest. The teachers had gotten together to form a list for a scavenger hunt but decided to call it a witch hunt for Halloween. All the teachers had hidden objects around the gym for the students to find and had a magnificent prize waiting for the one who found all the objects first. They had a large curtain covering the prize so no one could see it until all the objects were found. They would announce the winner before the party ended.

Mamaw had volunteered to make masks, and at her booth kids were elbowing each other to try and get the masks. Mamaw saw Leah and hollered for them to come see what she had been working on and handed Leah a mask that matched her dress perfectly. Mamaw also had a mask for everyone else in the gang and told the three boys who had joined them to pick out a mask to match what they were wearing. Josh, Christian, and Kurby did that and picked out the mask that matched their costumes. Mamaw was so pleased with the outcome of the masks that she volunteered to help with the winter dance in December.

Deni and the gang went up to the stage and grabbed a list from Ms. Linn. Ms. Linn was dressed as Dorothy from the *Wizard of Oz* and looked very young. She was smiling and laughing with Mr. Keen when Deni approached to pick up a list. Ms. Linn handed them the list and wished them good luck. Deni glanced at the list, as did the others, and they all started splitting it up so that everyone could participate and all get the grand prize. They all parted ways, wished each other good luck, and agreed to meet back there in an hour.

As they were hunting for the objects on the list, they would stop to play games along the way. There was dart throwing and a putting contest, along with other carnival game booths set up throughout the gym. Deni and Jack were the first to complete their part of the list, and Jack stopped to win Deni a stuffed dog. Cindy and Christian also completed their part of the list and met up with Deni and Jack. Cindy's arms were loaded down with stuffed animals Christian had won for her, so she had to give some of them to Deni to hold for her.

Mary and Kurby met up with Leah and Josh, and all finished finding their objects together. They made their way over to the stage and met up with the rest of the gang. When they presented the objects and the list to Ms. Linn, they were told that they were the only ones who had completed the list. Deni asked if they could all split the prize, and Ms. Linn said they would have to wait to see what the prize was before deciding on what to do with it. They all looked at Ms. Linn puzzled and walked off. Now there was nothing to do but play games and wait for the unveiling.

Finally, it was time for their names to be announced and to unveil the prize they had won. Ms. Linn's voice came over the loud speaker and requested that everyone come into the main part of the gym. As the other students filed in, Natalie finally caught a glimpse of who was with Christian. She looked mortified. She couldn't believe that Christian would be with *her*. Cindy was pretty, but Christian was her brother, and he should be with one of her friends. The only problem with that plan was that Christian didn't like any of his sister's friends and didn't like the way they all treated the other students.

They all took seats on the bleachers and waited till Ms. Linn called their names. As Ms. Linn made the announcement that the prize was won, she started calling the names of the winners. Deni and the gang made their way to the stage and stood beside Ms. Linn. Mr. Taylor was standing beside the curtain, waiting for the cue to pull it off at the right time.

As Ms. Linn was congratulating the winners, she turned to Mr. Taylor and said, "And here is your prize." Mr. Taylor pulled off the curtain and gasps swept through the gym.

The curtain fell to the stage as Mr. Taylor was doing his best Vanna White impression. He was trying his best to present the prize in a manner that was appealing. All Deni could see was a sea of pink and a lot of movement. When she finally calmed down, she looked at the prize and saw nothing but four little piglets walking around in a small coral on stage. She started laughing so hard that she couldn't see straight. Everyone in the gym burst out laughing. Then they heard Ms. Linn start speaking again. She was telling them that tied to the collars on the pigs were envelopes with the real prizes written inside. All they had to do was catch the pig and release the envelope to see what they had really won.

They all just stood there in shock and then quickly decided the guys should definitely be the ones going into that pen and catching those pigs. The guys decided to go along with this plan although they really wanted to see the girls doing this activity. They pulled off their costumes and stepped through the gate. Ms. Linn rang a bell signaling the start of the fight for the prize. Josh came up with the first envelope and gave it to Mr. Taylor, who gave it to Ms. Linn. Next was Kurby and then Christian and Jack. As they all got out of the coral, Ms. Linn announced that she would read the first prize won.

Josh stood by Ms. Linn's side as she opened the envelope and pulled out the piece of paper inside. As she unfolded it, Josh held his breath. He looked at Leah and grabbed her hand. Ms. Linn announced that Josh had won a free burger meal at Art's Drive-in. Everyone applauded and started laughing. Next was Kurby. He stood by Ms. Linn and she opened his envelope. She announced that Kurby had won the same thing. The crowd started getting the gist of these prizes and laughed at what was going on. Christian stepped up with his arm around Cindy and waited for their prize to be revealed. Ms. Linn announced that he had won the burger meal and then called Jack to the front.

Jack stood with Deni at his side, and Ms. Linn opened the envelope. She announced that Jack had won the best prize of all. She proceeded to tell the audience that the other prizes were really gag gifts and that one of the envelopes held the grand prize. Jack couldn't wait to hear what he had won. She unfolded the slip of paper from the envelope and read that Jack had won a $2,000 shopping spree at Shawna's Fashions at the mall. Deni was excited because that was her favorite store. Jack was let down but was happy for the girls. Deni told him they also had boys' clothes in there, and Jack felt a little relieved. Jack decided to split the money with his friends who had worked so hard alongside him. They left the Halloween party and went to Deni's house.

Once at Deni's, she invited them in for cake and to talk about when they could go shopping together. They all piled into the kitchen, where they found Cathy getting plates and forks out for the crew. Deni asked about her father, and Cathy said he was resting but was feeling a little better. She said the meds the doc gave him must be working because Stan was able to sit up for a bit. Deni was glad to hear that. Cathy looked at all the kids in her kitchen and asked how the party was.

Deni told her about the witch hunt and how they had won the prize and asked when it would be best for everyone to go shopping. Cathy suggested Sunday since everyone would most likely be available. Josh said he had to work but that he would get off at 1:00 p.m. if that was okay with everyone else. Everyone agreed and decided to pick Josh up from work and head to the mall. Jack volunteered to drive his mother's car so everyone could fit in it. He asked Cathy for permission to drive Deni to the mall the next day and Cathy agreed.

They all decided to break it up for the night, and all of Deni's guest left except for Cindy. Deni and Cindy went upstairs to get ready for bed and to stop and check on Stan. As they walked into her parents' bedroom, she saw her father turn his head. That was a good sign to Deni since he couldn't even move earlier. He held up his hand and told Deni to come sit down on the bed. Deni did and started telling her dad everything that happened at the party. Stan was excited for her and her friends. Deni kissed him good night and asked if he needed anything before she left and got him a fresh glass of water.

Deni and Cindy left and stepped in Deni's bedroom and saw a huge banner hanging from the ceiling, saying, "We love you." Cindy started crying and hugged Deni. Deni was overcome with emotion and hugged Cindy back. They both got ready for bed and lay there looking at the banner that Cathy had hung from the ceiling. Cindy told Deni that she was lucky to have parents like that. Deni asked what she was talking about. Her parents were the same way.

Cindy laughed and said, "Yeah, but sometimes my mom gets in a funk and forgets about everyone. But that's okay, I still have you." Deni laughed and drifted off to sleep.

The next morning Deni got up and went downstairs to fix her mom and dad breakfast. She remembered what had happened the previous morning and decided to make a lot more noise this morning when she went in their bedroom. Cindy came downstairs and started helping Deni. Cindy wasn't sure she wanted to go through that again either, so she and Deni decided to knock on the door before entering. They heard a faint "come in" and opened the door slowly. Cathy was still asleep, and Stan was starting to lift himself up a little. Deni sat the tray down between her parents, and Cindy started waking up Cathy. As Cathy turned over and saw the wonderful breakfast the girls had prepared, all she could do was hug Cindy.

Deni sat down next to her father to help him feed himself and realized that he didn't need that much help today. Stan was feeling better, but Deni knew it was just the meds talking. She gave her father his plate and set his coffee on the bedside table. Cindy did the same for Cathy, and both girls left. They both went downstairs to fix themselves something to eat. Cathy came downstairs with the tray in hand and set it on the counter. Cindy started cleaning the kitchen.

Cathy sat down beside Deni and started asking about the plans for Deni's birthday party next Saturday. With everything that's been going on, Deni had not even thought about her birthday party. All she could think about was what she did to her father and the party last night. Cathy told her daughter to start thinking about her own party and caught Cindy by herself, to tell her to watch and see if there was anything special Deni might want while they are at the mall. Cindy told her that she would be sure to watch and let Cathy know if there is anything Deni mentions or looks at that she might want. Cathy thanked her and told her to go get ready.

Cindy went upstairs to get ready to go to the mall and saw that Deni was just standing in front of her closet, staring. Cindy asked what she was doing. Deni said she didn't know what to wear today. She wanted something that would impress Jack and told Cindy that she needed to wear her electric-blue halter top to impress Christian. Cindy said she didn't even know if Christian was going but thought that would be a good idea anyway. Deni laughed and starting teasing Cindy about liking Christian.

They heard Jack pull up in front of the house and ran downstairs to let him in. The whole gang was there. Deni nudged Cindy. Cindy just pushed Deni and told her to shut up. Deni was laughing as the gang came up the walk. Jack looked at Deni and told her how pretty she looked, which immediately made Deni's face turn bright red. Cathy came into the foyer and saw everyone standing on the porch. She asked them to come in but they said they needed to go. Jack turned to ask if there was anything she needed while they were out. Cathy said no and told them all to be careful. Jack led them to his mother's Flex and had already pulled up the backseat so there was plenty of room for everyone. He opened the passenger door for Deni. She got in and fastened her seat belt. Jack ran to the driver's side and got in and fastened his seat belt. He then made sure everyone was buckled and started the car.

He stopped by the Pig-n-Tote to pick up Josh. Josh was standing outside waiting for them as they pulled up. He was impressed with the SUV and got in the backseat. Jack made sure Josh put on his seat belt before pulling out of the parking lot. They got to the mall just as it was starting to become very cloudy and parked in the covered parking lot. Jack opened Deni's door and helped her out of the vehicle. He then took her hand and led the way into the mall. Once inside, Jack told them to all pick out something at Shawna's Fashions and bring the clothes to him. He would then take them all up and make the purchases using the gift certificate that they had won. They couldn't split it because they had put the certificate in Jack's name, so he was the one who had to pay for it all.

They all ran into the store and split in different directions. Cindy went with Deni to help her pick out something that she thought Jack would like, and then Deni helped Cindy. This was the first time Deni had assisted Cindy picking out clothes, but she did all right for a first timer. Deni also made sure that she picked out something for Jack and told Cindy to go help Christian with his selections. Cindy approached Christian cautiously but was at ease when Christian turned and asked her opinion about the shirt he had in his hand. Cindy said she like the shirt and picked a great pair of jeans and a jacket to go with it.

Each person in the group was able to get two outfits apiece, and the girls also got shoes along with accessories that matched each of their outfits. They gave their selections to Jack, who took them to the cashier and overwhelmed the girl behind the counter. Jack presented the gift certificate and the girl started ringing it up. The total came to $1999.48. They were all surprised that they didn't go over budget, but the girls had kept close tabs on the total. They all walked out of the store with a bag in their hand, and Jack suggested they all go to the food court to DJ's Pizza by the Slice. They all headed upstairs to the food court and ordered their pizza.

While they were eating, Deni took out her cell phone and called her mother. She asked if there was anything Cathy wanted to pick up for supper so her mother wouldn't have to cook. Cathy told her what to pick up and thanked her. Deni went over to China Island Eatery and ordered what her mother had asked for. While she waited for the food, she turned to look at the table where her friends were sitting. She started reminiscing about the good times with each one of her girlfriends and thought of good times that were to come with them. She was so proud of her friends.

She picked up her mother's food and returned to the table. They all took their trash to the trash can and then headed to the parking structure. As they approached the door to the parking structure, they could see that it was pouring. The wind was blowing really hard, and they were worried that this was going to be a bad storm. Jack led them to the car and made sure everyone was secure before pulling out of the parking spot. Deni had put the radio station on a local talk station, hoping to get the latest weather report.

As the national weather bulletin came over the air, they all hushed to listen. The weatherman said there was a super cell over the town and that everyone should take cover, as conditions were favorable for a tornado. Everyone took out their cell phones to call home but were unable to make any calls.

"The cell tower must be down," said Jack and proceeded to speed up a bit to try and beat the storm home. They got to Jack's house first. Jack saw his mother trying to gather enough water, batteries, snacks, and blankets. She told all the kids to grab something to cover their heads with and run for the cellar.

The kids all grabbed the blankets Ruth had by the door and covered themselves before running out the back door. Harvey was standing at the cellar, instructing them to hurry and waited till everyone was in before closing the door and securing it. They all sat on the benches, and Harvey turned on the emergency radio. The weatherman came over the air again, instructing everyone to take cover because there was a tornado on the ground heading for Catfish Holler. All the kids were huddled together and looked scared. Harvey and Ruth assured them that their parents were safe and that they could all call once the threat was over.

They were down there for about thirty minutes before they heard the roar of the tornado. All Deni could do was pray that they would be safe. As they sat there listening to the roar and the wind outside, they could hear the debris hitting the door to the cellar. Deni sat there listening intently for the slightest sound of the storm letting up. No one could hear anything except for the debris that was pelting down on the door. Finally, the storm let up. Harvey told them to stand back as he opened the door. He opened the door to the cellar and found that someone's patio table was sitting on top of the cellar. The house was still standing but had some minor damage. They made their way to the house, and the kids immediately took out their cell phones to see if they had a signal. The cell tower had been taken out by the tornado. Ruth told them to go to the kitchen and try the phone in there. As Jack reached the phone, he looked up and saw a large hole in the ceiling above and could see sky through it.

He went upstairs to check and found that a large barbecue grill was lying on its side in his bedroom.

"Wow, come look at this!" he yelled. Harvey and Ruth ran up the stairs with the rest of the kids to look at the grill and to inspect any other damage to the house. Harvey inspected everything and found no other damage. He told the kids to call and make sure their parents were okay. The phone line was dead. Ruth told Jack to make sure everyone makes it home okay and to come back so they could cover the hole the grill had made in the roof.

Jack led them all outside and, one by one, took them home. He also wanted to go inside and make sure everyone was all right before returning home to his parents. He had dropped everyone off but Deni and saved her till last on purpose. He wanted to make sure her parents were okay since her dad was on bed rest. They pulled up in front of Deni's house and saw her mom sitting on the front porch, waiting anxiously. She ran to Deni as soon as Deni got out of the truck.

"Mom, are you and Dad okay? I'm so sorry I couldn't call or come home," said Deni as she hugged her mother.

Cathy inspected her daughter to make sure she was all right and said, "We are okay. Your father couldn't get out of bed, and there was no way we could have made it to the cellar. I was so worried about you."

Jack approached and told her that they had left the mall just as the storm was hitting and made it to his house just as the sirens went off. Cathy was grateful for Jack's fast thinking to get them all to safety and gave him a big hug. Jack hugged her back and told her she was welcome. He said he had taken on the task of driving his friends around that day and was therefore responsible for their safety.

Jack asked Cathy if there was any damage to the house, and Cathy told them there were only broken windows in the house. Jack went in to help cover the windows. Cathy led Deni inside, still holding her daughter. Deni took Jack to the basement and helped get the plastic wrap for the windows. After securing the broken windows, they both went in to see Stan. Stan thanked Jack for everything he had done to protect his daughter. Jack said it was his pleasure. He really liked Deni and hoped that she felt the same way. Jack asked Cathy if anyone had checked on Mamaw and left to go to her house.

Jack got to Mamaw's, and it appeared that some shingles had blown off from her roof. Jack asked if she needed any help with anything else and went to the shed to get a tarp to cover the roof where the shingles were missing. He told her he didn't want any more damage to occur and wanted that covered. Bea let him do what he had to do and tried to pay him for the trouble, but Jack just gave her a hug and went back home.

As he pulled up in his driveway, he saw his father with some of the neighbors on the roof, covering the hole that the grill had made. Jack ran in and up the stairs to see if there was anything he could do. His mother told him to pack a bag because they were going to have to stay in a hotel till the roof and floor were fixed. Jack packed his bag and went downstairs to wait for his parents. After finishing the roof, his father went over to see if they needed help, then came home to leave for the hotel.

The hotel was booked because it was the only one in town. The cell service had been restored and Jack's phone rang. It was Deni offering them a place to stay. They were grateful and headed over to Deni's house. When they arrived, Cathy had prepared a quick meal for all of them to eat and thanked Harvey and Ruth for keeping her daughter safe.

Ruth hugged Cathy and said, "You would do the same for me." Cathy hugged her tighter and told her, "Anytime."

After eating, Cathy showed them to the guest room and told them to make themselves at home. She told Jack there was an extra room in the basement for him and showed him where to put his things. She also told them that tomorrow they would all go over and get them more supplies to last till their house was fixed.

Ruth started to oppose this, but Cathy stopped her, saying, "It's the least we can do for the family that kept our daughter from harm. We will not take no for an answer." Ruth hugged her and thanked her for her hospitality.

Chapter 11

The beautiful glow of the morning sun was shining down when they awoke. Mamaw came down to check on everyone and to bring fresh baked goods to thank them for helping her. They brought her into the kitchen, and everyone hugged her. Mamaw had really become an adopted grandmother to Deni and to her family. She was the most loved lady in town, and she truly appreciated everyone. She made sure she told them, but more importantly she made sure she showed them how much she loved them.

Harvey and Ruth ate breakfast and headed over to their house to pack more supplies. Jack had checked the TV to see how long school was going to be closed and it was undetermined at this time. The code compliance officer in town and the gas inspector were trying to get to the school to complete the inspection but had other priorities first. Once at the school they had to each room and make sure there was no structural damage, water leaks, or gas leaks before letting the kids back in. The TV said school would be out the whole week, but to make sure, they all tuned in every day for updates.

Harvey and Ruth returned with a truckload of clothes and supplies for their stay. Harvey explained that it might take a while to complete the repairs due to all the damage around town. He told Cathy that as soon as the hotel had a room available they would be moving there so they would not be a burden to them.

Cathy told them, "Nonsense. I told you we are not taking no for an answer, and you are going to stay here till your house is totally done. I will not have it any other way. So just take all that stuff to your room and settle in for a good time." Harvey laughed and thanked her.

Deni finished all her extra assignments while she was out of school and decided to work ahead so she wouldn't get behind anymore. She called Cindy to see if Cindy could spend the night and make hair appointments for the next day. Cindy arrived, and they called Sabrina to see if she could fit them in. Since the tornado, she had a lot of cancellations and could get them in that day if they wanted. The girls decided to go that day, and Jack volunteered to take them. The girls told Jack it might take a while, but Jack insisted on going and said he could spend time at the music store next door. So they all loaded up the SUV and took off for the Hair Station.

Sabrina greeted them in her usual upbeat way and offered them something to drink. The girls decided on an orange-infused tea blend. It was very refreshing. Sabrina called Cindy over to the chair and started on her while Tasha started on Deni. Shelby rinsed the girls, and the other two ladies styled their hair. They met Jack on the sidewalk in front of the music store and looked at what he had bought. He asked if they wanted to go get something to eat and maybe take some supper home for everyone else. The girls agreed that he had a good idea and headed to Roscoe's Pizzeria to get pizzas to take home.

It was another sunny morning. They all watched TV to check the updates on the school. There was still no update on the school, and the news crew was continuing to say that the school was to be out all week and possibly longer. The kids were so excited they had an unscheduled vacation. They all walked down to Mamaw's house to check on her and to see if they could help her with anything around the house. Mamaw was baking a sweet potato pie, and the house smelled like a grandmother's house during Christmas. Grandmothers' houses should always smell like something sweet is baking. No matter what time of year it is. Oklahoma gets really hot in the summer and not everyone bakes that time of year. So most of the baking is done in the fall and winter months. Mamaw didn't care what time of year it was. If she wanted to bake, she was going to bake. That's another reason everyone loved Mamaw. She made the best baked goods in town.

The kids sat at the table, rolling out pie crust and mixing the filling to bake some more pies. Mamaw wanted to make pies to take around and was determined to get all these done today. She had been up since 5:00 a.m. to start on the pies. Deni looked around her kitchen and laughed.

"How many pies are you going to make?" asked Deni.

Mamaw looked at her and said, "Ever how many it takes."

"What does that mean?" asked Jack.

Mamaw looked at him and said, "Ever how many it takes to satisfy the people that are receiving them." They all just had that look on their faces that said, "Oh."

They spent the majority of the day at Mamaw's, helping her bake pies and tasting the filling that was so delicious that they couldn't stop eating it. At about 5:00 p.m., Mamaw was putting the last of the pies in the oven and sent the kids home with a pie for their families. Jack took Cindy by her house to drop off the pie, and they all headed back to Deni's to enjoy the burgers Stan was cooking on the grill and couldn't wait to cut into the pie Mamaw had sent home with them. Mamaw had also made them special homemade whipped cream to put on top of the pie, and the kids couldn't wait to show their parents what they had helped with today.

They finished with supper, and all the kids got up to retrieve the sweet treat from the fridge. Deni grabbed pie plates and forks, Cindy grabbed whipped cream, and Jack grabbed the pie. They all ran to the picnic table and showed the treat to the parents. All were shocked that their kids helped prepare something that looked like it should be in a restaurant dessert display. The kids gave everyone a piece of pie with whipped cream on top then sat to eat themselves. Everyone was mmm-ing and oh-ing so much that you couldn't hear if anyone said anything. After supper, the kids cleared the table and washed the dishes before going to the living room to try and coax the parents into letting them watch their favorite TV shows. The only problem was no one could agree on what to watch.

They all sat and watched Stan flip channels till everyone agreed on a show to watch. Stan was up for the first time since his fall and was feeling really good. Deni was shocked that her father felt good enough to prepare supper. She still felt bad about the whole ordeal, although her parents were still saying it wasn't her fault.

The kids started to get sleepy, and they decided to go to bed, so Deni and Cindy headed upstairs to fire up the computer and catch up on the latest celeb gossip. Cindy was still surprised to see Deni actually enjoying this activity and not trying to research something on the web. Cindy loved to see Deni happy and loved looking at fashion and gossip even more. They noticed that some of the clothes that they had picked out at the mall were in front of them, being worn by some of the hottest names in Hollywood. Deni was even more shocked to see that she didn't have to depend on Cindy as much this time and that she picked out some of the hottest fashions on her own.

Cindy was proud of her friend and shocked at how far Deni had come in such a short time with the latest fashion trends. Cindy did happen to sneak her journal into her overnight bag without Deni knowing and brought it over so she could write down anything that needed to be added. She spoke to Jack about the whole journal and what was going on and asked if he had anything to add. Jack had told her about an incident at Mamaw's while Cindy was in the bathroom. Cindy wrote everything down and thanked Jack for his input and thanked him for not only helping her but for helping Deni in the long run.

Jack said it was his pleasure and he would do anything to help Deni. He truly cared for Deni. Cindy thought of how lucky Deni was to have a boyfriend like that and how she longed for that in her life. Then her thoughts turned to Christian. She wondered if he could be anything like Jack. What worried her more than anything was that Natalie was his sister and the kind of trouble she was going to cause if she and Christian got close like Deni and Jack. Cindy wondered what was really going on with Natalie this year. She had always caused so much trouble in the past, and this year she was being so low-key about her existence. That wasn't the Natalie she knew, and she wondered what Natalie would do about her and Christian. Christian had made it very clear how he felt about his sister and her little Twit Clique.

Cindy went back upstairs and found Deni sound asleep, just as she was when Cindy left and went downstairs. Thank goodness Deni was a sound sleeper. Cindy lay down and stared at the ceiling. She lay there thinking about all the things that had been going on since school had let out in May, and now it was November. Her mind kept going even though she was so tired. She started having that same dream about the girl driving the convertible down an oceanfront road and looking at her reflection in the mirror. Cindy still couldn't figure out who she was and started dreaming about the car flying over one of the cliffs and landing in the ocean. She woke up breathing hard and grabbing thin air. Deni was still sound asleep. Cindy tried to go to sleep again.

The next morning was a cloudy day. It was not going to be good if it rained. There were still a lot of people in town who had not fixed their roofs. No new updates on the school and the newsman told viewers to stay tuned for the weather. Everyone was glued to their TV sets, not wanting to have a repeat of Sunday. The weatherman didn't say anything about severe weather, so that was a big relief. Everyone went into the kitchen when the phone rang; it was Stan's doctor wanting to set up the date for his surgery. The nurse said they would do it on Friday. Cathy wrote down the date on the calendar and asked what they needed to do. The nurse told them to come to the hospital for preadmission labs. The nurse told her to be at the hospital at 6:00 a.m. on Friday in the outpatient department and that Stan may have to spend a couple nights in the hospital.

Cathy hung up the phone and went upstairs to tell Stan about the nurse calling and what was going to happen on Friday. Cathy started crying and saying that they had never missed Deni's birthday in the past and didn't want this to be the first year. She was going to be turning fifteen. That was a special birthday for a girl. Not only was it Deni's birthday but also Cindy's birthday. She was like another daughter to Cathy and Stan. How could all this have happened? Stan tried to console his wife but found that to be impossible and just held her in his arms, saying he was sorry for all that is happening. Cathy knew it wasn't anyone's fault and felt terrible for feeling and carrying on the way she did, but she couldn't help it. This was going to be a special day for both the girls, and now he wasn't going to be there to share that with them.

Stan felt horrible but there was nothing either one of them could do about it.

Cathy went back downstairs to break the news to the girls, but the girls had already looked at what Cathy had written on the calendar. They had already made a plan to celebrate their birthdays with everyone in the hospital. Deni would make sure that her father was there for this birthday. Cindy made a mental note to make sure to alert the nursing staff at the hospital of the event and had already called her parents to inform them of the change in plans. Her parents were really behind this plan and started making plans to make a trip to the hospital on Friday to be with Cathy while she waited during Stan's surgery.

Cathy couldn't bring herself to tell the girls about all the changes going on. Deni looked at her mother and just hugged her. She told her mother about all the plans they had made while she was upstairs. Cindy told her that her parents would be there on Friday to sit with her. Cathy couldn't believe how strong the girls were and hugged them both. She was so proud of these two girls she could just bust. All she could think about then was how she had gotten so lucky to have such loving children. Yes, she was including Cindy in this family.

It started to rain about 3:00 p.m. and cooled everything off so much that Cathy had to build a fire. They all sat around the fireplace drinking hot chocolate and talking about the upcoming events. Deni didn't really want to make a fuss this year over her birthday anyway, and this was the perfect excuse. Cindy felt the same way as Deni but did have a little surprise for her.

Cathy was cooking homemade soup for supper that night and had called Mamaw to come join them. Mamaw showed up at 5:00 p.m. to help with last-minute preparations. Cathy filled her in on the surgery, and Mamaw said she would be there on Friday. Cathy asked her if she could stay with the kids and maybe spend the night. Cathy also told her about the girls' birthdays on Saturday and said that they were planning to have a little party at the hospital for them. Mamaw told her the kids could stay at her house and that she shouldn't worry about the party—she would take care of that. She asked what their favorite colors were. Cathy looked at her puzzled and answered all of Mamaw's questions.

Mamaw set the table and had made some homemade corn bread to go with the soup Cathy had made. They all sat at the table not saying a word, which was music to Cathy's ears. That's always a cook's dream. You can always tell how good the food is by the sounds coming from the guests. If the food is good, there's no conversation, just the yummy sounds everyone makes when they enjoy the food they are eating. That's the best sound in the world to a cook.

Mamaw asked the kids to stay with her on Friday and to have a sleepover. The kids got all excited about the prospect of staying with Mamaw. Mamaw would make sure this was a special weekend for the girls. She helped clear the table, and the kids volunteered to clean the kitchen. Mamaw sat in the living room with Cathy and Jack's parents. Mamaw asked if it was okay for Jack to stay with her also. She said she wanted this to be just like they were home. Everyone laughed because Bea only lived two doors down from Cathy. They all agreed that Jack could stay too.

Mamaw went home and immediately started writing down the plans for the weekend. She wanted to call Mike's Bakery because he had the best cakes in town. He had been there for about twenty-five years, and everyone in town recommended Mike for any occasion. Mamaw made a mental note to call him the next morning and order the cake for the girls in the colors they liked. Then she went to bed.

The girls said their good nights and headed upstairs. Deni couldn't wait to turn on the computer to see if any new breaking celeb news had been posted in the twenty-four hours they had been away.

Cindy asked Deni, who lay sprawled across the bed, "Do you think I should invite Christian to Mamaw's on Saturday?"

"If you want to, we could check with Mamaw first and see if that's okay with her. I don't think she'll mind though. I think that would be a great idea. Do you like him enough to invite him to your birthday party?" replied Deni.

Cindy laughed and said, "Yeah, I think I do. Why do you ask that?"

Deni laughed also, saying, "I don't know. It's just that a birthday party is very personal, and are you sure you want him buying you a present this soon?"

Cindy replied, "I didn't think of that. I guess I could tell him to come for cake and not worry about a present."

Deni said, "That would be cool but you know he won't. Just don't tell him it's my birthday too. I don't want him buying a present for me. Deal?"

"Deal," replied Cindy.

The next morning started with a boom, literally. It was stormy again and the thunder was so loud it rattled the windows. They immediately turned on the TV to see if severe storms were on the way. Luckily, there was no severe stuff, but this was Oklahoma. Tornados could pop up in any storm. The girls wanted to go to the mall but didn't want to go out in this mess. They decided to stay in for the day and make plans for the sleepover at Mamaw's. The girls decided to call Mamaw and see if it was okay to invite Christian to the party on Saturday.

Mamaw told them they could invite anyone they wanted. She also volunteered to invite Mary and Leah to the sleepover and to stay for the party on Saturday. The girls agreed with that and thanked Mamaw for all she was doing. Just two days till the party, and everyone had a lot to finish up before everything was perfect. Mamaw had ordered the cake and called Cathy to see if she would go with her to the Party Planner store to help with the decorations.

Mamaw told her, "I'll be there in five minutes to pick you up. This is going to be the best party for the girls. I hope it's okay with everyone that I'm throwing this for them. I wouldn't want to step on anyone's toes."

Cathy reassured her that everyone was more than okay with this arrangement. "You're family now, and it just wouldn't be a party without you there. This is going to be the best for the girls because you are here with us now." Mamaw thanked her again and said she was on her way.

Bea and Cathy got to the Party Planner store and couldn't decide what decorations to get. They asked one of the store employees to assist them. They didn't want to get the usual fifteen-year-old party stuff. This one had to be special because of Deni's father not being there this year. Mamaw thought it would be really cool to have a disco ball. She picked up the ball, and Cathy started laughing. Mamaw thought this was going to be the weirdest party ever, but she just had to get that disco ball. Then

Cathy decided to get the strobe lights and picked up some very bright and colorful ribbons to go with this disco theme they had going.

They walked out of the store laughing so hard they could hardly load the stuff into the car. This was definitely going to be the weirdest party ever for two fifteen-year-old girls. Bea asked Cathy if they were going to get Deni a car and asked if Cindy was getting one from her parents. Cathy said they haven't really had time to discuss anything about a car and had not talked to Hal and Sam about that yet.

"With the economy the way it is, I don't think anyone can afford to get anything extravagant at this time. I think we might wait till summer to get Deni a car or maybe graduation. Right now she's only fifteen, so a car can wait, and Stan would like to teach her to drive his truck, but with surgery tomorrow I don't know when that will happen," said Cathy.

Bea looked at her and said, "Why don't I help with that? I can take the girls out in this old car and teach them to drive. I wish I had a stick shift so I could really teach them something from the old days. It seems all the cars now are automatic, and no one knows how to drive a stick anymore. Back in my day, that's all we had were stick shifts. If you couldn't drive a standard, you couldn't drive." Cathy agreed and said that it would really be good for Bea to help out with the driving lessons.

They got home and unloaded the car at Bea's house and hid the decorations from the girls. Cathy gave Mamaw a hug and headed home. Mamaw was so exhausted from all the excitement that she decided to lay down for a nap on the couch, watching TV and dozing. She started dreaming about a red convertible and driving around a town while waving at everyone on the street. People were turning and pointing at the car and giving the driver a thumbs-up. She couldn't see who was in the car but had the strange feeling she was driving. This was fun—a four-speed on the floor, lots of power, beautiful red color, and the top down. She woke up with renewed energy that she had not felt in years.

Cathy went home to see the kids cooking supper for everyone. Deni was making something special for her father since she still felt responsible for his injury. She wanted him to have a good meal tonight since it might be a few days before he has another. Let's face it—hospital food is not that good. Cathy saw that Jack was being the man in the kitchen and was preparing steaks for the grill. He had been marinating them all afternoon, and everything smelled so great. The girls were busy preparing homemade soup for Stan and thought that it would be a great starter for the meal they were preparing.

They all welcomed Cathy home and then ran her out of the kitchen with a glass of red wine in her hand. They told her there were appetizers in the living room for her, could she please join the others and leave the cooking to them. Cathy saw Stan sitting in a chair, sipping wine and eating bacon-wrapped shrimp. She saw the appetizers the kids had made on the table and was shocked at the sophistication of this meal. She sat down to enjoy her wine.

She asked who made this when Harvey and Ruth spoke up. "Jack is a wonderful cook. Harvey's brother owns a bistro in Chicago. Jack used to spend every summer there. Ernie would take him to the restaurant every day, and Jack picked up a few things. He loves to watch the cooking shows on TV and picks up a lot of ideas from them. We are his guinea pigs, so to speak." Cathy was amazed at how this young man could cook. She had no idea he was this talented.

Ruth told her, "He plans on going to culinary school after graduation in California. He should do very well in that field. He already has such talent in the kitchen."

Cathy kept eating the food that was set out on the coffee table. She couldn't believe what Jack had prepared. He prepared coconut shrimp with orange marmalade sauce, bacon-wrapped shrimp, a tray of fruit cut in the shape of animals, a platter of cheeses she had never heard of, and a wonderful vegetable platter with homemade dipping sauce that was so delicious that they ate it all.

She told Ruth, "If I had known we had a chef staying here, I would not have cooked again."

Ruth laughed. "Don't be silly, your food is wonderful. Jack just does this on special occasions. He'll probably open a catering business after culinary school. He did ask if he could have the recipe to that soup you made the other night."

Cathy nodded and said, "Of course, but it's probably not as good as the soup he makes."

Ruth told her, "That's the one area he has a little trouble with. It's the soups. They all taste the same and have a little too much salt in them."

Cathy laughed, saying, "Oh well, you can't have everything. I don't think he'll have a problem serving his food."

They noticed Jack walk through the living room and out to the patio. He put the steaks on the grill and closed the cover. As he passed through the living room again, he asked if they needed anything and picked up the empty platter. He went into the kitchen to open another bottle of wine for the adults and took it to them. He wanted to set the table and make sure everything was perfect for tonight. He asked the girls to help him. He didn't know a formal place setting from an informal one. So the girls took charge . They set the table and went back into the kitchen to await orders from Jack.

Jack told them to go announce that supper was ready and to help seat everyone. Once everyone was seated, Jack arrived with the first course. He had prepared a salad with candied pecans, Gorgonzola cheese, and raspberry vinaigrette. He also placed garlic bread on the table for them to eat with the salad. Once everyone was through with the salads, he cleared the plates and brought out the second course. Jack had instructed the girls how to prepare roasted tomato and basil soup. He had made his own croutons to place in the soup for garnish along with a fresh basil leaf from his herb garden. After everyone had finished, he cleared these dishes and prepared everyone for the main course.

Jack brought out the plates with filet mignon, grilled asparagus with hollandaise sauce, sweet potato gratin, and homemade rosemary bread with butter. As he sat each plate down in front of the adults, you could hear the gasps from the parents. Jack was smiling and proud of his dinner menu. Deni's parents were quite impressed with Jack's cooking skills. The steaks were perfect along with the asparagus and gratin. Jack savored every bite. This was one of his favorite meals and soon became the favorite of the others. Jack cleared the table again and went to bring the dessert out. Jack had made crème brulee with fresh mint leaf and berries on top.

This was the ultimate meal for Stan. He felt that this was his last supper. If he ever had to have surgery again, he wanted to make sure Jack prepared his meals for him. He was stuffed and had to congratulate

Jack on a fabulous meal. Stan had never had anything that tasted that good in his life. He was sure Jack was going to make an excellent chef. Jack asked Stan what he might want to eat when he returned from the hospital.

Stan looked at Jack and said, "Surprise me. If it tastes that wonderful, I don't care what you make. My kitchen is yours." Jack laughed.

The girls cleaned the kitchen while their parents sat in the living room still discussing the meal that Jack had made. When the girls finished the kitchen they went in to watch TV with their parents. Deni wanted to spend as much time with her father as she could. She sat on the floor beside his chair and asked if he needed anything. He told her no and patted her on the back. He was starting to feel the pain from being in a chair for so long and needed assistance to go to bed. Jack jumped at the chance to help out again. He loved staying here and helping Deni and her family. He loved the sense of being needed. Jack didn't know how much he was appreciated by the Rosens. Stan was starting to look at Jack in another way also. He was starting to picture Jack as the son he never had. He was really getting close to this young man and could see why Deni liked him so much.

Everyone decided to go to bed. Deni and Cindy ran to her room and turned on the computer. They had to go on the computer and tell everyone about the meal Jack had prepared for them. Jack was truly becoming a hero in Deni's eyes. She was starting to really think of him as her boyfriend now. She had learned so much about him in his short stay at her house. She really appreciated Jack more than she could ever tell him. She was starting to get that funny little warm feeling all over every time she looked at Jack.

While they were on the computer, they found Christian online. Cindy asked if he wanted to come to her birthday party Saturday, and Christian accepted. She also told him not to bring a gift, that it wasn't that type of party. It was that type of party, but she really didn't feel that he owed her a gift. They had not been really dating, and she didn't know if they were officially dating or not. She didn't want to rush things and could not ask him these questions. She was nervous about Christian coming now. She didn't know what she should wear.

They turned off the computer and lay in bed staring at the ceiling. Deni started praying for her father to be okay and for him to come through the surgery without any complications. Then she drifted off to sleep. Cindy lay there unable to sleep, knowing that Christian was coming Saturday. *Oh my gosh, did I tell him it was at Mamaw's house?* Cindy couldn't remember if she told him that, so she made a mental note to call him tomorrow. Then she drifted off to sleep. She had a strange dream about a party. She could see some really strange decorations and could see Christian as he stood near a beautiful cake. He was getting a cup of soda and looking around the room. Suddenly he caught Cindy's eye and just stood there, locked in place, staring at Cindy. He wanted so much to hold her but couldn't move.

Cindy woke up when she heard a noise outside in the hall. She got up and crept over to the door and opened it just enough to see out in the hallway. She was startled to see Jack. He turned as she opened the door and told her to be quiet. She went out into the hallway and asked Jack what he was doing out there. He said he heard something and was following the sound. As they stood in the hallway in complete silence, they heard the noise again. It was a soft knock. They couldn't pinpoint where the noise was coming from; it seemed as if it was all around them. Jack asked Cindy if there was an attic entrance somewhere. Cindy pointed down the hall by the bathroom.

Jack opened the door beside the bathroom and found a narrow staircase leading to the attic. As he approached the attic he heard the knock again. Cindy was behind him and stopped when she heard the knock. She asked Jack if he saw anything and he said no. They made it to the attic landing and started looking around. Jack thought he saw something over in a corner and started heading there. Cindy was close behind and trying to hold a flashlight steady. Jack started laughing and turned to tell Cindy what he was seeing, when Cindy caught something out of the corner of her eye and then tried to scream. Jack caught the look on her face and grabbed Cindy and covered her mouth to stifle the scream. He told her to calm down and not scream. He let go of her mouth, and she immediately started telling him she saw something.

He was laughing and said, "Yeah, I saw something too."

"Then what are you laughing about?" said Cindy.

"Do you know what you saw?" asked Jack. Cindy shook her head and said she couldn't make it out. Jack told her, "That's because it's a shadow from the tree outside. The knocking is the limb barely touching the house as the wind blows." Cindy started calming down and looked where Jack was pointing and started laughing herself. They left the attic laughing and closed the door as softly as possible. They each crept back to their respective rooms and lay back down.

Cindy couldn't stop laughing at herself and thought how stupid she was being about a shadow. What really struck her as weird was how Jack could have heard that light tapping from downstairs. She would be sure to ask him tomorrow when she could catch him alone. Then she started dozing off.

Chapter 12

The next morning started early. They had to be at the hospital at 6:00 a.m., and everyone had to get ready. Cathy tried to get the girls to stay in bed, but they insisted on coming with them. Stan said it would be okay. As they headed downstairs they saw Jack standing in the foyer waiting for them. He said he was there to drive them to the hospital.

Stan said no but Jack held up his hand and told him to be quiet because his parents were still asleep. Stan lowered his voice and started to protest again, and Jack told him he would not take no for an answer. He wanted to be there for Stan and his family and thought that he could do the running for them while Stan was in the hospital. He told them that he had already arranged this with his parents and they would be by the hospital later to pick Cathy up and bring her home. But in the meantime, Jack said he was to be there to do anything that they needed. Stan hugged him and thanked him for coming into his daughter's life. Jack hugged him back and told him he was welcome and he would always be there for Deni and her family.

They all loaded up in Ruth's truck and headed to the hospital. Stan rode up front with Jack to make sure his driving was safe but couldn't find one thing wrong with his driving. Jack was slowly becoming the perfect future son-in-law. Stan chuckled a little under his breath and looked out of his window. Jack pulled up in front of outpatient department to drop everyone off while he parked the car. Stan needed assistance to get out, and Cathy got a wheelchair for him. Jack tried to park the truck as close as possible, but the parking lot was pretty full this time of the morning. He finally found a spot and parked.

When he got off the elevator to the outpatient registration, he saw Deni standing behind her father at the registration desk. Jack sat down beside Cindy. Cindy turned and asked about the noise last night.

"How did you happen to hear that soft knock from downstairs?" she asked.

Jack looked at her and said, "I have really good ears."

Cindy looked at him and said, "Yeah, so do I, but there is no way you could have heard that soft a knock downstairs."

Jack had to look around and tried to make sure no one else could hear him. Then he leaned closer to Cindy and started to speak so softly that Cindy could barely hear him. "I have a special gift," said Jack. "I have this ability to hear and sense certain things," continued Jack.

Cindy just leaned back and looked at him like he was crazy. "Yeah right, and I'm the Queen of England," replied Cindy.

Jack told her to keep her voice down and leaned in close again. "No, really. I have like this psychic ability, and it was working overtime last night," said Jack. He sat there telling her about the voices he was hearing, and he thought that she and Deni were still awake. So he went upstairs to see if he could hear if they were still awake, but when he got up there, he couldn't hear anything but the soft knock.

Cindy's eyes were starting to widen as he talked, and she was starting to really believe everything Jack was saying. She looked away, and when she looked back at Jack he was laughing so hard. Cindy hit him on the arm and told him he was a jerk. Jack told her he checked the house every night to make sure everyone was safe and to make sure the house was secure. It was a habit he got into as a child, and everywhere he stays he has to get up and check on the house. It's just one of his quirks. Cindy said it wasn't the only quirk he had but started laughing too.

Deni sat down beside them and asked what they were laughing about. They both started telling Deni about the adventure they had in the attic, and Deni had to laugh at what Jack had told Cindy about his "special gifts." Deni really started laughing at the fact that Cindy believed Jack.

The nurse called Deni's father back to the pre-op area to check him in for his surgery. Deni wanted to go with her father so she could spend as much time with him as possible before they took him to the surgery suite. They followed the nurse through the winding hall to a holding room that had a lot of gurneys that were partitioned off by curtains. The nurse showed him to the bed that would be his. There was a gown lying on the bed, along with a bag to put his clothes in after he changed. The nurse asked him to remove all his clothing and put the gown on and she would be back in a little bit to check on him. She did ask if he needed help before she pulled the curtain.

Cathy helped Stan get undressed and put the gown on. She put his clothes in the bag and helped him lay down on the bed before Deni stepped back through the curtain. The nurse came back and opened the curtain up and asked how he was feeling. She brought back a tray with equipment to start an IV. She asked Stan what kind of surgery he was having today. Stan answered all her questions and signed the forms she needed. The nurse started looking at his arms to start the IV. She placed the tourniquet and opened her supplies and then found the vein she wanted and stuck him. She got the IV started on the first try. When she was finished she told him she would be right back with his cocktail. Stan told her to make it a double. She laughed and said it would be much better than a double.

When she returned she had three syringes in her hand. She asked if he was ready to relax. He looked at her and was saying something while she was putting the solution from the syringes into his IV. His words were slurring and he was starting to get sleepy. That was after the first shot. Deni started laughing and held her father's hand. Stan looked at his daughter and smiled. Deni laughed again—her father's smile was just crazy looking. He had this really lopsided silly grin on his face. The nurse was still putting the solution from the other syringes into her father. As she finished with the last syringe, Stan was almost snoring. The nurse said it would be just a little bit before they came to get him. Deni ran back to the waiting room and got Cindy and Jack so they all could stay together.

The orderlies came to get Stan and told the rest of them they could follow till they got to the surgery doors. They all walked through the halls while Stan was in and out of sleep and stopped outside the surgery doors. They all said good-bye, and the girls kissed Stan and Jack shook his hand and hugged him. They all said they loved each other and off he went through the doors. The orderly came back out to show them the waiting room and told them where the cafeteria was and that the doctor would come in the waiting room to talk to them after the surgery was completed.

They all took a seat and sat there for a little while and then decided to go get something to eat. Jack volunteered to go to a nearby pizza place, but they all decided to go to the cafeteria to get something and stay together. Cathy thanked all of them for staying with her and especially thanked Jack for all he was doing for them. He had really stepped up and was helping out so much. He told her she was welcome and he would always be there for them.

They entered the cafeteria and were hit with a smell that didn't smell like hospital food. Jack was shocked that he could smell fresh herbs and spices cooking. As they walked in they were greeted by someone who looked like a waiter. He asked how many were in their party and seated them near the waterfall. They were so shocked that this was in a hospital. There was another waiter who came over to take drink orders and handed them a menu. As they looked at the menu, they were shocked to see what was being offered for lunch.

At the top of the menu were the specials. They offered a roast beef dinner with all the trimmings, turkey and dressing with all the trimmings, chicken cordon bleu, any kind of steak you wanted, and all the vegetables that could be offered. The menu was over six pages. The last two pages were things from the grill. The first four pages were prepared meals. Jack was impressed. The hospital boasted about being different, and by the looks of the cafeteria, it was living up to its claim. He wasn't a trained chef but could tell that some of the dishes offered were complex. At the top of the first page was the chef's name. He was even more shocked that the hospital had hired a world renowned chef.

Cathy ordered the wild mushroom risotto, the grilled broccoli with shaved parmesan cheese, and the grilled chicken breast with citrus rum glaze. Jack ordered braised short ribs, baked potato, and pureed cauliflower. The girls ordered cheeseburgers with fries. They all had sweet tea to drink, and the waiter had asked them why they were there and brought out a glass of red wine for Cathy. Cathy told the waiter she didn't order the wine, but the waiter told them that it was policy to bring a glass of wine to the patient's spouse or next of kin. This was a policy the hospital adopted to help keep nerves calm while the family was caring for their loved one. Cathy thanked him for the wine and drank it with her dinner. As they were getting ready to leave, they noticed they had not received the bill yet. They asked the waiter, and the waiter told them that the meal was free. Cathy asked why it was free, and the waiter told them that it was hospital policy.

Cathy made it a point to look up all the hospital's policies. The waiter knew what she was thinking and walked away quickly and returned with a book in his hand. He told her that the hospital had adopted this policy also as a means to keep patients' families calm and to help ease the stress the family was going through. The hospital felt that most families had enough stress with having a loved one in there, so they should not have to pay for meals for the length of the stay. This not only relieved emotional stress but also the financial stress that some families felt. Not every family can afford to pay, so in order to keep things equal for everyone, the hospital felt it would benefit them in the end to not charge families for meals. Jack stood up to offer to pay for his meal because he was not family, but Cathy told the waiter that he was their future son-in-law.

Deni looked at her mother with utter shock and almost fainted right there on the spot. Cathy told her to sit up straight and to stop slouching. Jack got up again, but the waiter told him there was no charge for the meal. Jack thanked him as well and they all got up to leave. Deni couldn't even look at Jack anymore. Deni couldn't believe her mother said that to a perfect stranger. Just because his family was staying with them doesn't mean she's gonna marry their son. Of course, Deni had thought about it before but had never told anyone about her feelings. She was just so embarrassed.

Jack couldn't look at Deni either. He knew what was going on in her mind because he was thinking the same thing. Since the tornado, Jack and his family had been staying with Deni and her family. It was a little odd but that's the way it was for now. He and Deni had not even had time to themselves or even act like typical dating teenagers.

They got back to the waiting room and saw Harvey, Ruth, Hal, Sam, and Mamaw sitting there waiting for them. Cathy hugged them all and told them the experience they had in the cafeteria. Everyone was very impressed with the hospital.

Cathy asked if anyone had come out to speak with them yet. Everyone said no, so Cathy approached the secretary desk to inquire about her husband. The secretary told her to wait a moment, and she picked up the phone to call the surgery desk in the back. Cathy waited there and listened to the secretary talking to the surgery scheduler. The secretary hung up the phone and told Cathy that the surgery was progressing well. Stan was doing well and the doctor should be out in the next ten to twenty minutes to speak with them. Cathy returned to their waiting friends and gave them the update and sat back down and waited with the rest of them.

It wasn't long before the doctor came out and the doctor walked to where the Rosen family was sitting. He pulled up a chair and introduced himself as Dr. Brock. He proceeded to tell them how the surgery went and told them that Stan was doing fine. He came through with flying colors. He also told Cathy that he removed the ruptured disc and replaced it with a new one that was synthetic. He also told them that Stan had several other bulging discs and asked how long his back had been bothering him. He said that this was not just a sudden thing that happened. He said that all of Stan's problems had happened over time, and that it was probably a good thing that he fell. He told them he went ahead and fixed the other discs and that Stan's back should be good from here on out. He told them that he would have to wear a back brace for six weeks, maybe longer, but that he should be better very soon.

They all thanked the doctor and shook his hand. He told them that it would be about another hour in recovery before he is taken to his room. So everyone decided that it would be best for Jack to take the girls home. Cathy said she would go with them so she could get her car and maybe pack a bag to stay overnight.

As they pulled up in front of the house, they noticed the door was left open. Jack told them all to stay in the car so he could go check out everything. He approached cautiously and slowly. Then he went inside. They could see him going from room to room and then appeared on the porch again. He came back to the truck and opened the doors for the ladies and told them everything was okay inside. They all got out and went into the house. As they got past the foyer, there was a loud surprise and people were everywhere. Cathy was scared out of her mind but quickly recovered. People had heard about Stan's surgery and had come over to help with whatever needed to be done.

Cathy was so overwhelmed that she started crying. These wonderful people had come over to help her family in their time of need. They had made her house so spotless that she was afraid to touch anything. She could smell something good cooking and saw that there were even more people in the kitchen cooking up enough food to last for a year. They all greeted Cathy with hugs and told her they were freezing the meals so she would not have to cook for a while. Cathy thanked all of them for this wonderful outpouring of affection. Then she broke down and cried. They all finished their jobs and hugged Cathy as they left.

Cathy went upstairs to pack a bag and take a quick shower. As she got back downstairs, she could see the kids eating what was left on the stove. Cathy knew everyone was in good hands. Mamaw said she would wait till later to take the kids to her house for the sleepover. Cathy told her be sure to take some of the food with her and make sure she took plenty. Mamaw told her that she wouldn't need it because she had everything planned. Cathy gave her a hug and kiss and left to go back to the hospital.

Mamaw went into the kitchen to see what the kids were up to and sat down to eat a bite. The kids were getting excited now about the sleepover and the party. Mamaw told them that Leah and Mary were waiting for them at her house, so they better get going soon. The kids finished eating and cleaned up their mess. They also went upstairs to pack bags for the weekend. Mamaw told them to load her car, with whatever they wanted to take. They had packed sleeping bags and extra pillows to take to Mamaw's. Bea told them that they didn't need the sleeping bags because she had plenty of beds, but the kids insisted on bringing the bags. They told her they all wanted to sleep on the floor in the living room tonight. She agreed with that but told them that she would have to sleep on the couch. She didn't think she could sleep on the floor anymore. They all laughed.

They got to Mamaw's house and unloaded the car. Mary and Leah were there waiting for them and helped them carry everything in from the car. Mary and Leah had ordered pizza from Roscoe's Pizzeria, and the delivery man pulled up right behind Mamaw. They paid for the pizza and finished unloading the car. They all headed into the living room to set up the "campsite" for the night. Deni, Cindy, and Jack went into Mamaw's room and took the mattress off her bed. They carried it into the living room and laid it right in the middle of the "campsite." They wanted Mamaw to be the center of attention while she wanted Deni and Cindy to be the center of attention. Oh well, whatever the kids wanted. Bea thought it was nice the kids even wanted to be around her, let alone include her in the sleep over. But to put her in the center of attention was really something to Bea. She felt really blessed to have these wonderful young people around her.

They all grabbed their pizza and a soda and went back in the living room. They asked Mamaw what she wanted to do, but Mamaw told them she didn't know what to do. Normally she would just sit in there and watch TV. Mamaw finally confessed to them that she had never been to a sleepover, and this was something she knew nothing about. The kids told her that she was in for a treat. They were going to show her exactly what to do and told her that they were pros at it. The girls asked Mamaw if she had a computer, so she showed them her computer desk. The girls were very impressed. Mamaw had all the latest equipment: a new laptop, a color printer, fax, and scanner all in one, a wireless router so she could lie in bed and still be able to work on her computer. She also had a wireless printer, so if she wanted to print while she was in the bedroom, she could.

The kids thought Mamaw was gonna be computer illiterate, but she was far from that. She was very computer savvy and wondered if the kids had the same equipment. The kids told her that she had a very cool setup, and they all wished they had the same thing but knew how expensive all that equipment was and they could not afford it. They were all so excited about the sleepover they didn't know what to do first. Jack was just along for the ride.

Mamaw gave them the laptop, and they all headed to the living room. Cindy immediately went on the Internet and pulled up the website for celebrity news. When they got together, that's what the girls usually wanted to do – check the popular websites and do girly things. The only problem with this picture tonight was Jack was there. What to do with him—that was the question. They didn't want him to be left out but didn't know how to quite do guy things. Jack told them to do what they usually do and he would go along with everything, just for tonight though. But he made each one promise to never tell anyone else about him being one of the girls even if it was just for one night.

He felt a little privileged right now anyway for being accepted in a girl's world. He felt a sense of insight into what girls do—the girl talk, the way they think, the way they feel about things, and what they wanted most at this point in their lives. Jack felt he could learn something very valuable about Deni and the other girls.

They all looked on their Facebook wall for any new posts and decided to set Mamaw up an account. This way everyone could stay in touch with her, and Mamaw could maybe teach her friends how to go on the Internet and stay in touch. Mamaw wasn't sure about all this but kept with her promise of whatever the kids wanted to do. So they set it up for her and asked if they could take a picture of her to put on the profile. She told them yes, but then they had to take pictures of all of them to put on there also. She also requested that they continue to take pictures throughout the night so she could print them off for the kids later and post it on her site for all to see.

They started snapping pictures and uploading them. Mamaw was having a good time. The pictures were showing a very happy little group tonight. The girls decided that they wanted to do makeovers next. They all got their bags out and started plugging in the curling irons, rollers, flat irons—anything they could bring for hair. Next came the equipment for the nails. They had to do all the beauty stuff to get ready for the party the next day. They all pulled out a bag full of nail polish and started picking out the colors they wanted. Leah was very talented with nails and could make them look salon-perfect. Leah had brought her acrylic nail stuff and offered to put on a set of nails for everyone. She had been to the beauty supply that day to stock up for tonight, so she had enough for everyone. Mamaw couldn't wait to get her nails done. She had to confess, again, to the kids that she had never had her nails done. Leah was shocked at the things her grandmother was confessing tonight and promised to never let that happen again. Leah told her Mamaw that she would do her nails tonight and be back every two weeks to do a fill for her and to make sure that her Mamaw always looked as beautiful as possible. Bea felt so privileged and was truly touched by the dedication her granddaughter was showing her.

Leah looked at Jack and told him he could have his nails done too but didn't think it was advisable since you can't just take them off. Jack said he would just watch and assist Leah with anything she needed. Leah and Mary had already brought over the foot massagers for the pedicures and asked Jack if he could get those ready for the pedicure portion of this nail fest. Jack did as he was told and waited for the cue to get them ready.

The girls started rolling and crimping each other's hair, and Jack was just sitting there watching the rollers fly. He was laughing at the girls and then had the bright idea to be the photographer. As the girls sat there with stuff in their hair, Jack started snapping pictures like a pro. He would not let any of the photos be deleted either. After the girls were through with their hair, they started on Mamaw. All four girls were around Mamaw with a clump a hair in one of their hands when Jack started snapping pics of what they were doing to the poor woman. Mamaw had a huge smile on her face in all of the pictures.

After the air cleared around Mamaw's head, the girls sat back to admire their work. Leah was the best at hair and nails. She stepped in to put the finishing touches on Mamaw. Jack thought she looked like a movie star. He was snapping pics like crazy so that everyone could see how gorgeous Mamaw really was. Bea looked at what the girls had done to her hair and was shocked to see that it actually looked wonderful. She asked if they could fix it in the morning for her, and they all agreed that they would do her hair and makeup for her.

Leah got a TV dinner table and set it up in the living room so she could get started on the nails. First were the birthday girls. Cindy stepped up and gave Leah a hand. Leah finished putting nails on her fingers and then started putting the acrylic overlay on. Leah was a perfectionist and was very precise about the whole thing. Leah was so good at it, you would have thought that she had already been through cosmetology school. She finished with Cindy, and then Deni took the hot seat. Leah went through the whole thing again and in no time was through with Deni. Next was Mary and then Mamaw.

Leah took her grandmother's aged hands and held them so gently that Bea could hardly detect anything being done to them. Leah took extra care with her grandmother and gave her a warm lotion massage to help relax Bea's stiff joints. Bea was so impressed with the precision and attention to detail that Leah displayed that she made an offer Leah could not refuse. Bea told her granddaughter that if this was what she wanted to do with her life after graduating high school, she would pay for the schooling herself. Not only would she pay for the schooling, she would even help put up the money to help open a shop. Leah was shocked. All she could do was hug her grandmother and accept with unrestrained joy.

Leah looked at Jack and told him to sit down. Jack looked at Leah and said, "No way. You're not putting nails on me. Those are for girls." Leah laughed and replied, "Just sit down. Men don't get nails, silly, they just get manicures. Trust me, you'll like it."

Jack reluctantly sat down in front of Leah and stuck out a hand. Leah put warm lotion on his hand and began massaging. Jack started relaxing and enjoying the massage he was getting. He had never had a massage before and felt he could certainly get used to it. Leah then took out her file and clippers and started cutting and shaping his nails. Jack was a little worried but then Leah would start massaging his hands again to calm him down. After she was finished, Jack looked at his nails and was very impressed with the job Leah had done. She then asked Jack if he could get the foot massagers ready and bring them into the living room. Jack set them up where Leah instructed him.

Cindy and Deni were the first again, and he watched Leah to see if he could assist her in any way. Jack then stepped in and asked if he could paint the girls' toenails. The girls looked at each other with total shock and agreed to let Jack do their nails. Before he started painting their nails, he had to go change out the water and set them back out for the other two ladies getting pedicures. He then started painting Cindy's toes and was really pretty good at it. He finished with Cindy's toes and grabbed Deni's feet and started painting them. Jack was so gentle with them. Deni was very impressed with all she was finding out about Jack. Was this guy too good to be true or what?

Once he was through with the birthday girls, he started on the other two and was just as gentle and attentive with them. Mamaw was so enjoying all this that she could hardly contain herself. Jack continued to snap pics while all this was going on, and when he was painting toenails, the girls were snapping pics of him. He couldn't wait to see these pics on the Internet. After everyone was done getting their nails painted, Jack had to confess something to them. When he was younger, his mother had hurt her back and couldn't bend over to paint her toenails, so Jack used to paint them for her. He was young and it was fun to him. So that explains why he was so good at doing these things. The cooking had started when he was young, and as he got older, he just continued building on the things he had learned.

After everyone's nails were dry, Jack had the ladies pose for a picture to hang in their rooms. He wanted Mamaw to remember this night forever. Now he was determined to make this as much about the ladies in front of him and to make this the most fun weekend possible.

They all went to Mamaw's room to change into their fun pajamas and give Jack a chance to change also. When everyone met back in the living room, Jack was standing there wearing a onesy that had clowns all over it. The girls broke out in a laughter so loud the neighbors could hear. Mamaw was laughing so hard that she was crying.

Jack just stood there with a red face and said, "Well, I thought if this was going to be a sleepover I better wear something that covers me up. I don't want anyone saying I wore something indecent." They were all laughing so hard they could hardly hear him talking.

Once they were calm again, they were all laying on their sleeping bags and asked Mamaw what she wanted to do. She couldn't think right now because she was so happy with the evening. All she wanted to do was lay there and listen to the kids talking about teen things, and then she said, "I can't think of anything I want to do, but is there anything y'all want to talk about?"

The kids lay there, thinking, and finally Mary spoke up. "Do you care if we ask you questions about stuff?"

"What kind of stuff?" asked Bea.

Mary was hesitant and finally said, "I don't know, about you and just stuff."

Bea laughed and said, "Ask away."

The kids starting bombarding her with questions. Obviously, they had been thinking about this stuff for quite some time. Bea stopped them and said, "One at a time, please. If you kids had so many questions for me, why haven't you asked them before now?"

They all just shrugged their shoulders and said they didn't know. Bea told them if they ever had another question to please just ask instead of keeping it bottled up inside. They all agreed and said they would from now on.

Mary was first. "How old were you when you first fell in love?"

Bea sat there a minute and said, "I think I was about eighteen. He was wonderful. He was twenty and was home visiting before he went off to war. He was the man I ended up marrying and stayed with for over forty years."

The kids sat and soaked up every word like a sponge. Leah was next. "What was it like growing up in Tennessee?"

"Well, it was hard. I didn't always live there, but when we moved there it was during the Depression. Times were really hard then. You couldn't always go to town and just buy what you wanted or needed. Supplies were hard to come by because there were no jobs," replied Bea. She could talk about this stuff for hours, but she was sure this was not the only things the kids wanted to know.

Jack asked, "Do you have any siblings?"

Bea nodded her head and told them she was the youngest of three and was the only one still alive. Her parents died when she was only twenty, and her sister and brother died years ago from cancer. Jack told her he was sorry for her losses. Bea sat there reflecting and got up to go get something. When she returned she had a huge box that was full of old pictures. The kids had a wonderful time going through the pictures and asking who were in them. Leah never got to spend this kind of time with her grandmother and was having a wonderful time looking at her family heritage.

Bea decided it was time for everyone to get some shut-eye since it was 1:00 a.m. As soon as the lights went out, they saw something glowing. It was Jack's pj's. They all started laughing again, and Mamaw had to hold her sides. This was definitely turning out to be one of the best moments of Mamaw's life. She still couldn't believe the time. The only time Bea had ever been up this late in her life was when she was in labor with Louise. Leah thought that was funny. She couldn't imagine her mother being as young as her, but Mamaw had the pictures to prove it. They all lay there, still mumbling questions at Mamaw and trying their best not to go to sleep. Mamaw was exhausted and was sure going to sleep good tonight. She did manage to ask what time they all wanted to go to the hospital tomorrow and got no answer. They were all sound asleep. Mamaw went to sleep with a happy heart and thanked God in her prayers that night for bringing her to this wonderful place. She talked to Harold a little and so hoped that he was watching at this moment. She missed him at times like these and wanted so bad to have him there, but if he was watching, she knew he would be proud of Bea and of his granddaughter.

Chapter 13

The next morning, the girls all woke up to a wonderful smell that filled the house. They rolled over, thinking Mamaw was already up and cooking breakfast. Mamaw was still asleep on her mattress and didn't really want to get up. They all looked around and saw that Jack was missing. Jack thought he heard some noise coming from the living room and quickly put together a tray of coffee, cups, creamer, and sugar to take to them. He didn't want the ladies to have to lift a finger today.

Mamaw woke up just as Jack was setting the tray on the coffee table. She rolled over and opened her eyes to find everyone staring at her. At first she wasn't sure where she was but quickly remembered she was in the living room. Jack asked how she liked her coffee and handed her a cup. He then fixed the girls their cups and returned to his cooking. He was still wearing his clown pajamas, and the girls still couldn't stop laughing.

Bea sat up to drink her coffee and to try to wake up. She told them she had never had that much fun in all her life. She thanked them for all they did for her and invited them all back in two weeks for another round of hair and nails. The girls all agreed to return, and Bea asked Jack to return as well. Jack said he would check with everyone's parents first before he returns to make sure it is okay with everyone. He wasn't sure he would be able to come but thanked Bea for the invitation.

Jack had set the table and had made a wonderful breakfast of eggs Benedict, homemade biscuits, fried ham, fried bacon, homemade gravy, fried eggs, and freshly squeezed orange juice. Bea was shocked at what Jack had made and thanked him for all his effort. She sat down and started dishing up almost everything on the table. The eggs Benedict were to die for. Jack had made homemade hollandaise, and it was the best Bea had ever eaten. They all ate the fantastic breakfast and decided to start getting ready to go to the hospital. Jack had placed a candle in two of the biscuits and placed them in front of the birthday girls, and they all sang "Happy Birthday" to them. He told them to just wait and see what he was going to do next.

They all told Jack to take his shower first while they clean the kitchen. Jack started to protest but thought he better go with this one since he was outnumbered. As he gathered his things and headed for the shower, he overheard Mamaw telling Deni what a wonderful boyfriend she had. Deni wasn't quite sure what to say because Jack had never asked her to go steady or anything. All Deni could say was, "Yes, yes, he is."

Jack took his shower and the others followed. After everyone was ready, Mamaw told them to load the car so she could take them to the hospital. Jack walked out with them but doubled back so the girls wouldn't know what he was doing. Jack called Christian, Josh, and Kurby to come over and assist with the decorating. Once everyone showed up, the work began.

Mamaw arrived at the hospital just in time for the lunch trays and saw that Stan was having soup, tea, juice, and Jell-O. Stan was feeling very well due to the pain meds he was receiving through his IV. He was laughing and talking to everyone, and Deni was happy to see her father in good spirits. He hugged all the girls, Mamaw included, and wished his daughter and her best friend a happy birthday. He could not believe that his little Deni was fifteen today. It seemed like yesterday they were bringing her home from the hospital.

The nurses had heard about the girls' birthday, and all came in to sing "Happy Birthday" to them. The nurses had gone to the cafeteria and brought back cupcakes with candles for the girls. Both girls were very grateful for the attention the nursing staff were showing them.

Deni and Cindy shared the cupcakes with everyone in the room. Stan was due to be released from the hospital on Monday and was anxious to get home. He wanted to sleep in his own bed and eat real food. He really wanted to ask Jack to cook something for him, but the doctors put him on a liquid diet for a couple of days.

Cathy had noticed something different about Mamaw and told her how pretty she looked. "Did you have a good time last night?" she asked.

Bea looked at her and smiled. "Yes. We stayed up till 1:00 a.m. this morning talking. It was the greatest. I can't wait to do it again. We decided to do it every two weeks due to the nail schedule."

She showed Cathy the nails that her granddaughter had put on and how professional they looked. Cathy was impressed and then asked Leah if she could do hers. Leah told her that she would come over tomorrow if she wanted but then looked at Stan and told Cathy to just call her when she was available. Cathy told her it would probably be better if she came over the next weekend, or she could wait and have them done at Mamaw's next time they have a sleepover. Leah said that would be good too.

Mamaw said she had to run an errand and would be back as soon as possible. The girls were talking so fast that Stan could not keep up with them. They had to tell him about the night they spent at Mamaw's and how much fun they had fixing Mamaw's hair and nails. Stan chuckled and told the girls he was glad they had such a good time. They asked if he needed anything from home or if he wanted something to eat. They told him they could fix whatever he wanted and offered to make something to bring the next day. He told them he didn't need anything and told them to hold off on the food to see what he could have tomorrow. They all sat in the hospital room waiting for Mamaw to return and found a movie on TV to watch.

Deni climbed in bed with her father, snuggled up close to him, and they watched TV together. Deni thought it felt like it did when she was a little girl. She would crawl in bed with her dad on Saturdays and watch cartoons with him. Cathy would bring breakfast up, and they all ate in the bed. Stan was reminiscing about that also but didn't dare tell Deni for fear it would embarrass her too much. They both lay there watching and laughing like old times. The movie was almost over when the door to his room opened. One of the nurses came in to tell the guests that their grandmother was downstairs waiting for them in front of the hospital. She also told Cathy to come down with them if possible.

The girls and Cathy thought it was really odd behavior for Mamaw. They took the elevator down to the first floor and headed for the front entrance. When they got to the front door, they saw Mamaw standing beside a red convertible Mustang. What was going on? Was this a joke? They couldn't figure out what was going on and ran to her beside the car. The girls were shocked and couldn't say anything and just pointed to the car and looked at Mamaw.

Bea was standing there smiling and told the girls to get in the car. They all just stood there. Leah was the first to speak up. "Mamaw, what do you mean, 'get in the car'? Is this your car?"

Mamaw stood there smiling and said, "Yes. I just bought it. What do you think?" They all started walking around the car. They couldn't believe she bought this car.

She looked at Cathy and told her, "Now I have a stick shift so I can teach the girls how to drive."

Cathy laughed and said, "You didn't have to go buy a new car just to teach the kids how to drive."

"Oh I know that, but this way I have a car that will last me the rest of my life, then I can give it to Leah," replied Bea.

Leah looked at her grandmother and could only hug her. The girls all started piling into the car. Leah got to ride shotgun. Bea turned the key and the car roared to life. The girls all giggled because of how bad the car sounded; they loved the low roar. Cathy stood there telling the girls to put on their seat belts and Mamaw told them to hang on. She let out the clutch and the tires squalled on the pavement in front of the hospital. She held up a hand to wave good-bye as she pulled away. Cathy was laughing and waved good-bye to them.

Mamaw was having the best day of her life. She had people around her who loved her, she bought her dream car, and she had the most wonderful granddaughter and her friends with her. Something Bea always wanted was to spend more time with her granddaughter, and now she had the opportunity to spend as much time as she wanted with

Leah and her friends. This was the best thing Bea had ever done in her life. Now she could teach young ladies to be young ladies and still have a good time without compromising their morals and integrity.

Leah asked her grandmother what had possessed her to buy the car, and Mamaw told her that she had always wanted to have a car like this but never thought she would have it. It's just something she had to have, and now was the time to do it. Leah was so proud of her grandmother.

Mamaw was at a stoplight when a young punk pulled up in a vintage muscle car and started revving his engine. Mamaw revved her engine too, and both took off in a cloud of smoke. Mamaw beat him to the next light and looked at him with a quirky smile. Next light he gave her a thumbs-up and just waved at her. The girls were laughing and congratulated Mamaw. They couldn't believe they were riding with someone who can drag race, especially one Bea's age.

Mamaw pulled into her driveway and honked the horn. Jack was looking out the front window and was shocked to see Mamaw driving a Mustang. Jack didn't want the girls to see him peeking through the curtains but was excited at the sight of a new car. He wanted to rush out the door and have a look at the car but didn't want anyone to know he was waiting inside. When Mamaw came in the front door, she saw that all the decorations were up. *Perfect*, she thought. She wanted this to be a big surprise for the girls. Mary and Leah walked in first and told Deni and Cindy to close their eyes. Mary and Leah escorted them into the house and told them to open their eyes. As Deni and Cindy opened their eyes, the boys jumped up and yelled, "Surprise." The girls were blown away by the surprise and started looking around at all the decorations.

The boys rushed to them, saying "Happy Birthday" to both the girls. The girls were overwhelmed with all the excitement in the room. They were looking around and started laughing. They almost didn't recognize the boys because of the costumes they had on. They were all dressed in disco clothes. One looked like John Travolta in *Saturday Night Fever*, and one looked like he was wearing a bird on his head. He had long feathers coming out of his purple hat and had on a bright purple suit. Josh was the funniest. He had on a bright orange suit with rhinestones on the collar. He stood out like a sore thumb. Christian was the most sophisticated among them. He wore a bright blue suit with yellow lapels. The girls were looking at the disco ball and laughing at the music that was playing on the stereo.

The guys escorted them in, and on the table was a huge cake decorated with their favorite colors. Their parents were hiding in the kitchen and finally came out to join in the party. Even the parents got into the disco theme. The kids were all enjoying themselves when Cathy walked through the door. Deni ran to her mother and hugged her so tight. Cathy hugged her daughter and wiped a tear from her eye.

Deni told her, "I thought you were staying at the hospital with Dad." Cathy looked at her daughter and said, "I couldn't miss your special day. Your father said he's sorry he can't be here but was glad you came to him. You know how much we love you. I will never miss your birthday."

Deni hugged her mother again and told her, "I love you. Thank you."

The party began and everyone was dancing around. Mamaw brought out the punch and immediately started filling glasses. The birthday candles were lit and the girls were told to make a wish. Everyone ate cake and the dancing began again. Finally, around 9:00 p.m. the party started to die down and the girls were getting tired. Cathy left to go back to the hospital and took the pictures back with her to show Stan. Christian finally got up the nerve to approach Cindy and wish her a happy birthday. He then pulled a little box from his pocket and presented it to Cindy.

Cindy looked at the box and then at Christian. "I told you not to bring a present," she said.

"I know, but don't tell Deni I gave you this," he said.

"Why not?" asked Cindy.

Christian looked at her a little embarrassed and said, "I didn't bring anything for Deni. I didn't know it was her birthday too, so I just brought this for you."

Cindy looked a little embarrassed now and took the little box over to a corner. She opened it very slowly and took the lid off the box. She couldn't believe her eyes. She saw a small locket inside. She looked at Christian and said, "I can't accept this. It's too expensive."

Christian told her it wasn't expensive and told her to open the locket. She gently removed the locket and found the latch to open it. When she opened the locket, she saw a picture of Christian and a small piece of paper folded up inside. Christian told her, "Read it. It's something I thought you might like."

She unfolded the paper and found a poem inside. It was poem describing how two strangers meet and instantly fall in love. It was such a beautiful poem. How did he know that she would feel the same about him? She liked him—actually, she liked him a lot. She was so afraid he didn't feel the same way, but this just confirmed that he felt as she did. She turned around and hugged him and thanked him. He helped her put it on and told her to never take it off. That way he could be with her always.

Mamaw was cleaning up, and the rest of the kids were carrying in plates for Mamaw to put in the dishwasher. Deni heard Cindy laughing with Christian. She wondered what was going on between them. Jack wandered over to Deni and told her to follow him. She followed Jack to the backyard. Jack had made a special place for them under the peach tree. He then pulled out a large box from under a blanket by the tree. He gave it to Deni and said, "Open it. I've had this for a while now." Deni sat down on the blanket and started opening the box. She gently removed the paper so she could save it. This was her first present from a boy and wanted to save as much as possible so she could put this in her scrap box.

She had the paper all folded neatly and Jack started laughing, "What are you laughing at?" she asked.

Jack looked at her and pointed to the paper. "I've never seen anyone open a present as gently as you. Most people just rip into them. But you save everything," he replied.

Deni was too embarrassed to tell him why and just laughed with him. She pulled the lid off the box and pushed back the tissue paper to reveal a beautiful leather coat. She looked at Jack and was shocked. She pulled the coat out of the box and tried it on.

"Jack, this is too much. Why? How? When?" stammered Deni.

Jack told her that the first day he saw her, he remembered her commenting on how she wanted a coat like the girl in the library at school. He told his mother, and she took him to the store to help him pick it out.

Deni was shocked that he would remember something like that. Jack also told her to look in the pocket. She put her hand in the pocket and found a small box. She took out the box and gently opened it. She found a beautiful ring in the box. It was her birthstone, a topaz with diamonds around it. She took the ring out with a shaky hand and told Jack, "This is too much. I can't accept this. You spent too much money on my …"

Jack looked at her and told her, "I didn't spend too much money. That ring was my grandmother's ring. My mother told me to give it to you for your birthday. You see, my grandmother's birthday is the same day. Her father gave that ring to her on her fifteenth birthday. My mother saw how close we are and decided to give this ring to you for your fifteenth birthday since you're also the closest thing to a daughter to her. This way the tradition keeps going."

Deni looked at him with tears in her eyes. She had no idea that Ruth felt that way about her. She would make sure when she got home to be sure and thank Ruth for this wonderful present and tradition she was entrusting to Deni.

Deni hugged Jack and thanked him for the presents. She was so happy that he was there. She was even happier that Jack felt that way about her to buy her such an expensive gift. Deni was sure that he loved her, and she was starting to have strong feelings for Jack. This was stupid since she was so young. She should not be feeling this for anyone until she was at least twenty-one. That was always her plan, but then again, she didn't plan on Jack coming into her life. Now that he was there, her plans had changed.

Deni and Jack walked back into the house holding hands. This was the first time she had ever held hands with Jack. Deni could tell that Jack had strong feelings for her, and she was starting to have those feelings for him, but she didn't want him to know that because she was afraid it might push him away. Jack was the happiest young man on the planet tonight because he had made his girlfriend happy.

Mamaw saw them come in together and looked at Ruth and said, "Aw, young love. What I wouldn't do to relive that moment when I fell in love with Harold. We were about that age and so much in love. Don't tell the kids that I was that young. I told them I was about eighteen and didn't want them to think it was okay to fall in love so young. Nowadays it's different than in my day."

Ruth looked at her, shaking her head. "I know what you mean. I was about that age too. But I would never tell Jack that. I always wanted him to be older, but now that I know Deni, I have no problem with the way they feel. The only problem is that this is young love, and we both know how dramatic these young girls can be. I just hope that eventually they end up together. I would love to have Deni as a daughter-in-law, but when the time is right. I would never condone for them to get married this young. Maybe when they are thirty." Mamaw and Ruth laughed and just watched.

Everything was put away and all the others went home. Mamaw told the kids it was almost time for bed. Jack and Deni carried Mamaw's mattress into the living room again. Mamaw asked them what they were doing, and all the kids replied that they were going to sleep over again. Mamaw laughed and went to put her pajamas on. The girls ran Jack and Christian out of the room so they could change and put on their funky pj's. Jack walked back into the room and had on a different set of pajamas. This time he had on a pair of neon green pj's that had bright pink and orange flowers all over them. The girls and Christian were laughing so hard they were crying.

Christian told him, "I didn't know there were six girls at this sleepover." Jack just turned red and hit Christian on the arm.

Christian was saying his good-byes and took some pics on his phone to take with him. He could not wait to post these on Facebook and wait for all the comments.

Jack told him that he better not post those pics and that he better delete them from his phone, but Christian told him, "I'll keep them for an emergency."

Jack settled into his spot on the floor and asked Mamaw about her car. "What possessed you to get a car like that?" he asked.

Mamaw told him that this car had always been a dream of hers and that she always wanted a car that she could drag race down Main Street. Now she had that car and told him about the boy that raced her. She told him how she beat the boy and that the boy gave her a thumbs-up.

Jack laughed and shook his head. Mamaw seemed like such a schoolgirl. He had a hard time believing she was over the age of seventy when she talked about that car. They all went to sleep laughing about Mamaw drag racing.

The next morning they woke to the smell of coffee and sat up to find Jack sitting there with a cup ready for them. Mamaw was the last to sit up. She took her cup of coffee and took a deep breath. She could tell there was something cooking but couldn't make out what the smell was. She took another deep breath and asked Jack what he was cooking. Jack just smiled and told her that he ran down to Mike's Bakery for a little surprise for everyone. He went into the kitchen and brought out a large platter full of donuts, bagels, scones, and something no one recognized. They saw something wrapped in a tortilla and asked what it was. Jack wouldn't tell them anything but told them all to try one of the little wraps. They all grabbed a wrap and began to take a bite.

Mamaw was the first to speak. "This is really good. Mike's Bakery had these? I'm gonna have to make a trip down there in the morning sometime."

Deni told him, "It's different but really good. I taste the eggs but can't make out what's with them. There's something else mixed in there, but what is it?"

The other girls agreed with Deni and were all still eating their little wraps. Jack waited till everyone finished the breakfast wrap and finally stood up. "Now does everyone want to know what they just ate?" Everyone's head was bobbing, and Jack cleared his throat. "It was scrambled eggs with squirrel brains." All the girls started coughing and acting like they were going to get sick when Mamaw reached for another one.

Deni told her, "You're not going to eat another one, are you?"

Mamaw looked at her and took a big bite of the wrap. Deni started choking and gagging.

Jack asked her, "What's wrong? Didn't you like the one you had? I thought you liked it?"

Deni said, "Yeah, that was before I knew what it was. I can't believe you fed us squirrel brains. I'm not sure I'll ever trust what you try feeding me again."

Jack told her, "I'm sorry. I thought you should just try new foods in a way that was appealing. I've eaten these for a long time. You know, they are a good source of protein and iron. Consider it to be brain food." Everyone burst out laughing and thanked Jack for feeding them something horrible for breakfast.

Jack said, "Not really, what I really fed you were breakfast burritos. I just wanted to see if I could convince all of you that you were eating brains." They all started beating Jack with their pillows. Jack lay on the floor laughing and taking his punishment.

After breakfast, Mamaw told them all to get in the car so she could take them to the hospital. Jack told them he had to go home because his family was going back to the house to check on the work that had been done so far and to see how much longer it was going to take before the house was complete. He watched as they all took off, with Mamaw squealing the tires. The girls were all yelling and laughing at how Mamaw drove her car. They squealed to a stop at the hospital and all got out of the car.

They saw Cathy walking across the parking lot, looking in her purse for her keys. Deni ran to her mother and asked what was going on. Cathy hugged Deni and told her that her father was coming home.

Cathy said, "Your father is doing so well that the doctor decided to send him home a day early. Isn't that great?"

Deni hugged her with a sigh of relief and told her mother that they would go back home to wait for them.

Mamaw squalled the tires when she left the hospital, hoping she could get someone to race her, but there was no one out on the road this morning. They got to Deni's, and went inside to help clean up before Cathy and Stan got home. Deni wanted this to be the perfect home for them when her father stepped through that door. Deni stepped in and found that Jack and Ruth had already cleaned and they had left a note on the banister. Deni grabbed the piece of paper and read aloud, "We heard about Stan coming home and cleaned for you. Enjoy this time with him. Be back soon. Love, Ruth and Jack."

"Isn't that nice?" replied Mamaw. Deni shook her head and went to the kitchen.

She wanted to start her dad's favorite pot of soup but found that Jack and Ruth had already prepared a roasted chicken noodle soup with fresh rolls.

"Wow, I wish I had someone living at my house that could cook like this," said Cindy. Mary and Leah told Deni they were going to move in with her. Mamaw smelled how wonderful the soup was and took one of the rolls and smeared butter all over it before taking a bite. She told them how wonderful they were. The girls all grabbed a roll, put butter on it, and started eating. By the time Stan got home there were no more rolls left. Deni felt horrible about eating all the rolls and thought about warming the bread Jack had made for dinner that night. She opened the oven to put in the bread and found another pan of rolls.

Cathy pulled up just as Deni was removing the other pan from the oven. Deni ran in to help with her father and took over for her mother. She helped her father up the stairs and into bed.

She asked if he was hungry and Stan told her, "Something smells so good down there. Did Jack make something for me to eat?"

Deni smiled and nodded her head. "Do you want me to bring you some?" she asked.

Stan told her to bring it on. Deni placed the tray on his lap and stood back as her father started eating. He told her how wonderful everything was. Deni took the tray and headed downstairs just as her father was turning to get some sleep.

She put the tray on the counter in the kitchen and went into the living room. She found everyone sitting there, enjoying the soup and rolls, and sat down on the floor. Cathy was filling everyone in on the progress Stan had made and why he got to come home so early. She was so proud of him for the attitude he had about moving around so quickly after surgery. She was convinced that was why he was sent home early. Deni was glad to have him out of the hospital.

Chapter 14

The repairs were coming along nicely. Most had been completed, and the school had been approved for the students to return. Things were getting back to normal, and everyone was getting back to the life they led before the tornado. The kids in town were looking forward to going back to school to find out all the latest gossip that happened while they were out. The kids couldn't wait to see how their school looked and to see if they could figure out how bad the damage was without asking anyone.

Classes started again and the teachers picked up right where they left off but gave extra work to the students to help make up for the week they had been off. The kids all went home with extensive homework and long faces. Jack was still living at Deni's, and every girl in school was jealous. But what they all didn't know was how close she and Jack had become. Deni was afraid that she would start looking at him as a brother instead of a boyfriend. You know, once a guy is looked at as a brother, he can never be anything else.

They all went home with a book bag packed to the brim. Jack and Deni sat at the table to start on the massive mound of homework. They never heard Cathy come down and start cooking or even notice when Jack's parents came home from work. All they could focus on was the homework. They finally finished at about 9:00 p.m. and realized they missed supper.They were famished and went to the fridge to find something to eat before going to bed. Deni was so happy she finished

154

the extra work that Mr. Taylor had given her while they were off. There was no way she could have finished it on time now with all the extra homework.

Deni went to her room exhausted and fell into bed. That night she had the dream again about the strange person driving down the oceanfront road with the wind in her hair. She couldn't fully make out the face in the dream but knew it was someplace she had never been. All she wanted to do was drive and let the sun shine on her beautiful blonde hair. The wind was whipping her hair around and blew hair in front of her eyes. When she pulled the hair from her eyes, all she could see was the car veering toward the ocean. The car went off the cliff and was flying over the water. Deni woke up gasping for air and coughing as if she were drowning. She was sweating and couldn't believe the dream she was having over and over again. Deni didn't know this person but then again she thought she remembered herself driving the car at some point. Why was she having this dream? Was this a premonition or was this just a weird dream? Deni didn't want to think this could actually happen to anyone.

School was hopping along uneventful and the months flew by. Finally it was approaching Christmas break. Thanksgiving break was short due to their time out of school but now it was Christmas break. Deni couldn't wait to get home and start decorating for Christmas. She wished Jack and his family were still there, but they had moved back home last month. She wanted Jack to be there to cook Christmas dinner and wondered what he was planning to cook for his family.

Deni ran through the front door and found her mother in the kitchen baking Christmas cookies. She saw all the different shapes and all the different bowls of icing and couldn't keep her fingers out of them. Cathy spat her hand with a wooden spoon and laughed at how icing makes people seem like little kids again. Deni tried to grab a cookie and Cathy swatted her hand again. Deni laughed and asked where her father was. Cathy told her he wasn't home from work yet but that he should be anytime.

Cathy also told her, "Ruth called today to invite us over for Christmas dinner. Jack is cooking and has already started baking treats. What do you think?"

"I want to go over there. I can't wait to see what he's making," said Deni.

"Me either," replied Cathy. "I love his cooking. It was so nice when he was here and cooking all the time," said Cathy. Deni agreed with her.

Stan came in with a huge Christmas tree and asked where he was supposed to set it up. Cathy told him where she wanted it and got the tree stand for him. Stan put the tree in the stand and placed it in front of the picture window in the living room. Stan stood back and looked at the tree to make sure it was straight. He had done a good job this year and got it straight the first time. Stan had been back to work for about three weeks and was doing really well. He had no problem recovering from his surgery and was feeling great. His back had not felt that good in years.

Cathy told them to come eat and then they would decorate the tree. She had already carried down the ornaments from the attic and had them in the living room. Deni was trying to hurry up and eat so she could get started on the tree. Cathy told her to slow down because the tree can wait. After supper was finished and the table cleared, they started decorating the tree. Deni was the first in the living room and was pulling ornaments out of boxes and putting hangers on them. She would hand them to her mom and dad, and they hung them on the tree. This was tradition since Deni was a little girl.

Her father put the lights on first, and then Deni handed them ornaments. Next they would put the icicles on and then put the topper on the very top. They had gone to the Christmas shop and found a Victorian Santa to place on the top of the tree. They had bought that tree topper years ago and had taken such good care of it that it still looked new. Deni made sure that it was wrapped every year and stored in a place where it was protected from the mice. She cherished that Santa and looked forward to having a topper like that of her own someday. Deni often dreamed of the day when she would be decorating a tree with her own daughter.

They finished the tree and plugged in the lights. Deni sat on the floor and watched the lights twinkle for about an hour. She went up to her bedroom and climbed into bed. She was so tired and excited about the Christmas season she could hardly sleep. She lay in bed that night dreaming of the tree she would decorate with her daughter. She had boxes and boxes of decorations and a big beautiful tree. Her daughter had long wavy brown hair and big blue eyes. How did she get those blue eyes? Deni had dreamed this dream a million times but never remembered seeing her husband. She had remembered seeing the silhouette of a man decorating the tree but couldn't make out the face. Who was she married to?

Deni woke up that morning feeling confused but unable to remember why. It didn't matter. She woke up late and had to get ready for school. It was only two days before Christmas break. She couldn't be late now. She had a perfect record and wasn't going to tarnish it now. She was determined to make it there on time. She showered, put her hair up, and threw on some clothes. She was out the door within fifteen minutes after waking. All she could think of was getting to school.

She ran into the school and made it to the first period just as the second bell rang. She sat down breathlessly. Cindy and Jack just stared at her and shrugged their shoulders. Deni couldn't talk yet, she was breathing too hard.

Finally, when she calmed down, Jack leaned over and asked, "What happened?"

Deni explained that she overslept. Jack told her that from now on he was going to call her and make sure she was up and even come by and pick her up. He told Cindy the same thing, that he would swing by and pick her up for school. They didn't even want to know how he was going to do that because the only vehicle he had was his mother's. But never question a free ride to school. They both thanked Jack and concentrated on their studies.

When school let out, Deni was surprised to find her tires flat on her bike. Now what was she supposed to do? Jack offered to ride his bike home and pick up a vehicle. He told the girls to wait there and he rode off. Deni and Cindy waited there for about thirty minutes until a big four-wheel-drive truck pulled up and stopped right in front of the girls. They couldn't see through the windows because the windows were tinted so dark. The truck was tall so the girls couldn't see in it anyway.

They stood there waiting for the truck to go forward when the passenger door opened and out peered Jack. Deni and Cindy stood there.

Jack laughed and said, "Well, are you gonna get in or just stand there with your mouths open?"

Both girls stood there and finally said, "How do we get in?"

Jack laughed and climbed down, put the girls' bikes in the back, and helped the girls climb in the cab. Jack climbed up behind the wheel and asked if they were ready.

Deni asked, "Where have you been hiding this massive truck?"

Cindy asked, "Did you do this to this truck or did it come this way?" The girls were firing questions at him so fast he could hardly hear them all.

Jack told them, "Wait, wait, wait. One at a time. I bought this truck and fixed it up. I like it being this big. I can pretty much go anywhere I want. I can run over other cars in this thing if I want. I haven't been hiding it either. It's been in the garage out behind the house. We had to build a bigger garage so I could fit my truck in it. I haven't driven it because it only holds three to four people. I couldn't drive this to the mall with all our friends, and I couldn't take it to the hospital because I didn't want Cathy to have to climb up and down. So now that you know I have a truck, we can start driving this to school." The girls thought it was cool and couldn't wait to show up at school the next morning in this beast.

Jack dropped the girls off and came into Deni's house to see her parents. Cathy hugged him and told him how much they all missed him. Cathy told him to thank his parents for the invitation to Christmas dinner, and Jack asked to make sure they would be there. He was fixing something very special for all of them. Deni thanked him for the ride home and asked if she could do anything to help him with the preparation of the dinner. Jack told her no, but he would keep her in mind if he needed any help. He told her to just show up looking beautiful like she always does. Deni turned red and said okay. Cathy was starting to get a little queasy from all the mush floating around the room and laughed when Jack said that last line to her daughter. Cathy had not heard a line like that in years.

Jack left and Deni started fixing supper with her mother. Stan came in and greeted both his ladies with a hug and a kiss. He set the table and helped serve the food. He asked Deni about her day and sat and listened to every word. He didn't know Jack had a truck either, and Cathy didn't pay any attention to a vehicle in the driveway when Deni came home from school. She was shocked to hear that part of the conversation. She was just so happy to see Jack that she didn't even notice the monstrosity in the driveway. Deni continued to tell them about Jack coming to pick her up every morning. Her parents said that isn't necessary. Don't take advantage of him, then the phone rang. Stan left to answer it in the living room.

Deni and Cathy continued to talk about Jack's huge truck and how it was going to freak everyone out at school. Cathy was laughing when Deni told her that Jack had to practically throw them into the cab and was laughing even harder when her daughter told her how she was speechless when Jack first drove up. Cathy had never seen her daughter speechless except the first time she went to the mall.

Stan got off the phone and told the ladies that the call was from Jack. He was asking if it was okay to drive Deni to school every morning. He also told Stan that he was contacting Cindy's parents so he could drive her to school also. Stan told him it was okay and that he wanted to see this monster of a truck and maybe go for a ride one weekend. Jack told him that it was a deal and offered to take him in the spring when the weather is better. Stan took him up on that offer. Both laughed before hanging up. Stan told Deni that it was okay with him for her to ride to school with Jack if it was okay with her mother. Deni looked at her mom, and Cathy said that was fine with her.

Deni finished her supper and called Cindy to ask if she was given the green light to ride to school with her and Jack in the morning. Cindy told her it was okay with her parents and that she would see her in the morning. Deni got off the phone with her friend and went to bed. She started dreaming about decorating her tree with her daughter again. This time she would make sure to look for the face of her husband. She still couldn't make out his face and could only see silhouettes.

Her daughter, on the other hand, was gorgeous. She was having so much fun decorating with her daughter, when she heard a faint sound in the distance. She was dreaming about looking for this sound, when suddenly she awoke and answered the phone. It was Jack giving her a wake-up call. She told him he was lucky this was the last day of school till after the New Year, and she wasn't sure he was going to make it to the next year if he kept calling this early in the morning.

Jack laughed and told her, "Get up and get ready."

make a hair appointment for the weekend before Christmas. Cathy told her daughter that she would call Sabrina today and make the appointment. Deni thanked her and kissed her mother good-bye. Deni heard Jack coming down the road and stood on the porch with her mother.

Cathy was laughing hard when he pulled up in the drive. All she could do was bend over and laugh and couldn't wait to see how Deni got up in the cab of that truck. Cathy stood there waiting for Jack to climb down and hoist Deni up in the truck. She wondered if Jack was going to climb up with Deni on his back or if he would just throw her in the cab. Cathy stood watching and laughing. She bent over double just thinking of all the ways Jack was going to get Deni in there, when she noticed that Jack had equipped his truck with small step ladders. How brilliant was that for him to think of ladders. She watched as Deni climbed up the ladder and settled into the middle part of the seat beside Cindy.

Jack climbed in and pulled out of the driveway. Deni and Cindy were waving so fast that Cathy could hardly see their hands. She waved back still laughing at how small the girls looked sitting in that big truck. All Cathy could do was shake her head and go back inside. She stood by the window in the kitchen and looked out at the street, watching as all the kids heading to school walked by. Cathy started remembering Deni as a little girl walking to school with all her friends, and now she was grown up enough to ride with a boy to school. Cathy wiped a tear from her eye and started cleaning the kitchen.

Jack pulled into the parking lot at school. Most of the kids were just arriving, and all stopped to see who was driving the monster. Jack revved the engine and squalled the tires. The other kids in the parking lot cheered but couldn't see who was driving the truck. Jack pulled into a parking spot and opened the door. Everyone cheered when they saw who was driving.

Cindy opened her door and climbed down out of the truck. Jack turned to help Deni climb down. The girls in the parking lot were all cheering for Jack until they saw Deni and Cindy get out of the truck. Jack was only interested in one girl at his school, and that girl was Deni. She was the lucky one, thought all the other girls. Jacks friends came up to inspect the truck and to ask Jack about the truck. The girls started walking toward the school when they heard a familiar laugh.

Natalie was close by. They heard her laugh before they saw her and turned to find that Natalie was standing beside Christian, who was talking to Jack. Natalie was asking questions about the truck and running her hand over the smooth lines of the truck. Jack was answering her questions but that's about it. He turned his back on her and was talking to Christian.

Deni stood there and watched as Natalie put her arm inside Jack's arm to turn him around. Jack removed his arm immediately and asked Natalie what she was doing. Christian apologized for the way his sister was acting and told her to leave them alone. Natalie refused to leave, so Jack stepped away from her and asked her to kindly leave and to not scratch the truck. Natalie walked off in a huff and saw Deni and Cindy watching her. She made a beeline for Deni and laughed at her when she approached. Natalie looked at Deni and said, "Well, you're not the only one who gets to ride in the massive truck. Jack just asked me to the lake this weekend and for a ride home this afternoon. Sorry if you were depending on him, but I guess he doesn't have time for you anymore."

Deni looked at her and laughed. "You are such a sad person. You honestly think I'm going to believe a lying, conniving, sneaky little shrew like you. I think I know who Jack is and who Jack will be with this afternoon. Oh, and about this weekend, Jack is busy at my house helping me with the outside decorations. Sorry if you thought he had time for you, but that's too bad. He's all booked up for the rest of the year, and he doesn't have time for scum like you." Deni and Cindy turned to go and left Natalie standing there just staring into space.

Jack caught up with them as they walked through the door to the school and asked what all that was about with Natalie. Deni told him it was nothing, and Jack proceeded to tell her what went on at the truck. Christian caught up with Cindy and told her he was sorry for his sister being such a horrible to them. Deni told him it was no problem, and Cindy told him that Deni put her in her place. Christian told her that it was a good thing and totally supported Deni standing up for herself. Jack told her that she didn't have to stick up for herself because he would put a stop to it, but Deni told him that she was used to Natalie being that way. Deni told Jack that Natalie had been that way since grade school, and what Christian had said about his sister confirmed that story. He told them that she was that way ever since she was a baby and was trying to push his parents around since birth. He also told them that Natalie was a pushover for mushy movies. Deni told him not to talk about his sister behind her back.

"That's not the way to handle the problem with your sister. You should confront her and let her know how you feel. Not here at school though. You should always be considerate and not talk about people behind their backs, especially your sister," said Deni.

Christian said he was sorry and that she was right. "Even though she is evil at times, she's still my sister. Maybe someday she will actually realize what she has done to people and apologize for all the hurt she has caused." Deni told him that was the spirit and to make sure he told his sister that sometime.

Jack was proud of Deni and was proud to call her his girlfriend. He grabbed her hand and walked down the hall holding her hand. Deni was beaming this morning and was in good spirits. They all decided to skip the last hour and quickly found that it was the wrong thing to do. Mr. Taylor had made assignments for everyone to do over the break and made sure that no one in class told the others what the assignment was. He knew that his last hour was going to be thin, but he didn't realize how many students would skip. So those who attended his class received extra credit and homework for the holidays. Anyone who completed the work and had the highest score would get something extra special.

They got to Deni's house and all climbed out of the truck. Jack came in to tell Cathy how the kids reacted to his truck. Cathy laughed and said that she was proud that Jack got to show off his truck. Jack laughed and said he wasn't really showing it off but felt proud when he pulled up in the parking lot and all heads turned. Jack was not a show-off and wasn't going to start now. Cathy laughed and gave them all a snack.

Cindy asked if she could call her mother and told her mom what had happened at school and what Deni had said to Natalie. Cindy's mom was laughing at them and then asked to speak to Cathy. Cathy and Sam just burst out laughing about the girls climbing that beast. Cathy hung up the phone still laughing and told them to go in the living room so she could start supper. They all went into the living room and turned on the TV. They had settled on a show when Stan came in and asked whose monster truck that was in the driveway. Jack asked if he needed to move it, but Stan said no. Stan asked if he could look at it, and Jack went outside with Stan.

Cathy walked into the living room and started asking the girls about Natalie. She asked if she needed to make a phone call, but the girls discouraged Cathy from calling Natalie's mom. They told Cathy that the phone call would only make it worse for them, so Cathy decided not to call. She kept questioning them about school, and the girls wondered where this was leading to. Deni was starting to worry that her mother knew she had skipped school. How could she know? The phone hasn't rung and no one had been to the house. Who could have told her they had skipped?

Finally, Cathy admitted that Ruth had called and asked if it was okay for the girls to skip school with Jack. Jack had called his mother to approve the skip with her and asked his mother to make sure to call Cathy and Sam. Ruth called everyone and texted Jack to let him know that everyone was okay with the girls skipping with him but told him to be careful and that she loved him. Jack had received the text while in the cafeteria, and while they were eating lunch, he suggested they skip last hour.

Cathy had called the school to let Mr. Taylor know that the kids would not be in class and asked for any missed assignment. Mr. Taylor had given the extra work to Cathy and told them to have a merry Christmas. She told the girls about the extra work Mr. Taylor had given them.

Jack and Stan came back in from looking at Jack's truck, and Jack told the girls good night. He needed to go home and help his mother cook supper. He also wanted to double-check the grocery list for the special dinner he was making in three days. He wanted to go over the menu again and make sure it was perfect and then go to the grocery store and try to find everything he needed.

Jack left, and Deni watched TV till supper was ready. Stan asked what she was going to do while she was out of school, and Cathy answered for her. "She has homework to do. Mr. Taylor gave everyone extra work for extra credit. So she's going to be very busy."

Deni laughed and said she would finish that work quickly so she could go shopping with her friends and spend time with Jack. She asked her mother, "Did you call Sabrina and make my appointment for me?"

Cathy told her that her appointment was for the next day at noon, and she also made one for Cindy. Deni excused herself and called Cindy. Cindy was so excited to go with Deni and to have her hair colored again. They decided to call Jack and have a phone conference. Jack asked if they wanted to go shopping afterward. Both girls agreed and said they needed to go and pick up presents. They asked Jack if he had anything else planned for the day, and he told them he had to stop at the grocery store. He also told them that he needed to go to the mall to check out the specialty food stores. The girls were delighted that Jack was going to take them. It's always best to have a guy with you when you go to the mall. That way no one bothers you and Deni knew that her mother would feel better knowing Jack was with them.

Jack told them he would be by to pick them up at around ten thirty and wished them both a good night. Deni was still on the phone with Cindy, and Cindy started teasing her.

"He likes you. He likes you," sang Cindy.

Deni replied, "Stop it. Yes, he likes me and I like him. But you like Christian, so what's the problem here?" Deni was laughing as she said that to her best friend.

Cindy laughed and said, "No problem there. I think he wants to spend time with me over the break. Do you think I should call him and see if he wants to go tomorrow?"

Deni told her, "Why not? He could keep Jack company while we are in the salon."

Cindy got off the phone with Deni and immediately called Christian. Christian told her he was going to be with friends tomorrow, but he would try to see if he could sneak off. Cindy hung up with Christian then turned on her computer.

Deni went to ask her parents if it was okay for Jack to take them tomorrow, and just as she figured, Cathy was delighted that Jack was going with them. Stan didn't have a problem but told Deni to make sure to be home by 7:00 p.m. He wanted her home so she could catch the carolers that would be coming around in the neighborhood. Deni told him that she would be there and asked if Jack and Cindy could stay for the carolers.

Deni went to bed thinking of the next day. She had good dreams that night and was dreaming of having her hair a little blonder. She had been neglecting her hair lately. She didn't want to become the person she used to be.

Deni awoke the next morning refreshed and realized she had to start getting ready. She wanted today to be a special day. She was spending the day with the two people that meant a lot to her. Jack and Cindy were there at ten thirty and Christian was with them. Deni asked what he was doing and he said he was just trying to throw Cindy off. He wanted to surprise her. Jack had called and asked if he could go with them today so Christian could spend the day with Cindy. Christian couldn't resist spending the day with Cindy.

They all piled inside Jack's mother's SUV and headed downtown to the salon. Deni and Cindy were greeted by Sabrina and Tasha. The girls were the only ones there, so Sabrina and Tasha were able to get right to them. The ladies disappeared behind the curtain to start mixing the color and reappeared to start working on the girls. Sabrina started on Deni and was talking up a storm about her new boyfriend in town. He had been her high school sweetheart and had moved away. Now he was back, and Sabrina couldn't stop talking about how gorgeous he was. Deni was laughing at Sabrina and wondered if that was how she sounded. Sabrina and Tasha finished applying the color, and the timers were set.

Cindy and Deni sat there waiting for the timers to chime. Deni was reading a gossip magazine while Cindy was trying to talk to her about something she was reading in a science magazine. Deni wasn't paying attention because she was reading something about the newest hairstyles. This year short hair was in and long hair was out. Deni thought about all this and decided to have her hair cut short. The timers went off, and the girls were escorted over to the washing bowls. After the rinse was complete, the girls went back to their chairs.

Sabrina and Tasha took the towels off the girls' head and all gasped. The colors had gotten switched, and the girls now had their natural hair color back. Deni had been trying to dye her hair blonde and now she had brown hair. Cindy was trying to dye her hair brown and now she was blonde. Sabrina was shocked. How could she have mixed up the wrong color? Tasha was embarrassed and looked at Sabrina tearfully. Deni and Cindy started laughing and just went with the flow. Both the girls told the hairstylist not to worry about it because it could be fixed the next time. The two stylists were grateful for the girls' attitudes and gave them a coupon for a free day of beauty. The girls thanked the stylists for the free day and told them to cut their hair short.

Sabrina was surprised by this request since Deni had long hair and had insisted on keeping it that way. Now she wanted it cut and told Sabrina to cut it like the picture in the magazine she had been reading. Deni showed the picture to Cindy, and Cindy told Tasha to do the same. The stylists started cutting. Hair was falling, and the girls couldn't believe they were actually cutting their hair. The girls had never had their hair cut short in their lives. The most they had ever done was have their hair trimmed.

The stylists finished with the haircuts and styled the girls to look like the picture. They turned the girls around to the mirrors and revealed two of the prettiest girls they had ever seen. Deni and Cindy didn't even recognize themselves. They thanked the stylists and made return appointments. Deni loved her hair. It was so light and carefree. Now she would be able to get ready in five minutes. The girls walked outside to try and find Jack and Christian.

The guys were in the music shop next door, and the girls found them in the country section. The girls walked up to them without saying a word and stood there to see how long it took the guys to notice them. Jack turned around, saw that two girls had walked up beside him, and noticed how gorgeous these ladies were. He didn't recognize who they were and walked right past them. The girls giggled. Jack knew that laugh.

He turned around to the ladies and said, "Excuse me, do you know Deni Rosen? You have a laugh that sounds like hers."

"Really. I wonder why that is. How long has it been since you have spoken to this Deni?" replied Deni. She was trying to hide her accent and had changed her voice so Jack couldn't tell it was her.

Jack stood there looking the ladies up and down and finally looked into her eyes, and his mouth dropped. "Deni, is that you? Wow, you look amazing," said Jack. Christian walked up and stood there, wondering why Jack was talking to two strangers. Then he looked at Cindy's eyes and his mouth dropped open. The boys looked like frogs trying to catch flies. The girls laughed and told them to stop staring. Christian didn't think Cindy could look any better, but now here she was looking like a movie star.

Chapter 15

T hey arrived at the mall at 3:00 p.m. and it was packed. They had to walk a mile to get to the door. They walked in and made their way to Shawna's Fashions. Deni wanted to get her mother a new outfit and look for something for her father. She also was on the lookout for anything that her friends picked up and secretly wanted. Deni would have to buy these things secretly but knew that she could do that fairly easily. They all paid for their purchases and left the store. Jack wanted to look at the specialty food store upstairs and told the others to meet him at the food court in an hour.

Deni told Cindy she had to go to the restroom and headed in that direction. When she saw that Cindy wasn't watching, she then turned and went back to Shawna's Fashions. She had seen Cindy pick up a coat and wanted to check the price. She went into the store and was browsing, not noticing how many other customers were there. She turned around and saw her friends gathered at the cashier counter laughing. They had all split up only to end up in the same place. It was so funny for all of them to end up at Shawna's.

They made additional purchases and headed to the food court. Deni called her mother and asked if she needed anything. Cathy told her what she needed, and Deni took home a pizza from DJ's. Jack called his mother to let her know that he would be at Deni's. They left with the pizza and packages and headed for Deni's house. They got there in plenty of time to see the carolers and then headed to Mamaw's house.

Mamaw had decorated her house with everything she could get her hands on. She had animated figures in the front lawn and lights everywhere. She had been making the rounds to all the yard sales in town and to every sale she could to get all the decorations for her yard. She had even attended a police auction then a storage auction. She had extension cords everywhere. Jack was laughing at all the lights.

He whispered, "I bet you can see this thing from space."

Deni laughed and said, "Yeah, but let's hope no one tries to land a plane on it. Look at this thing. It's a good thing the airport is on the other side of town." Jack was laughing so hard he could barely walk.

They walked to the front door and heard Christmas music playing and Mamaw singing at the top of her lungs. Jack laughed even harder then and grabbed his side. Mamaw answered the door in an apron that looked like a Santa suit, and she had on a hat. She honestly looked like Mrs. Claus. They couldn't contain the laughter anymore. Mamaw had a bowl in her hands and told the kids to come in. As Mamaw walked through the living room, she turned down the music on the stereo. The kids looked around and weren't surprised to see the inside of Mamaw's house just as stuffed with decorations. She had everything you could imagine in that house and yard.

Mamaw had homemade candy, cookies, cakes, pies, and fudge in dishes all around the living room. The cakes and pies were on the table waiting for someone to cut into them. Everything looked so good and she was still baking. Deni asked if she was okay.

"I'm fine. I just love Christmas. Do y'all want me to bake anything special for ya?" she asked. Deni was still giggling and said no. She told them that she had to box up the candies and stuff for presents. She had so many to box up that it would take her a week. Mamaw had plans of giving a box of goodies to almost everyone in town.

Mamaw was touched by a lot of people in town. Everyone loved her and she felt the same about them. She wanted to express her thanks by giving goodie boxes to all her friends. So the kids decided to help her and asked where the boxes were. Mamaw was delighted for the help and gave them a stack of boxes to put together and a list of people that were to receive the boxes. The kids formed an assembly line. Jack put the boxes together, Deni filled them, and Cindy wrote out the tags. They finished in about two hours and were exhausted. Mamaw came out of the kitchen to check on them several times and finally came out to help stack the boxes near the door. Jack asked if she needed help distributing the gifts. Mamaw told him that it would be great if he could help.

The kids went back to Deni's. Jack said good-bye and left for the night. Cindy and Deni went upstairs to wrap presents. Cindy had left Deni's present in Jack's truck so that he could wrap it at home for her. Jack was going to wrap the present so Deni couldn't shake it to try and guess what it is.

The girls lay in bed talking. They always had a good time together. Now they both had boyfriends and were talking about what they were giving them. This was a first for both girls. They had never had boyfriends before, at least not like this. Deni thought of how Jack was too perfect to be true. She told Cindy how Jack was the kind of guy you only read about in books.

Cindy told her, "Yeah, but he is pretty terrific. I think you're thinking too much about this. I think he's that way cause that's the way his momma taught him to be. I mean, look at his dad. He's that attentive with Ruth. So why wouldn't Jack be that way with his girlfriend?"

Deni replied, "You're probably right. I do have a tendency to overthink things. Jack is wonderful. My parents love him, your parents love him—heck, everyone loves him. I just think there's something going on, and I can't quite put my finger on it."

Cindy told her, "Just forget about it. There's nothing going on there. He's just a good guy and his momma taught him right. Just lie down and go to sleep."

Deni lay there staring at the ceiling and still couldn't get it out of her mind. Cindy rolled over and was thinking that since they got their hair colored again, Deni seemed more like herself—overthinking everything and being suspicious about things. Cindy made a mental note to write it down in her journal. She also wanted to put in her journal how the colors got switched and how Deni was changing again.

The next morning started with rain and a possibility of snow. The girls were hoping it would snow. They wanted a white Christmas this year. They hadn't had a white Christmas in years. The most they always got was ice. That's the way it is when you live in Oklahoma. You never knew what the weather was going to do. Snow, sleet, rain, ice, or God only knows what.

Jack got up to help his mother prepare breakfast, and he wanted to start printing up the menus and start on preparations for the Christmas dinner he was serving. After breakfast, he looked on the computer and was trying to decide on how the menu should look. He finally decided and started printing the menu. He looked it over and was quite surprised how well it turned out. He went into the kitchen and got out the ingredients for his fourth course and started working away. He was finished with that quickly and decided to call Deni.

Deni answered and asked him, "What's up?"

Jack told her he needed to go back to the mall and asked if she wanted to tag along. Deni said she needed to go back to the mall too and asked her mother if it was okay to go with Jack. Jack told her that he would be there in ten minutes, so Deni scrambled to get ready. Usually, Christmas Eve was a day for Deni to sit around in her pj's and not do anything, but today she was going to be spending it with Jack. This was going to be a perfect day.

Jack showed up in his monster truck, and Deni ran out to climb in. They took off and Jack told her he needed to find a deli. Deni suggested, "How about Guido's on Main Street? We pass it on the way to the mall." Jack replied, "Do they have prosciutto?"

Deni looked at him with a funny look on her face. "What's that?"

Jack laughed. "It's Italian ham. It's cut really thin and it is so good."

Deni told him, "Probably. I don't really know. I've only been in there one other time and it wasn't for that." Jack laughed and asked her to make sure to point it out so he could stop on the way to the mall.

They got to the deli just in time and Jack got his prosciutto. He got extra and made Deni try it.

"This stuff is pretty good. It's really thin though. I'd have to pile a bunch of this on my sandwich to even call it a sandwich," she said.

Jack laughed and said, "Well, you'll see what it's really used for tomorrow evening." They laughed and continued on to the mall.

They pulled into the parking lot of Swaying Pines Mall and were shocked to see the parking lot so full that the line to get into the parking garage formed around the block. They couldn't find a parking spot, and Jack was worried the mall would close before they could even park. He finally found someone walking out who showed him where she was parked so they could have that spot. Jack thanked her as she pulled out and he immediately pulled in. He told Deni she could stay there or make a run with him. He was in a hurry and it was raining. Deni decided to make a run since she still had to pick up something special for Jack.

They ran to the door of the mall and were soaked. The rain was so cold, and it felt like the temperature was dropping. Deni asked him if he would mind her going to some of the shops on her own. Jack told her to be very careful. He also told her that he would meet her back by the front doors in an hour. She said that was fine and that he needed to be careful too. He kissed her cheek and ran up the escalators to the second floor. Deni ran to Shawna's Fashions and was looking around. She found a nice necklace and wondered if Jack would wear it. She had never seen him wear jewelry and was afraid he would be embarrassed to wear it.

She kept looking around and couldn't decide on anything to get him. Finally, an assistant came over to help.

Deni told her, "I'm trying to find something for my boyfriend. He's a wonderful person, but I don't know what to get him." The girl asked what size he was, and Deni told her she didn't know. The assistant asked other questions, but Deni didn't know the answer to any of them. Now she felt horrible. Jack was her boyfriend, and she didn't know anything about him. What were his likes or dislikes? What size clothes did he wear? She just couldn't remember any of the things she thought she knew. The assistant finally recognized her and asked if Jack was the boy who had won the gift certificate at the Halloween party. Deni said yes and was so happy that the girl remembered her. This was going to be a big help.

The assistant told her that Jack was in there a couple of days ago and was admiring a leather jacket. She took Deni to where the jacket was hanging, and Deni was shocked at the price. She couldn't afford it, so she asked the girl if there was anything else that Jack was admiring in the store. The assistant took Deni to a rack of clothes and showed her what Jack had been looking at. Deni picked out something great for him to wear. The assistant showed her the shoes that Jack was looking at, but

Deni decided to get the outfit instead. She took it to the counter and paid for her purchase. She headed to the front door and then stopped at one of the jewelry stands in the middle of the mall. She found a nice inexpensive bracelet and bought it. The man at the stand asked Deni if she wanted it engraved. Deni said yes and told him what to put on the bracelet. The man wrapped the bracelet for Deni and she put it in her bag.

Jack was waiting by the front door and told Deni to stay there. He wanted to go get the truck and bring it to the door. She waited inside for Jack to bring the truck around. She finally saw Jack inching his way through the parking lot and ran out to the truck. Jack had warmed up the cab, and Deni was happy for the heat. While they were in the mall, the temperature had dropped, and the rain had turned to sleet. Jack told her it was going to be a fun ride home if the roads were starting to ice. He wanted to show Deni what his truck could do in this type of weather.

They made it back to Deni's without incident, and Jack told her that he needed to get home. Deni said good-bye and walked into her house. Her mother was in the kitchen making fudge.

Deni asked, "Is Mamaw going to the Wilsons' for dinner tomorrow?"

Cathy replied, "I think so and I think she's bringing someone."

Deni smiled that little quirky smile, saying, "Really. Who is it?"

Cathy turned and replied, "I don't know. She was very mysterious about the whole thing. I wonder who the lucky man is. Who do you think it is?"

Deni looked around, saying, "I think it might be Mike from the bakery. They have a lot in common."

"Yeah, but he's so much younger than her. I don't think it's Mike," replied Cathy. "

I don't know, but whoever it is will have to put up with us," laughed Deni.

Jack got home and ran straight to the kitchen. He needed to marinade his steaks, and that was going to take time. He started on the dessert part of his menu. He wanted everything to go perfect tomorrow. Ruth came in to check on him.

"It smells so good in here. Is there anything I can do?" she asked. Jack shook his head and ran her out of the kitchen. Ruth left the kitchen laughing and shaking her head.

Mamaw called Deni and asked if she could come by to drop off their presents. Deni told her it was the perfect time because she was just itching to open something. Mamaw was there in two minutes and knocked on the door. Deni let her in and showed her to the living room. Cathy came out of the kitchen and offered Mamaw something to drink. Mamaw handed the presents to Cathy and told her which ones needed refrigeration. Cathy laughed and took them to the kitchen. Mamaw turned to Deni and handed her a big box. Deni looked at Mamaw in wonder. Cathy returned from the kitchen and saw Deni with the big box on her lap. Cathy sat down beside Mamaw and waited for Deni to open her present.

"Well, are you gonna open it or just look at it?" asked Mamaw. Deni started ripping paper, took the top off the box, and folded back the tissue paper.

Deni sat there with a tear in her eye. Cathy was trying to see what was in the box. Deni took out the most beautiful dress she had ever seen. Cathy gasped and told Mamaw that she didn't have to buy such an expensive dress for Deni. Mamaw told them that she had made the dress. She found the material on sale and had to get it for Deni. Deni sat there looking at the dress. It was so gorgeous she was afraid to touch it. Deni remembered picking out this same dress in a magazine the night they had the slumber party at Mamaw's. She couldn't believe that Mamaw made that dress. It had only been a little over a month. This dress looked like it had taken months to make. How did she do that?

Mamaw asked if she liked the dress and asked her to put it on. Deni ran up the stairs and shortly came back down with a grand entrance. Deni felt like a movie star in the dress. Mamaw had picked out an electric-blue color with a black lace overlay. She had also hand beaded the bodice of the dress and some of the skirt. She had added tulle underneath the dress to make it fuller. This was the most sophisticated dress Deni had ever worn. Mamaw wiped a tear from her eye as Deni came down the stairs. It looked perfect on Deni. Cathy was in awe of the dress and how it fit her daughter. Deni ran up and hugged Mamaw so tight that Mamaw thought her ribs would break. Deni could not thank her enough for the dress and promised to wear it tomorrow to Jack's house.

Mamaw opened her present from Deni. Deni had taken all the pictures that were taken at the slumber party and put them in a digital picture frame. Deni had also taken the best picture of her and Mamaw and put it in an old Victorian frame. Mamaw was so overcome with emotion that she started crying. Deni hugged her, and Mamaw told her that it was the nicest gift that anyone had ever given her. She cherished the time that they spent together, and Deni felt the same way about Mamaw. Mamaw hugged them both and left to deliver more presents.

Deni could hardly sleep that night. All she could think about was the dress Mamaw had made and how Jack would react. She wanted to curl her hair in the morning and make sure that her makeup was flawless. She was going to make this a Christmas Jack would not soon forget. She fell asleep dreaming of Jack's reaction and the wonderful food that Jack was serving tomorrow. She also had a dream about the stranger Mamaw was bringing. Who was the mystery person? She could only imagine the outline of the person but not the face.

The next morning, Deni got up and ran down the stairs. She couldn't wait to open her presents. There were presents stuffed under the tree and most of them were Deni's. She couldn't wait anymore. She ran upstairs and burst through her parents' bedroom door and jumped on the bed, begging them to get up. Her parents were laughing at this "grown-up" lady jumping on their bed like a five-year-old. Stan finally got up and put on his robe. He told Deni to wait downstairs, and they would be there in a minute.

Her parents finally came downstairs. Deni had already separated the gifts into piles. She had a pile for her mother, her father, and her pile in the middle of the floor. Stan and Cathy laughed at their daughter sitting there with presents all around her. This reminded them of when she was five and she got a bike for Christmas. She was riding the bike around the living room when they came downstairs. The only difference is now she is fifteen and not riding a bike around the living room. Deni immediately started ripping paper. She got through her presents before her parents even opened on of their own.

Cathy started cleaning up and Deni went to make breakfast. Stan came in to get another cup of coffee. He hugged and kissed his daughter and greeted her a merry Christmas. She hugged her dad and told him, "Merry Christmas." Stan asked if she could come outside with him because he had a surprise for her. She followed her father to the front door and he covered her eyes. She walked onto the front porch and Stan uncovered her eyes. What she saw was atrocious. She couldn't believe her eyes. She looked at her father and stood there.

Stan asked, "What's wrong? Don't you like it? I got a really good deal on it and thought you would like it. I've got some work to do on it, but it should be ready by the time you get your license."

Deni stood there looking at something that kinda looked like a car. "What exactly is it? Is this a car or a train wreck? Is this some kind of joke? Dad, that's really funny. Now where is my surprise?" she asked.

Stan stood there. "This is your surprise. It's not a joke."

"But it doesn't even have a fender. Look, there's no back glass. How am I supposed to drive this thing if there're no seats? Dad, you have got to be kidding," replied Deni.

Stan laughed and told his daughter that it would be drivable by the time she got her license.

Deni told him, "Thanks, Dad, but I don't think that thing will be presentable, ever."

They went back into the house and found Cathy in the kitchen. She looked at Deni's disappointed face and hugged her daughter. She whispered into Deni's ear, "Please don't be too disappointed. Your father wanted to get you a new car, but this deal just fell in his lap. He thought that it would be something that he, you, and Jack could work on so that the car would be personalized. Please say you like it for his sake."

Deni looked at her mother and kissed her cheek. She then turned to her dad and hugged him as tight as she could and thanked him for the car that was going to be the most beautiful car in town. Stan kissed the top of her head and told her of the plans he had for the car. Deni sat and listened intently.

Jack called and asked if they could be there at 4:00 p.m. Deni told her parents what time Jack needed them to be there. Deni ran up the stairs and grabbed her towel and ran to the shower. She bathed in a soft-scented floral bath. When she got out, she applied the matching lotion. She went to her room and sat in front of the mirror. She took her hair down and started brushing it. She dried her hair and decided to spiral curl it for the evening. Cathy came in and helped her daughter get ready. She rolled her hair and assisted with putting on the dress.

She looked at her daughter as if looking at her for the first time. The love that Cathy felt for her was unimaginable. Deni could see tears welling up in her mother's eyes. She sat down again and started putting on her makeup. She brushed a light dusting of sparkle powder on her shoulders and across her chest. Cathy left to get ready. When Deni came down the stairs, she saw her parents waiting in the foyer for her. Cathy was dabbing her eyes, and Stan was so proud that he was left speechless.

They knocked on the door, and Kurby escorted them to the living room. He took their coats, and Josh came around with a tray of hors d'oeuvres. Deni looked at the silver tray and saw something on a piece of bread. Josh saw all of the confusion in their faces and proceeded to hand them a piece of paper. On the paper was the menu for tonight. Deni looked at the paper and started reading.

Welcome

First Course

Artichoke Puree with Goat Cheese Bruschetta on Toasted Baguettes Crostini with White Truffle Oil and Olive Paste

Second Course

Mini Crab Cakes with Orange Sauce
Shrimp Cocktail

Third Course

Poached Garlic Soup
Insalata Caprese

Fourth Course

Champagne Grapefruit Sorbet

Fifth Course

Cabernet Filet Mignon
Hasselback Potatoes

Sixth Course

Chocolate Jalapeno Cake
Cognac-Laced Truffles

FINALE

Decaf Latte'

Deni looked at the menu and didn't know what half those things were. Stan and Cathy both said at the same time, "Impressive." Just as they were about to ask about some of the dishes, there was an announcement. They saw Jack standing in the doorway to the dining room, and he was clinking a glass with a spoon.

He said, "Welcome. My name is Chef Jack Wilson. What you are enjoying is artichoke puree with goat cheese bruschetta on toasted baguettes, and the other is crostini with white truffle oil and olive paste. I hope you enjoy what you are eating, and there is a lot more to come. Again, welcome and I will be explaining the dishes as we go along." Everyone applauded and thought it was spectacular. He was dressed in a chef outfit with the tall hat. Deni thought he looked handsome.

Jack reappeared at the door and proceeded to tell them, "I forgot— these are your servers tonight. So if you need anything, please feel free to ask Kurby, Josh, or Christian. Thank you."

Deni was looking around for Cindy and found her talking to Christian and what appetizer they liked best. The doorbell rang, and Kurby promptly answered and escorted in a pretty lady with a very handsome man. Deni didn't recognize the couple at first and then did a double take and realized it was Mamaw with Orville. Orville was the town farmer. He had a large farm just south of town. He always provided fresh vegetables to the stores in town an always had a stand on the side of the road by his farm. He was a nice man. Deni never realized how handsome he was, for a man his age.

Mamaw made her way around the room introducing Orville to everyone. Nobody recognized him in a suit. Everyone had only seen him in overalls. He always wore overalls wherever he went. They really didn't know him that well. But it looked like Mamaw did. She looked like a schoolgirl while introducing him. Deni caught her blushing when Orville paid her a compliment. Mamaw finally made her way over to Deni and Cindy.

Mamaw introduced Orville to them, and he shook their hands. "It's nice to meet you. Bea has said nice things about you two."

Deni shook his hand and couldn't say a thing. Did he say she had said nice things about them? Just how long has she been seeing him?

Deni thought about all this and decided to ask during dinner. They stood and talked for a moment, and Jack arrived at the door again.

"Ladies and gentlemen, I would like to invite you into the dining room. Please look for your place card," Jack announced. He then opened the doors to the dining room, and everyone took in a surprised breath. He had set the table formally with crystal glasses, actual silver flatware, and the most beautiful china you have ever seen. They all walked into the dining room and found their places. Once seated, the servers came around with water and wine. Josh had the water, Christian had the wine, and Kurby had tea. The servers then set plates in front of each guest, and Jack started announcing what they were eating.

"This is miniature crab cakes with an orange sauce and classic mini shrimp cocktails. Hope you enjoy," announced Jack. Again, Jack and his servers disappeared back into the kitchen. Josh came back out to refill glasses.

Jack and the servers appeared again. "Next we have poached garlic soup and insalata Caprese. The Caprese is tomato slices with fresh mozzarella, fresh basil with olive oil and balsamic vinegar drizzle. Enjoy," Jack announced and then he disappeared.

The guests were enjoying the food as much as they were enjoying the show that Jack and the other boys were putting on. Everyone was eating as fast as they could to try to get to the next course. Each course just got better and better. Deni couldn't wait for the main entrée to arrive.

Deni was too far away from Orville to ask him the questions she wanted, so she recruited Cindy to ask him. Cindy looked at Orville, who had been telling a story about his rabbits.

Cindy asked, "How big is your farm?"

"Oh I forget how big it is. I have twenty-five acres for growing vegetables, twenty-five acres for the cows and horses, couple acres here and there for whatever I want to do with them," replied Orville.

Cindy then asked the question Deni wanted to know. "So how long have you known Mamaw?"

Orville looked at her hard and then smiled and said, "About a month. We ran into each other at the car dealership, and she looked like a firecracker. I just had to meet the hot-rod granny who was buying the Mustang. She's a looker, you know."

Cindy laughed and replied, "Yeah, I know."

The servers cleared the dishes then Jack announced.

"This next course is champagne grapefruit sorbet. This is to simply clean the palate to prepare for the main course of the evening. Thank you and enjoy." The servers put down the crystal bowls and silver spoons in front of everyone.

Deni was the first to take a bite. "Um, this is so good." She couldn't stop eating it and got a brain-freeze. She should have eaten it slowly, like she was told to do. The servers next brought out the most delicious looking and smelling steak that Deni had ever seen.

"This is filet mignon in a cabernet wine reduction. Made with wine, sugar, peppercorns, and fresh herbs. With that we have Hasselback potatoes. These are potatoes with thinly sliced garlic, sour cream, and a Greek yogurt sauce on top. I hope you enjoy," Jack told them.

The steak was cooked to perfection and so tender you didn't need a knife. The potatoes were unusual at first but turned out to be so good that one wasn't enough for Deni. She was too embarrassed to ask for another one but would make sure to ask Jack to show her how to make them.

The guests were starting to get full. The servers brought out plates that had a small piece of cake and two truffles on it. Jack came out again to announce the dessert.

"Now we have a little different dessert from what most of you are used to. This is chocolate jalapeno cake. Trust me, it's good. And the truffles are cognac laced so be careful. For those under twenty-one, we have raspberry mint truffles. Enjoy."

Deni couldn't resist the cake even if it had jalapenos in it. If it was half as good as the other courses, it was sure to be magnificent. She took her little piece of cake and popped it in her mouth. The chocolate was so decadent, so smooth, it melted in her mouth. Then at the very end of the taste was the kick from the jalapeno. Then she grabbed a truffle. Truffles had always been Deni's favorite. She wanted to save them but couldn't resist the call of the chocolate ganache inside. *This is heaven*, she thought.

Jack came back into the dining room and asked his guest to please report to the veranda for the finale of the meal. They followed Jack and saw the servers waiting for them with decaf lattes in hand. This was absolutely the best meal Deni had ever had. She had never been to a formal dinner party and never eaten food like this before. She was so proud of Jack. All the other guests were congratulating him on the meal, and some were asking for recipes. Deni approached Jack and lightly touched his arm.

He turned and looked into her eyes. "You are so beautiful tonight. I had a hard time staying in that kitchen." Deni blushed and giggled. She took his hand and told him what a terrific meal he had made. She also told him about the potato thing. He told her he would teach her how to make those so she could have them anytime.

Deni agreed with that and asked Jack if he knew anything about Orville. Jack told her he didn't know anything about him but heard that he was a hard worker and a very nice man.

Jack told her, "I know you care about Mamaw, and so do I, but does it really matter as long as she likes him and he's good to her? I just want her to be happy. She deserves that, and if Orville makes her happy, then so be it. Look, she's not getting any younger and neither is he. If they make each other happy for whatever time they have left, then I say go for it."

Deni looked at him. "You're right. I guess I just think of her as my mamaw and want the best for her. If Orville is who she wants to spend time with, then I'm happy for her."

They looked at Mamaw and Orville in the corner talking, laughing, and said, "I don't think you could stop it anyway. Look." Deni looked at the corner and saw how happy Mamaw was with Orville. How could she deny Mamaw such happiness?

Chapter 16

Christmas was nice, so was the New Year, but now it was back to school. Deni had finished all the homework that she was given over the holidays. She just kept looking at the monstrosity in the driveway and dreaded the day she would be driving it to school. She was already made fun of because she was so smart. If she drove that thing to school she really would be the laughing stock of the school and possibly the whole town. How could her father do this to her? She couldn't even look at it anymore. She turned her back to the driveway to try and forget her car.

She waited for Jack to pick her up for the drive to school. It was sleeting out, so they didn't know how long they would be in school today. If it started snowing they would be let out early and maybe miss the rest of the week. The only problem with that was if school was out another day they would have to add days to the end of the school year to make up for the snow days. Although the tornado took a week of that time, and they still had the rest of winter and spring to go through before summer break. The school had already taken their spring break. If they add days to the end of the school year, that would shorten their summer break.

Jack was five minutes late. Deni climbed in next to Cindy. The truck was all warm and cozy. Deni didn't want to get out of the truck when they got to school. Jack let the girls off at the front door and parked the truck. He made a run for it, and Deni opened the door just as Jack reached for the handle. They made it to first period just in time. During last hour, Mr. Taylor asked for all the special assignments to be turned in. Some of the kids looked around and didn't know what the teacher was talking about. Mr. Taylor began to explain, and the kids who didn't get to participate were highly disappointed. The kids that did know about the assignment handed it to Mr. Taylor.

As school let out, Jack told the girls to wait by the front door and he would pick them up. The girls waited there and heard a familiar giggle come up behind them.

Natalie was walking toward them. "Well, well, well. Where is your robot boyfriend? You got him on a short leash, Deni. What's wrong? Afraid someone might steal him from you?"

Deni looked at her and just shook her head. "What's wrong, Natalie? All the guys here figured out that you're a lowlife and won't have anything to do with you? Poor little rich girl. I guess money doesn't buy everything," said Deni. Cindy was standing there just giving Natalie a look that could set Natalie on fire.

Natalie starred at Cindy and said, "I don't know what my brother sees in you. Maybe he lost a bet and this is how he has to pay—by scraping the bottom of the barrel. What a shame that he doesn't really like you. He's just pretending so that he won't hurt your feelings." Cindy looked at her with a red face.

Cindy was so mad that she could have bit a nail in two. She could barely even speak. "Poor Natalie, can't find a guy this year. You know, Natalie, I feel sorry for you. You feel you have to put down other people to make yourself look good. That's a bully in my book. You are such a pathetic person. You are not even worth the time it would take to scrape you off my shoe. It would be just better to throw the shoes away." Natalie looked at her, seething now. She had no comeback and pushed past them out the door.

Deni looked at Cindy and gave her a high five. "Way to go, girl. I can't believe we scared off Natalie. That wasn't so bad. I can't believe you said that to her. I'm so proud of you."

Cindy looked at her friend and said, "I'm so proud of you too. I can't believe she's like this. She has left us alone for so long. I guess because

Christian is interested in me, she has to include you too. I'm sorry, Deni, I didn't mean to drag you into this."

Deni told her best friend, "You didn't drag me into anything. I went in willingly. You know I would do anything for you. I'm not gonna stand by and let Natalie get to us. Most of all, I'm not gonna stand here and be quiet while she treats my friend like crap. It's not gonna happen. You got that?" Cindy nodded her head and gave Deni a hug of thanks.

Jack pulled the truck to the curb, the girls ran for it. Jack had the truck all warm and cozy again. She liked the warmth of the truck and the warmth of having her boyfriend and best friend with her. Deni couldn't imagine her life without her friends and without Mamaw now. She always looked at Mamaw's house before entering her own house and would often come out at night to check on Mamaw's house before going to bed. Today, she noticed a truck in Mamaw's driveway. It must be Orville visiting.

Deni said, "Look. How cute is that?" She pointed to Mamaw's house. Cindy and Jack saw the truck. They both agreed with Deni.

"You know, Valentine's Day will be coming up soon. I think we should do something nice for Mamaw," said Deni.

Jack told her, "We should. That will show our appreciation for her and how much we love her."

Cindy agreed. "I think she needs something extra special." Deni and Jack agreed with Cindy. Jack had something in mind for her and wanted to surprise even the girls with it.

He told them. "Let me take care of it. I think I know what she needs."

The girls told him, "Okay."

They all got out of the truck and ran into the house. Cathy was standing there with the door open, waiting for them. She told them she had hot chocolate in the kitchen for them. They all headed to the kitchen and grabbed a mug. Cathy had also made homemade biscotti for them. Jack sat there drinking his hot chocolate, saying it was the best he ever had. He asked how she made it and asked for the recipe of the biscotti. Cathy felt an overwhelming pride swell up in her. Jack had asked her for a recipe, how was that? She made something so good that this fabulous chef had to ask her for the recipe.

Time seemed to pass quickly for Deni, and before she knew it, it was Valentine's Day, and she had not even gone shopping for a present for Jack. Cathy saw the way Deni came downstairs and pulled out a big box of chocolates for Deni to give to Jack.

Deni hugged her mother and said, "Thank you. I don't know what's gotten into me. Can you call and make a hair appointment for me for Saturday? I'll make sure and tell Cindy to be here to go with us."

Cathy told her, "No problem. That will be nice for us. I haven't gotten to spend a lot of time with you two lately. I've missed that. I'm sorry I haven't gotten to spend time with you. There's just been so much going on."

Deni shook her head and replied, "I know, Mom, but I understand. You have been really busy and unable to do a lot of things. I'm sorry I haven't made you spend more time with me. Mom, it's okay. It's no big deal." Cathy hugged her daughter and sent her on her way.

Jack was waiting in the driveway. It was so nice that he picked her up for school. This was so much easier for Cathy. She didn't have to worry about getting up early, but it was her habit to get up early. She stood in front of the kitchen sink, looking out the window, watching her daughter ride off with her boyfriend. Her daughter was growing up. Soon she would be graduating and going off to college.

Around 10:00 a.m., Deni received a dozen lavender roses that were delivered to her in Mr. Larson's class. The girls at school had been receiving flowers, chocolates, balloons, and cards all day long. Mr. Larson was getting tired of being interrupted. He told Deni to try and see around her flowers. She read the card, and it said, "Happy Valentine's Day. Love, Jack." Deni kept reading the card and started blushing because Jack had used the word "love." Jack didn't really know how to sign the card and thought that "love" was the best word to use since it was Valentine's Day. Deni thanked him for the flowers. Jack told her she was welcome and asked both girls if they wanted to go with him after school to Mamaw's house. They both agreed, and Jack told them he needed to stop at his house to get Mamaw's present. Last hour seemed to drag by. Jack and the girls stopped by his house, and Jack ran in to get the box. He came out and put it in the backseat. The girls kept looking at the box because it was shaking every now and then.

They got to Mamaw's house and saw that Orville's truck was there in the driveway. Jack parked behind Mamaw's car. The girls got out and Jack grabbed the box. They walked to the door and heard music playing. All three started laughing. Jack rang the doorbell, Mamaw answered the door, and asked them all to come in. They went into the living room and saw Orville sitting there sipping a glass of tea. Orville didn't drink and preferred tea to anything else.

Jack looked at Mamaw, held out the box, and said, "Happy Valentine's Day." The girls told her the same and Mamaw took the box.

She noticed it was awfully light and wondered what was in such a big box to be so light. She sat on the sofa next to Orville and removed the top. Mamaw held a small black-and-tan fur ball. It was so small you could barely make out what it was. Then she held it to her face and a tiny tongue came out and licked her nose.

Mamaw asked Jack, "What kind of dog is this?"

Jack scratched the dog's tiny head and told Mamaw, "It's a Yorkshire terrier. Most people call them Yorkies. Isn't he cute? I knew the moment I saw him that you had to have him."

Mamaw stood with the tiny bundle in her hands and hugged Jack so hard he thought he heard a rib crack. Then she came over to Deni and Cindy and hugged them just as hard. The girls were all over the puppy. He was the cutest thing they had ever seen. Jack also presented her a book on Yorkies and the papers on him. Mamaw watched as the tiny thing ran around the girls. She told Jack she needed a collar with a bell for the puppy. Jack laughed and brought out a bright red collar with tiny bells on it and gave it to Mamaw. She thanked him again. Orville looked at the puppy and laughed.

"What exactly is that thing?" he asked. "Are you sure that's a dog? Looks like a walking hair ball that a cat coughed up," Orville said.

"I know. Isn't he cute? I think I'll call him Alphie. Do you like that name, little britches? What do you think?" Mamaw asked the puppy as she picked him up. She held him up and looked at his face as she was talking. He licked her nose again as if he understood what was said.

"That's it then, Alphie. That's gonna be your name," she said to the puppy.

Orville laughed and said, "I ain't never seen somebody talk to a dog like that. Do you really think he can understand you, Bea?"

Mamaw laughed and said, "Yeah. I think people don't give dogs enough credit."

Orville laughed and said, "You know, when I was growing up, we had a dog that was smart. She would sit, roll over, fetch, and she was a darn good bird dog."

"Well, Alphie is gonna be a better dog than that. He's gonna be doing all sorts of things. I used to have a dog named Gizbeau. He was so smart that I had to spell things around him. Then he learned how to spell and I had to come up with a new way to talk about things around him. I really miss that dog, but now I have Alphie, and he's gonna learn all the tricks I taught Gizbeau," said Mamaw.

Jack dropped Deni off and left to go home himself. Deni ran in to tell her mother about the dog they had gotten Mamaw. Deni also had to tell her mom about Orville being there at Mamaw's.

Cathy laughed and said, "I think it's cute. Mamaw and Orville becoming friends."

Deni laughed and told her mother, "I think they're becoming more than friends. You should see how she acts in front of him. It's gross." Deni didn't want to think of Mamaw with anybody. That was her mamaw, and she didn't need a papaw to go along with it. Things were fine just the way they were.

Mamaw honked her horn as she passed by Deni's house, and Deni saw a small black bundle in Mamaw's arms. She knew that Mamaw was going to the pet store to get supplies for Alphie. Cathy was so happy for Mamaw and Orville. It reminded her of when she and Stan first met.

Cathy and Deni were fixing supper when they heard a knock on the door. Mamaw and Orville had stopped by on their way home from the pet store. It looked like Mamaw had bought the whole store. They came in to show Cathy the puppy. Cathy held the little bundle in her arms and the dog went to sleep. Stan came home and made so much noise that Alphie woke up.

He looked at Cathy and asked, "Why are you holding lint from the dryer?"

Cathy shushed him and said, "This is Bea's Valentine's present from the kids. Isn't he cute?" Stan looked at how little he was and still thought he looked like a small ball of lint.

Cathy put him down on the floor, and Mamaw gave him a toy to play with. The toy was bigger than the dog. It didn't take long for Alphie to find the squeaker in the toy, and soon the house was filled with squeaks. Stan laughed at the puppy while it played with the toy trying to pick up something twice its size and walk across the floor with it. Puppies are so clumsy and Alphie was no exception. He would fall on his head, take a tumble, then get back up and take off again.

Orville was sitting there talking to Stan when Alphie walked up to him and barked. Orville looked at the tiny dog. "Was that a bark? I think that was a bark. I'm not sure though." Alphie was trying to play with Orville, but he wasn't quite sure how to play with Alphie. He was so afraid he would hurt the little guy, so he just sat there. That aggravated Alphie more, so he ran around and barked at him. Finally, Orville reached down to pet the dog, but Alphie growled at him. Orville rolled the dog over to scratch its tiny belly and Alphie started having fun with Orville.

Orville was getting a big kick out of watching Alphie play with his toy parrot. He picked up the toy and tossed it across the room. Alphie looked at Orville and took off for the parrot.

Orville told him, "Bring it here. Bring it to Papaw. Oops, didn't mean to say that. He reminds me of playing with my granddaughters when they were babies. I've heard that pets can become like children, but I never thought I would feel that way about a dog. But he's just so cute. Kinda gets in your heart."

Bea laughed at Orville and said, "You're just a big softie. Alphie likes you. Didn't you ever feel that way about any pets you've had?"

Orville hung his head and said, "I didn't really have a pet. The only one I ever had, my father got rid of him while I was at school one day. He didn't like to have pets around and decided to get rid of my dog. I've never really had a little dog. I have dogs on the farm, but they are all big outside dogs. I would like to have a little one that lives in the house, but that's just something else to clean up after. I always thought that was a chore because of the sheddin', but the man at the pet store said these here dogs don't shed. He said their hair is like people hair, and they shed like people shed. Ain't that something? I never heard of that."

Stan looked at Orville and was shocked at how the man felt about this dog. He must really like Bea to like her dog. Stan could tell that this man must have had a hard life. Stan thought Orville grew up in a house where animals didn't matter that much. Today people put too much into their animals, thought Stan. Stan had always thought people that treated their pets like kids were weird, but after looking at Alphie, he was starting to change his mind.

Mamaw and Orville loaded up the packages from the pet store, grabbed Alphie, and headed to the car. Orville had to squeal the tires as he pulled out of the drive. Mamaw was waving and grabbed Alphie's paw and waved good-bye to the Rosens. Deni thought they looked so cute. Mamaw and Orville looked like a cute little family with their little dog. The only thing was they were riding around in a muscle car and drag racing down the street.

Deni was getting tired and started to wish her parents a good night when her father asked her to run to his truck. "I think I left something in the front seat. Can you get it for me?"

Deni ran out to her father's truck and grabbed a package out of the front seat. She returned and gave it to her father. Stan pulled out a big box of chocolates and gave it to Deni. She was shocked her father would give it to her. He was supposed to give that to her mother. Then Stan turned to Cathy and pulled out a small box. Cathy opened the box and began to cry. Inside the box was a diamond heart-shaped necklace.

Stan helped Cathy put the necklace on and Cathy hugged him, saying, "You remembered. All these years, I thought you had forgotten." Deni wondered what her mother was talking about.

Stan hugged his wife and told her, "I know you thought that. That's why this was the perfect time to get it for you. I love you very much. Happy Valentine's Day."

Cathy kissed her husband and told him, "I love you too. Happy Valentine's Day." Deni thought it was getting yucky and went to her room.

The next morning Cathy was downstairs, sipping her coffee and looking out the front window. Deni came down and poured herself a cup of coffee and stood by her mother, also looking out the window.

"That thing out there has got to go in the backyard, garage, or something," Cathy said. Deni knew what she was looking at and told her mother, "Can't we just get rid of it and say the police came by and towed it for being so ugly?"

Cathy laughed and told her daughter, "No, that would hurt your father's feelings. Besides, he got that thing so you two could spend time together."

Deni replied, "Yeah, but Mom, I don't work on cars. Why did he even think that I would want to work on this?"

Cathy looked at her daughter. "He thought this was a way for you two to bond more. You're getting older and soon will be out of the house. This was the only thing he could think of to keep that bond with you. He loves you very much and wants to spend time with you, even if you are just standing there handing tools to him. Please, Deni, for me. Do this for me and for your father. You'll appreciate it in the end, trust me. Someday you will look at that car and think about all the time you and your father spent on that thing. Trust me, please."

Deni couldn't resist her mother's pleading and finally gave in. "Okay, but I'm not getting greasy. Can I call Jack and ask him to help us out with it? You think that would hurt his feelings?"

Cathy told her daughter, "I think that would be okay. Jack seems to be serious about you, and maybe this would be a way for your father to get to know him better. Do you feel the same way about Jack? I mean, you are really young, and I wish you wouldn't get serious with a boy till you're, like, thirty. But I know that's not gonna happen. So if this is the boy, then this is the boy. Just remember, you're gonna be going to college, and there will be a whole slew of boys there that are just waiting for a smart beautiful girl like you to come along. Just keep your options open."

Deni told her mom, "I know what you're saying. I like Jack a lot, but I don't know if it's more than that. Time will tell, but I don't want to tie myself down either. I hear you, Mom, and for now, this is how it is. I'll ask him today if he would help Dad."

Jack showed up to drive Deni to school, and she left with a heavy heart. She felt that it was time for her to break up with Jack but also loved the fact that Jack was really a good friend. She did not want to lose that over something stupid like breaking up. Fact was, she was developing feelings for Jack and was scared to admit that, even to herself.

School was as boring as usual, and they couldn't wait till summer break. They were all counting down the days, even the teachers. People think teachers don't look forward to those breaks as much as the kids, but they are wrong. Mr. Taylor had been teaching a long time and was beginning to burn out. All he could think about was how long it was till the next break. The kids were thinking the same thing. How long till summer break?

Time passed for Deni, and she was doing really well in school despite the little memory lapses and strange kooky behavior she was showing every now and then. Cindy was still keeping the log and noticed that when Deni had her hair color darkened, things seemed to subside. She was becoming her old self again. Now that she was dyeing her hair blonde again, things were becoming weird. What was really going on? Was it Deni or something else?

Cindy called Jack to get his thoughts on things and to ask if he had noticed the difference in her behavior when her hair went back to being dark. Jack told Cindy that he had indeed noticed the difference and asked if they could get together so he could look at her journal. He had some things to add but didn't want to talk to Cindy on the phone. He told her he would be there in five minutes. Cindy hung up the phone and told her parents that Jack was on his way over.

Cindy was waiting for Jack in the kitchen so they could be alone. She gave him the journal to read. He sat there studying the journal and told Cindy she had done a good job.

"This is not a job, this is my best friend. She's like a sister to me. I just want to figure this thing out and help her. I don't know what is going on. Did you hear her in science class today? It's like she had never heard of the human heart. That's not Deni. Deni would have been all over that and probably would have already known everything they were going over," she told Jack.

Jack replied, "Yeah, that is weird. Have you noticed any other classes that she might be having trouble with? I don't see anything in the journal about all the classes."

Cindy thought and said she hadn't really noticed anything but would certainly pay more attention to Deni. Jack suggested she start writing down everything that Deni does. "It would be better if you could observe her from the time she got up till she went to bed."

Jack told Cindy, "If we really want to help Deni, we need to start looking at every minute of her day. This will take some time, but I really think we can do it. Are you in?"

Cindy looked at Jack with determination. "Of course I'm in. This is Deni we're talking about. I'll have Mom call Cathy and work it out. That won't be a problem." Jack told her this was the only way they could do this for Deni.

Jack left and Cindy went to bed. She lay there thinking about everything Deni had done and wondered if she had left anything out of her journal. Cindy made a mental note to read the journal again and add anything that she could think of that Deni had done. Cindy was determined to get to the bottom of her unusual behavior. Sam had called Cathy and told her what the kids were up to, and Cathy agreed with Cindy coming over to help Deni. If this is what they needed to do then Cathy was okay with it. Sam agreed and told Cathy that she would help in any way that she could.

Cindy had to start spending time with Deni, so the next morning she packed a bag to take over to Deni's. Jack picked her up for school and threw her bag in the backseat. He went to Deni's house and unloaded Cindy's things, and they went off to school.

Chapter 17

Time seemed to pass quickly for Deni, and soon it was prom time. Jack had asked her to the prom and was making plans with the other guys for the limo. Christian was going with Cindy, Kurby was going with Mary, and Josh was going with Leah. They were all together and hoping to have a good time. Deni had always wondered what happens at a prom, and now she was going to find out. Cathy had made hair and nail appointments for the girls, and all the girls were coming over to get ready. Cathy was going to have a house full of kids.

Deni and Cindy were looking forward to the prom. This was the first time they were going. They had always heard stories about the dancing and how funny some of the kids looked out on the dance floor, but this time they would have a firsthand look. The hair salon was full the day of the prom. Deni and Cindy needed to have their color done along with the styling. Deni knew exactly what dress she was wearing and had gone to the mall and found black rhinestone-studded heels that matched her dress perfectly.

Sabrina greeted them at the door as they walked in the salon. She was happy to see them and was super busy. She and Tasha immediately took Deni and Cindy over to their chairs and draped them. Sabrina and Tasha disappeared behind the curtain and came out with color. They reassured the girls that the colors were not mixed up this time. Deni had the blonde and Cindy had the brunette.

The timers went off and the girls went to the wash bowls. They heard the familiar sound of the doorbell. Deni and Cindy both heard that familiar giggle and looked at each other.

"Well, well, well, what do we have here? The bleach blonde idiot and her interpreter," said Natalie.

Deni and Cindy looked at her and laughed. Her hair looked like a rat's nest. She didn't even bother combing it before coming to the salon.

"You know, you could have at least brushed your hair, Natalie. You're scary enough as it is, but now you look like the bag lady down on Third Street," said Deni.

Cindy burst out laughing, "Do you have a mouse in there somewhere?" Natalie was shocked at the response from the girls and stalked away. She sat down on the bench at the front of the salon and grabbed a magazine to hide her face.

Deni told Cindy, "Wow, I've seen bad hair days, but jeez." Cindy looked over at Natalie sitting there trying to hide and laughed. The girls were finished and were turned around to the mirror. They both looked so sophisticated. They thanked Sabrina and Tasha for the excellent service and gave them a big tip. The girls were making return appointments, and Tasha went to get Natalie.

Cindy told Tasha, "Good luck with that hair. She's gonna need some serious help." Deni laughed and both waved good-bye to Natalie.

They met Jack on the sidewalk, and Jack offered to take them home. Deni called her mother to let her know that Jack was bringing them home and asked if she needed anything. Cathy told her daughter no and to be sure to thank Jack for the ride. They got home right before Mary and Leah showed up. Deni couldn't wait to see what Mamaw had made for Leah to wear. The girls all piled into Deni's room and started an assembly line to get everything done. Leah set up the nail station, Cindy set up the pedicure station, and Deni did the makeup. Then they would all switch, except for Leah. She was the only one who could do nails. But all the other girls pitched in to make sure that Leah looked fabulous.

They all finished with the manis and pedis, then ran downstairs to get something to snack on. They finished with their snacks and Cathy laughed at the way the girls were walking because their toenails were wet. They all went back upstairs to Deni's room and finished getting ready. Leah took out her dress and everyone just froze. It was simply gorgeous. Mamaw had made Leah a dress out of a salmon satin material. Mamaw had also hand beaded the bodice and the front of the dress. The dress was so gorgeous that it looked like one off the red carpet.

Leah put the dress on and she was so stunning. The rest of the girls paled in comparison until they put on their dresses that Mamaw had made. All of the dresses had hand beading on them and were made to flatter the girls. Mamaw had also picked the colors that looked best on them. They descended the stairs into the living room. Stan was sitting there reading, he immediately dropped the paper and starred at the stunning beauties coming down the stairs.

"Since when did we have supermodels move in upstairs?" asked Stan. The girls blushed and continued down the steps. They stood at the foot of the stairs.

All Stan could do was smile and whistle. "Boy howdy, you young'uns clean up good. Did y'all put on that stink 'em stuff? Shore smells like it. I ain't never in my whole life seen nobody that looked as good as y'all."

Deni laughed, saying, "Dad, stop it. Really, do we look okay?"

Stan looked at his daughter, smiled, and said, "If you looked any prettier, you would be on the cover of a magazine." They all blushed and stood there while Cathy snapped pictures.

Their dates showed up wearing tuxes and a Hummer stretch limo was waiting on the street for them. Deni was stunned by the limo and Jack's ability to get a car like that whenever he wanted. The boys brought each of the girls a wrist corsage to wear, and the tuxes matched their date's dress. Stan and Cathy were impressed with the boys and told them all to have a good time. Mary and Leah both had curfews at eleven thirty while Deni and Cindy had midnight curfews. So they all decided that the group curfew was going to be eleven thirty. Christian was the only person Deni was worried about. Would he think that all this was stupid or would he go along with it and then make fun of it all? Deni was worried that Christian would tell Natalie about everything and she would take it all wrong then make fun of them at school.

Christian did tell them that he had a midnight curfew but went along with the earlier curfew. Christian was cool with them and was nothing like his sister. Hopefully he was not going behind their backs and reporting everything back to Natalie. Then again, maybe she was just paranoid. They got to the prom, had pictures taken of each couple, then as a group. Deni thought this was the best picture. She wanted to remember this night forever.

They walked into the cafeteria, which had been turned into a banquet hall. There were decorations everywhere and balloons attached to anything that was tied down. Streamers hung from the ceiling, extra lights were hung up, and there was a disco ball hanging right in the center of the ceiling. Deni and the gang started laughing at the disco ball. They wondered if there was gonna be disco music playing. They found their table and sat down. An announcer stepped up the podium on the stage. She said that food was now being served. Waiters came through the kitchen doors with trays on their shoulders.

The food smelled great to Deni, but it was nothing like the Christmas feast they had at Jack's house. Jack was a fantastic chef and was sure gonna be a hit at culinary school. He would have no problem opening up his own restaurant. It would be an instant success, Deni just knew it. The servers set down a plate of rosemary chicken, rice pilaf, steamed broccoli, and fresh yeast rolls. There were butter plates on the tables, water, and tea glasses along with silver flatware. The servers had already come around and poured water and asked what drinks they wanted. Some ordered soda while the others ordered tea.

The kids dug into the chicken like they had never eaten before. The food was good but, again, not as good as Jack's. Once you've eaten one of Jack's meals, nothing else compares. But for a catered event, it was good food. They ate without talking and soon were interrupted by an announcer.

"Now, please, help me welcome Natalie Whitcomb and Alisha Nelson. Your class president and vice president," the announcer said.

The two walked up on stage and stood behind the podium. Alisha took out a piece of paper. "It's customary for the juniors to roast the seniors, but the two classes are so close that we decided to combine them. We will be roasting the seniors, but we have a few juniors that need to be included in this. Now, Natalie, who is our first victim?" said Alisha.

Natalie stepped up to the mic. The girls alternated in announcing who was most likely to succeed, most likely to go to college, the class clown, and so on.

Finally, the dessert was served, and the girls on stage were concluding their roast with the teachers. They did have some juniors in the mix, but thank goodness none of Deni and her friends were included. The announcer came back up to the mic and announced that the tables would have to be removed and if everyone could make room for the teardown team. Most people stood close to the walls, and some who didn't want anything to do with the dance left. Deni and the gang stood close to the walls and waited for the tables to be cleared. They wanted to take part in the dance. Deni wanted to experience everything she could about the prom. She had waited fifteen years for it and was not going to leave early.

The DJ came out on the stage and set up his machines. Then the music started. Deni and Jack were the first out on the dance floor, followed by the rest of Deni's friends. Then everyone came out on the dance floor. It was so much fun. Then the ceiling rained balloons down on their heads. Deni thought it was such a magical night. She couldn't see how it could get any better. They danced till they couldn't dance anymore and realized it was getting late. They said good-bye to their other friends and returned to the limo.

Deni and Cindy were so tired when they got home that all they could do was fall into bed. Deni dreamed of the dance and how attentive Jack had been to her every need. He was such a great guy that she couldn't believe he had chosen her to be his girlfriend. It seemed he had chosen her from the very first day. He was such a gentleman. How lucky she was to have such good friends and a boyfriend like Jack.

Deni and Cindy got out of bed late the next morning and went downstairs to find Cathy warming up breakfast for them. She poured the girls a cup of coffee and sat it in front of them. She was afraid to ask how the prom was last night. From the look of things, it went pretty good but the girls looked like they had been put through the ringer. The girls finally looked like they were waking up, and Cathy got up the nerve to ask the girls about the prom. Cathy tried to brush back Deni's hair from her face, but there was so much hairspray on it that it just hung in a clump.

"Well, are you gonna tell me how it went or do I have to drag it out of you?" she asked.

The girls looked at her and told her every detail of the prom. They even told her every word that was said during the roast and how long it took to clear the tables before they could dance. Cathy was impressed. The girls told her that they were still tired. Cathy told them that they could take it easy today and reminded them that they only had a week left of school before summer break.

As the girls headed upstairs, Cathy thought about the past year, when Deni had gotten out of school for the summer, and how she had begged Deni to get off the computer. Now look at her daughter. One thing she found a little disturbing was Deni didn't do a science fair project this year. She had forgotten all about it and told her mother that she couldn't think of anything to do for a project. Cathy thought it was a little strange since Deni was always thinking of something to do for a science fair project. This was a first for Deni. Cathy would make sure and talk to Cindy about it later.

This last week of school was going to be the longest week for Deni. She was so looking forward to the summer and getting a tan. This year she was going to buy a bikini. She wanted to spend every day at the lake so she could lay out by the water. She had already been begging her dad for a pool.

Stan had told her, "If you can get into the accelerated summer program, I'll put in a pool."

Deni had agreed with that and had been working her butt off for the last four months. Hopefully she would hear something this week about the accelerated program.

Cindy asked about the summer program and asked Deni if she was ready to go to school for the summer. Deni told her that if it meant graduating in August, yes. "I can always lay in the pool in the afternoon and on the weekends." Cindy told her she was ready too. She wanted to get out of school early, and to graduate two years early was no small feat. Cindy couldn't wait to hear from Principal Worden.

The week was filled with excitement and tests. Deni, Cindy, and Jack were exempt from the semester tests. They only had two days to go to turn everything in and get their library releases. This was the first year that Deni didn't have tons of books to hand in. She had not checked a book out all year. Still, she had to go get her release signed. The librarian asked where she had been. Deni told her she'd been around but had a busy year.

They got home from school on Tuesday and Cathy told her Mr. Worden called. "He wanted to know if you would be interested in attending the accelerated summer program. He said that you only needed two classes to graduate."

Deni had to ask and was almost afraid to hear the answer. "What classes do I have to take?"

Cathy looked at her and said, "Math with Mr. Foltz and PE with Ms. Lyons." Deni thought that it was okay and told her mother that she wanted to go.

Cathy said, "Good. I already told him you would. Oh, and, Cindy, he called your mother as well." Cindy and Deni were jumping up and down and screaming.

Stan came in and asked what all the noise was about, and Deni told him so quickly that he didn't understand a word. The girls ran upstairs to call Jack. Cathy looked at Stan and told him about Mr. Worden calling and offering the summer program to both girls.

"Those two are pretty fantastic, you know," said Stan.

"Yeah, I think their pretty terrific myself. Can you believe she will graduate in August now?" said Cathy.

Stan shook his head, saying, "No. I can't believe our little girls are all grown up."

Cathy laughed. "You said 'girls.' Stan, we only have one daughter."

"Not really, if you think about it. Cindy has been with her from the get-go and been here most of the time," Stan said.

Cathy agreed and said, "Okay--girls."

Jack told them that he was going to be taking math with them and that was the only class he needed to graduate. He also told them that he would take them to school and wait for them to get out of PE. Graduation went off without a hitch. Usually the graduation is scheduled to be on the football field, but every year it rains on graduation day so the ceremony is always moved inside the gym. But this year, it did not rain, and they actually had the ceremony on the football field. Deni asked if Cindy or Jack wanted to go this year. Both said they didn't and decided to go to a movie instead.

The girls lay in bed that night and talked about all the fun they were going to have over the summer.

Deni said, "I've heard Mr. Foltz can be tough but that he was really kinda cool about it all."

Cindy said she had heard the same thing. Since they only had school three days a week, they decided they would spend the rest of the time by the pool that Stan had promised Deni. She wondered if her father had remembered that promise. If not, she was determined to remind him. The next morning the girls came downstairs for breakfast. Deni looked at her father and said, "Dad, when is the pool going in?"

Stan put down his paper and said, "I was wondering when you were going to get around to that. I thought you had forgotten."

Deni laughed and replied, "Yeah, right."

"I've already called the guy and he's gonna start this weekend. What we have to do is pick out what shape it's gonna be and what color tile we want," replied Stan.

He threw pamphlets on the counter with some tile samples attached. Deni and Cindy were so excited that they couldn't help but pick out the brightest tile to show her father. Stan said no to the pumpkin color.

Deni and Cindy picked a rather modest, medium-sized pool with gorgeous blue and red tiles. There was also a neat design on the bottom of the pool. Deni didn't know they could do a bottom design and picked out the turtle design.

Stan had one last question for Deni. "Do you want a chlorine pool or saltwater?"

Deni thought about this for a moment. "I think I want saltwater. It's not as harsh on my hair or skin."

Stan laughed. "Are you kidding me? This is what you are concerned with? Hair and skin? Well, we wouldn't want to damage that hair color, would we?"

Cathy was standing by the stove, laughing at the exchange. Stan told the girls he would be sure to call the pool guy this morning and let him know what they had picked out. Deni thanked him and so did Cindy.

Cathy wanted to make sure to talk to Cindy today about Deni's behavior. Cathy had noticed that Deni had been forgetting again and that she was becoming shallower. Deni had never been shallow in her life. She had never been forgetful either. What was going on with her daughter?

The pool man came the next day and started digging. Deni was so excited about the pool and was hoping that she could get through the summer classes. She couldn't believe she had to take PE class. How could she be short on PE? Guess it just slipped her mind. She had heard what the summer PE classes were like and was really looking forward to it. She had heard that the teacher would take the kids to skating rinks. Deni was looking forward to ice-skating and roller-skating. The ice-skating rink was about thirty minutes away, so she didn't know how often they would go there, but the roller-skating rink was right here in town.

Summer classes began on Monday. The pool was coming along. The men had it dug in two days. Then started pouring the concrete. Next would be the tiles and the design on the bottom of the pool. Deni was watching the pool builders with great anticipation. She loved watching the men pour the concrete. They worked hard to make sure that the concrete was smooth as glass.

The week passed so fast that Deni was now facing just two months of school and then college. Now she had to get busy and decide on a college to go to. She asked her mom where her acceptance letters were so she could start reviewing the colleges. Her mother went to the hutch and retrieved a stack of letters and set them in front of Deni. Deni fanned out the brochures on the counter. She saw nothing in the state of California and decided to take the brochures upstairs. She booted up the computer and immediately went online.

She typed in California universities, and thousands of links came up. How was she going to get through all these links? She decided to narrow the search and just research top Southern California universities. She immediately found Pepperdine University in Malibu, California. They offered the degree that Deni was interested in, so she immediately looked up the criteria and admissions requirements. She filled out the online forms and e-mailed a short video of herself to the admissions office. She included her contact information, her school transcripts, and her offers from other schools. She was sure to get into this college since she had been accepted to Harvard, Yale, and other top universities.

Deni checked on the pool builders and saw that the tile guy was there. She watched as they unloaded the tiles and began placing them in the bottom of the pool and numbering the pieces so he would know where to place them for the design. Deni watched how careful the guy was in handling the tiles and how meticulous he was. This pool was going to be gorgeous, Deni thought. She couldn't wait till it was done. At the rate the builders were going, the pool should be finished in about two days.

Cindy returned from her house and asked Deni what was up. Deni told her that she had applied to Pepperdine in Malibu. Cindy looked at Deni in shock.

"Why would you want to apply there when you have all these offers on the table?" she asked. Deni told her that she thought it would be fun to go to a college where there was sunshine all the time and no tornadoes.

Cindy told her, "Yeah, but they have, like, earthquakes and fires and stuff. Are you sure about this?"

Deni told her friend, "Yes. I'm very sure about this. There's not a doubt in my mind about this school. It's where I'm supposed to be."

Cindy said okay and told her, "Let me at that computer so I can fill out the forms. Show me what to do." Deni pulled up the site and walked Cindy through the admission paperwork.

That night at supper, Deni told her parents that she had filled out the paperwork for Pepperdine and to please look for a letter in the mail. They told her that they were proud of her and that she was soon to be a college student.

That night, Deni checked her e-mail and made Cindy check hers to see if she had received anything. Deni couldn't wait for the letter. She just had to be accepted to this school. Jack called to see what time summer school starts. He wanted to make sure what the proper dress for summer school was and asked if he could wear shorts.

Deni laughed and told him, "I didn't think guys worried about things like this."

Jack laughed and said, "Well, that's where you're wrong. Guys worry about this stuff all the time. Especially, if there're girls involved." Deni couldn't help but laugh.

Deni lay in bed that night, dreaming of college life in California. All she could think about was lying on the beach, watching the surfers, rollerblading down the sidewalk at the beach, driving her monstrosity of a car, and the clothes she was going to wear. All she could think about was the shopping and the fashions. She had heard about the fashion district in Los Angeles and couldn't wait to go there to check out the prices.

The next morning the pool builders were there early, checking to see if the tiles were dry. The temperature outside was a hundred degrees. It was so hot and humid that Deni was watching to see if they were going to start filling the pool today. She could just imagine floating in the pool on these hot days and getting the deepest tan she could possibly get. She called Jack to see if he could take them to the mall. Jack told her he would be over right after breakfast.

Deni ran upstairs to tell Cindy that they were going to the mall. Cindy was ready in twenty minutes and waiting for Deni. Deni was standing in front of her closet, staring at her clothes.

"What are you doin'?" asked Cindy.

"Trying to find the right outfit. Get up and help me," replied Deni.

Cindy looked at her closet and said, "Why don't you wear that blue halter and the cute shorts with the flowers? That looks so good on you."

"I can't believe you would suggest that outfit. I've worn that, like, a million times. I need new clothes," Deni said in a frustrated tone.

Cindy stood there looking at Deni, wondering why she was getting mad about clothes. This was a new behavior that Cindy would have to write down in her journal.

Jack came over to pick the girls up to go shopping. Just as they were pulling out of the drive, Deni saw a fire truck pulling up. Why was a fire truck at her house? She saw the pool contractor talking to the firemen and saw that they were hooking up one of their hoses to the fire hydrant across the street and stretching it out to her backyard. She always wondered how they filled a pool so quickly. Jack drove off, and Deni watched the firemen adding more hoses so they could reach the pool.

They got to the mall and found a parking spot close to the entrance. They walked into the mall, and Jack suggested they go get a slice of pizza, but all Deni could do was run to Shawna's Fashions. Cindy and Jack ran after her and saw that she was at the bikini rack and had five in her hand to try on.

Jack looked at Cindy and asked, "Why is she in the bikinis? I thought she only wore one-piece suits."

Cindy shrugged and looked confused. She approached Deni with caution and asked, "What are you doing? The one-piece suits are over there."

Deni looked at Cindy with a fiery look in her eyes, "Are you gonna help me pick out suits or give me a lecture about the appropriate suit to wear? I'm so sick of people being holier-than-thou. Why are you treating me this way? I'm just trying to be cool like everyone wanted."

Cindy looked at her sternly asking, "What is wrong with you? You've been acting weird all morning. I've never seen you like this." Deni turned around and stormed off to the dressing room.

Jack approached Cindy and asked, "What's up?"

Cindy told Jack what had happened that morning and now this. She needed help with this dilemma. She decided to call Cathy and fill her in on what Deni was doing. Cathy told Cindy that Deni had been short with her for the past week also and wondered if there was something going on. She asked if Deni was worried about anything, but Cindy told her that Deni had not talked to her about anything but fashion and hair for the past three months. She also told Cathy about Deni applying to that college in California and why she wanted to go there. Cathy was so surprised at her daughter's behavior and asked if there was any way that the three of them could meet and discuss what to do next.

Deni came out of the dressing room and decided to buy all five suits. Cindy stood there looking at Deni, wondering what was going on in her mind. She approached cautiously and asked Deni if she could help her pick out a couple suits. Deni's attitude changed, and she turned around smiling. "Sure, what kind of suit do you want? A one-piece? That would probably be your style. I can't believe you tried to put a one-piece on this body. I need to show it off. I'm not going to cover up just because you say I need to. You sound like my mother."

Cindy thought she was going to have to apologize, and hopefully that would change Deni's attitude. Cindy grabbed Deni and turned her around. "I'm sorry if I have upset you in any way. But you have to admit that something is changing in you. We have never had a fight in our lives. You have never acted like this. I'm sorry if it upsets you that I'm concerned and worried about my sister. I love you and am trying to help you."

Deni wrenched her arm from Cindy's grasp and took a step back. Deni stood there looking at Cindy, "I know. I'm sorry. I don't know what happened. I don't know what's happening and I'm scared. Please, help me through this."

She grabbed Cindy and hugged her. She was crying and hugging Cindy. Jack watched this exchange and made a mental note to write this in his journal.

Jack approached them and hugged both girls. The sales lady came over and asked if everything was okay. Jack told her, "Yeah, just a little upset that you don't have a couture line of bathing suits."

Both girls laughed. Jack asked if everything was okay now and asked if they could help him pick out some summer clothes. The girls were on a mission now and brought Jack everything they could find that would look good on him. Cindy picked out a bikini also and asked Deni what she thought about it. Deni laughed and showed Cindy the same suit she had picked out for herself. They both went into the dressing room and tried on their bathing suits. Cindy did approve of all the suits that Deni had picked out for herself and went out and picked out more for Deni to try on.

The girls finished up their shopping and looked for Jack. Jack had made his final selections and told the girls he was ready. They paid for the clothes and headed for the parking garage. They loaded everything in the backseat. It was nice coming to the mall when it's not so crowded. Deni liked the mall now and couldn't believe she hated it at one time.

Chapter 18

They got to Deni's house and looked at the pool. It was full of water now, and the contractor was adding chemicals to it. Deni approached him and asked how long it would be before she could swim. He told her she would have to wait for twenty-four hours before going in.

She then asked Jack to take her to Walmart so she could pick up floaties for the pool. Jack laughed and told the girls to get in the truck. The girls were in the truck before Jack even made it out the door. They got to Walmart and saw why the mall was so empty. Everyone in town was at Walmart. They couldn't find a parking spot so Jack dropped them off at the front door. He told them he would drive around and pick them up. The girls ran to the pool department and picked out what they. They ran to the nearest cashier and out the door. Jack was there waiting for them. He saw the cart full of bags and got out to help. People started honking and tried to pass him, but the parking lot was so full it was gridlocked now. The girls climbed in and waited for Jack to get in. The gridlock was moving now, and Jack looked for the nearest exit.

Cathy was waiting for them to get home. Stan had called and said that he wanted to have a pool party, but Deni told her mother what the contractor had said about staying out of the pool till tomorrow. Cathy called Stan, and he asked Deni to plan for tomorrow night. He also asked Jack if he could help with the grilling. Jack agreed to that eagerly and told Stan that he would do everything if that was okay. Stan told him that was not a problem because Jack was the best cook around.

The kids decided to go see Mamaw to invite her over and ask if she could bake some sweet potato pies for the party. Mamaw was playing with Alphie and trying to teach him to sit up. The girls knocked on the door, and Alphie ran to the door barking, if that's what you could call it. It sounded like a high-pitched soft bell. Alphie saw who it was and started jumping on the door. He wanted to get to the girls. Mamaw told him to sit down and he sat down. She opened the door for the kids, and Alphie immediately started jumping on their legs. Deni bent down to pick up the tiny dog. Alphie started licking her and trying to climb her face. He wanted to lick her face. Deni laughed at the tiny dog.

Cindy tried to grab him from Deni, and Alphie jumped into her arms. He did it so fast that both girls almost dropped him. Mamaw told them that he was doing that a lot, and she dropped him the other day. The girls felt better knowing they weren't the only ones. Mamaw invited them into the living room. The girls told her about the pool party, and Mamaw got all excited about making pies. She said she would definitely be there and asked if she could bring a guest.

Deni laughed and told her, "If you mean Orville, then yes. We really like him."

Mamaw told her, "That's good cause I like him too. He hasn't been able to come around as much because of the crops that he has to tend to, but I think I can convince him to come to a cookout." They all thanked her. Then kissed Alphie and Mamaw good-bye.

The girls left talking about how cute Alphie was and told Mamaw to bring him too. Mamaw told them that she doesn't go anywhere without Alphie. So she promised to bring the dog and her "gentleman friend" to their house tomorrow. She did ask what time they wanted her there, and Deni told her anytime she wanted to come over would be fine, but she thought they would be ready to eat by 6:00 p.m.

Deni went home and looked at the pool again. The water looked so inviting. She showed her mother the bathing suits and told her she had bought one for her. She pulled out a bikini and gave it to her. Cathy looked at the thing and laughed.

Deni asked her mother, "What's wrong? Don't you like it? Cindy helped me pick it out."

Cathy held the thing to her body and looked at the girls. "You really expect me to wear this thing," she said.

The girls chimed in together, "Yes, it's perfect."

Deni told her mother, "It's just for right here at the house. No one is going to see you in it but us. What's wrong with it? You have a great body, and it's time you showed it off."

Cathy continued to look at the girls and shook her head. "Okay. But you have to promise that the only people who will see me in it are those that are in this room and your father." The girls agreed and said that they would not invite anyone over unless her mother approved first.

School was starting in two days, and Deni wanted to enjoy her pool first. She went to bed dreaming about the sunshine, tanning and laying out by the pool with her friends. Cindy lay across the bed talking about the day with Deni. Deni had never shown signs of aggression in her life, but today was different. Deni was so aggressive that Cindy was actually scared of her best friend. Deni had turned on her like a pit bull. What was going on with her?

Deni finally fell asleep, and Cindy got up to go downstairs and write in her journal. She found Cathy sitting at the kitchen table and sat down beside her.

"What do you think is wrong with my daughter? I can't stand this anymore. I think she needs to be checked out," said Cathy.

Cindy grabbed her hand and told her, "Look, I don't think it's come to that extreme but something is going on. I want you to look at my journal and tell me what you think and if there's anything I've left out. Have you noticed any other behavior changes?"

Cathy took the journal and started reading. She was shocked at how her daughter had acted today and was even more shocked to see what Cindy had written. She noticed the different handwritings in the journal and asked Cindy who else had been writing in it. Cindy told her about Jack coming to her and writing things in her journal. Cathy thought that was a good idea and asked if she had figured out when they all could meet and discuss this. Cathy also thought that Stan should be told about this and get his input.

Cindy agreed and told her that she had not even thought about that because Deni had her so upset that she was unable to think about anything else. Cathy told Cindy that she was sorry for her daughter's behavior toward her and that she hoped it would never happen again. Cindy told her that they worked it out, but the look in Deni's eyes was something Cindy had never seen before.

Cindy asked Cathy, "Can you call Jack tomorrow and ask if he can come by tomorrow night? You'll have to act like you're talking to Ruth, but I think you can pull it off. I hate sneaking around like this, and we are gonna have to be really quiet tomorrow night. We can wait till Deni is asleep and go down to the basement. Can you tell Jack to ride his bike and to come in through the back?"

Cathy replied, "Sure, I think we can pull this off. I'll be sure to tell Jack everything. I hate this sneaky stuff too, but I don't see any other way around it."

Cindy closed the journal and headed back upstairs. She was very quiet when she opened the bedroom door. She expected to see Deni in bed asleep but instead she found an empty bed. She walked in looking around and wondering if Deni went downstairs. She thought that if Deni had gone downstairs, she may have heard everything, and that would blow everything.

Deni came in the room asking, "Where have you been? I woke up to go to the bathroom and you were gone."

Cindy looked at her in surprise. "I thought I heard a noise downstairs and went to check it out. Why? Is there something wrong?"

Deni yawned and asked, "Should there be something wrong? Why are you so jumpy?"

"Who? Me? I'm not jumpy. You just frightened me, that's all. Why are you asking me all these questions?" asked Cindy.

Deni started getting aggravated. "I'm not the one asking questions, you are. Let's just go to bed and try to get some sleep. I can't believe you're acting like this, I don't know if I can sleep in the same room with someone acting like they did something wrong."

Cindy looked at her. "What do you mean I'm acting like I did something wrong? I haven't done anything to make you ever think that."

Deni replied, "Well, you're acting like that now. You should have seen your face when I walked in. What exactly have you been doing? Did you sneak out to see Christian? If my parents found out, they would freak. Don't do this to me. I don't want to get in trouble because you two can't control your hormones."

Cindy climbed in bed. "I didn't sneak out to see Christian. I've never done anything like that in my life and I'm not starting now. I told you that I thought I heard something downstairs and went to check it out. Now go to bed, please."

Deni climbed in bed, saying, "I'm sorry. I should know better. I know you would never do anything like that. I'm really sorry for thinking that. Will you forgive me?"

Cindy rolled over and told her, "Of course I forgive you. We've been friends forever. I'm not gonna let this come between us."

Deni rolled over and said, "Thanks. I don't want this to come between us either. I don't know what's going on with me, but whatever it is, I'm starting to get really worried. Do you think I need to see a doctor or something?"

Cindy looked at her, "I don't think it's that serious. I think you've just had a lot on your mind. We just need to sit out by the pool every chance we get and relax this summer."

Deni rolled over on her side and said, "I think you're right. Sitting out by the pool sounds really nice. I can't wait to get out there tomorrow."

Cindy mumbled something inaudible and was snoring before Deni went back to sleep. Deni turned on her ocean sounds and quickly went to sleep. She started dreaming about lying by the pool and getting a fantastic tan. At one point in the dream there was a guy who brought a tropical drink to her with an umbrella in it. Deni looked at the man and tried to tell him she was not old enough, but he reassured her that the drink had no alcohol in it. Deni took the drink from the tray, he stepped in front of her so she could see his face and saw that it was Jack. He had made her a fantastic tropical drink and brought it to her on a silver tray. Wow, what did she do to deserve this? She was in a bikini and Jack was there. She would never expose herself like that to a boy, let alone Jack.

She didn't recognize herself though. She looked so different lying there on the lounger. She realized that the pool she was sitting at didn't look like her pool. Where was she at? All she could do was look around to see if she recognized anything. Deni started getting up to explore her surroundings. She went into the building and saw Jack talking to someone who looked like a doctor. The doctor was telling him that she was going to be fine. She just needed to relax. Jack looked worried and turned around to catch Deni's eyes. Jack wandered over to her and told her to go relax by the pool, but all Deni could do was look around to try and remember where she was. She asked Jack where she was, and Jack told her everything was going to be okay. She just needed to go back to the pool and relax.

Deni woke up in a cold sweat and couldn't catch her breath. She recognized her room. That was a big relief to Deni. She saw Cindy lying there sleeping and looked at her clock—4:00 a.m. Deni got up to go to the bathroom to wash her face. She had the weirdest dream and was trying to make sense out of it. She was really shaken up by this dream. She went down to the kitchen to get a snack and saw her dad sitting on a bar stool.

He looked up when Deni approached. "What's up, kiddo? Couldn't sleep?"

Deni stumbled over to another stool and sat down. "No. I had a bad dream. I don't know what's been going on with me, Dad. Have you noticed anything different? I mean, I keep getting mad at Cindy and we have never had a fight. Yesterday we had a big fight at the mall. I can't believe I got so mad at her. I just had this feeling come over me that I couldn't control. I felt like I wanted to hit her or throw something at her. I wanted to tear that place apart. I was so mad. What's wrong with me?"

Stan hugged his daughter and said, "Deni, I know this is a stressful time in your life. I don't know what's going on with you. But I promise we will get to the bottom of this. I'm not gonna quit till I find out you are okay. I know you think I don't notice things around here. Sometimes I notice things before your mother does."

Deni looked up at her father, wiped her eyes, and said, "Mom knows. How come no one has said anything to me? How long have y'all known I was screwed up?"

"You are not screwed up, you hear me? You are just going through a tough time right now, that's all," Stan said. He just sat there hugging his daughter while she cried.

Deni finally was able to form words again and asked, "How long have y'all known? Why didn't y'all talk to me about my behavior? Dad, I feel so all alone."

Stan told her, "We have known for quite some time now that you haven't been yourself. We haven't said anything because we didn't want to upset you any more than you already are. We also didn't tell you because you were having a tough year, and this would just stress you out even more. We kept this from you to protect you. It wasn't to hurt you or anything like that. We kept this from you because we thought that it was just a phase you were going through and because we love you. I would never do anything to hurt you or cause you more stress. We talked to other parents, and we feel this is normal behavior for a girl your age. They assured us that you were just growing up and it would pass."

Deni looked at him. "Great, you told other people about this before you told me. How could you do that to me? Now people are gonna look at me like I'm a drug addict or something. I can't believe you would do this. Thanks a lot, Dad. Now I don't know who I can trust. It's like all y'all have turned against me. Why? That's all I want to know is why? Why did you feel you had to spread it around town that your daughter is losing her mind? Thank you very much for all the protection you've given me."

Stan looked at his daughter stunned and wondered where he had gone wrong. Suddenly she just turned into a raging maniac. What was really going on with his daughter? Now Stan saw what the others were talking about. Stan thought to himself, *What have I done?* He was going to have to fix this, but now he didn't know how.

Deni stomped up the stairs and slammed her bedroom door behind her. It was 4:30 a.m., but Deni didn't care; she was mad and she didn't care who knew it. She wanted people to know she was mad; she wanted to scream at all of them for going behind her back and talking to other parents. Now what if they told their kids and it got around school? She would be the laughing stock of the whole town. She was so mad. She just wanted to hit something. She put on her clothes and ran downstairs and out the front door. Stan ran after her, but Deni had grabbed her bike and was pedaling up the street. Stan was in his pj's, running down the street and yelling for her to stop, but all he heard was her screaming to leave her alone.

Stan went back to the house and woke Cathy up and told her what had happened. Cathy jumped up and got dressed as fast as she could. She ran out the front door and jumped in her car. Stan told her which way Deni was pedaling, and Cathy backed out of the driveway. Cindy heard all the commotion and came running downstairs. Stan told her what had happened and that Cathy was out looking for Deni right now. Cindy told him that she might know where she was headed.

"Does Cathy have her cell phone?" she asked Stan.

Stan said, "I think so. She usually keeps it in her purse."

Cindy started dialing the phone number, and Cathy answered on the first ring. "I think I know where she might be heading. Do you remember when we were little and we would ride down to the old bridge? Well, we would hide our bikes in the tall grass and sit under the bridge and hide from the passing cars. That was our secret place, and when we would get stressed, that place would always calm us down. Go to the old bridge," said Cindy.

Cathy hung up the phone and sped up to see if she could catch Deni, but Deni knew all the shortcuts to the bridge. Cathy finally arrived at the bridge and parked her car. She yelled for Deni, but there was no answer. She looked in the grass where Cindy had said they would hide their bikes and found Deni's bike. She looked under the bridge, but Deni wasn't there. *Oh God*, she prayed, *please let her be all right. I couldn't go on without her. Please don't take her from me, not now when I need her so much.*

Cathy heard a noise from behind her and saw Deni standing there in the tall grass, looking at her. The look she saw in Deni's eyes was frightening. She had never seen Deni look so mad. Deni ran at her and knocked her over. Cathy yelled at her, "What are you doing?"

Deni yelled back, "You betrayed me by talking to other parents about my problem. How could you? I trusted you. I can't believe you would do this to your own daughter."

Cathy got up and walked toward her daughter. "I can't believe you're acting like this. You will never touch me in that manner again, young lady. I don't know who you think you are, but you will never treat me like this again. Yes, your father asked some of his coworkers about their daughters, and they told him that their girls acted the same way. He thought he was trying to help you. He loves you so much. We love you so much. We couldn't stand to see you suffering like this. It drives us crazy not knowing what to do to help you. We don't know what's going on any more than you do. So calm down so we can talk about this. Okay?"

Deni was crying so hard by now that all she could do was crumple to the ground and bawl her eyes out. Cathy approached her with caution but soon realized that this was a little girl who needed her mother. Cathy sat down beside her daughter and hugged her. Deni leaned on her mother and told her she was sorry. She was crying so hard that Cathy could hardly make out what she was saying. Cathy told her it was going to be all right, and they were going to take her to the doctor Monday after school and have him check her. She told Deni that it was something she should have done a long time ago, and she was sorry that she didn't.

Deni felt so bad for raising a hand to her mother. She didn't know why she did that. This thing possessing her was out of hand. If this was normal behavior, she didn't want it anymore. She wanted to be abnormal, like she used to be.

Cathy sat there just holding and rocking her daughter. Cathy cried with her and told her everything that had been going on with her behavior. She also told Deni about Cindy noticing it and keeping a journal on her. She told her daughter about Jack knowing and offering to help out in any way and asked her to please not be mad at them for the concern they showed for her. She continued to tell her daughter how much her friends love her and that all that was going on was done out of love for her and to help her with this.

Deni promised she would not be mad at anyone if they all promised to not keep this from her anymore. Cathy promised her that they would not hide anything anymore and made Deni promise the same thing. She told her daughter that you don't get that mad unless you're harboring the feelings. They both pinkie swore that they would never keep secrets again, and then Cathy told her daughter to get in the car. Cathy put her bike in the trunk. She also told her daughter that she is grounded for a month. Deni agreed with that and said that she was going to ground herself an extra two weeks for coming after her mother like that. She apologized to her mother again for coming after her; she told her mother that she had felt so angry it was as if she had been possessed. She felt like she had lost herself and that the person who was doing all that weird stuff wasn't her. She felt like she was having an out-of-body experience. Cathy told her that sometimes people can get that mad but told Deni she didn't care if she was in her body or not—she was still grounded.

Cathy pulled up in the drive and saw Jack's truck there. She led Deni in the house with her arm around her. They walked into the kitchen and found everyone standing there, waiting for them to come home. Deni hugged her father and told him she was sorry.

Cathy explained, "I've told Deni everything. Everything including the journal that Cindy's been keeping, Jack's input on her behavior, and the meeting we were going to have tonight. We are taking Deni to the doctor Monday after school and getting her checked out. I've had all I can stand."

Deni stood there and apologized to her friends and parents. She hugged them all, and Jack gave her a kiss. Right there in the kitchen and right in front of her parents. Deni wasn't embarrassed by this. She kissed him back and told him she loved him. Jack told her he loved her too. Cathy also told them that Deni was grounded for the next month and that Deni had tacked on another two weeks. Cathy didn't elaborate on the incident but assured them everything was all right and that it was nothing to worry about.

Stan said to his daughter. "I'm so sorry I didn't have you at the doctor's office a long time ago. I'm so sorry that you had to have a meltdown to open our eyes. This will never happen again. Now what does everyone want for breakfast? I'm starving."

Jack stepped up then and said, "I'm sorry I didn't tell you about the journal and that we were watching you so close. We just didn't want this to happen and was doing our best to protect you. Also, Mr. Rosen, I'm sorry you had to see that kiss, but I can assure you that this was the first kiss Deni and I have ever had. And as far as breakfast, let the chef at the stove."

Stan shook Jack's hand and told him, "You know if you keep kissing my daughter like that, you might just have to marry her one day. But not till both of you are through college. Deal?"

Jack looked at him and held out his hand for Mr. Rosen to shake. "Deal."

Jack put on an apron and shooed them all out of the kitchen. Cindy went with Deni to her room and sat on the bed while Deni sat on the floor.

"What exactly happened out there?" she cautiously asked Deni.

Deni looked at her and tears started welling up again. "I attacked my mom. Can you believe that? I actually attacked my own mother. I don't know what came over me. I was downstairs talking to Dad, and then all of a sudden it's like I was taken over by an alien and was so mad all I could do was leave. I've never done that before."

Cindy sat there looking at Deni. "Wow. I never thought you would ever do anything to hurt anybody. Is she okay?"

Deni sat there crying. "She says she is, but I know deep down that she's not okay. How am I ever gonna make this up to her? I would never hurt anyone, let alone my own mother. It's like I was possessed or something. I don't like this feeling at all. I can't wait to see that doctor on Monday."

"Wow, you really are shook up if you are looking forward to seeing a doctor. I'm so sorry I didn't say anything before," she told Deni.

Deni wiped tears from her eyes and asked, "Can I see that journal? Maybe we can pinpoint when this started happening."

Cindy got up and got the journal out of her overnight bag and handed it to Deni. She said, "I think we may have already done that. You see, Cathy and I started noticing things happening the very day you got your hair colored for the first time. I don't know what that has to do with anything but you might mention that to the doctor on Monday."

Deni looked at her and said, "I won't have to because you're coming with me. I want you to tell him exactly what has been going on and let's just see what he says about all this. But for right now, let's go eat breakfast."

The both headed back downstairs and saw Jack preparing breakfast. They offered to help him. He poured them a cup of coffee and told them to sit down.

Cathy was in the bedroom with Stan, telling him everything that had happened out by the bridge. Stan got mad about Deni attacking Cathy. Cathy explained what she thought was happening to Deni and said she really thought a doctor could help. She said she had heard about girls doing this when they got that age and just needed to be on antidepressants. It was a simple pill that Deni would have to take at bedtime. She may not have to take it for the rest of her life, just till she got through this growing spurt. Cathy explained that their daughter was going through a lot. She was looking at graduating in August, two years ahead of the rest of the kids her age, and that was a lot to handle. Cathy could completely understand what Deni was going through and told Stan not to be mad at Deni. If anything, he should be mad at her for not doing what she wanted to do in the beginning—take Deni to the doctor. Stan assured his wife that he was not mad at anyone and was glad for Cathy. Glad that Cathy could understand what their daughter was going through and for being there for her. He also told Cathy how much he loved her and how much he loved Deni.

Chapter 19

Everyone met in the kitchen to eat the breakfast that Jack had so meticulously prepared. Deni was still so shocked at how Jack could have hidden such a talent. Jack was pouring coffee and making sure everyone had enough to eat that he had forgotten to eat. Deni made him sit down and waited on him for a change. Stan elbowed Cathy and told her to watch. Cathy just grinned and told Stan to quit staring.

Jack had told Deni he loved her, but the best part was that Deni had told him first. She was so afraid that her parents wouldn't agree with their relationship because of their age. Deni knew he was the one for her, and she didn't care about her age. All she knew was that she loved Jack and he loved her. Jack had also made a deal with her dad to marry her when they both got out of college. Wow, she just remembered that part. Does that mean she's engaged? Surely not. Her parents would never go for that. She was too young to be that attached to someone.

Deni and Cindy cleaned up the kitchen and went back upstairs to change clothes. The sun was up now, and it was already ninety degrees outside. Deni and Cindy put on their bathing suits and asked Jack if he had his with him. He told them he did and went to change. They went out beside the pool and started blowing up the floaties they had bought at Walmart. It seemed that it took forever to blow those things up, but once they did, it was time to get in the pool.

Deni jumped in first, followed by Jack and Cindy. The water was cold, but the girls didn't care. It was nice to them. It was getting hotter outside and the pool felt so good. Stan came out of the house and had on the most outrageous swimming trunks anyone had ever seen.

Deni covered her eyes. "Dad, what are those things?"

Stan stood there with his hands on his hips, so proud, and said, "These, my dear, are my swimming trunks. Don't you like them? I went yesterday and bought them."

Cindy and Jack were laughing so hard they almost drowned. Stan had on theses bright-pink and lime-green floral swim trunks. The base color on the shorts was a bright orange. They were so ugly that Deni thought they were just a joke, but she remembered seeing some like that at Walmart. That's where he got them, at Walmart.

Stan was still standing there so proud when Cathy came out the door wearing the new bathing suit Deni had bought for her. She had a towel wrapped around her and was embarrassed to take it off. She flashed Stan and he was shocked.

Cathy covered her eyes and threw a towel to Stan and told him to cover up. She told him those shorts were atrocious. How could he buy something like that? Cathy was embarrassed for him, but he stood there so proud that all they could do was laugh at him.

Stan told Deni to call all her friends and invite them over for a pool party and to be sure to bring their parents with them. He wanted help cooking for the masses. Jack stepped up for that one and told him he would help as much as he could. Deni looked at her father and reminded him that she was grounded. He told her what she did was very bad and that her grounding could start tomorrow, but for today they were having a pool party.

Deni called all her friends to come over for a pool party and to bring their parents. Jack and Stan threw on shirts and left to go to the store. Deni laughed because Jack had to go to the store with her father looking like a circus freak from the seventies. Jack was a little put off by the outfit Stan was wearing, but Stan didn't care about the shorts and put on a bright green shirt to make sure that he stood out as much as possible.

They got to the Pig-n-Tote and Homer met them at the door. He told Stan to stand outside to bring in help. Stan looked at him funny. Homer laughed and said, "I thought you were a neon sign. Isn't that the look you're going for? If it is, you certainly achieved it."

Stan laughed, saying, "No, I'm not a neon sign. Don't you have work to do? I can't believe you treat customers like this. Off with your head. Now be gone, peasant."

Homer looked at him with an odd look on his face. "Now you're a king. You have serious problems there, Rosen, serious problems."

Jack watched this exchange and tried to sneak past Stan, but Homer called after him and said, "Hey, Jack, you might want to try and ditch this guy somewhere and make sure you chain him in place so he doesn't come back."

Jack just held up his hands. "I don't have a dog in this race so, please, just let me go on about my business and get the stuff needed for the cookout."

Homer told him, "You can shop here, but you have to leave this thing in the car so it won't scare my customers."

Jack went about his business and tried to ditch him in the aisles. Stan kept running after him and yelling, "Don't you dare try and ditch me in here. If anyone sees Jack Wilson, please, stop him. He's my ride home. I want everyone to know that I am here with Jack Wilson."

Jack was trying to find the bathroom so he could hide in there for a while. Homer went in his office and got on the intercom, announcing, "Please do not use the restrooms, they are out of order for the next hour for cleaning."

Jack saw him looming in his office high above the cash registers and shook his fist at him. He went to the meat counter to check out the steaks. Stan finally sauntered up beside Jack and hit him on the back. Speaking as loud as he could possibly talk without shouting, he said, "Boy, this stuff looks mighty good. Whatcha think we need to pick up for all them there peoples comin' over? I wasa thinking maybe about them there steaks or some of them ribs. Whatcha think, Jack?"

Jack noticed that Stan was standing there rubbing his belly, which he had stuck out the whole time he was talking. This has got to be the most embarrassing moment of Jack's life. Stan was a cut up but this was downright embarrassing.

Jack tried to reply, "Can you keep it down and just be normal, please?"

Stan slapped Jack's back again and said, "Boy, speak up. I can't hear a dern thing yer sayin'. What's that again?"

Jack just hung his head in shame and tried to get out as soon as possible. All Jack could do was point. Stan finally told the butcher to get the rib eye steaks and some ground sirloin. The butcher got his order ready and handed Stan the steaks. The butcher knew Stan very well and laughed the whole time Stan was standing there. He knew that Jack was Deni's boyfriend and knew what Stan was trying to do but tried not to encourage Stan in any way. Jack had obviously been humiliated enough.

They walked to the front of the store, and Jack ran out into the parking lot. When Stan finally emerged from the store, Jack was leaning on the side of the car. Stan unlocked the car, and Jack got in, sinking as low in the seat as possible. Stan was continuing to walk and talk like he was from the furthest reaches of civilization and doing a great impression.

Stan got in the car laughing and told Jack that he had done a great job in there and to please forgive him for making a fool of himself. "If I have to wear this stupid getup then I guess I'll be the one to make fun of it first, or at least the person wearing it."

Jack told him it was okay and that he knew what he was doing. Jack tried to play everything off, but Stan knew he had embarrassed Jack. Jack could not wait to get home and tell Deni what her father had done at the store and how Homer played along with it all. Jack did tell Stan to just get prepared for the revenge humiliation of his lifetime. "When you least expect it, expect it," he told Stan. Stan looked at him and simply told Jack to bring it on.

They got to the house and noticed some people were starting to show up, so they quickly unloaded the car and Jack went to work in the kitchen. He wanted to try and marinade the steaks for a bit and to pat out the hamburgers and put them in the fridge. He also wanted to prepare a special dip for the chips they had bought.

Deni was still in the pool, greeting all her friends as they jumped into the cool water. Cindy was there with floaties, and all the girls got on the floaties to tan and float around the pool. The only problem with that was that Stan thought the girls could use some cooling off. He did a cannonball dive and splashed them all. The girls yelled and screamed, telling him to get out. Cathy just stood back, laughing. Stan grabbed one of the games the girls had picked up for the pool and asked how many people wanted to play. The girls decided it was time to get out and see how soft their skin was. After all, this was a saltwater pool. Deni had definitely done her research on this subject, and the girls were so shocked that their skins were not dried out.

Stan finally got out of the pool and told the girls they could have it back. The girls were so happy they all jumped in at once. Jack came out to the patio and greeted everyone and immediately went to the grill. He started the coals and left to go back into the kitchen. Jack wanted to prepare the dish of chips and dip to serve. He wanted to make other platters to serve as appetizers and to help tide people over before the main course.

Deni was having so much fun that she had totally forgotten all the events of the morning. She and Cathy were back on good terms. She thought that her mother would never forgive her. Deni couldn't figure out how her mother had forgiven her so fast. See, what Deni didn't know was the power of a mother's love. Mothers love their children so much that they could forgive them for almost anything. A child may hurt her mother and make her question how she raised her child sometimes, but a mother's love is unconditional. Deni will later learn this when she has her own children.

Cathy stood visiting with her friends and didn't even know that Deni was still thinking about those events. She looked at her daughter and was trying to figure out what had made her daughter act in such a way. Deni had never been that angry about anything. Deni had never been angry enough to hurt a fly. Why now? What has happened to cause this kind of behavior? Cathy was determined to figure out what was going on and see what the doctor had to say.

Jack came through the sliding glass doors with two platters in his hands. He sat them down on the picnic table and went back in to get another one. He came back out with another platter in hand and with the meat for the grill. He sat the appetizers on the table and went to the grill. He loved cooking and loved these kinds of gatherings. He was with people that he really cared about and a young woman who he has true feelings about. For the first time in Jack's life, he was falling in love and with a girl who was soon to be sixteen. What was he thinking? If they found out the truth about all this, he would not only lose his love but lose the people he cared so much about.

Deni watched Jack as he was preparing the food and couldn't help but think of him saying he loved her this morning. Was he nuts? He said that right in front of her parents and didn't think anything about it. Deni had also told him she loved him but now was having second thoughts. She didn't even know what love was and couldn't really tell if this was love she was feeling or just a strong like. This was going to take some time. Maybe Mamaw could help her.

Jack cooked the meat to perfection and put the platter on the table. Cathy and Ruth had set the table and were waiting for the meat to finish cooking. Jack went in to bring out the rest of the food, which included his world-famous potato salad. He had made a potato salad with dill and capers along with other secret ingredients. He sat all the food on the table and took his seat. He started passing around the food and remembered he had forgotten a few things. He got up to go to the kitchen to get the rest of the things for the table. He had made a dipping sauce for the meat and rolls for the feast. He brought them out, and everyone was so busy eating they didn't even notice that he had left.

Jack took a seat beside Deni and kissed her forehead. Cathy nudged Ruth and they both smiled. This was the best for the moms; they loved that their kids were so close, and Ruth looked forward to seeing her son with someone so special. Ruth had never seen Jack so happy. She had seen her son date girls in the past but had never seen him this serious about a girl in his life. Ruth could only think about what would happen if everyone finds out the truth about her son. Would she continue to be friends with any of these people?

They all raved over how tender the meat was. The taste was just too good to describe. Jack could certainly cook, and he enjoyed seeing people eat. He could not get over how easy it was to make people happy with just a good meal. He loved having the ability to make people happy and savored the camaraderie. He loved having friends like this and loved living in Oklahoma.

The party was winding down, and the girls were starting to get tired. Deni was just getting out of the shower and went looking for Cindy. She had asked Cindy to stay with her today and to go to the doctor with her after school tomorrow. She wanted Cindy to be there to be able to tell the doctor exactly what had been happening. Cindy was in Deni's room looking on the computer for anything regarding the rage that Deni had been experiencing. She had found that there are a number of problems that could cause this, such as depression, bipolar disorder, ADD, ADHD, intermittent explosive disorder (IED), and countless other disorders. Thinking of all the disorders that Deni could have developed in such a short time was giving her a headache.

Deni asked, "What are you looking up?"

Cindy quickly closed the web browser and replied, "Nothing. You scared me. Where have you been?"

"In the shower. Why? What were you looking up on the Internet? It looked like you were pretty involved," said Deni.

"Nah, just looking at the next gossip rag coming out. I think I'll go jump in the shower," said Cindy.

Cindy gathered her stuff and headed down the hall. Deni was still drying her hair and wanted to see what Cindy was so involved in on the computer. She waited till she heard the shower going before pulling up the history on her computer. She saw that Cindy was checking out rage problems. *What was she doing looking that up?* Deni thought and then got really mad at Cindy for thinking she had a disorder of some kind. She was certainly going to confront Cindy about this, and she was going to do it now.

Deni stormed into the bathroom and demanded Cindy to tell her why she was looking up those disorders. Why would she be looking that up?

Deni demanded, "Do you honestly think there is something wrong with me? I can't believe this, my best friend, thinking that I have some kind of disorder. I am not crazy, I'm just really mad."

Cindy replied, "Deni, look at you. This is not like you. This is what makes us think you have developed some kind of disorder. I was just trying to help, we all are, and you're too *mad* all the time to realize that. There is something wrong with you, and I wanted to try and figure out what's wrong. So sue me for trying to be a good friend and trying to help you."

Deni was starting to calm down now and was listening to Cindy. She started crying and turned and walked out the door. She went to her room and bawled her eyes out. Cindy found her lying across the bed, crying in her pillow. Cindy sat down next to her and tried to console her but was afraid to move. Deni was so touchy that Cindy was becoming a little afraid to say anything to her.

Cindy tried to console her friend. "Deni, I'm sorry if I upset you. I was just trying to help. I am concerned about you and just want to find out what's wrong. I love you so much and don't like to see you this way."

Deni rolled over. "I know. I don't know what's wrong with me. I can't stand this. I can't believe that I got so mad about all this. It's like I can't control it, like I'm having an out-of-body experience, you know. It's a little scary."

Cindy could do nothing but hug Deni and pray for the best. The girls were exhausted from the day they had. Deni went to bed with her hair still wet. Cindy went downstairs to get something to drink and saw Cathy sitting at the bar. Cathy asked if everything was okay, but Cindy just started crying.

Cindy sat down and told Cathy everything that had happened upstairs and how mad Deni got. She also told Cathy what Deni had said about the out-of-control feeling she had when she got mad and how everything was scary. Cathy held Cindy and gave her a drink of water. Cindy was starting to calm down and went upstairs. She went to bed and fell fast asleep. She had a dream about the doctor telling Deni that she was going to have to go into the hospital for further testing and that he thought that Deni had a serious brain condition. Cindy woke up crying and yelling for Deni to not go.

The next morning Cindy woke up exhausted. She didn't know how she was going to get through the day. This was the first day of summer school, and she needed to be on her toes. She went to take a shower, and hopefully she would wake up. She met Deni downstairs and saw Jack in the kitchen eating breakfast with Deni. She pulled up a stool and Cathy handed her a plate. Cathy asked if she was all right but Cindy was still exhausted. Cindy ate what she could and left to go to school.

Jack pulled up and found a parking spot right up front. There are only a few kids who attend summer school, and most of them attend to graduate early. Most kids spend their summers at the lake or goofing off. Deni was never that way and was so proud that the school offered her this opportunity.

They got to Mr. Foltz's class and took their seats. Mr. Foltz came in and introduced himself to the class and began the roll call. He told the class what he expected out of them this summer. Jack raised his hand to asked to go to the bathroom.

"May I go to the bathroom?" asked Jack.

Mr. Foltz told him, "Sure, come get the hall pass." He pulled out a large toilet seat that had been painted gold. Jack looked at him curiously.

Mr. Foltz said, "How bad do you need to go? This is the hall pass and make sure you bring it back."

Jack looked at him and said, "I don't have to go that bad." He sat down and told Deni that he couldn't believe that Mr. Foltz had spray painted a toilet seat for his hall pass. Deni was laughing so hard that she could hardly stand it. Jack had heard things about Mr. Foltz's class but had never seen or heard anything like this about him. Deni and Cindy were still laughing so hard that they couldn't talk to him about the toilet seat right now. Jack sat in an embarrassed slump and tried to get past this little moment.

Mr. Foltz was explaining the syllabus for the class and asking if anyone had any questions. No one raised their hand for fear that Mr. Foltz would bring them to the front of the class and pull something else out from under his desk.

Mr. Foltz handed out the books and told them to read the first chapter tonight. Then do the assignment at the end of the chapter and hand it in on Wednesday. Then he dismissed class. Deni and Cindy walked over to the track at the football field and met up with Ms. Myers. She had them all run the bleachers and run ten laps around the football field. The football team was practicing the whole time the class was running. Deni felt so self-conscious about the football players watching them, and some of the players were making comments and yelling at them. One guy whistled when the class ran by and Cindy almost fell.

They finally got through PE class and Jack picked them up for the drive home. He told them that Ms. Myers had put them through some pretty harsh drills today. He said he had heard that she was pretty easy but had no idea that she would have them doing all that in this kind of heat. Deni and Cindy were exhausted and couldn't wait to get home and jump into the pool, but Deni had a doctor's appointment.

They got home, and Cathy told Deni that her appointment was made for tomorrow. "The doctor didn't have any openings for today, so I had to make it for tomorrow at eleven," Cathy said.

Deni was so happy about it she ran upstairs and put on her bathing suit and jumped into the pool to cool off. Cindy was right behind her and jumped in the shallow end. Jack ran to his truck to get his bathing trunks and also jumped into the pool. Cathy watched as one by one the kids ran through her house and jumped into the pool. Cathy got caught up in the excitement and ran upstairs to put on her bathing suit. She ran outside, and all the kids looked at her, wondering what she was doing. Cathy ran to the deep end and jumped in, splashing the kids. Deni got the lounge floaties out, and all three girls picked out which one they wanted and jumped on to start tanning.

Jack was laughing at them and decided to work on his tan too. They were all floating around the pool and almost fell asleep on them. They all turned over at the same time and splashed water on themselves to help cool them off. Jack followed suit and turned over. Jack thought he heard the doorbell ring but wasn't sure. He heard a noise and got out of the pool to check it out, when he ran into Mamaw and Alphie coming through the sliding glass door.

Jack and Mamaw were startled, and Alphie barked his little bark at Jack. Mamaw put him down and he ran to Deni in the pool. He hit the water and sank. Deni was shocked that the little dog couldn't swim and grabbed the dog before he hit bottom. She brought him up to the surface to see if the dog was okay. Deni thought all dogs could swim. Mamaw was throwing a fit because she saw her little baby sink and almost drown. She grabbed him and grabbed a towel to wrap him in.

She inspected him from head to toe and made sure he was okay before putting him down again. He immediately ran over to Deni, who was still in the pool, and slid to a stop before hitting the water.

Deni grabbed him and slowly took him to her floatie. She put Alphie on her stomach to see what he would do, and Alphie just laid down to take a nap. Deni couldn't believe he wanted back in the water after almost drowning. He didn't seem to mind though because he was with Deni.

Mamaw stood there and watched Alphie like a hawk to see what he was going to do. When she saw that he just wanted to be with Deni, she smiled. She told Jack she was sorry for scaring him, but she didn't get an answer when she rang the doorbell so she let herself in. She knew they were probably in the pool and couldn't hear her so she just headed to the back.

Jack told her he was sorry too and that he would be sure to check next time before running through the house. Mamaw also apologized to Cathy for just coming in. Cathy told her it was okay and that she was sorry she didn't hear the doorbell.

Cathy got out of the pool when she saw Mamaw come through the sliding glass door and offered her a chair. She also offered her something to drink. Mamaw told her she wanted sweet tea. Cathy went in to get the drinks, and when she returned, she heard Deni asking Mamaw if she could come spend some time with her tomorrow after seeing the doctor. Mamaw told her she didn't have to ask to come see her. All she had to do was show up. Deni thanked her and told her she would be there at about 1:00 p.m. and asked if she needed to bring anything. Mamaw said no and that she would be waiting for her.

Cathy gave her the tea and sat down to talk to Mamaw. "So what's been going on in your busy life?"

Mamaw laughed and replied, "I'm not busy. I just take care of Alphie and visit with Orville. But I am here on a mission. Orville wanted to know if it was okay for the kids to come down for the weekend and help him on the farm. I know you need to talk to Stan about it so just let me know before the weekend. Deni, did you say you have to go to the doctor tomorrow? I hope nothing's wrong."

Deni told her, "No, I just have to go in for a checkup."

Mamaw told her, "Good, but I'll pray anyway that everything turns out okay. Well, I better get going and get this little stink home for his supper." She had walked over to the pool and picked up Alphie and rubbed his head. Alphie licked Mamaw on the chin and almost jumped out of her arms again.

Cathy and the kids said good-bye to Mamaw, and Jack went in to fix everyone a snack. Cathy sat by the pool with her daughters and wondered why Deni was going to talk to Mamaw instead of talking to her. She remembered when she was a girl and wanted to talk to someone like Mamaw about things. She tried to shake off the feeling that Deni was growing apart from her. She also knew that whatever Deni needed to talk to Mamaw about, Mamaw would give her good advice. She shouldn't worry but was because it was her daughter.

Jack brought out the snacks and everyone sat at the table eating. Deni was still laughing at Alphie almost drowning. It wasn't funny when it happened, but now it was a little funny because he couldn't swim. She asked Jack if they made life jackets for dogs and where she could get one. Jack told her that he thought they had them at Walmart and asked if she wanted to go later. Deni said she did and finished eating the sandwiches that Jack had made.

Chapter 20

Stan came home from work and asked Deni about her first day of summer school. Deni told him it was good and had to tell him the story about Mr. Foltz's hall pass. She told her father about Jack asking to go to the bathroom and the pass that Mr. Foltz had given Jack and how embarrassed he was.

Stan laughed and told Deni to make sure to ask Mr. Foltz where he got that pass because he wanted to get one to tease Jack with. Deni said no and told her father that he was being a meanie.

Cathy told Stan, "Mamaw came by today and asked if the kids could go spend the weekend at Orville's farm. She said Orville had asked her to ask us if they could come help out. What do you think?"

Stan studied this for a moment and turned to the girls. "Well, what do you two want to do?"

Both girls thought this was a good idea. "I want to go for the weekend. I like Orville and think he is a nice man. I think it will be fun," said Cindy.

Deni agreed with Cindy, saying, "Yeah, but it sure is gonna be hot. I wish we could take the pool with us."

They all chuckled. Stan said that Orville had a pond out there for them to swim in if it got too hot. The girls curled up their noses at the thought of swimming in a dirty pond. All Deni could think of were turtles biting her toes.

They all decided it was a good idea for the girls to go to Orville's for the weekend, and Deni told them she would tell Mamaw tomorrow. Cindy called her mom to let her know what was going on for the weekend, and Sam told her that Mamaw had called her and asked earlier. Sam thought that it would be okay for her to go with Deni and learn more about farm life. Cindy didn't want to let herself get excited over it till later in the week, but she couldn't help herself.

They finished supper and all went into the living room to watch TV. Deni was getting excited for the weekend now and couldn't wait to see Orville's farm. Deni wanted to see how Alphie was going to be at the farm. She didn't know Alphie had been there every week and that he loved going to Orville's farm because he had other dogs to play with and chickens to chase.

The next morning, Deni got up bright and early to get ready to go to the doctor. She was a little nervous and didn't know what to expect today. She woke Cindy up to get ready, and Cindy was slow to respond but got up and took a shower. Deni went downstairs to find her mother sitting at the bar, reading the paper.

"Aren't you gonna get ready? Mom, hello. Are you awake? Please, get up and get ready. We don't have time to be dragging this morning," said Deni in a rush.

Cathy looked up at her daughter and smiled. "Yes, dear, I am awake, and slow down. There is plenty of time to get ready. It's only seven o'clock. What are you doing up so early anyway?"

"Mom, please, this is so important to me. I feel like today I'm gonna find out what's wrong with me. Cindy looked on the computer last night to research what is possibly going on with me. There were some things on there that really upset me. I just don't want any of those things to happen to me. Mom, some of those things are really scary. I just want to get there early to see if the doctor can get me in and find out what's going on," replied Deni.

Cathy looked at her daughter with concern and said, "I know, sweetheart. I want to find out too. Sometimes it doesn't pay to research things on that darned computer. When are you gonna learn that sometimes that thing can be wrong or misleading? I hope and pray that there is nothing wrong with you. I think you are just a normal teenage girl going through a rough time and it's stressing you out."

Deni replied, "Yeah, I guess. I hope that's all it is, I really do. I'm just really scared."

Cathy hugged her daughter and told her everything was going to be fine. She got up to start fixing breakfast and asked Deni what she wanted to eat. Deni thought for a moment but couldn't make up her mind. She told her mother it didn't matter what she made, she didn't think she could eat. Cathy told her she would make her favorite breakfast and knew she would eat that.

After breakfast they all cleaned up the kitchen, and Deni had to wait for her mom to get ready. She went out to the pool and used the skimmer to get the leaves out. She had to do something to keep her mind busy. She took care of the pool and washed off the patio and then sat there waiting for her mother. Cathy finally came downstairs and found Deni on the patio, pacing.

Cathy told her daughter to get in the car so they could leave, and Deni practically ran through the house. Cathy and Cindy followed and drove downtown. They found a spot to park right in front of the building. Deni walked into the office and told the receptionist she was there. The receptionist asked her to sit down. Deni had to wait even longer now. Deni had a hard time sitting still and had grabbed every magazine in the office and tried to read. Finally, the nurse came to the door and announced that the doctor was ready for her. Deni followed the nurse to the room and sat there waiting again.

"What is with doctor's offices? They make you an appointment and you never get in at that time. They make you wait and wait. Why tell people to be here at a certain time if you're not going to see them at that time," complained Deni.

Cathy and Cindy laughed secretly and Cathy just shook her head. The doctor came in and shook Deni's hand and sat down on his little stool.

"What can I do for you today, Miss Deni?" asked her doctor.

Deni got so nervous that she couldn't remember what she was there for. She was looking at her mother in a panic now and wondering why she was there.

Cathy spoke up and told the doctor everything that had been going on. She told the doctor that the latest problem had been the rage that Deni was experiencing. Cindy spoke up and told him that she had been keeping a journal and handed the journal to the doctor. Dr. Belle Mahoney took the journal and thumbed through it. She could see that there was more than one person writing in this journal and asked who the other person was that had been helping with the journal. Cindy told her about Deni's boyfriend, Jack.

Dr. Mahoney continued to listen to everything and looked at Deni. She got up to start her examination, and Deni stopped her. She wanted to explain what was going on and how it made her feel when these things would happen. Dr. Mahoney listened intently and then went about examining Deni. She went through the usual routine of listening to Deni's lungs, heart, and stomach and examining it for any tender areas. She looked in Deni's ears, nose, and mouth and then sat back down on her stool.

She looked at Deni and Cathy and then spoke. "I'm not sure what's going on because her exam was fine. I want to do a series of blood tests and see if anything shows up there. Some of the symptoms you are describing to me are indicative of teenage depression. I want to start you on an antidepressant and see if that helps alleviate some of the problems."

Cathy asked, "What drug are we talking about here and how much?"

Dr. Belle Mahoney answered, "I think I want to start her out on one of our new drugs at a very low dose and gradually increase if necessary. I have some samples I'll give you to see if this works."

Cathy thanked her for all she had done and waited till the doctor returned with the samples. Dr. Belle, as Deni called her, told Deni to make a return appointment in six weeks for a recheck. Deni thanked her and hopped off the exam table to leave. Dr. Belle asked Cindy if she could keep the journal until the return appointment. Cindy gave it back to the doctor and they all left. They stopped and made the return appointment and left the office.

Cathy made it home in time for Deni to go see Mamaw. Deni left as soon as they came home and walked the two houses to Mamaw's house.

When she got there, she saw Mamaw holding Alphie and waiting at the door. Mamaw opened the door to let Deni in, and Alphie jumped out of Mamaw's arms into Deni's. He made his way up to her face and licked her chin. His little tail was wagging so fast it looked like he was having a seizure.

Mamaw led her into the living room and offered her something to drink. Deni told her she wanted sweet tea and played with Alphie while Mamaw got the tea.

"Well now, this is a special treat for me. I love having company and especially the kind where all we do is talk. What can I do for you, sweetheart?" asked Mamaw.

Deni put Alphie down on the floor and turned to Mamaw. "I've been having some problems and wanted to talk to you about them. I've talked to my mom, but you know how that is—she's my mom and has to say certain things. I just want to know if she went through this and how long it took her to get over it."

Mamaw told her, "Well, I'm here so ask away. I'll give you straight answers if that's what you want, but I must warn you, these answers may not be what you want to hear."

Deni looked her straight in the eye and said, "I know that but I want to know the truth. I started having problems with forgetting things last summer. Then when school started, I had to drop my honors classes. I had a little trouble with my classes this year and had to ask for help. Now I'm starting to have problems with anger. I don't know what it is, but when I get mad, I completely lose it. It's like I don't even know what I'm doing. I attacked my mom over the weekend because I got so mad. Is any of this making sense to you or am I just losing my mind?"

Mamaw sat her tea on the table and replied, "I do know what you're talking about, and yes, every teenage girl goes through this. I don't know about attacking your mother but we'll cover that. When I was a teenager, I had this phase that I went through where I was just mad at everyone. I couldn't understand why everyone was getting on my nerves so bad and then I just stopped one day. I was so mad all the time that I almost lost my friends. Now about attacking your mom, that's something that is never okay to do. I don't care how mad you get. You should never attack your mom. I know you were mad, and one thing you have to do is when you feel yourself starting to get upset, think about what made you mad. Is it worth getting mad over? Or is it something that you should be getting mad over? If it is something to get mad about, you have to sit down and talk yourself into calming down and thinking about what you're going to say. Don't go overboard. Is any of this helping?"

Deni nodded her head and told her, "I was hoping I wasn't the only one going through this. How'd y'all come out of it? Dr. Belle put me on medicine today for depression and said that might help. She wants me back in six weeks to check on me. What do you think?"

Mamaw replied, "I wish they'd had that when I was a kid. Maybe it would have helped to have some medication. I think it's a great idea. How do you feel about it?"

Deni told her, "I'm not sure yet. I don't know how I should feel about any of this. I just don't feel right and don't know how to fix it."

Mamaw hugged her and said, "I know you don't, but maybe this will fix everything that's been going on. Just think positive about it and it will help."

Deni hugged Mamaw and asked, "Can I talk to you about another problem I'm having?"

Mamaw said, "Of course, you can talk to me about anything. You know that."

Deni started right in. "Jack told me the other day that he loved me. Without thinking, I told him that too. The only problem is I'm not sure I do love him. I'm not sure I even know what love is."

Mamaw told her, "I know what love is. It's when you can't stand to be away from someone longer than a minute. Love is when you see that person's face everywhere you look. It's when no one, I mean no one, can tell you that you are too young to care for that person. It's when you see that person and your palms start to sweat, your heart races, and your whole world is turned upside down. That's what love is like. Is that how it is for you?"

Deni thought for a moment. "Yeah, I guess it is. When I'm not with Jack, I wonder what he's doin'. Is he thinking of me as much as I am him? I wonder how he feels about everything and wonder what he would do in situations. I guess I do care more for him than I thought. Thank you so much for talking to me. I feel so much better."

Mamaw gave her another hug and told her, "You are so welcome. Don't be afraid to come talk to me about anything. Whatever is said in this house stays in this house. Is that understood? Whatever we talk about is between us. I'm proud of you and love you very much."

Deni told Mamaw she loved her too, and then they went into the kitchen to make something for lunch. Mamaw had made some homemade bread that morning while Deni was at the doctor's, and she had fresh-baked ham sitting on the stove. Deni asked what all this stuff was, and Mamaw told her she cooks when she gets nervous or worried about anything. Deni said she hated to see Mamaw upset but at the same time was glad that she was baking.

They made sandwiches, and Mamaw had potato salad in the fridge to go with them. She poured more tea for them and sat down next to Deni. Deni kept talking about different things throughout the lunch, and Mamaw listened intently. They finished their lunch and Deni helped clean the dishes.

Deni left to walk home, and Mamaw immediately called Cathy to let her know that everything was okay. She didn't tell Cathy anything that Deni had talked about but told her that everything was okay now. Deni walked home feeling like a load had been lifted off her and decided to call Jack as soon as she got home.

Deni walked into the kitchen to find Jack there eating lunch with her mother. Cathy had already filled him in on what the doctor had said and showed him the medication Dr. Belle had given them. Deni walked in and kissed Jack straight on the lips.

Cathy interrupted them. "I will not have any of that in my house. You two are too young to start that kind of nonsense and right in front of your mother."

Deni turned around and said, "I'm sorry, Mom, but I just had to check something out. Technically, that was an experiment."

Cathy told her daughter, "I don't care what it is. You will not be doing that in my house. Is that understood?"

Deni and Jack both understood clearly and told her they were sorry. Cathy accepted that and told them to go change into their bathing suits and meet her at the pool. Everyone changed and met Cathy at the pool. Cathy had a surprise for them and was happy to show them the floaties that she had gotten. Cathy had called Mamaw while the others changed and asked her to bring Alphie. Cathy told Mamaw to meet them at the pool. Mamaw walked up behind the girls with Alphie in her arms. Cathy uncovered a floatie for Mamaw and a life jacket for Alphie. Mamaw's floatie had a little pocket in it for Alphie, and his life jacket matched the floatie.

"Where did you get this?" asked Cindy.

"I went to the pet store and saw them last week. They are special order, so I ordered one for Mamaw and Alphie," replied Cathy as she scratched Alphie's belly.

"How did you know that Alphie couldn't swim though?" asked Mamaw.

"I didn't really. I just went and picked up the life jacket, and it happened to match the floatie," replied Cathy.

Jack was impressed with the pool products they had available now and started putting the life jacket on Alphie. Alphie was so excited and was wiggling so fast that Jack could barely put the thing on him.

Mamaw went in to put on her bathing suit while Alphie was busy trying to fit into his pocket. Mamaw emerged from the house in a beautiful one-piece bathing suit that really flattered her figure. She got on the floatie with such ease. Jack handed Alphie to her. He fit perfectly in the pocket of the floatie, and Mamaw took off floating around the pool. It felt so good on this nice hot day. The heat index today was supposed to be 112.

Cathy told the kids to not get in the pool yet because she had one more surprise to reveal. She had really gone all out on this surprise thing. She went and got a slide to put up next to the pool. The kids were so excited to see the slide. Jack went to the shed to get the tools to install the slide. He found everything he needed and went to the side of the pool to start work. The pool contractor had already installed bolts for the slide, and all Jack had to do was put the slide on them and bolt it down.

Cathy helped him as much as she could, and they got the slide installed. Cathy hooked up the hose to the slide, and it was up and running. Cathy was the first to go down the slide. She had so much fun on the thing that she just kept going down the slide. Mamaw was having a blast watching the kids, including Cathy, go down the slide and make a big splash. Alphie watched as they went in, and every time they would hit the water, Alphie would cover his eyes and hide his head. Everyone got a big laugh out of how smart Alphie was and how he always hid his eyes.

The afternoon was filled with so much fun in the pool. By the time they got out, they were all burned to a crisp. Mamaw was the only one not burned, and Alphie was just along for the ride. Mamaw pulled out the blister cream and started smearing it on the kids. Cathy definitely got the worst of it all. She was so red that Mamaw was afraid that Cathy might need to see someone for the severe burns. There wasn't going to be any more fun in the sun for them this week. It would take a while for them to get over their sunburns.

Stan came in and saw how everyone was burned and took over for Mamaw. Now it was Stan's job to smear the blister cream on each of them. Deni wasn't that bad, but the rest were awfully burned. Mamaw took Alphie home to get him his supper. She asked if there was anything else she could do for them, but they all said no and sent her on her way.

Stan went in to call Roscoe's Pizzeria to have a pizza delivered and needed to take Jack home. Jack had ridden his bike over and was unable to ride his bike back home since his legs were so burned. Jack could barely sit down in Stan's truck and tolerate the ride home. Stan dropped him off and hurried home. He got there just as the pizza delivery man was walking up to the door. Stan paid the man for the pizza and took it into the house for all the red babies, as Stan called them, to eat.

The red babies were in so much pain they were sorry they spent so much time in the pool now. Cathy made a mental note to buy sunscreen and told the girls to try and take a cold shower to help the sunburn. The girls ate and went upstairs to take the showers. They all were moaning and groaning as they went up the stairs, and as the water hit their sunburned skin they would scream.

The weekend was rolling around, and they were gearing up to go to Orville's farm. Cindy called Mamaw to see what she should pack, and Mamaw told her to pack something that was old and wouldn't matter if it got dirty. She did tell Cindy that Orville had livestock on his farm so she should make sure to pack some old boots they could stuff their pants down into. Mamaw also told Cindy to be sure and tell the others to pack the same, and she would be by to pick them up at around 7:00 p.m. Friday night. Cindy said she would tell them and thanked Mamaw.

The girls told their parents what Mamaw had said and started packing for the trip. Deni had to pull out old clothes that she hadn't worn in over a year. As she pulled them out, she stood there looking at the clothes like they were from another era. Cindy asked what she was looking at, and Deni just started laughing. Deni told her to look at the clothes she used to wear and asked Cindy why she let her wear those awful things. Cindy laughed and pulled out Deni's favorite shirt. She told Deni she didn't know why she let her wear that stuff, but it happened.

Deni got all her clothes together and was ready to go. She and Cindy worked on her their homework and would have to take their homework with them to Orville's over the weekend. Deni said she hopes Orville is good at math because she was going to need help. Cindy agreed with her and they both started to work. They finished the homework around 10:00 p.m. and got ready for bed. Mr. Foltz was really loading them up with homework, and she couldn't figure out why, but she knew that they had to get everything in over the summer to be able to graduate.

School was okay the next morning, and Mr. Foltz told them the usual about homework, except this time he gave them four chapters to do over the weekend. Deni was just exhausted from all this work and asked Jack if he had any problems doing all the work. Jack said he had a little and asked if they knew anything about how good Orville was with math. The girls laughed and said no but was thinking the same thing last night. The girls made it through PE okay and found they were not as tired following the drills as they used to be at the start of class.

Jack gave them a ride home and went in to see Cathy before heading to his house to finish packing. He told Deni that if she wanted to ride with him to Orville's that she would be more than welcome and proceeded to tell her that he was taking his truck with him so he could do errands for Orville during the day. Deni told him that it would be nice but said she would ride with Mamaw in her Mustang convertible. Jack laughed and said he had figured that she would ride with Mamaw.

The girls had just finished supper when Mamaw knocked on the door. The girls ran to the door to let her in and were met by Jack. He had just driven up and decided to wait there for Mamaw to pick up the girls, and he would just follow her from Deni's house. Mamaw came up behind Jack with Alphie in her arms, and Alphie almost got away again, jumping for Deni. Deni caught him just in time. She was used to Alphie jumping for her and was prepared this time. Mamaw laughed and said she had to make sure she kept a firmer grip on him from now on. The girls let Jack put the bags in his truck and loaded up with Mamaw. She took off with the tires squealing while Stan stood there shaking his head at her. You could hear the girls laughing a mile away at Mamaw squalling the tires.

Orville was waiting for them at the gate and waved as Mamaw came through. He knew that Mamaw drove fast and was a speed demon but had no idea that she was even worse with the girls in the car. He heard the car coming and the girls laughing before they even got there. He was laughing at the girls and was glad to see that Jack had driven his truck up there. He had some hauling that needed to be done and wanted Jack to help him. Orville closed the gate and joined everyone on the porch. He was so glad to see the kids. The kids were happy to see Orville and gave him a great big hug. Orville was so overwhelmed by the greeting that he started to tear up.

He told them that he had a surprise for them and opened the door to a living room full of people. Mamaw was so surprised to see them and started hugging everyone in the room. Everyone who was in there knew Mamaw and was trying to hold Alphie, who was jumping from one person to the other. Deni, Cindy, and Jack walked in and stood there. They didn't know what to say, so Orville starting making the introductions.

"This here is my daughter, Janet. She came to spend the summer with me. She hasn't been able to do that since the girls were babes. This is Micah, Mel, and Lissa. These are my granddaughters. Girls, this is Deni, Cindy, and Jack. These are kids that live close to Mamaw—oh what the, these are Mamaw's grandkids."

Deni, Cindy, and Jack all stepped forward to shake their hands and to try and get to know the girls. They found out that the girls were their age. Janet had triplets—no wonder she hasn't been able to come visit. Orville explained that this is the reason he asked us out.

"I was wonderin' if young'uns wouldn't mind showin' them around a bit and showin'em what the kids do here," said Orville.

"Of course we can. We can take you to the mall tomorrow and see a movie if y'all want to. Do y'all like to shop? Cause I love to shop. I can show you all the latest fashions and *the* best place to shop in the mall," said Cindy.

Orville's granddaughters looked at these country bumpkins like they were speaking a foreign language. Orville told them to go with Cindy tomorrow to check out small-town life. The girls sneered at him and reluctantly agreed.

Orville told Deni that his family lives in California. "They're not used to the country ways. They live in a big city that never rests and are used to things bein' open all hours of the night. Can you believe that? Things open twenty-four hours a day. What is this world comin' too?" Orville said as he shook his head.

Deni told him, "That's okay, we'll show them around and make sure they feel welcome."

Orville thanked them and told them all to come in for a snack. Deni looked around the living room and saw there was no TV anywhere in this small room. She wondered what they did at night to keep themselves entertained.

Chapter 21

The next morning, Deni, Cindy, and Jack got up to Mamaw and Orville singing in the kitchen. The kids stood there watching the couple dance around while Orville sang to Mamaw. He had the most soothing beautiful voice Deni had ever heard. He was whirling Mamaw around, and she was laughing with delight. Deni thought she heard Mamaw singing along with Orville, and the way their voices mixed made the most beautiful sound. It was like angels singing.

The kids walked into the kitchen and cleared their throats. Orville had just dipped Mamaw and was holding her there, smiling at the kids.

"Oh, I didn't hear you come in. How long you been standin' there?" Orville asked.

Jack replied, "Long enough to know that you two are meant to be together. I had no idea that y'all could sing like that. It was gorgeous. Can you sing us a song later?"

Orville laughed and pulled Mamaw back upright. "I think that can be arranged. What do think, Bea?"

Mamaw blushed and said, "I think that would be great. I didn't know you could sing like that either. You have a beautiful voice. It's so soothing and smooth. I will gladly sing with you."

Orville asked the kids what they were planning for the day, and Jack told them that he was going to drive everyone into town, and they were going to spend the day at the mall. Orville told him that sounded like a good idea.

"Well, we better get this breakfast cooked," Mamaw said.

Orville and Mamaw were such a cute couple cooking in the kitchen together. They were already so close they were finishing each other's sentences. Orville decided pancakes would fill everyone up and had made enough to feed an army. He sat down a huge mound of pancakes on the table, and Mamaw sat down a platter heaping with breakfast meats.

The kids looked at the large mounds of food and sat there staring. Orville told them it was from one of his pigs he had slaughtered last week and that the meat should be really good. He had cooked ham steaks, bacon, sausage, and Canadian bacon. The kids didn't know where to start on the piles. Deni finally dug in first and took a little of everything, and Mamaw had put a basket of biscuits on the table. Jack took one of the warm biscuits, and Orville turned and got his butter. He told them that he had made that butter and wanted everyone to try some. He said it was fresh and that he tried his best to make everything from scratch on the farm.

"Nothin' goes to waste around here," said Orville.

Janet and her mob came into the kitchen and sat down with a thud. Orville looked at her with a funny look on his face and sat a cup of coffee in front of her. His granddaughters looked at the mound of food on the table and asked if there was any granola. Orville laughed and told them this is how they eat on a farm and to sit down and dig in.

Deni thought it was going to be a trying and long day if these girls were as big a snob as she thought they were. Cindy was thinking the same thing and passed the platter of meat to Micah or Mel or whatever her name was.

Micah looked at the platter and took as little as possible, but her grandfather was there to make sure she got her fair share of the meal. He loaded her plate with meat, pancakes, biscuits, and anything else he could grab. Mamaw had been cooking eggs, and asked Orville's family how they wanted them. This was a big mistake, thought Deni. The other kids curled up their noses and told Mamaw they only eat egg-white omelets.

Mamaw laughed and said, "Well, you're in God's country now, so we eat hearty. It's time you girls learned about farm life and the benefits the land can give you."

Janet sat there looking at her children and told them, "You girls have got to quit being snobs. I didn't raise you that way, and don't turn up your nose at every little thing. You girls don't behave and I might just leave you here with your grandpa."

Orville laughed and told his daughter, "That would be fine with me. I'll put them to work on the farm. Teach 'em how to grow the food they eat and harvest it. It's a great feeling when you bring those crops in and sit down to fresh food. I got a cow that I'm takin' to the slaughterhouse later this week. You girls can go with me."

Mel spoke up then. "You have got to be kidding. I am not going to a slaughterhouse and watch anything be killed. That has got to be the grossest thing I have ever heard of."

Janet told her daughters to straighten up again and to please try to consider other people's feelings. Her daughters looked at her with a look that told their mother they were trying. Janet rolled her eyes at them and told them to straighten up. Her daughters tried to eat but just wasn't used to the good country cooking that Orville and Mamaw had prepared. Deni and her friends sat there looking at these snobs and couldn't wait till they got them away from here. Deni could just feel a fit coming on and it might just be aimed at these snobs.

Deni, Cindy, and Jack cleaned the kitchen and finished getting ready to go to the mall. They got ready in record time and asked the others if they were ready to go. They loaded up in Jack's truck and took off for the mall. The mall wasn't crowded and Jack found a spot up close. The snobs got out and laughed.

Lissa said, "You call this a mall? It looks like a strip mall, not a real mall. Is the real mall behind this one or what?"

Deni looked at her and let go. "Okay, that's it. Look, we may not have the biggest malls, greatest fashions, the best cars, or even movie stars here, but there's something we have here that you won't find anywhere else. That's love. Love for your neighbor, family, friends, and even people who work at the mall. We also have respect. Something you three need to learn. I will not walk in that mall with any of you until you check your attitude. I cannot believe you don't see what your grandfather is doing for you. Your grandfather loves you very much. He gave you a place to stay here, he got up early this morning to fix breakfast, and he gave you something that he helped feed and grow on his own, and you three just threw it back in his face like he was a low-life. Well, guess what, he is one of the best men in this county and very well respected here. You three are not going to screw that up for him. He has worked hard to be where he is today, and how dare you treat him like he's nothing. I should just scratch your eyes out now and call it a day. Don't you dare let me hear one more bad thing come out of any of your mouths about that man or the place where he lives." With all that said, Deni turned and walked off.

Jack and Cindy were shocked at the way Deni talked to those girls but were so proud of her. They turned and ran to catch up with Deni and left the three snobs to stand there with their mouths wide open staring in disbelief.

Mel started first. "You know she's right. We came thinking that we could show these people that not everyone from California is a snob, and instead we turned into them. I'm so ashamed."

Lissa agreed and Micah stepped up. "We should probably try and find them and apologize for the way we acted. Mom didn't raise us to be snobs and took us to California because of Dad. I can't believe we acted like that. Dad would be so upset. If he knew how we treated Papaw and these kids, he would have whipped us and grounded us forever. Now I bet he's rolling over in his grave. We should do this for Dad and the way he wanted us to turn out."

Her sisters agreed with her and ran to catch up with the other three. Deni, Cindy, and Jack were already in the mall and trying to avoid the snobs by going upstairs and watching the front door. Deni was still so mad she thought she could shoot daggers out of her eyes if she tried hard enough.

Jack spotted the triplets come through the mall doors. He watched as they looked from store to store but couldn't find them, and then he saw them head toward the escalators. He told Deni and Cindy to get a seat on the balcony at the Burger Stop. He thought the triplets would never find them there, but he was wrong. The triplets had spotted them while going into the restaurant and made a beeline for them.

Deni got a seat on the balcony as far away from the doors as possible. The triplets watched as Deni led the others through the balcony doors and waited till they were seated. The hostess came over and asked how many were in their party, and the triplets told them they were meeting friends there and they would sit with them. The hostess led the triplets through the balcony doors, and the triplets approached the others and grabbed seats.

Lissa started. "We are sorry for everything and want to ask for your forgiveness. We didn't mean to be so awful. Our parents didn't raise us to be mean, and if our father was still alive, he would be so mad at us."

Deni looked at Lissa and asked, "You don't have your father anymore? What happened to him?"

Mel told her, "He worked on an oil rig and there was an accident. It's been about two years now. Daddy was a very loving man and thought so much of Papaw. Daddy wouldn't allow anyone to act the way we did, and he certainly wouldn't approve of the way we spoke to Momma and Papaw. We have a lot to fix when we get back to Papaw's."

Cindy, Jack, and Deni told the triplets how sorry they were about their father dying. Deni asked them if they were hungry since they really didn't eat any breakfast, and the triplets told them they were starving. The waiter brought water and menus and waited to get their order.

When the food was served, everyone at the table was friends and the triplets were being so nice. Deni imagined this was the way it should have been from the beginning. She really liked the triplets and thought it was fascinating that they lived in California. Deni sat and listened to the girls talk about the ocean, the dolphins, the seals, and the whales. Deni was amazed that you could stand on the beach and watch as they swam by. Deni has never seen the ocean and wanted to go even more now after hearing the triplets talk about the place they lived.

After lunch, Cindy led the girls down to Shawna's Fashions. Micah assumed that Jack would not stay with them as they shopped and asked where he wanted to meet them.

Jack looked at her a little confused. "What do you mean? I'll meet you right here."

Now Micah looked a little confused and said, "I just thought that you did your thing and the girls did theirs. I'm sorry if I offended you."

Jack chuckled and said, "It's okay. I like shopping at Shawna's. They have guy clothes, and usually, the girls use me to carry all the clothes around that they buy. So I'm here at your disposal, to carry whatever you need carried."

The triplets giggled and said they were glad to have him there and thought they might pick out some clothes for him. Jack agreed and escorted all five girls into the store. The triplets were surprised that Shawna's carried the latest fashions and the most up-to-date shoes. They were also shocked at the couture line that Shawna's had. They were having a blast and loading Jack up with all the clothes they had picked out.

Cindy and Deni headed to the dressing room for the fashion show, and Jack took a seat outside the dressing room door to hold all the clothes the girls picked out. Jack laughed at all five of the girls ,who looked like kids in a candy store, throwing clothes at him from every direction. The store clerk came over to rescue Jack and could barely find him under all the clothes.

Finally, two hours later they were ready to head to the cashier. Jack took all the clothes up to the register and went to look for something for himself. Mel, Lissa, and Micah followed Jack to the men's fashions and began throwing items at him for him to try on. They positioned themselves outside the dressing room and waited for Jack to come out. Jack liked everything so much that he bought everything the girls picked out for him.

Deni was so happy with the way the events of the day turned around all she could do was stand back and watch these girls in action. They were good at this fashion stuff. Deni thought Cindy was the best, but these girls were pretty close to passing her.

They went to the truck to load the packages and noticed the sun starting to set. They decided they better get back to Orville's before night and took off for the farm. The road was deserted on the way to the farm, and because everyone was starting to calm down from the shopping, Deni could finally watch the landscape. She watched as field after field passed and the cows grazed in the pastures. Everything was so beautiful; she had a new outlook on life now and knew that if anything tried to stand in her way that she could overcome it. She felt so invincible and saw all the fields with the flowing wheat and thought they looked so majestic. All you could see for miles were rolling hills and fields of wheat. It was gorgeous. Some of the farmers had planted fields of corn or soy beans. She admired all this as if for the first time. Then out of a clearing she saw something she had never known was there. A building with a sign that had a plane on it. It read, "Kenny's Aeronautics." Why had she never seen this before? She wanted to make sure she asked Orville when they got home.

They pulled up to the farm just as the sun went down, and Alphie came running out to meet them. He was jumping up and down, turning in circles, and doing pretty much anything he could do to get someone's attention. Deni laughed at his little antics and picked him up to love on him. Alphie licked her face and cleaned her ears for her and then almost jumped out of her arms trying to get to Cindy.

Orville met them on the porch and saw all the packages and immediately went to relieve the girls of their bundles. Mamaw stepped out on the porch along with Janet, and they were talking about how many packages the kids had with them. Janet told Mamaw that sometimes the girls went a little crazy with the shopping, and this looked like one of those times.

Orville took the packages to the living room and asked, "Did y'all buy the mall or what? Where do I need to put these things?"

His granddaughters told him to leave them there; they wanted to show everyone what they bought. Orville chuckled and said it would be better if they modeled it all so that way he could decide if it was appropriate or not. His granddaughters laughed and told him that everything was appropriate, but Orville told them that he would be the one to decide what's appropriate.

His granddaughters took the bags to their room as did Deni, Cindy, and Jack. The adults sat there waiting for the fashion show, and Orville got up to get everyone some popcorn and sweet tea. Bea sat there talking to Janet about how her girls seemed different. Janet told her she was hoping they would come to their senses and straighten up.

The kids filed down the stairs to start the fashion show. Jack rounded out the group and looked amazing in the pants and shirt that the triplets had picked out for him. The adults clapped and loved what the kids had picked out, and Orville had to agree with them that everything was appropriate. Nothing too short, no tops too low, no shorts that were too small, and no dresses that showed everything. The clothes were very appropriate, and Orville told them they could go to the mall anytime.

Deni had to ask Orville about the place she saw down the road. "Orville, do you know anything about Kenny's Aeronautics? I've never noticed that before. How long has he been there?"

Orville chuckled and said, "Well, let's see. He built that building last year. He used to work out of his home that's further back than where the building sits, but he's a hoot. I'll take you to meet him tomorrow. Y'all will really get a kick outta him. He's been doin' crop dustin' for all us farmers for years and loves to fly planes. You'll see him in the skies, buzzin' the house sometimes. He's a good man and so funny, but don't ever play cards with him."

Deni laughed and couldn't wait to go meet a real crop duster. She couldn't wait to see his plane and to ask if it was scary to do that line of work. They all ate supper that night, and the triplets had really changed their attitude. Deni was shocked at how quickly it took to snap them out of their snobbish way. Orville was having such a wonderful time having all his girls back with him. He was so happy that he had met a woman who was so wonderful and let him into her world and become part of her extended family. The kids that Mamaw had grown close to were so wonderful and so loving he couldn't believe that these children had been here all along and he had never met them. He so enjoyed the kids. Mamaw was lucky to have them.

They arose the next morning to the sound of the music from the kitchen. Deni snuck downstairs to watch Orville and Mamaw dancing and singing together. She loved seeing this happy couple—it reminded her of her own parents. She stood there watching and thought she would go wake up Jack. She woke him up and asked if he wouldn't mind cooking breakfast so Orville and Mamaw could dance and sing for the kids. Jack so eagerly agreed to this that he nearly knocked Deni over while coming out of the door.

Jack, Deni, and Cindy all approached the kitchen and watched for a bit before walking in there to interrupt the wonderful moment. Jack cleared his throat and appeared in the doorway. Orville was dipping Mamaw, and Alphie had jumped on her chest and was licking Orville's chin. Somehow he brought her out of that dip without dropping Alphie and with such ease.

Jack asked him if it was okay if he cooked breakfast. Orville told him to have it. Deni asked if he could play some music for them while they cooked. Orville told him that wasn't gonna be a problem and went in the living room and grabbed his Martin guitar. He came back into the kitchen and asked Bea to sing a song with him and whispered in her ear. She laughed and said she knew the song and asked him to start it off.

Orville pulled up a kitchen chair and started playing. When both of them started singing, it was so beautiful. The kids stopped what they were doing and listened. Orville and Bea sounded like a band of angels. The others in the house came downstairs and stood in the doorway to the kitchen.

The song they decided to sing was a song about ugly kids. Orville's guests were laughing and cracking up about the song, and when the two finished, the place erupted with clapping and yelling. Everyone told them how good they were and requested they sing another. Orville started playing a slow song, and everyone pulled up a chair, except for Janet who stayed in the kitchen doorway.

Orville started singing a beautiful song about an old home with a wagon wheel out front. Deni saw that Janet was wiping tears from her eyes, so Deni went to her. She asked if she was okay but Janet couldn't talk.

The song was so gorgeous and Orville was singing his heart out. Bea started singing the harmony with him, and it was amazing.

When the song was over, there wasn't a dry eye in the kitchen. Janet approached her father and hugged him. She stood and said, "I haven't heard you play and sing since Momma passed. You are so wonderful. I love to hear you sing. Please promise to never stop singing again."

Orville hugged his daughter and wiped a tear from his cheek. He promised her that he would never stop singing again. He asked Bea to always sing with him, and the kids looked on in surprise. Deni wondered if that was his way of asking Mamaw to marry him. Mamaw told him that she would sing with him anytime he wanted. Orville bent down and kissed Bea on the cheek. He told her that her singing was gorgeous and their voices blended so well. It's like they had been singing together for years.

Jack told him that he better get started on breakfast and asked what everyone wanted. They all started yelling their request, and Jack tried to remember as many as possible. He started in on the orders and recruited Deni to help out. Mamaw and Orville continued to sing and dance around the kitchen. Everyone was enjoying themselves so much that they almost didn't hear the front door slam.

Orville turned around to see Kenny wheeling into the kitchen. Orville walked up to Kenny to shake his hand and told him, "We were gonna come see ya after breakfast. I wanted you to meet Bea and her adopted grandkids."

Kenny wheeled over to Mamaw and shook her hand, and then Mamaw started making introductions. Kenny shook each of their hands and wheeled over to the end of the table. Deni just stood there staring as if mesmerized, and Jack whispered in her ear, "It's not polite to stare."

Deni shook her head and turned around to help Jack with the cooking. Deni said, "Sorry, but I thought Orville said Kenny was the one who flew the planes. He can't mean this Kenny. He's in a wheelchair. How is that possible?"

Jack whispered back, "Yeah, so he's in a wheelchair. There are some extraordinary people out there that can do extraordinary things from a wheelchair. Don't be so narrow-minded, Deni. Wow, what's with you?"

Deni looked at him. "I'm sorry. I'm just wondering how, and I think that's really special that he can do that. I would love to go up with him sometime. I just want to see how he does it, that's all. I didn't mean anything by it."

Jack gave her a hug and reassured her that he knew she didn't mean anything by it and that he had an uncle who was a paraplegic and was a little touchy sometimes about people feeling sorry for them. Deni, in turn, reassured him that she was not feeling sorry for him; she just had a lot of questions about it. Jack laughed and said, "Always the researcher." And she agreed.

Kenny told them to break up the hug fest by the stove and come over and sit down. Jack told him that he was cooking breakfast and couldn't sit down right now, but he could spare Deni for the time being. Deni thanked him and sat down beside Kenny.

Kenny looked at her and asked, "So how old are you, young lady?"

Deni blushed and said, "Fifteen. How old are you?"

Kenny laughed and said, "Old enough to know better. I like you. You're quick on your feet. Have you ever flown before?"

Deni looked him straight in the eye and said, "No, but I would love to. Can I ask you a question?"

Kenny looked at her and said, "You can ask me anything. I told my nieces years ago that if they ever had any questions or was wondering anything about me or this chair, that I would rather them ask me than sit and wonder. So ask away."

Deni laughed. "How can you fly?"

Kenny looked at her and simply said, "Why, in a plane of course. How do you fly?"

Deni laughed a hearty laugh and blushed. "That's a good one. I like you too."

Kenny looked at her seriously and explained, "I have special hand controls for my airplanes. It's really pretty cool. The man who taught me to fly helped me design them, and we made some modifications to the foot controls to accommodate the hand controls. You should come fly with me so I can show you. It's easier to show you."

Deni told him, "I would love to come fly with you. Just say when."

Kenny looked at her and unlocked his wheels and said, "When."

Deni looked at him with big eyes and simply said, "Okay. Let's go."

Kenny asked if it was okay to take Deni up in one of his planes, and Orville and Mamaw told him to take her. Kenny told them all to listen for him as he goes over the farm. Orville grinned, told Kenny to be careful, and the two of them went out to the runway to the plane .

Jack kept cooking, and when he was done, he set four platters of food on the table. Everyone started passing the plates and began to eat when they heard a plane. They all ran outside and saw Kenny heading for the house. He got as low as he could to the ground and buzzed everyone in the front yard. Jack could have sworn he could hear Deni laughing. Mamaw was outside with her camera, snapping as many pictures as possible. Kenny made a few more passes and headed back to his runway.

Kenny touched down with such ease Deni could barely feel the wheels touch the ground. Kenny taxied to the hangar and Deni got out. She watched as Kenny got out of the plane. She watched as he used his arms to scoot over to the wing and got a blanket from the backseat. He threw the blanket over the wing and reached behind the seat and grabbed his wheelchair. He slid his wheelchair down the wing and propped it up. He then slid himself down the wing to where his wheelchair was still folded. Deni watched as he opened his wheelchair, sat it on the ground, and slid himself in the seat of the chair. She was very impressed with how independent Kenny was, not allowing anyone to really help him.

They got back to the farm, and Kenny wheeled into the kitchen with Deni following him. Everyone asked Deni how she liked flying, and Deni told them it was the greatest. She also told Kenny that she would fly with him anytime he wanted company. He told her he would take her up on that and gave her his card. Deni tucked the card in her back pocket and thanked him with a hug.

Orville wanted to hear all about her first experience flying and asked Kenny how the rookie did. He told them she didn't throw up at all and he was trying to make her get sick. Everyone laughed and Deni couldn't stop talking about the flight. Jack sat down next to Deni and gave her a plate. She dug into the food as if she hadn't eaten in a week, and Kenny told her to slow down because sometimes the stomach upset doesn't hit till a person is on the ground. She listened to him but couldn't stop eating; she was so hungry.

Orville asked Kenny if he could stay for a while and maybe sing a song for the kids. He said yes and left the kitchen to go get his guitar out of the van. When he returned, he had his guitar case with him and set it down on the couch. Orville and everyone moved in the living room with him, and Orville had his guitar with him. Mamaw sat close to Orville so she could sing the harmony with him.

They started out singing a fast song, then Orville and Kenny started singing a beautiful slow song that was so touching. Kenny sang lead and Orville sang tenor. Mamaw joined in singing alto, and the three of them made such wonderful music. Deni didn't want them to ever stop.

Finally they wound down the music. Orville was acting crazy, making everyone laugh. Deni felt so at ease with Orville, Kenny, Janet, and the triplets that she truly felt these people were her family. How much fun this family was going to be, she could only imagine. Deni hugged Kenny so tight when he left and thanked him again for the flight lesson. Kenny told her to call anytime she wanted to go up or just come on out to the hangar and climb in. Deni said she would do that and hugged him again.

Orville told them all finally that Kenny was really his brother, and they had been playing music most of their lives. He also explained how Kenny was involved in a car accident, and that's what paralyzed him. Deni felt so bad for him. But Orville told them all the wonderful things Kenny had accomplished while being paralyzed. Jack thought that this man was really amazing, and was surprised no one had ever realized the treasure they had right down the road from the middle of town.

Chapter 22

I t was time for Cindy, Deni, and Jack to leave; and the triplets were sad to see them go. Janet was glad to hear her daughters say that and said, "Well, I'm glad you girls have made friends here."

Her daughters looked at her a little strange. Janet added, "I'm buying the house next door, I mean across the field."

It took a little while for it to hit her daughters, and then they started jumping up and down and screaming. They all ran over to Jack, Cindy, and Deni; but Jack quickly wiggled out of the jumping match. Orville laughed and told Jack that he had some quick moves. Jack told him that he used to be a wrestler, and it taught him a lot. Orville chuckled and shook his head.

Janet told the girls that she had already sold their home in California and that the real estate company was overseeing the packing of their belongings. She said the moving vans should be there in a week. Her daughters kept jumping up and down and screaming. Deni and Cindy got so caught up in all the excitement that all they could do was scream and jump too.

Jack drove the girls home and gave Deni a kiss on the cheek. He told her he would be there to pick her up for school the next morning and drove off. Cindy and Deni were dragging when they got up to their bedroom. All they could do was hit the hay, as Orville would say. They both had the most wonderful dreams. Cindy's was of the six of them shopping and buying loads of clothes again. Deni's was of flying, with

Kenny at the wheel. She loved that feeling so much that she felt that her life had a new direction now.

Kenny had told her to not just look at the sky but to feel the peace and serenity it brought with it. Deni dreamed of soaring so far above the clouds and hearing nothing but the peace that came from flying. She could tune out everything except that piercing noise. Where was that coming from?

Deni was slowly pulled out of her slumber by her alarm clock going off. She slammed the snooze button and didn't know that she had really turned the alarm off. She woke up startled, looked at the time—8:00 a.m. Oh my God, they were late. Where was Jack? Had he overslept too? She picked up her phone and called Jack and got no answer. She woke up Cindy and told her the time. The girls ran to take quick showers, and Deni tried to call Jack again—still no answer. Where was he?

Cathy got up and asked the girls what was going on, and Deni told her they were late and asked her if she could please take them to school today. Cathy grabbed her daughter's shoulders and spoke very slowly. "Deni, calm down. You don't have school today."

"What are you talking about? It's Monday. Of course we have school," said Deni just as slowly.

Cathy laughed and told her daughter to look at the schedule. No school today due to teachers' meetings. Deni looked at the schedule and found that her mother was right. She couldn't believe that she had forgotten this. She quickly asked her mother if they could invite the triplets over to go swimming. Cathy said yes and handed her the phone.

Deni tried to call Jack again and told him what was going on and invited him over to go swimming. Jack still wasn't answering, so Deni tried calling his parents. There was no answer there either, so she tried Jack's cell number. Jack answered, sounding a little strange. Deni wasn't quite sure how to handle this side of Jack. Jack heard her voice and told her he couldn't talk right now and hung up. Deni just looked at the phone and slowly hung up.

"Did you get a hold of him? Is he coming over?" asked Cindy.

Deni still had her hand on the phone and looked at Cindy with tears in her eyes. "No, I didn't get to invite him. He said he couldn't talk and hung up."

Cindy threw down her bagel and said, "Hung up? What do you mean *hung up*?"

Deni said, "He just hung up. Jack has never hung up on me. He sounded so strange when he answered the phone then he just hung up. What do you think that means?"

Cathy entered the kitchen to find the girls sitting there with a weird look on their faces. "What's up? The girls coming over or what?" she asked.

Deni told her what had happened with Jack, and Cathy was baffled by the behavior. She told Deni that Jack could have been at the doctor's or something and couldn't talk. She reassured her daughter that it was nothing and that he didn't mean for it to sound the way Deni is taking it. She was sure there was an explanation for his behavior. Deni shook her head but didn't believe it for one minute. She could feel something was going on but didn't know what yet.

The triplets came over and they all headed to the pool. The phone finally rang, and it was Jack asking for Deni. Deni told her mother that she didn't want to speak to him and told her mom to tell him she wasn't there. Jack could hear Deni in the background as Cathy delivered the message. Jack tried to ask Cathy what was going on, but Cathy told him she didn't want to get in the middle of it and then hung up.

Jack kept calling most of the day but Deni refused his calls. The triplets asked what was going on, and Deni had no problem telling them what had happened. The triplets told her she should talk to Jack because he had seemed like such a nice and attentive guy. They thought that Deni should give Jack another chance and to please go call him.

Deni didn't have to call Jack. He showed up on her doorstep, demanding to talk to her. She let him in, and he was so upset that he could barely contain himself. He was pacing back and forth and grabbed Deni and just hugged her. He told her he was sorry and that it would never happen again. He tried to explain everything to her but all she could hear was rambling. She told him to calm down and to slow down so he could tell her what was going on. He did just as she said and started from the beginning. After he finished telling her what was going on, she naturally forgave him.

They walked to the pool holding hands, and everyone cheered when they saw Jack. Cathy asked if everything was okay, and Jack told them that he had to take his mother to a specialist in the city, and that's where he was at when Deni called. He said that his mother has a rare heart problem and the nearest specialist is in the city. When Deni called, the doctor was in the room talking to them about the new medication he was adding to her regimen. Deni apologized for getting mad, but Jack told her he completely understood and that it would never happen again.

Cathy told him, "Now that all that is settled, let's go swimming." She then jumped into the pool with the kids.

Deni and Jack were still talking, and Cathy could tell that Jack felt really bad about hanging up on Deni and felt Deni should understand the situation. Cathy asked about his mother, and Jack told her that she was okay and the new meds the doctor gave her were going to help eliminate frequent doctor visits. Cathy told him she was happy to hear that and to be sure to tell his mother that she would be praying for her full recovery. Jack thanked her and hugged her.

The triplets were having fun in the pool, and when Jack joined the crowd, it made it even better. Jack mentioned Fourth of July to Cathy. She invited everyone over for a swim party, but the triplets told them that they should be moved into their home by then and wanted everyone over there. Deni asked if they had a pool, and the triplets all chimed in together, "Yes."

Deni was ecstatic and asked if it was okay to go over to their house for the Fourth. The triplets also told them that they could shoot off fireworks there since they lived so far out in the country. They also told them that Mamaw and Papaw was coming and their mother was planning a big party. Jack asked if it was okay if he did all the cooking. They said they would ask their mother but didn't see a problem with it. Cindy, Cathy, and Deni chimed in and told the girls that he was the best cook, and they really wanted him to cook for them. Lissa got out of the pool and picked up her cell phone to call her mother. She explained what Jack wanted to do for the party, and Janet quickly agreed to have

Jack cook. Lissa handed the phone to Jack, and he asked if he could come over early to prepare his meal. Janet told him he could come spend the night on the third if he wanted, but anytime would be fine with her.

Jack was planning his menu and was already shopping for the freshest ingredients to make his award-winning meal. He did tell Janet that he was going to be up most of the night on the third and that he would stay at his house that night due to the cooking and prep he needed to do.

On July the 3rd Jack got up and started working on marinating the meat for the cookout. He also had to get the smoker going to smoke the pork for the party. He was busy in the backyard when his mother came out and asked if she could help. Jack said no and asked how she was feeling. Ruth told him she was fine and asked if he and Deni had worked everything out.

"Yeah, we worked it out. It's getting harder and harder to come up with excuses here. She was really mad about me hanging up on her," said Jack.

Ruth asked, "What excuse did you give her? Does she have any clue about what is going on?"

"No. She's totally in the dark still. I don't know how she's going to take this when everything comes out. Her moods have been so up and down that it's going to be tricky to keep her calm," Jack replied.

Ruth told him, "You have to keep this going and don't give up. You know how she's going to react, and that's the way she's supposed to react."

Jack said, "Yeah, I know but I just hate all this."

Jack showed up at Janet's at 8:00 a.m. on the Fourth to start cooking. He was finally ready to put the meat on the grill, and everyone started showing up at around 1:00 p.m. Jack had a tray of appetizers for everyone to enjoy, and he took out the fruit platter that he had in the freezer overnight so they would be frozen for this hot day. Everyone enjoyed the frozen treat and couldn't wait to see what else Jack was making.

The kids immediately went to the pool and jumped in. Orville and Mamaw came up with Alphie. Orville asked Jack when he was gonna come back out to the farm for a weekend, and Jack told him he could come out next weekend if that was okay. Orville told him that was fine and to bring the girls with him. Kenny wheeled up on the patio and said hello to everyone and introduced his wife, Suzie, to Deni and her family.

Suzie was a joy to be around. Her smile lit up the room, and her laugh was so contagious. Kenny truly loved her. You could see it in his eyes and she felt the same about him. The two of them together was so amazing. They had a love that would transcend time. Deni watched the two of them and told her mother that they had a love that she dreamed of having someday. Her mother told her that she would find it but she should make sure to remember this day and how she feels when she sees them together.

Jack put the platters of food on the table and called everyone over to eat. There was so much food. He had made smoked pulled pork sandwiches; grilled chicken, hamburgers, hot dogs, homemade sweet potato chips; rainbow slaw—and he had not even brought out the dessert yet. Mamaw had made homemade buns for Jack and potato salad. Everything was so good. The pulled pork just melted in your mouth. It was so tender and juicy. Deni was shocked at how good it was. She had never eaten pulled pork before. Jack had made his own barbecue sauce and had extra on the table.

Everyone was so full after eating that Jack didn't bring out his dessert till everyone was ready for it. He wanted everything to be perfect today as he always did when he was cooking. He had also put out his regular veggie and cheese platters. Everyone was munching. He would wait till almost dark to bring out the dessert. Janet had set up a volleyball net in the yard, and Orville had made a horseshoe pit.

Orville, Kenny, and all the other men were playing horseshoe, and the kids were in the pool, so the mothers decided to start up a game of badminton using the volleyball net. It was a blast to see the moms out there trying to hit the birdie and having such a blast. Alphie was running around trying to steal the birdie and causing more problems. Deni had never heard Mamaw laugh like that, and it was good to see Ruth up and playing games.

As the sun started setting low in the sky, Jack went in and brought out his special dessert. He had made fruit tarts and arranged them in the shape of the flag. He had small tartlets with strawberries on some and blueberries on the others. It was a perfect-looking flag and looked so good. He had promised there were enough for everyone because he had another tray full in the fridge. Janet asked that everyone bring their dessert and chairs out by the pool, and she would start setting up the fireworks. The gentlemen jumped in then and told her that it was their job and made her sit with the rest of the women.

The firework show was simply amazing, and everyone thoroughly enjoyed all the festivities of the day. Alphie was the most worn out of everyone there. He loved the fireworks and ate all the food that everyone dropped or just gave him. Everyone started loading up for the evening, and Janet was hugging everyone and saying good-bye. She also told them to come back soon and to not ever forget where she lived.

Deni got home just in time to fall in bed and go to sleep. She had wonderful dreams about the fireworks and watching Jack cook over the hot grill. She liked to watch Jack when he was concentrating on something, watch the way he would move with such precision.

School the next day was long. She just wanted to go home and didn't even want to participate in PE class, but she knew that if she didn't, she would flunk and not be able to graduate. It was hard for her to believe that she was going to be graduating in a month. Then what was she going to do? She had all these colleges requesting that she attend their college over all the other colleges and just didn't know which to pick.

Jack saw her daydreaming and told her she better pay attention or Mr. Foltz might just give her the golden toilet seat to wear around her neck. She snapped out of the daydream and started paying attention just in time for the class to be over. She couldn't help but look for the hall pass every time she entered or exited the room. She wanted to make sure she knew where it was for fear he might make her carry it for some reason.

Jack had been asking around about Mr. Foltz since the first day in class. He heard that Mr. Foltz used to coach a little league team, when his sons were small, and he would drive his big car to pick up the team for the games. After he picked up the last kid, he would roll all the windows up, lock the doors, and light up a big fat cigar. The kids would show up in a car that was filled with smoke and reeking of cigar smoke.

Deni told Jack that there was no way Mr. Foltz could do that because of the laws they have now about kids and second-hand smoke in the vehicles, but Jack told her that this was long before they knew anything about second-hand smoke. Jack also told her that Mr. Foltz just did that to torture the kids while he drove them to the baseball game. Deni laughed at what he used to do and told Jack that she hopes she never makes him mad.

After school that day, Deni couldn't wait to get in the pool. She ran in to change into her bathing suit and started for the pool. She stopped in her tracks and realized her mother wasn't home. She started looking around for her and found a note on the banister of the stairs. It read that Cathy had driven out to see Janet and check on them after the party the day before. She also wanted Deni to be careful while swimming and told her that she loved her.

Deni ran out to the pool and didn't worry about her mother after reading the note. She was floating around the pool and thought she heard a plane close by. She started searching the sky and finally saw Kenny's plane flying toward her house. He saw Deni in the pool and got as low as he could to buzz her house, and Deni could see him waving from the cockpit. She was standing out in the backyard, waving her arms as high and wide as possible and saw that Kenny had seen her by the way the wings of the plane were waving at her. She loved flying now and wanted to go up in that plane again soon.

School flew by that week and the weekend was approaching. Deni wanted to go back to Orville's for the weekend and called Mamaw to get his phone number. She also asked Mamaw if Orville would mind if they came out that weekend. Mamaw told Deni she thought it would be fantastic, so Deni called Orville and asked if they could come out over the weekend. Orville told them to come out Friday after school, and she could ride on the tractor as he fed the cows. Deni told him that they would be there.

Finally, Friday came around and Deni was so excited. She kissed her mother good-bye and told her she would be home on Sunday. She ran to Jack's truck and jumped in like it was a little truck, and they took off for Orville's farm.

Orville was standing at the gate to let them in and ran to the truck to help unload bags. The girls hugged him and thanked him for having them there. Orville said he had something planned for them tomorrow, but for now he needed to go feed the animals.

Deni followed him to the barn and saw the big tractor parked around the side. Orville went over to the tractor and climbed up with ease. Deni tried to watch how Orville climbed up but couldn't do it without help. Orville reached down a hand and helped her up. He told her to sit on the fender over the back tire. Deni was a little reluctant but sat down where he told her.

Orville started the tractor and put it in gear and pulled out with a lurch. Orville pulled over to the hay barn and grabbed a round bale of hay and took off for the pasture. Deni was having a blast on the tractor. She sat there and took everything in, feeling the wind in her face and the smell of the hay and the cows running to meet Orville. Deni watched as Orville stopped and ran to the hay to pull it off the fork on the back of the tractor. The cows were mooing and running to meet him and slowed when they saw he had stopped. The cows saw someone new on the tractor and stopped there, watching to see what Deni was going to do. They watched Orville pull the hay off and place it in front of the cows. The cows mooed, and one small calf approached Orville to have his head scratched. Orville had names for all his cattle, and this little one was Red.

The little calf had the prettiest red color with white spots on him. He butted Orville in the rump and pushed him into the hay bale. Orville chuckled and told him to wait a minute, but the calf was not having that. He pushed Orville again and Orville had to turn around to scratch his head. The calf stood there turning his head so Orville could cover as much area as possible. Orville hollered for Deni to come and scratch him, but when she jumped down, it startled the other cows, and they jumped, causing Red to jump. They mooed at Deni and stood there watching her.

Red stood there, letting Orville continue to scratch his head and saw Deni approaching. He raised his head higher and watched Deni. He jumped as Deni got closer, but Orville kept telling him that everything was going to be okay. Deni finally made her way over to Orville and reached out her hand to scratch the calf when the calf turned and licked her whole arm. Deni had never been licked by a cow.

The calf's tongue felt rough and dry. She had never felt anything like it. The other cows had started to move in closer to get to the hay, and Red moved closer to Deni. She reached her hand out again and Red hit it with his nose. Deni started rubbing his nose. He lowered his head, and Deni's hand slid up to the top of his head. She started scratching between his ears and moved her other hand up to scratch under his chin. Orville told her to be careful because Red would go to sleep on her with her scratching him like that.

Red was closing his eyes and moving his head so Deni could get all the spots Red wanted scratched. Finally, Orville told her it was time to go, and Deni reached out and hugged Red before she climbed back up on the tractor. Red followed her and mooed at her to keep scratching, but she told him she would be back tomorrow to give him another scratching.

She took her place on the tractor and Orville took off for the house. Orville parked the tractor and jumped down. Deni jumped off the tractor and fell flat on her heinie. Jack and Cindy were waiting for them, and Jack went to help her up, but she was laughing so hard she couldn't move. Jack started laughing with her and tried to help her up at the same time. It was nice to see Deni laughing again, especially at herself.

They went into the house to help prepare supper, but Orville already had that taken care of. Mamaw was at the stove, taking the last of the chicken out of the pan and had already set the table for them. They all came in and hugged Mamaw and sat at the table. Alphie ran over to Deni and stopped short of jumping on her, and then he started smelling her. He must not have liked what he smelled because he looked at Deni, blew out at her and walked off.

She laughed. She asked Mamaw what was going on with Alphie. Mamaw told her that Alphie could smell the cows on her and didn't like it. She explained that he blows at you when he's mad. Deni and the rest started laughing at the little dog as he went over in the corner and lay down. Deni felt sorry for him and tried to give him treats to come to her, but he wouldn't budge.

After supper, Alphie started to calm down about the cow smell on everyone and started coming around. Deni sat down in the living room, and Alphie jumped up beside her. She told him she was sorry for "cheating" on him with a calf, and Alphie got all excited and jumped in her lap. She thought that was funny. All he needed was an apology for not coming to him first. Funny little dog.

Orville told them to get a good night's sleep 'cause he had a job for them tomorrow and asked Jack if he could go into town for more feed. Jack told him that would not be a problem. They all went to their rooms and were so tired that all they could do was go to bed. Deni was still talking about the little calf and how he didn't want her to leave.

She lay there thinking of that little calf and the way Alphie treated her when she came in. Alphie had never been mad at her, and she didn't know a dog could get mad at you, but Alphie wasn't like any other dog. Mamaw treated him like a little kid and talked to him like a person, so it would only seem reasonable for Alphie to act like a human. Deni still chuckled at how Alphie blew at her because he was mad, and all Deni had to do was apologize to the little dog for him to come to her. She had never in her life met a dog quite like Alphie.

The next morning was a beautiful day. They got up to find Mamaw cooking a hearty breakfast for them and Orville dancing in the kitchen with Alphie. The kids laughed at him and took their places at the table. Mamaw sat all the food in front of them and sat down to dig into all this wonderful food.

Following breakfast, Orville called the feed store to let them know that Jack would be coming to pick up his feed. Orville told Jack where the store was and what to pick up. He gave him the money for the feed and sent him on his way. Orville looked at Deni and Cindy and asked if they were ready to go. The girls followed Orville to the old barn behind the house, and he swung the doors open. The girls saw something covered up with a tarp. Orville uncovered the precious truck, and the girls saw something that made them giggle. Orville had covered up a yellow truck that was not in the best of shape. The paint was fading, and the old truck looked like it had been in the barn for years. The girls opened the doors to the truck, and the squeak from the hinges reminded them of fingernails on a chalkboard.

Orville told the girls to hop in, and he climbed behind the wheel of the truck. He told them that this truck was very special to him because this is the truck he used to teach his kids how to drive. He asked the girls if they were ready, and he stepped on the clutch and turned the key. The old truck sprang to life with a loud roar. Orville looked at the girls and grinned, and then he slowly released the clutch and took off. He revved up the truck, and when he stepped on the clutch, the pipes started popping. The girls laughed with delight, and every time he changed the gears, the pipes would sing and pop.

Deni was beginning to understand why Orville had held on to the truck. She understood why he liked this truck so much. The floorboard was starting to get hot under her feet, so she was fidgeting and moving her feet all over. Orville pulled over on the side of the road and smiled at the girls.

"Okay, are you ready?" asked Orville as he looked at Cindy.

"Ready for what?" she asked.

"To drive. Scoot over, and I'll show you how to change the gears," he told Cindy.

Cindy scooted over, and Orville told her how to start the truck. Cindy got behind the wheel and did what Orville told her to do. She stepped on the clutch and started the truck. She put the truck in gear and released the clutch slowly. The truck leapt forward and died. Cindy stepped on the clutch again and started the truck. This time she released the clutch slowly, and the truck lurched forward just a tad and kept going. Cindy went through the gears, and then Orville told her to stop and try everything again. Cindy did this for about thirty minutes. Orville told her she did very good. Next it was Deni's turn to try and drive the truck.

Deni slid behind the wheel of the big yellow truck and did just as Orville told her. She pushed in the clutch and started the truck. She put the truck in gear and released the clutch slowly. She had been watching Cindy very closely to see how slow she had to release the clutch and what she needed to do when it came to her. She released the clutch, and the truck lurched and kept going. She went through the gears and stopped and started again. She got really brave and tried to make the pipes sing but instead almost ran into a ditch. Orville laughed and told her that in due time she would be able to make those pipes rattle.

Orville got back behind the wheel, and both girls told him to make the pipes pop. Orville laughed, and the pipes rattled all the way back to the farm. The girls laughed so hard they could hardly contain themselves. Orville pulled into the barn and made the pipes rattle one last time, and the girls started laughing again. The girls thanked him for the driving lesson and asked when they could go again.

Orville told them, "Anytime you want. Me and Old Yeller will be waiting."

The girls said in unison, "Who is Old Yeller?"

Orville laughed and said, "That's what I call the truck. When I was teachin' my girls to drive, we all nicknamed it Old Yeller. So that's been the truck's name for years."

The girls laughed and said, "That's a good name for this truck."

The girls thought that the drive reminded them of that country song, where the man talked about teaching his daughters how to drive. They laughed and said that now they understood the song better.

Chapter 23

School had flown by so fast. Deni was already preparing for graduation. Cathy had made hair appointments for the girls, and this time Deni's hair will be the blondest it had ever been. She still didn't want to go platinum blonde, but this color was close. She had so gradually colored her hair lighter and lighter that she didn't realize how close to platinum blonde she really was. Cindy's hair was the color of Deni's before she started coloring her hair and was so pretty.

Both girls were so pretty and their parents were so proud. The girls had sent out invitations to the graduation and had already been receiving graduation gifts. Deni was happy that her life was going as planned and was happy about all that she had been going through for the past year and a half. She had picked her college but decided to wait and start in January. She wanted to spend this time with her parents and her friends. She was going to be going off to college soon and wanted to spend as much time with her mother as possible before moving out of the house she grew up in. She didn't know how this was going to affect her mother or how it would affect her.

The last week of school was busy but it was really fun. Mr. Foltz was so much fun, and now she could tell people what a teddy bear he was in class. She had heard so many stories about how hard he could be, and now she knew that he was hard but so much fun. She remembered that first day in class and how intimidated she felt, but now he was one of her favorite teachers.

Deni had brought home the cap and gown that the school had ordered for them, and Cathy cried when she unfolded the gown. She couldn't believe that her little girl was old enough to graduate high school. She held the gown and remembered when she brought Deni home from the hospital. She was so tiny. Cathy had such big hopes and dreams for her baby girl, and now those dreams were coming true. She had no idea that Deni would be graduating two years early and that her daughter would be going all the way to California for college. She was so overwhelmed at that moment with emotion. She couldn't stop crying.

Mamaw told Cathy that some of her friends from Tennessee were coming in to see the girls graduate. Cathy asked Mamaw if there was anything she could do to help, but Mamaw said no because Orville was giving some of them a place to stay. Cathy told Mamaw that Orville sure was getting close to her and wondered where their relationship was going.

"Oh, I don't know. I like where I live here in town, and he likes living on the farm, so I don't know if it will ever go any further than it is right now. We like it the way it is. You know what they say, if it ain't broke, don't fix it," she told Cathy.

Cathy laughed and said, "Yeah, I've heard that before. I just think you two could be very happy together. You know, married together."

"I know what you mean, but at our age, we are both so set in our ways, and I'm so afraid that if we got married that it would mess that up. That's something I don't want to take a chance of screwing up," said Mamaw.

The day passed quickly, and with each passing day, Cathy had mixed emotions regarding the upcoming graduation. She saw everyone getting ready for the big event and was getting anxious. She saw Mamaw's company coming in from out of town and saw that Orville was at her house more frequently. Deni was asking her mother what was wrong with her, and Cathy couldn't answer her. Every time Cathy looks at Deni, she began to cry. This was one reason why Deni wanted to take that time off after graduation to spend with her mother.

Deni was getting excited about her graduation and asked her mother what kids do after graduation. She told her that there were some kids who were planning a party after graduation, but Deni and her friends didn't want to do any of that. She wondered what else they could do, and her mother suggested for everyone to come back to the house and have a pool party. She told her daughter that her father could cook out for them, and they could all just camp out in the backyard and stay up all night if they wanted. Deni thought that it was a good idea and decided to make invitations for her own "party."

She went to the computer and started searching for pool party invitations and found some that had a beach scene on the front and told of the events of the day and the location on the inside. Deni printed them off and made the envelopes out to give out to her friends.

The next day, Deni handed out the invitations, and they handed in their books. The PE class was still going strong, and Ms. Myers was not going to cut them any slack. She made them run the drills and do all the stuff they usually did just to make sure they got as much exercise as possible. The last day was mostly practice for the graduation ceremony. They went through lining up and where they were going to sit. Then they faked all the speeches and sent everyone on their way.

Deni got home to find her mom ironing her gown and crying. She asked her mother when she was ever going to quit crying, and Cathy told her that it would never stop. Deni hugged her as tight as she could and asked her to not cry. Cathy told her she would try to stop crying but couldn't promise anything.

It was time to get ready for graduation, and Deni's friends all came over to get ready. Deni had picked out a sundress to wear under the robe, and most of the girls had all picked out sundresses that were similar. They got ready and descended the stairs to see Cathy and Stan standing on the landing, and Cathy was crying still. Stan started tearing up a little when he saw Deni in the graduation robe. He told her how proud he was of her and for the accomplishments she worked so hard for.

They all loaded up and headed to the football field. Deni and her friends got out of the car and told her parents they would see them after the ceremony and left to go line up. Stan and Cathy found Mamaw and Orville sitting in the stands, surrounded by Mamaw's friends from Tennessee. Janet and her daughters were there, and so was George. George had known Leah since she was a little girl coming to visit Mamaw every summer. He felt part of the family and was a little jealous that Mamaw was so close to Orville.

Kenny wheeled up the ramp and found Orville waiting for him. He wheeled him over to the wheelchair spot and sat down beside him. Mamaw and everyone else moved down to sit by Kenny, Suzie, and Orville. Cathy thought Kenny coming was a nice gesture and didn't realize how much Kenny cared for her daughter.

Finally the ceremony started, and the kids filed in and took their seats. The principal came up to make his speech and introduced the valedictorian of the class. As each speaker was introduced and approached the podium, everyone was clapping. As the speakers droned on and on about their life as a high school student and how many opportunities lie ahead of the graduates, Cathy started thinking back to her graduation and how she wanted to be a photographer but was unable to live that dream due to financial problems.

Finally, it was time to hand out the diplomas. The kids filed up on stage as their names were called and received a piece of paper explaining their diplomas would be mailed to them. Deni was a little disappointed that she didn't get her diploma, but at least she was graduating. After the ceremony and all the kids filed back out, the chaos began. Where were Deni, Cindy, and Jack? It was so hard to find the kids. Cathy finally found Jack and asked where Deni was at, and Jack told her that he saw Deni taking pictures with some of the other kids. Cathy told him she needed to get home to set up for the party, and Jack told her that he would bring Deni home. Cathy left and got home with little time to spare.

Mamaw, Orville, Kenny, Suzie, Janet and her girls, and everyone Mamaw had invited from Tennessee came over to help Cathy set up the backyard. Mamaw thought it would be funny to have the disco ball there as a joke. George helped string the lanterns around the backyard, and Kenny had made a banner to string up outside.

As the graduates came through the house, they were met with a chorus of "For He's a Jolly Good Fellow." Jack laughed and was amazed at how fast Cathy had decorated. Stan was preparing the grill and was waiting for the kids. All of Deni's friends were there along with their parents and all the people that had come in from out of town to see the kids graduate.

Once everyone started calming down, the kids went around and thanked everyone for coming. George was standing next to Mamaw and Orville but thought he recognized Jack.

"How long you known that kid?" asked George.

Orville turned and replied, "Oh, 'bout a year now. Why?"

George was studying Jack's face and told Orville, "I could swear I've seen that kid before."

"Well, he kinda has one of those faces, I guess," replied Orville.

George still was watching Jack and was trying to figure out how he knew Jack. George kept thinking while visiting with everyone and still couldn't shake the feeling that he knew Jack.

Stan yelled for everyone to listen up and made the most perfect speech Deni had ever heard. He cleared his throat and said, "I would like to thank everyone for coming here tonight to not only honor my daughter but to honor all these kids— excuse me, young adults—for graduating high school early. They have all been working their butts off to get to this point, and now it has paid off. Deni, sweetheart, I want to say how proud your mother and I are of you. Not just for this accomplishment but for being our daughter. You have truly given my life a new meaning. You are not just a smart, intelligent kid but the perfect daughter. You worked hard to get here, and I think that needs to be rewarded. I don't know what I would do without you in my life. When you were born, I held you in my arms and wondered what in the world I am gonna do now. She's so little and dependent on me to provide for her, for guidance, for love, and for the affection and support that you deserve. Now you are all grown up and I'm wondering what I will do *now*. I feel lost, and every time I have doubts about things, you show up and make those doubts disappear. You not only light up a room but you light up the universe for me. I love you very much and will always be here when you need to be held, helped, or just for support. I will always be here and always be your daddy. I love you and am very proud of you."

Stan had a hard time making that speech and started crying when he mentioned the part about Deni being born. Deni's parents loved her very much, and now they showed everyone just how much. Deni ran to him and hugged him so hard. They both stood there with tears streaming down their faces, and Stan couldn't stop telling her he loved her. Deni told him she loved him too.

Cathy stepped up, wiping her tears, and added, "Now that the cry fest is calming down, I would like to invite everyone to the front yard for Deni's surprise."

Everyone walked through the house. Deni was still arm in arm with her father and stood on the porch. Stan made her cover her eyes when they reached the porch and led her to the front yard. Stan still had Deni's eyes covered and told Cathy, "On the count of three." They both counted, and on three, Stan removed his hand from Deni's eyes, and Cathy pulled a large tarp off of something. Deni couldn't see anything yet and finally was able to focus enough to realize that it was the junk car that her dad had given her at Christmas.

Deni stood there with her bottom jaw on the ground, and everyone was oohing and aahing so much that Deni couldn't say anything. The car had been totally restored and was a beauty. Jack was so amazed that he stepped over to the car to inspect it for any flaws. He was very impressed with the work and asked Stan where he had restored this beast. Stan told him that he has a friend at work that knew a guy, and that guy was the one who restored it for him. Jack whistled and opened the door to the car.

Deni slid into the driver's seat and still had her jaw on the ground and was speechless. She couldn't believe that her parents had done this for her. She was supposed to go take her test next week for her driving permit. Now she couldn't wait. Mamaw stepped up to the muscle car and told Deni to just call her anytime she wanted to race. Deni laughed and said okay. Jack turned around and asked Stan about the motor and the paint job and all the stuff that girls don't usually think about or care to hear about.

Deni wanted to take it out for a test drive and asked her father to get in and take her for a drive. Stan slipped into the passenger seat and handed Deni the keys. Deni looked at her father and was stunned again. Her father was never one to break the law in any way and was shocked that he was willing to break the law this easy. She put the keys in the ignition and started the car. The car roared to life. Jack threw his head back and was impressed with sound of the motor.

Deni backed out of the driveway and did a burnout in the road before rocketing toward the middle of town. She cruised the local drive-ins and circled town the way the older kids do during football season and visited all the popular places to show off her car. Everyone was looking to see who was driving the hot rod. Deni felt so cool driving this car and for making everyone look. She was almost sorry she was out of school and wasn't going to get to drive this beast to school this year. She wanted so bad to make Natalie jealous.

She pulled back up in the driveway and parked the car. Deni and Stan walked back to the pool and saw everyone was still there, and everyone cheered Deni for the burnout. George had been talking to Jack and still trying to figure out where he might know him from. Finally he looked at Orville and said he had figured it out.

George hollered at Jack, who was across the yard from him and said, "I know who you are now. You work for that hair colorin' company in Memphis. I used to pass by there all the time when I worked construction, and I seen you coming out of the plant."

Jack's face went white and told George, "I don't think that was me. I'm too young to work at a job like that. I think you are mistaken."

George told him, "No, I don't think so. I saw you come in the diner across the street. Only you was wearin' a suit, a tie, and had on a white coat. Do you 'member? You came in there with some of them other white coats. Y'all was talkin' 'bout new products and how it might affect people. You don't remember that?"

Jack was getting whiter by the minute, and Ruth stepped beside her son and whispered something in his ear. Jack turned to look at George and said, "I am sure, sir, that you are mistaken. How could I be in Memphis and here at the same time? I think you have mistaken me for someone older."

George said, "Nope. I got your face embedded in my brain. I know it was you. You sat at that corner booth and was talkin' all fancy with them other men in white coats. I know it was you."

Jack looked at him again and tried to convince him. "I have never been to Ruthann's Diner, and I don't know what you're talking about."

Deni stepped up then and said, "Jack, George didn't say the name of the diner. How would you know that name if you've never been there?"

Jack stood there with a blank face and turned away from them. Ruth was standing beside him, trying to talk to him, but Jack wouldn't have it. He turned around and found the whole group staring at him, waiting for him to say something.

Jack cleared his throat. "You are right, George. I work for that company. I work in product development and research. My job is to help develop the products and to observe for any side effects. I was sent here to watch Deni and Cindy for any side effects from the hair dye that Sabrina uses."

Deni looked at him, stunned by this confession, and said, "You were sent here? What does that mean?"

Jack approached Deni. "I was sent here to observe you and Cindy and to write down everything you do. Then I take it back to the lab and decipher what is actual behavior and what are side effects from the product."

Deni was starting to turn red in the face now. "You mean all this that has been going on with me, you knew? You knew the whole time what was going on and didn't say a word. I don't believe you. You told me you loved me."

Jack started pleading with her. "Deni, please, I do love you. You have to believe that. I am telling the truth."

Deni pushed him away and said, "How old are you really? What is your real name? Did you ever mean anything you said? I can't believe this."

Jack turned to address the silent crowd. "My real name is William Jackson. I am twenty-three years old. I have a bachelors degree in chemistry. I live in Memphis and work at Natural Hair. We make products for the hair from all natural materials. We have a new line of hair color out that is being tested on humans. Deni was the test subject for the blonde color. We have a new chemical that was put in the dye that alters intelligence. Deni's was to alter her intelligence to be below normal standards. Cindy's hair color was brunette and was to alter her intelligence to be above average. I was sent here to observe these two young ladies and write down their every move. Then report back to the rest of the team and decipher what we needed to do to improve the product so there are no side effects. Cindy helped me a great deal by keeping her journal and staying here with Deni. The doctor you saw was in on the whole deal and gave Cindy's journal to me so I could report back to my company. When Deni called me the other day, I was in a meeting and didn't want her to know where I was. We were discussing Cindy's journal and trying to decide what plant could have caused this problem."

Cathy stepped up then and asked, "Are Ruth and Harvey your parents?"

Ruth stepped up to answer that. "No, we work with Will and are on the team with him. We have been observing all this from the start. As soon as Sabrina used the products on you two girls, the company rep was notified, and they immediately got us together to come here and observe. It wasn't just a coincidence that Will was in all your classes and wasn't into all the things the other kids are into because he is not a kid anymore. He is also a chef in training and has many accomplishments under his belt. Harvey and I have been working with Will since he came to the company a year ago. The company thought that we could pass as his family and that he could pass as a high school student. So they sent us here and bought that house so that we could be close to the two girls."

Cathy looked at her with betrayal in her eyes. She couldn't believe that the only reason Ruth had gotten close to her was because of her job. Cathy grabbed the two girls and walked into the house. Before she slammed the sliding glass door, she turned and thanked all her guests for coming and wished them good night.

The others were standing there staring at Jack or Will, whatever his name was, and wanted to kill him for betraying the town. Mamaw looked at him with tears in her eyes. She slowly walked up to him and stroked his face and then reared back and slapped him.

Orville just looked disappointed in him and walked off. Cindy's parents were almost as bad as Deni's parents. Sam walked up to them and told them to run as fast as they could and to never return to this town and walked off. Jack was so hurt, so he walked away from the rest of the guests before anyone else could inflict any more pain on them.

Cathy took the girls up to Deni's room and was sitting there fuming over Jack's revelation. "No wonder he seemed too good to be true. Now it all makes sense. He was playing them all for the fools they were. The worst is how everyone here seemed to really care for that family and took them in as our own. I feel so betrayed."

Deni just sat there. "You feel betrayed? All the things he said to me. All the things we did together. It was all a lie. I hate him for doing this to me. I hate him for developing whatever it was he developed."

Cindy was wiping tears, saying, "I still can't believe all this has happened. The only plus is I was onto something and he was afraid I would expose the damage he was doing. I can't believe that a company would do this to people without their permission. I think we should sue them for all their worth."

Cathy turned around and said, "You know you might be on to something there. Let me handle all the specifics on that. I used to work for an attorney and can contact them in the morning."

It took a long time for everyone to settle down from the news they learned earlier. Thank God for George. If it wasn't for him, they would have never known what was really going on with Deni and Cindy. What Cathy couldn't figure out was why Deni was affected and Cindy wasn't. I guess this would come out in the trial.

Deni couldn't calm down enough to sleep and was up most of the night trying to figure out what to do with these feelings she had for Jack or Will. It was really weird to call him Will. She had called him Jack for so long. How was she supposed to deal with everything and also deal with the fact that the doctor she saw was in on the betrayal? This was too much for Deni to swallow.

Chapter 24

Will had tried to call Deni for the past week but was unable to talk to her. He left her message after message, saying he was going to be leaving and wanted to talk to her before he left. Deni didn't even listen to the messages and didn't want to know what was going on with this guy she thought she knew but didn't. She wanted to talk to him but didn't at the same time. She was so confused. She did call Sabrina to tell her what was going on with the hair color, and Sabrina told her that she did not know anything about the company and what they were doing. Sabrina immediately threw out the hair color and told Deni that she would never buy from that company again. Deni thanked her for her help and told her she would be in for a different hair color.

Cindy was still at Deni's because they really needed each other right now. Cindy had heard some of the messages that Will had left on the answering machine and was still torn about him. She didn't trust him anymore, and her parents didn't want her having anything else to do with him. Cindy was steering clear of Will and didn't want to see him for fear she might scratch his eyes out. Deni didn't know about all the late-night meetings with Will and didn't really want to bring all that up right now.

The days turned into weeks and the weeks turned into months. Finally one day in November she heard a knock on her door. She answered the door and saw Will standing there with balloons that read

Happy Birthday. She had completely forgotten it was her birthday. She should have been excited about this one, but was still upset for all the stuff Will had put her through. Deni stood there looking at the man who had lied to her. She didn't know whether to slap him or hug him.

Will presented the balloons and asked, "Can I please talk to you? I need to see you and explain what happened and what was going on."

Deni looked at him. "I don't know, Will. I really liked you but I can't be around you anymore. I'm only sixteen and you're twenty-three. I can't believe you lied to me, to all of us. I never want to see you again. I do want to ask how many others have there been? How many others have you betrayed and lied to? I can't even look at you anymore. Just leave and never come here again."

Will stepped back and looked at the closed door. He felt terrible. He knew this assignment was going to be a big risk, but what he didn't count on was falling for the girl he was to be observing. He didn't care about the age difference and was determined now to make things right. He swore he would never do anything like this again. He took out his cell phone and called his boss.

Cathy came down the stairs and asked who was at the door, and Deni told her it was Will. Deni told her mother everything that was said and walked up the stairs to her bedroom. Cindy was waiting there for her and wanted to know everything. Deni just couldn't tell the story anymore and told Cindy that she had sent him away. Cindy told her best friend that she would eventually get over him, but for now she wanted to think about the college they had selected and what they were going to pick for their major.

Deni told her that she just couldn't talk about it now and grabbed her things to go soak in a tub. She walked to the bathroom in a daze and ran a hot tub of water. She put in the bubble bath that she liked and slipped into the tub. She just wanted to get away from everything. She sat there crying and thinking about how Will had deceived her. Deni had been this way since he left months ago. She wished she had never met Will and had her hair dyed to begin with. This all started because she wanted to change, and now she knew that change was not a good thing. She was so confused and upset by the events that she didn't know what she was thinking anymore.

The attorney that Stan had hired was a shark. Will's company had settled with Deni and Cindy outside of court, and the girls were set for life. Deni just didn't think that the money would make any difference because it didn't fix her feelings or the betrayal she felt. She had finally found someone that was her equal and was the most attentive person, only to find out that it was all an act. Natural Hair had also agreed to pay for college for both the girls in addition to the money they paid to the family.

Deni had been in the bath for over an hour, soaking and thinking, hoping it would wash away all the feelings she had for Will. How many times had she soaked in a tub thinking this would help? She couldn't get past this and was so hurt by all the events. How could she get past these feelings and move on to healing?

Cindy burst into the bathroom. "All right, I've had enough of you moping around, feeling sorry for yourself. It is not the end of the world, it's only the beginning. We have so much ahead of us and you don't see it. We have the chance of a lifetime here. We can go to any college in the world and it's paid for, in full. What other kid has that chance? Get out of that tub and dry off. While you're drying off, think that with each wipe of that towel, you're wiping away all the feelings you have pent up right now. This is our chance, and I'm not going to give it up because you're in this funk. It's been months now, let it go."

Deni got up and grabbed a towel. She did just what Cindy said, and when she was through, she felt a sense of renewal and new life. Change was a good thing, and this was her chance to do just what she always wanted to do. She should be seizing every opportunity that was being handed to her. She was going to take the bull by the horns and take control of her life now.

She walked to her room with confidence. She looked at Cindy and said, "Let's pick where we want to go to college and our major." Cindy had the brochures spread out on the bed and looked at Deni and told her, "This is more like it." She liked this strong person standing before her and thrust the brochures at her.

Deni and Cindy sat there looking over the brochures, and Cathy walked in to check on them. She sensed the change in Deni and immediately changed her mood to match Deni's. Cathy sat on the bed and looked at the brochures with the girls.

Deni held up a brochure and stood up to make an announcement. "This is it. I found the one I want to go to and what I want my major to be."

Cathy and Cindy both said, "Which one?"

Deni laughed and said, "Pepperdine, of course. It's a great college, and I want to major in acting with emphasis on theater and television."

Cathy looked at her daughter and said, "Are you serious? I thought you would major in something like biomedicine or engineering. Not that you can't do acting, but I just thought, as smart as you are, that you would do something that was in research or development for eco stuff."

Deni laughed. "I know, Mom, but I want to make a difference, and the best way to do that is to be an actress then use that fame to make a difference in the world. Like Angelina Jolie or Ashley Judd, you know."

Cindy said, "Yeah, I know what you mean, but that's a long shot. You just don't get famous just because you want to. You have to be really good and still that's a long shot."

Deni said, "Well, I thought that's what you wanted to do for your major. I thought you were going into acting. What's your major then?"

Cindy said, "Well, I do want to be an actress too, but I think I'll do something else. I just have to look at the programs and find something I like. You want me to go to Pepperdine with you?"

"Of course, we can't be separated. We never have been before, why stop now. I thought you would like going there. It's right on the ocean. It's sunny and the weather is nice. Why not go there? Mom, will you go with us when we tour the campus?" Deni said.

Cathy looked at the girls. "Of course I'll go with you. You think I'm gonna miss a chance to go to California? Never. The best thing is the hair dye company has to pay for everything. That's the only good thing that came out of this whole mess."

Cindy looked at them and said, "I think we need to look at more than just one college while we are there. They have so many there that

I think it would be in our best interest to look at as many as possible while we are in California. We could spend a week and look at a different college every day."

Cathy told her, "That's a good idea. Why don't you two look on the Internet and see what interests you and make a list so we can go there. I'll call the colleges and let them know we are coming and arrange for a tour."

Both girls agreed to that and sat down in front of the computer. They stayed on the computer for hours and finally found another college in California they would be interested in. They were looking at the smaller colleges and found UCSB (University of California, Santa Barbara). They ran downstairs and told Cathy about the other college they wanted to tour. Cathy asked if there were any others, and the girls said they had looked and looked, but these were the ones that appealed to them the most.

Cathy got on the phone and started making arrangements for the tours of the campus and possible registration for the spring semester. The colleges were eager to set up the tours and made them for the first week of December. Now the girls could celebrate their sixteenth birthday the way it should be celebrated—happily.

Stan came in with a cake and balloons, and behind him were the rest of the girls' friends. Mamaw, Orville, Kenny, and Suzie rounded out the group. The girls were surprised at everyone coming over but felt that someone was missing and ignored the urge to say who it was. They both knew and felt it but didn't say a word to anybody.

The party was fantastic, and the girls were exhausted from the day's events. Both girls had appointments to go to the local tag office and get their driver's license the next day. They were excited about the prospect of getting to drive on their own now but were too exhausted to think about anything else but sleep.

The next morning was a beautiful sunny day. The girls went downstairs and found Cathy cooking a big breakfast. The girls sat down at the bar and asked if there was anything they could do. Cathy was in a good mood and told them to sit there and try to relax before they left to take the driving test.

They finished breakfast and cleaned up the kitchen. All three got ready to leave, and Cathy asked them if they had been reviewing the driving manual. Deni told her she had been reviewing it for the last couple days, and Cindy said she was afraid to look at it for fear it would confuse her even more.

They got to the tag office to find it crowded. Cathy tried to check the girls in and tell the receptionist they had appointments but couldn't get to the desk. An hour later, Cathy finally was able to tell the receptionist what they were there for, and the lady brought the girls back to fill out the proper paperwork and told them to take a seat. Shortly after, an officer came out and called Cindy's name and told her to follow him.

They went to Cathy's car and got in. Cindy was so nervous that she couldn't remember what to do and the order in which to do them. She dropped the keys in the floorboard and had to fish for them. The officer was sitting as stiff as a board and waiting for Cindy to get the keys in the ignition. Once she got the keys off the floor, she put them in the ignition and put on her seat belt. The officer sat there watching every little move she made, and when she turned to see if he had his seat belt on, he asked her what she was supposed to do next.

Cindy stopped to think about it and then adjusted the mirrors. He told her to start the car and exit the parking lot. Cindy did just as he asked and when they got to the stop light, he told her to turn right and take the side road. Cindy did everything he asked. She even parallel parked perfectly, but when she got back to the tag office, the officer told her to park the car in a space that was impossible to park in. The car that had just pulled in was parked crooked, and Cindy turned to tell the officer that she couldn't park there without hitting the other car, but the officer told her to park there anyway.

Cindy didn't try to argue with the officer but asked him how that was possible when the other car was halfway over the line into her space. The officer insisted she park there, and when she pulled in, she hit the other car. She looked at the officer and said, "I told you I would hit that car."

The officer was trying not to laugh and got out to inspect the other car. There was no damage to either car, and the officer told Cindy that she had been his best driver all day until now. He said he was sorry but he had to fail her and that she could come back next week to retake the test.

Cindy was devastated and sat there crying. The officer went back into the office and called Deni's name. She followed him to the same car where Cindy was still sitting, crying. Deni opened the door and helped Cindy out, and Cathy was waiting to console her. Deni got into the driver's seat and put her seat belt on. The officer got back into the car and put his seat belt back on.

He told her to start the car and back out slowly and try not to hit the other car. Deni did as she was told and backed out slowly. She did so with such ease that the officer was impressed. He took her through the same test as Cindy. Deni was pulling back into the parking lot and pulled into a space where no other cars were parked close to her. She passed with flying colors, but poor Cindy was still crying.

Deni followed the officer into the office, and the receptionist took her picture and handed Deni her license. Deni walked out thinking she could conquer the world, but Cindy was still so distraught that all she could do was fall into the backseat. Deni got to drive home and told Cindy that she would bring her back next week to take her test again.

The girls got home, and Cindy called her mother to let her know that she failed her test, and Sam felt so bad for her. She told her she could take the test again and that Deni had passed hers with flying colors. Sam told her to congratulate Deni, but she still felt bad for her daughter. Cindy said she loved her and hung up the phone.

The next week Cindy went back to retake her test and passed with flying colors. She couldn't believe that she had failed and the same officer gave her the retake. He even asked her if she was there last week. Cindy laughed and said yes, that she was the one who hit the car, and he laughed and told her that in all the years he had been doing this, no one had ever hit a car. They both laughed about it now, but last week it was not funny.

The weeks went by so fast, and now it was time for the girls to go on their trip to California to see the two schools the girls wanted to see. Cathy had set up tours at Pepperdine and UCSB. They were going to spend a week in California and wanted to be able to sightsee. Stan said he didn't know what he was going to do without them for a whole week, but he would make do somehow.

The flight was a little bumpy at first, but once they reached cruising altitude, it was smooth sailing. They landed at LAX, and Deni was shocked at how huge the airport was. There were people everywhere. It looked like a zoo. She turned to her mother and asked if they could go home. Cathy laughed and said that she was the one who wanted to come here and see these schools, so she should suck it up and go to the baggage claim.

They got their baggage and went outside the airport; it was even more of a zoo there. Cathy had arranged for a limo to pick them up and take them to the hotel. The hair dye company had arranged for a limo to drive them anywhere they wanted to go for the whole week, so this limo was theirs till they go home. Cathy saw the man holding the sign and headed in his direction.

They got in the limo, and the driver asked them if this was their first time in Los Angeles, and all of them said yes in unison. The driver told them to sit back and enjoy the ride. Cathy told him that she didn't know what hotel to go to; the company that made the arrangements for this trip said it was to be a surprise. The driver chuckled and told them that it would be a great surprise for them then and said he had the hotel they would be staying at. He also told them that he would take them through LA and let them see some of the sights on their way to the hotel. He asked what time they would need him tomorrow morning, and Cathy was at a loss.

"What do mean tomorrow morning?" asked Cathy.

The driver informed her that the company that had made flight reservations and hotel reservations had also made reservations for him with the limo all week. "I am at your disposal, ladies."

The girls were very impressed and were all raving about all this posh treatment. They asked the driver his name and he told them his name is Armand. He was a very nice man with a thick, heavy accent that they later learned was from Italy. He recommended several restaurants for them to try while they were there and pointed out all the major sights on his way to the hotel.

Armand finally pulled into the driveway of a place that looked like a castle. It was so large; Deni had never seen anything so big in her life. The drive was lined with statues, palm trees, and fountains. The driver pulled up to the door and got out to open the door for the girls. As he opened the door, a gloved hand thrust into the car to help the ladies out. Cathy grabbed the gloved hand and got out of the car.

They got out of the car and looked at the hotel grounds. The doorman grabbed the bags and escorted the ladies through the lobby to the desk. They checked in and the bellman asked the ladies to follow him. He led them through the lobby and out through the gardens to a villa on the back of the property. It had a private entrance and the limo had pulled around to the entrance.

Pierre opened the door to the villa, introduced himself, and told them he would be their personal valet. Deni looked at her mother and mouthed the words, *"What is that?"*

Cathy shrugged her shoulders like she didn't know, and Pierre showed them the villa. He led them into the living room, where there were sliding glass doors leading to a private patio with a private pool and a hot tub. He took them to the master bedroom, through a pair of sliding glass doors off the patio. The room had its own private bath, a king-size bed with Egyptian cotton sheets, and a posh comforter. The bathroom was all marble with a Jacuzzi, separate shower stall, and a large vanity with a chair in the middle. The closet was a large walk-in just off the bathroom with a built-in dresser along one wall. In the center were two sofas that were back to back for sitting and dressing.

Pierre led them back to the patio and walked to the other end, where another pair of sliding glass doors stood. Pierre opened the doors to a room with two queen beds. It was just as posh as the master bedroom. The bathroom was all marble, and the vanity had two sinks. The walk-in closet wasn't as big as the master bedroom and didn't have the sofas in it. Instead it had two large chairs that were placed back to back and had no built-in dresser. It was still a very large and was a nice room. The girls were so excited they could hardly contain themselves. Cathy did ask Pierre what was across the hall from the front door, and Pierre told them that was a room for the valet, chef, and chauffeur. Cathy was even more impressed, knowing they had all those people at their disposal.

Pierre took them back to the living room and into the kitchen. There stood a stocky man with a white coat and a tall hat. Pierre cleared his throat and the man turned around. Pierre introduced him as their personal chef, Buck. Buck had a big smile and a nice face. Buck shook their hands and asked what they might want to eat during their stay. Cathy told him they were just simple folks from a small town, and anything he wanted to make would be fine with them. Although she did add that they didn't want anything raw, live, or bleeding in the kitchen. Buck laughed and told her that she would not be seeing any of that in his kitchen.

Buck opened a nice chardonnay and handed Cathy a glass. He also pulled out a tray of assorted cheeses and fruits and then pulled out another tray of finger sandwiches for the ladies to eat for a snack. He pulled out sodas for the girls and poured them in a wine glass. The girls thought they were in heaven here and took the trays to the pool. Buck told them that dinner would be ready at 8:00 p.m., but Cathy told him they like to eat at 6:00 p.m., so Buck nodded and told her, "Six it is then."

The girls went to put on their bathing suits and found that their luggage had been unpacked and put away. Deni found her bathing suit and ran back to the pool to tell her mother that Pierre had put everything away. Cathy ran into her bedroom to find that all her things had been put away as well and put on her bathing suit too. She went into the living room to look for a book of events or attractions and couldn't find anything. Pierre appeared out of nowhere and scared Cathy. She asked him if they had books like that in the hotel rooms, and Pierre told her they did not. This hotel was too nice to have such things like that in its rooms and said that if there was something they wanted to know about in this town, they should just ask him and he would make the proper arrangements.

Cathy was laughing to herself when she walked back out to the pool and sat down to find that her wine had been refilled. She wondered how all this happened without anyone being seen. She also wondered if this was how movie stars felt when they go to a hotel. Then she had the crazy thought that movie stars are probably used to this kind of treatment. Pierre did show up to announce that the masseurs were there and asked where they wanted the tables. Cathy told him that it must be a mistake because she didn't ask for a masseur and wanted to know who ordered them.

Pierre said he wasn't at liberty to say but that there were special instructions when the reservation was made to take care of the special people in the room and to give them anything they wanted. He also told Cathy that the massages were set up for today and for every other day during their stay. Cathy was even more impressed and thanked Pierre and told him to set the tables up on the patio.

The girls were told what to do to prepare for their massage and did just as they were told. They went out to the tables and slid under the sheet. All three of them were lying there waiting when they heard footsteps coming up behind them. The music was turned on, and the ladies' sheets were pulled back to their waist. The massage oils were applied and the relaxing began. All three ladies were so relaxed by the end of the massage that they didn't want to move. Next, there were manicurists that came in to give them mani-pedis. The ladies really thought they were movie stars after all this.

Buck came out to tell them that dinner was served and escorted them to the dining room that had been set with candles and a very formal, very shiny table. The ladies were so awestruck that they ran to their rooms to get their cameras. Buck at first didn't know what was happening and looked at Pierre. Pierre couldn't figure out what was going on. The ladies came back with cameras, snapping pictures of everything. They asked Pierre and Buck to stand together at the head of the table and took their picture.

Cathy ran across the hall and knocked on the door. Armand answered the door. Cathy asked him to please come and eat with them because she was sure Buck had made plenty of food. Armand declined the invitation, saying it was not proper for the help to eat with them. Cathy asked him to please come with her because she needed to get something straight with them.

Cathy walked back to the dining room and called in Pierre and Buck. All three of the workers stood there looking at each other like something was wrong. Cathy began by telling them that they are not help. She told them that she had not hired them; therefore, they were not her help. They were her equal. All three of the workers stood there with a questioning look on their faces, and Cathy continued.

"I would like it if we could all sit down and eat together. We are simple people from a small town. We are not better than you and you are not better than us. We are all equal here and I will not have it any other way. Now, Buck, did you make enough to feed us all?"

Buck nodded and headed in to get the other place settings for the table. Pierre followed him and told him that they could not do this, that the hotel would have them fired if they found out. Buck told him he didn't care. If that's what the client wanted then that's what the client got. Buck also asked Pierre if they were there to please the hotel or please the guests of the hotel. Pierre told him, "To please the guests." Buck told him that if that's what pleases them and makes them happy and it gives them a good review, then that's what they should do. So Pierre grabbed the glasses and followed Buck into the dining room.

They set the plates on the table, and Buck returned to the kitchen to get the food and serve it family style. He liked these people and wanted to make sure they ate well the rest of the week. They all sat down to dinner that night and treated like Royalty.

The next morning Cathy got up early before Buck and started fixing breakfast. She set the table in the breakfast nook with six plates and poured orange juice for everyone. When Buck and Pierre came in they were not only shocked but they were also very touched at the effort Cathy had made to make them feel they were part of the family. Buck and Pierre had never had a guest that went through this much trouble for them and who made the effort to get to know them. Most of the guests who stayed in these villas were complete snobs and didn't care what they looked like and didn't even ask their names. But this lady was different. She cared about people and made them feel welcome, even if it was in a hotel villa.

Breakfast was delicious, and the girls were all laughing about some of Buck's and Pierre's stories about the other guest. They had funny stories to tell about almost every Hollywood star there was. Cindy and Deni were eating this up. They loved gossip about Hollywood, and this was really the inside scoop. Cathy asked if they were married. Buck told her he was still looking for that special someone, Pierre told her that he was divorced, and Armand told her he was a newlywed. Cathy insisted that he bring his wife to dinner tonight and asked the others to bring a special someone too.

The three ladies went to get ready for the tour of Pepperdine today and didn't know what to wear. Apparently, Pierre had slipped in early in their rooms and laid out the clothes for the outing. How did he do that? He knew exactly what to lay out for this occasion.

Armand was waiting at the limo when the ladies came out and opened the door for them. He had a smile on his face and thanked Cathy for all she was doing for him. She told him to make sure he brings his wife tonight and to let her spend the night while he was here. She needed a night out at a fancy hotel too. He laughed and closed the door. He knew exactly where they were going and took the scenic route so the ladies could marvel at the ocean. It was their first time to see the ocean and couldn't believe the beaches here. He took them by the place where movies, TV shows, and commercials were filmed and showed them as much as possible before their appointment.

He got them to the school on time and had called ahead to let the tour guide know that they were on their way. When he pulled up in front of the school, the tour guide was standing there waiting for them. They got out of the limo and thanked Armand for the fabulous ride, and he said he would be waiting for them. The tour guide started the tour with the view of the ocean, which was spectacular. Deni could get used to all this special treatment. The tour proceeded throughout the school, and when they got to the science building, they recognized a familiar face in one of the labs.

Chapter 25

Ruth stood at the head of a class, showing them how to mix the chemicals to get the desired effect, when she looked up and saw Cathy standing in the hall. She told her class to read their books and that she would be right back. Ruth walked out in the hallway to carefully approach Cathy. Deni and Cindy didn't see her till she was out in the hallway. Cathy stood there looking at Ruth, not believing it was really her.

"You look good," said Ruth.

Cathy replied, "So do you. What are you doing here?"

"Well, that's a long story. When you have time, I'd really like to talk about it," Ruth told her.

"That would be nice. Why don't you come by the hotel after you finish up here and we can talk?" asked Cathy.

Ruth said, "That would be nice. I'd like that."

Cathy gave her the address of the hotel and went on with the tour. After the tour, Armand was waiting right where he said he would be and opened the door for the ladies. When they were on their way back to the hotel, Armand heard the two girls talk at once. He asked Cathy how she does it. And Cathy told him that you get used to it and get bits and pieces. He laughed at how excited the girls were and shook his head at them.

He took them through Bel Air on the way back to the hotel and showed them some stars' homes. They were so impressed with the homes there and could only dream of living there someday. Armand laughed and told them everyone had that dream. He finished the tour through Bel Air and headed to the hotel. He took the back entrance to the villa and parked the limo there. He let the ladies out of the car and walked them to their door. Cathy reminded him to go pick up his wife for dinner tonight at 6:00 p.m., and again he thanked her.

They were greeted by a wonderful smell when they entered the villa and found Buck in the kitchen making lunch. He had made a wonderful grilled chicken salad with candied walnuts and feta cheese and a wonderful soup. The ladies had never eaten anything like it. He served them by the pool, and Cathy told him to sit and eat with them, but he insisted he had already eaten.

Ruth showed up at around 2:00 p.m. and was led back to the villa by a bellman. She was impressed with the accommodations and told Cathy so. Cathy told her that the hair dye company had agreed to pay for all and also told her the settlement the company had given them. Well, not all the terms of the settlement, just the part about them paying for the girls' college and paying for the accommodations.

Ruth told her, "After what happened at your house that night, no one wanted to continue working with the company. We all quit and went our separate ways. We didn't think when we took that assignment and didn't realize how much it hurt us or the people that were being observed. It was just too much for us, as it was for you too."

Cathy told her, "After that night, the girls just slipped into a deep depression and are just now coming out of it. This is the most I've seen them smile in months. I know what happened seemed harmless from the company's point of view and they need their research, but they need to know they are dealing with real live human beings that have feelings and can get hurt. Deni really fell for Jack or Will, whatever his name is, and he was her first boyfriend. I don't know if she'll ever trust again. I've tried putting her in therapy, but she refuses to go, saying she'll get through this on her own, but I don't know. I'm afraid that this has had a bigger impact on her than she wants to admit."

Ruth told her, "I know what you mean. Companies don't think about the impact their research might have on people. They just want to make money, and if this is how they do it, then that's how they will do it. We have rallied to get the research stopped for that intelligence-altering chemical, but I'm afraid it's hit a wall. I truly am sorry for all that happened. I miss you. We hit it off so well."

Cathy grabbed Ruth's hand and told her, "I've missed you too. I want to stay in touch with you, and if you ever need someone to talk to then you call me."

Ruth told her, "Back at cha. I'm so glad we worked this out. I just couldn't stand everything that happened."

Ruth got up to leave, and Cathy told her that they would be there all week if she could stop by again and visit. Maybe they could all go out for a nice dinner or something. Ruth told her that they could come to her house for supper one night, and Cathy told her that would be nice. They exchanged information, and Cathy hugged her as tight as she could. Ruth returned that hug and told Cathy she would see her later.

The girls jumped in the pool and splashed Cathy by accident. Cathy told them what happened with Ruth and told the girls they were going to go over to Ruth's for supper one night. The girls were a little apprehensive but agreed. They swam a little longer and got out to get dressed for dinner. Cathy had told them that Armand was bringing his wife over, and they wanted to look presentable.

Pierre had laid out clothes for them and was waiting for them in the dining room. They knew there was company coming and had set the most beautiful table possible. Armand knocked on the door, and Pierre immediately let him in and led him to the living room. Armand introduced his wife to Pierre and Buck, and then Cathy and the girls walked into the room. Armand introduced his lovely wife to the ladies, and Cathy gave her a big hug. Armand looked at his wife and said, "I told you she was different."

Buck served them appetizers in the living room and a very nice red wine. When the dinner was ready, he announced the dinner and escorted them to the table. Cathy insisted they all sit and eat with them, and each worker took their seats around the table. Cathy got up to thank everyone for making them feel at home in this huge room and Armand for bringing his lovely wife to meet them. She continued around the table, thanking each one for their contribution to this fabulous feast. Buck brought out the roast leg of lamb.

Buck carved the leg with such precision and served each one exact portions. They sat there eating and enjoying the company. Cathy felt like this was a new family she had come out to visit and wanted to take them all home with her. She felt that this hodgepodge of people was just the ticket to breathe new life into their lives at home. She asked them all to come to Oklahoma to visit sometime and gave them all her address and phone number.

Of course, they all promised to come out at one time or another, but Cathy knew that they probably wouldn't. They finished the meal still laughing and talking like old friends, and the girls cleared the table. Buck tried to stop them, but the girls insisted on clearing and cleaning up.

The next day was to be an early day, and they all said good night. The girls fell into bed, exhausted from the events of the day. They lay there talking about the school and what they may want to study there. They talked about the chemistry class that Ruth was teaching. They were a little shocked to see her there but thought that it was a sign. A sign that they should start healing and forgiving the people that had hurt them so bad. They talked about all the things they went through and how they could start the healing process with Ruth.

The next morning came early for them. They had not gotten to bed till midnight and had to get up at 5:00 a.m. to get ready to go to Santa Barbara for the day. Pierre had come in while all the ladies were in the bathroom and laid out their clothes for the day. He also put out comfortable shoes for them because he knew when people go to Santa Barbara (SB) they always had to walk down State Street and shop. Buck had gotten up extra early so that the ladies would have a great breakfast, and he wanted to pack them a picnic lunch to take with them.

They finished getting dressed and ate the great breakfast Buck had prepared, and Armand went to get the car. They all loaded up and got in the car. Armand was going to take the famous Pacific Coast Highway (PCH) to Oxnard then hit the 101 Highway to S B. The scenery was magnificent. The girls wanted to sleep so bad but couldn't stop looking out the windows at the ocean and the mountains. Armand was getting a kick out of the girls' reactions to seeing the dolphins playing in the surf.

They hit the 101 Highway at Oxnard and headed to SB. The scenery there was just as breathtaking. They could see there were islands off the coast that were so clear. They asked Armand about them, and he told them that it was the Channel Islands and told them some history about the islands. When they finally arrived at UCSB, the tour guide was waiting for them and immediately started the tour.

He took them through every building and explained the scholarships that were still available. The girls like this school because it was smaller and felt more like home. They had a hard decision to make. Armand told them that they may want to do some shopping here and took them down State Street. They were all so excited about the prospect of picking up some California fashions, and Armand told them to call him when they got hungry so he could pick them up. Buck had packed a nice picnic lunch for them. Cathy thanked him, and he stopped in the middle of the street and let them out.

The girls were ecstatic to finally get to shop. They went into every store on both sides of the street. There were restaurants everywhere and specialty stores up and down the street. They had a blast shopping and finally had to call Armand to come get the bags. This was a good time to have that picnic, and Armand had picked the perfect spot at the beach.

The girls wanted to pick up souvenirs for their friends back home and wanted to get Christmas presents for their families. Cathy told them not to spend all their money here because they still had the rest of the week to shop and sightsee. Armand promised to take them shopping in LA this week and told them that he had planned something special for tomorrow, so they needed to leave it open. Cathy looked at him and grinned, wondering what Armand had planned for them.

The ride back was relaxing and both the girls fell asleep. Armand laughed to himself and told Cathy that no matter how old they get they still fall asleep on the ride home. Cathy laughed and asked for a little hint about the plans tomorrow, but Armand was not giving that one up. He liked these people and wanted to show his appreciation. He had heard about all the trouble they had been going through and wanted to do something nice for them.

They got back to the villa and found a note from Ruth on the counter. Pierre's handwriting was impeccable. Ruth had asked if they wanted to have dinner tonight at her house, but if that wasn't possible then they would reschedule for Thursday. Cathy called her to let her know that Thursday would be better for them and asked Ruth if she would like to go shopping with them on Thursday. Ruth said yes and asked what time she should meet them.

Cathy was exhausted from the day and Armand was still bringing in bags. Pierre helped them put everything away and told them that dinner would be ready in about ten minutes.

The girls went to the bathroom to freshen up and change clothes. When they emerged from their room, the aroma from the kitchen was intoxicating. Pierre led them to the dining room while Buck was putting the finishing touches on the table.

Everyone took their place and Armand came in to eat with them. The girls were still curious about the plans for tomorrow, but Armand wasn't even giving a hint of what was in store for them. He would just laugh and grin when they bombarded him with questions, but he stood firm on not telling them anything.

They all went into the living room to watch TV after dinner, and Buck served them dessert. He had made a wonderful Dutch apple pie and served it with vanilla bean ice cream. It was fabulous. Cathy could not get over how good everything tasted here. Buck was such a great cook, so she started reminiscing about the meals that Will made for all of them. She did miss having him around and knew that Deni missed him. The girls didn't say much about him anymore, but Cathy knew he was still on Deni's mind.

They sat and watched some of the programs that Stan wouldn't let them watch at home. They were having such a good time but were so tired from the day. They finally went to bed and saw that Pierre had turned down the beds, laid out their pajamas, and put a chocolate with a rose on their pillows. Cathy thought it was so thoughtful. She was going to make sure she did something nice for these three gentlemen who were making their stay so delightful. She wanted to get them something to remember her by and made a mental note to get them all something special when she went shopping again.

The next morning came with a bright beautiful sunlight shining in the bedroom, waking up Cathy. She had not felt that refreshed in a long time. She got up and put on her robe and shuffled to the kitchen to find that a cup of coffee had already been put on the bar for her. She thanked Buck for everything and asked him how he knew she was up. She was trying to be quiet. He looked at her and grinned and said that Buck knows everything. She laughed along with him and sipped her coffee.

The girls finally got up and came into the kitchen looking like zombies. Buck looked at them and jumped a little at the sight of the two teens. He handed them both coffee and told them to go into the living room. He served them breakfast there and asked if there was anything else they needed. They said no and he disappeared into the kitchen again.

Armand knocked on the door and Pierre let him in. He found the ladies sitting on the sofa, eating breakfast. He told them to be ready in thirty minutes because he had a big day planned for them. Armand had let Pierre and Buck in on the plans, and Pierre had gone down to the lobby of the hotel to borrow some fancy clothes for all three of them to wear. He had laid the clothes on the beds along with the shoes he had also borrowed.

When the ladies walked into their rooms, they found the nice clothes lying across their beds and the shoes set right beside them. They were shocked at how nice the clothing was and asked Pierre to explain how those clothes got there. He told them that the hotel sometimes lends clothes to guests who need them, and he had taken the liberty of getting these clothes for them to wear today for their outing with Armand. This made Armand's plans even more suspicious to the girls, and they got even more excited.

They hurried and got ready and heard a knock on the door. Pierre had let three ladies in and led them to the living room, where they set up chairs and tables and had a bag full of makeup and hair products.

Cathy came out to see who was there and asked, "What's going on?"

Pierre introduced the three ladies to Cathy and asked her to have a seat. "This is all part of the outing today. Please, do sit down and let these ladies work their magic."

Cathy sat down, and when the girls came in, they took their seats too. Deni was a little reluctant to sit in the chair after all that had happened to her, but Pierre assured her that these ladies would only be styling their hair and that they were very trustworthy.

Deni sat there and watched the ladies work her hair and watched as her mother was transformed into a movie star. Deni then couldn't wait to see how she was going to look and couldn't wait to see Cindy. When Deni's stylist finished with her, Deni looked in the mirror and didn't recognize the woman looking back at her. Cindy looked at Deni and Cathy with her mouth open. Cindy couldn't believe that the other two ladies were her best friend and her best friend's mother. They all looked like movie stars.

Armand reappeared and asked the ladies if they were ready to go for their outing. They all looked at Pierre to see if he had any other tricks up his sleeve, and Pierre told them they were now ready. They followed Armand out to the limo and got in the backseat. Armand started the car and took off.

Cathy was wondering if this guy was an axe murderer or what and was starting to worry when she saw that he was pulling into Rodeo Drive in Hollywood. He pulled up in front of one the stores and told the ladies to ring the bell and tell them they are there to see Dalton. Cathy looked at him with a questioning look and he told her to trust him. She did and did as she was told.

She walked up to the store and rang the bell. A woman's voice came over the intercom and asked who was there. Cathy told her they were there to see Dalton, and the lady buzzed them in. They were met in the foyer of the store by a nice-looking lady with beautiful red hair. She smiled and welcomed them in the store and shook Cathy's hand. Cathy introduced herself and told the lady again that they were to see Dalton.

The assistant's name was Tiffany, and she led them to a white room with a round chair in the middle of the floor. There was champagne waiting for them, and Tiffany told them to have a seat, sip some champagne, and that Dalton would be with them shortly. They took their seats, and Cathy told the girls they could try one sip of the champagne. The girls took a big sip and realized it was sparkling cider in the glasses for them. The girls enjoyed drinking from the champagne glasses and were a little reluctant to ask for more.

Tiffany returned with the bottle of cider and the bottle of champagne for Cathy. Shortly, there was sound from behind the door, and they could hear someone barking orders at other employees. The door swung open and there stood a man who was so beautiful Deni thought he was a girl. He had on a flowing pair of pants—at least Cathy thought they were pants—and a bright beautiful shirt that matched perfectly with his skin tone.

He approached them with his hand out, saying, "I'm Dalton. It is so nice to meet you. I have the most magnificent clothes to show you today. Now you relax and the show will begin."

Cathy looked at him and said, "What show? We were brought here by a friend, and all he told us was to ask for you. I'm Cathy and this is Cindy and Deni."

Dalton shook their hands and asked them to sit and enjoy the show and then he would tell them why they are there. They sat back down, Tiffany refilled their glasses, and the music started. The models that came out were so tall and gorgeous. The clothes they were modeling were absolutely the best. Luckily, Deni had brought her camera and was taking pictures of everything. She wanted to remember this moment forever.

The models just kept coming through the door and walking around the circular chair. Cathy was so overwhelmed by the fashion show. She wanted to take every piece of clothing with her but knew they must be expensive. Finally the last girl walked out, followed by Dalton. The models surrounded the circular chair and stood there while Dalton made his announcement.

Dalton cleared his throat and said, "Now the reason you are here is because your friends at the hotel wanted to give you something special. They asked me to do this little show for you, and now each of you is to pick one outfit to take with you. It has all been taken care of by Buck, Pierre, and Armand. Now, please, look at the models and pick something."

Cathy was so overwhelmed by this gesture all she could do was cry. She hugged Dalton and told him this was just too much. She could not accept something that expensive from anyone. Dalton hugged her back and whispered in her ear, "This is something that these three gentlemen insist on doing for you. You have been such a special person to them they want you to have something to remember them by, and this was the one thing they could think of that is as special as you. They told me to thank you for making them feel like part of your family. You accepted them as friends, not as servants. No one has ever done that for them, and they have grown to love you and your daughters. Please, do this for them."

Cathy walked around, looking at the models and the clothes and finally settled on a flowing dress that was very flattering. Dalton was moved when he saw Cathy wearing his clothes. He asked her if she could model for him in a show they were having over the weekend, but Cathy had to decline because they would be leaving Saturday morning.

Deni and Cindy picked out their outfits, and Dalton told them all that if they ever needed a job to look him up. He could use them as models for his show. It's as if he had made all those clothes just for them. He had never seen anyone more suited to his collection than these three women. They thanked him and grabbed their packages to leave. Dalton gave them his business card and had put his personal cell number on the back of the card so they could call him and model for him. If they decided to go to school there. They hugged him and told them they would call as soon as they decided what school they were going to and when they would be back. He told them to be back in time for fashion week so they could walk for him in the shows.

They walked outside the shop and found Armand waiting beside the limo for them. They all ran to him and hugged him. Cathy looked up at the driver with tears in her eyes and thanked him. He hugged her back and wiped tears from his eye and thanked her for being herself.

Next stop was a posh restaurant for lunch. They were escorted to a table on the balcony that overlooked Rodeo Drive. The waiter told them to watch for stars that were shopping down below. The waiter served them and told them the bill had already been paid. Cathy thanked him for the service and attention he had given them, and he told her that he knew now why this was so special.

They returned to the street to be overtaken by cameras and a mob of paparazzi. There was a star on the street, and the paps were not going to leave whoever it was alone until they got the shot they wanted. Shortly, they were in the center of the circle of paps and looked around to see Mason Rounds standing there smiling at the three ladies. Deni and Cindy started screaming because it was Mason Rounds. They loved him. He was the hottest actor out there right now, and he was so dreamy. He stopped and asked if they wanted a picture with him, and Deni immediately gave her camera to the closest person and posed by Mason. The pap was nice and took the picture of them with Mason and asked if they would pose for him. They posed for the nice pap guy and asked for Mason's autograph. Deni whipped out a pen and paper for him to sign. Mason walked off and hugged them as he left.

The girls were all smiles on the ride back to the hotel, and when they walked in, they immediately hugged Pierre and Buck for all they had done for them. Cathy told them that no one had ever done anything this nice for her and thanked them for all they had done today. Pierre looked at her and told her it was his pleasure. No one had ever acknowledged him like she had and was grateful for all she had done for *him*.

The girls went into their rooms to put on the clothes that the workers had bought for them and put on a fashion show for them. Pierre, Buck, and Armand sat and clapped for the girls, and then the girls told them what Dalton had said to them about modeling for him. The three workers were pleased that the girls had a job opportunity but were happier to see the nice clothes the girls had picked out. The girls also told them about meeting Mason Rounds on the street and how nice he was and showed them the piece of paper that he had signed.

The three workers got wrapped up in the excitement, and when Cathy came out of her room, their jaws dropped at how beautiful she was in the designer clothes. Cathy walked in with a humbled look on her face and thanked them for all they had done for her. They clapped for her and told her how beautiful she was in the new outfit. They were happy to do this for their special guest, which told Cathy how special she was to them.

The rest of the week was going to be relaxing, and Deni wasn't sure what school she was going to pick. Cindy was pretty set on Pepperdine but was listening to Deni's comparison of the colleges they had toured. Then it hit Deni. She got up and ran to the living room to find a phone book. She couldn't find a phone book anywhere and got out her laptop and connected to the Internet. Cindy was standing behind her and asked what she was looking for but Deni wouldn't tell her.

She finally found what she was looking for and turned to look at Cindy. "You remember how fun it was helping Jack, I mean Will, cook those wonderful meals? Well, I've been thinking about that and thought why not check out culinary schools. What do you think?"

Cindy looked at her friend like she had lost her mind and said, "What? You want to go to culinary school? Are you nuts?"

"What's wrong with culinary school? I love cooking and learning about the different foods and spices that are available out there. I think I want to check out culinary schools while we are here," replied Deni.

Cindy told her she was crazy but would go with her to check them out, and they started looking for culinary schools in Los Angeles. Deni asked Cindy if she had decided to go to Pepperdine, and Cindy said she would probably go there since they offered the classes she wanted. Deni told her that she wanted to go to the Culinary Institute of California in Santa Monica. She said that it would be close to Cindy's school, and maybe they could get the hair company to pay for housing. Cindy told her that would be great and went and told Cathy their plan.

Cathy thought that was a good idea if that's what Deni wanted. Deni went to bed that night dreaming of being a chef and opening a private restaurant like the one they visited today on Rodeo Drive. She thought that was the best place to open a posh restaurant. She dreamt of movie stars coming in or calling for a table and how nice the place would be for production meetings and so forth. She dreamt of Will standing beside her, showing her a new recipe and helping her in the kitchen. She missed him so much and wished that things hadn't turned out the way they did, but what could she do now?

They got up the next morning late and relaxed by the pool. They wanted to rest up before the dinner tonight at Ruth's. Ruth had already called to let them know what time to be there, and Cathy offered to come by earlier to help get everything ready, but Ruth told her she had plenty of help at home.

Chapter 26

They arrived at Ruth's house precisely at 5:00 p.m. They knocked on the door and were greeted by a lady dressed in a maid's uniform. The lady led them into a parlor and disappeared to let the lady of the house know they were there. Ruth came out of the kitchen and brought with her a plate of appetizers. The maid followed her with a tray of drinks. Ruth offered them a seat and asked how they liked the house.

Cathy told her the house was beautiful and asked for a tour. Ruth gladly obliged the request and took the three on a tour of her house. Deni and Cindy couldn't believe they were in a mansion up in the hills of Bel Air. They were taken from room to room and wondered how many rooms this place actually had.

After the tour the butler announced that dinner was being served. They followed Ruth into the dining room and sat down. The first course was served, and the second course was on its way out the door, followed by the chef.

Deni, Cindy, and Cathy almost dropped their glasses when they saw Will follow Ruth through the door. Ruth turned and said, "I trust you all remember the chef, Will."

Cathy spoke up and said, "Yes, we do, and we were hoping to never see him again. What is he doing here?"

Will spoke up then and said, "After what happened, I quit my job and went to culinary school. I teach there now, and Ruth has been good enough to let me stay here till I get on my feet."

Deni threw down her fork, making an awful sound, and said, "You're what? Staying here? That's sick. She's not even your mother."

Will said, "I know, but I don't have parents anymore, and she's the closest I have to a mother. My parents died years ago, and I got really close to her in Oklahoma, so I love her like a mother."

"Mom, can we leave here now, please," said Deni.

Cathy looked at her and said, "I think it's time to sit down and talk this thing out and forgive the people who have hurt or wronged us in some way."

Deni sat there and finally asked what culinary school he went to and told him she was thinking of going to culinary school but wasn't sure. Will sat down beside her and told her that she should go to culinary school because then they could open up a restaurant together. Deni wasn't sure about all this and told him she would have to think about it some more. As the evening went on, they all sat and ate great food and talked about all the things that had happened. Will and Ruth apologized again for everything and asked them to forgive them for all that was done to them.

Cathy couldn't resist asking the question the girls wanted to know so bad. "How can you afford this home if you quit your job at the hair company?"

Ruth laughed and simply said, "I was filthy rich before I even got that job. I don't have to work, but I like it, so I go to work three days a week, and the rest of the time I shop or whatever I want to do. Will moved in here because he needed a place to stay while he went through school, and he is getting ready to graduate. I thought I'd invest in a restaurant, and Will was my first choice for executive chef. I wouldn't have it any other way. I love Will, as a son of course, and I love his food, so it's a perfect match."

Cathy was stunned at the possibility here and asked if it would be okay for the girls to stay there while they went to school. Ruth accepted that at once and told them they could stay there as long as they wanted. She asked them what school they had chosen, and Cindy told her

Pepperdine and Deni said she was looking at culinary schools but wasn't sure yet. Ruth told Cindy that would be good because she could ride to school with her and not have to worry about a car for a while. Deni told her she had a car, and Ruth remembered the beautiful car that she had received on her graduation day.

So it was set. The girls had a place to live with good, loving, decent people to stay with while they were in school. Ruth asked them if they wanted to spend the next day in Rodeo Drive, and Cathy told her what the staff at the hotel had done for her and the girls. Ruth told her that it was very special what those employees had done, and to help repay that generosity, she would come up with something extra special for the gentlemen. Cathy thanked her but told her she would do something for them herself. Ruth told her that it was fine but asked her to please let her help out. Cathy agreed to let her help.

They finished the fabulous dinner and sat in the living room to talk. As they continued to talk and work things out, the girls got more excited about going to school out here in California. Will had convinced Deni to go to culinary school and open a restaurant together. He had already picked out the place and had some plans written down for the decorations.

The night passed fast, and the girls were getting tired. Will asked if he could come see Deni tomorrow, but Cathy was a little reluctant. She told Will that Deni was only sixteen now and still too young to date someone in his twenties. She asked if Will could wait till Deni was eighteen, and Will gave her his solemn promise that he would wait till Deni was of age to start dating her. She thanked him for that and hugged Ruth good-bye.

The next day was their last full day in California, so the girls decided to go shopping. They wanted to get something nice for the three gentlemen who had made their stay so wonderful. They couldn't believe that a week had passed and wanted to go somewhere nice without Armand knowing about it. They asked Armand to let them off at the nearest mall, so he took them to the best mall in Hollywood. Cathy shopped around for the best gift for her "helpers" and decided to get each one an Oklahoma Sooners shirt, and then all three girls got into the photo booth and took pictures. They wanted to give them to the gentlemen at the hotel, and Cathy went and picked out a nice frame and wrote a beautiful poem to go with the little picture she had placed at the bottom of the frame. She had each wrapped them and put them in her bag. When they returned to the villa from shopping, they found that Pierre had packed everything for them except for the things they would need for the night and the morning. Cathy didn't want to give the gifts to the men till the morning but had to give in to the excitement and gave it to them following dinner.

The gentlemen all wiped a tear from their eyes and thanked all the ladies for coming to stay with them. Pierre was so touched by the thought that he had to leave the room to gather himself. He returned with a big hug for all three ladies and told them he loved them and would miss them so much. Cathy reminded him and the other two gentlemen to come see them when they had the chance. She meant that, and all three gentlemen knew Cathy had meant that from the bottom of her heart. She hugged them all again the next morning and left to catch her plane.

The days passed fast in California, and when they returned home, it was snowing. The girls had gotten so used to the weather in California they didn't want to come home. Deni sat down with Stan and told him her plans of going to culinary school. Stan told her he didn't care what she did as long as she was happy. Deni also told him about seeing Will and what he had promised her mother. Stan agreed with that and told Deni he wanted a promise from her to not date him until she was eighteen. Then he made her promise to not date anyone till she was eighteen. Deni laughed while making that promise.

Christmas passed quickly as well as New Year's, and it was approaching the time for Deni and Cindy to leave for college. They had agreed to take Deni's car, but only if Cathy and Stan could go with them to pull the moving trailer, and then they would fly back once the girls were settled.

Stan went and got the moving trailer the day before moving day, and the girls were busy packing. Cathy was crying every time she walked into Deni's bedroom. She couldn't believe her daughter was going off to college at sixteen. This was going to be a great time in her daughter's life, and she didn't want to put a damper on things, so she stayed out as much as possible.

They loaded everything up and put the last of the girls' things into the trailer. Deni climbed behind the wheel of her car and backed out of the driveway to start her new life, but there was one thing she had forgotten to do. She turned around and ran to Mamaw's house. Mamaw was waiting on the porch for her, and Deni ran into her open arms. Mamaw was crying so hard Deni could hardly understand her. Mamaw told her she loved her and to be good while she was out in California. Mamaw also told her she was going to come visit her in the spring to make sure she was behaving and kissed the girl on the cheek. She had packed some goodies for the family to eat on the road and waved good-bye to everyone. Cindy hugged and kissed Mamaw, and all of them said they loved each other. The girls ran back to Deni's car and backed out of the driveway to start their new adventure.

If you enjoyed The Blonde Effect
be sure to watch for Deni's next adventure in:

Deni's Couture Cakes

This will be a Caketastrophe for Deni
And her friends.